Praise for Dying Is My Business

"Crazy, dark inventiveness on every page. Reminiscent of Roger Zelazny's Amber books." —Mike Carey, author of *The Devil You Know* and *X-Men: Legacy*

"Urban fantasy-noir at its finest, full of marvelous imagination, snarky humor, Whedonesque romance, inventive mythology, and badass monsters! Fans of Richard Kadrey's Sandman Slim will love it."
—Christopher Golden, *New York Times* bestselling coauthor of *Father Gaetano's Puppet Catechism*

"Nicholas Kaufmann is the Christopher Moore of urban fantasy. *Dying Is My Business* is a smart, gleeful page-turner by an expert in the genre."
—Sarah Langan, Bram Stoker Award-winning author of *Audrey's Door*

"Brilliantly conceived . . . kept me enthralled from the first page to the last."
—Tim Lebbon, author of *Coldbrook*

"*Dying Is My Business* is hot-paced adventure mixing the criminal underworld with otherworldly magic, and introducing a hero who is both cold-blooded and compassionately heroic."
—Laura Anne Gilman, author of *Dragon Justice*

"Tremendous fun, packed with magic, plot twists, and thrills. Nicholas Kaufmann is an author to keep an eye on."
—Harry Connolly, author of the Twenty Palaces novels

"Kaufmann spins his yarn with relish and a gift for making the fantastical seem completely plausible—the perfect combination for an author of urban fantasy."
—Charles Ardai, Edgar and Shamus Award-winning author, editor of Hard Case Crime, and consulting producer of *Haven*

Dying Is My Business

NICHOLAS KAUFMANN

ST. MARTIN'S GRIFFIN
NEW YORK

DYING IS MY BUSINESS. Copyright © 2013 by Nicholas Kaufmann. All rights reserved. Printed in the United States of America. For information, address St. Martin's Press, 175 Fifth Avenue, New York, N.Y. 10010.

www.stmartins.com

Design by Steven Seighman

The Library of Congress Cataloging-in-Publication Data is available upon request

ISBN 978-1-250-03610-0 (trade paperback)
ISBN 978-1-250-03609-4 (e-book)

St. Martin's Griffin books may be purchased for educational, business, or promotional use. For information on bulk purchases, please contact Macmillan Corporate and Premium Sales Department at 1-800-221-7945, extension 5442, or write specialmarkets@macmillan.com.

First Edition: October 2013

10 9 8 7 6 5 4 3 2 1

For Alexa, always

Acknowledgments

An enormous amount of thanks are due to Daniel Braum, M.M. De Voe, Ben Francisco, Sarah Langan, and David Wellington for their invaluable help. Many thanks as well to Richard Curtis and Michael Homler for making this happen. And, as always, to Mongo Bettina for lighting the way.

Out of the waters it rose at twilight; cold, proud, beautiful; an Eastern city of wonder whose brothers the mountains are. It was not like any city of earth, for above purple mists rose towers, spires and pyramids which one may only dream of in opiate lands beyond the Oxus. . . .
—H. P. Lovecraft describing New York City, 18 May 1922

Ain't found a way to kill me yet.
—Alice in Chains

Dying Is
My Business

One

It's not as easy as it looks to come back from the dead.

It's a shock to the system, even more than dying is. The first new breath burns like fire. The first new heartbeat is like a sharp, urgent pain. Emerging from the darkness like that, the sudden light is blinding, confusing. Coming back from the dead feels less like a miracle than like waking up with the world's most debilitating hangover.

When I gasped my way back to life that night, it took a moment for my eyes to adjust, and for the fuzzy, greenish smear in front of me to come into focus. When it did, I found myself staring into the grinning face of a dragon. It was fake, obviously. Even in my groggy, fresh from the dead state I was pretty sure there were no such things as dragons. The smiling, cartoonish head was attached to a green plastic body with a cracked wooden saddle on its back. Where its legs should have been was a big, rusted metal spring embedded in the dirt beneath it. A spring rider, I realized, the kind kids rode on in parks. Was that where I was? A park?

I lifted myself up onto my elbows and looked around, trying to remember where I was and why I'd come here. This wasn't the first time I'd died—in fact, it was the ninth; I was keeping count—but that didn't mean it had become any easier or less disorienting. It was night. The stars above were hidden by thick, smoggy clouds that turned the moon into a feebly glowing smudge. There were sodium streetlights nearby, close enough to light my surroundings in a sickly yellow pallor. I saw another spring rider behind the first, a unicorn this time, and in the distance a seesaw, a rusted merry-go-round, and a half-broken jungle gym.

A playground. What the hell was I doing in a playground?

Oh, crap. It all came back to me then. Bennett. I'd come here looking for a man named Bennett. I sucked in a deep breath, my lungs still aching. There was a small, ragged bullet hole in my shirt, right over my heart, rimmed with blood and gunpowder. I stuck my finger through it and touched the smooth, unbroken skin beneath. The bullet wound had already healed. There wasn't even any blood, except for what was on my shirt and what had spattered in the dirt around me. The rest had been reabsorbed back into my body, neat and clean.

I was a freak, but at least I was a meticulous freak.

Groaning, I turned onto my side. Something small rolled off me, landing softly in the grass. I picked it up. It was a bullet. *The* bullet, in fact; the one that had killed me. My body had spat it out as it healed itself. I tossed it away. The bullet landed on a patch of bare dirt, rolled a few inches, and came to a rest against the worn leather shoe of a dead body that sat slumped at the base of the swing set.

I should have been surprised, but I wasn't. I'd gotten used to seeing corpses when I came back from the dead. Way too used to it.

This one's head drooped toward its shoulder, its jaw hanging slack. Its skin was as brown and paper-dry as a mummy's, as if it'd been sitting there undiscovered for centuries, but the black silk shirt hanging off its withered frame and the cheap gold chain around its neck told a different story. He'd once been a beefy psychopath named Maddock, Bennett's bodyguard. Now he was more like beef jerky, emaciated and dried out, as if he'd been dug out of an ancient pyramid in Egypt. Only he'd just died a few moments ago, and this wasn't Egypt, this was Queens.

I got to my feet and stood over Maddock's body. The son of a bitch hadn't just shot me dead, he'd done it with my own damn gun. I pulled my chrome-plated Bersa semiautomatic handgun from his dead fingers. I glanced around the playground, looking for Bennett. I hoped I hadn't lost him. For the past couple of months, ever since the little boy in the crack house died, I'd been off my game, like my heart just wasn't in it anymore. I still did my job. I still broke into warehouses, vaults, and homes, and stole priceless objects for a low-level crime boss in Crown Heights named Underwood to sell on the black market, but I was losing my touch. After botching a recent job by setting off a silent alarm I should have known was there, I suspected Underwood was running out of patience with me. I'd heard enough agonized screams coming from behind his black door to know that an angry Underwood was a dangerous Underwood.

So when he asked me to bring Bennett in, I figured this was my chance to show him I could still pull my weight. My mistake was thinking the job would be an easy one. I thought I had the element of surprise on my side, but when I followed Bennett to the old, deserted playground in Queens, he was less than surprised. It was an ambush. The moment I passed through the gate, Maddock came out of the dark and wrestled the gun out of my hand. *Next time, Underwood should come for me himself, not send some half-wit errand boy,* Bennett had said, and then Maddock shot me with my own gun and I'd died for the ninth time.

The ninth that I knew about, anyway. It's hard to be sure about these things when your memories don't go back more than a year.

I hurried through the open playground gate and onto the sidewalk outside. Bennett couldn't have gotten far yet. I never stayed dead for more than a couple of minutes. The brisk late-September night air nipped at me. This time of year in New York City, the days were still warm but the nights grew cold, as if winter were trying to sneak up while no one was looking. Bracing myself against the chill, I looked up and down the empty street, past the boarded-up windows of the vacant buildings to either side. I spotted Bennett in his blue pinstripe suit ducking around the corner, and sprinted after him. As I rounded the corner, he stopped next to a parked black Porsche and reached into his pocket for the keys.

"Bennett!" I yelled, and ran at him.

He saw me. His eyes widened in surprise, and the color drained from his face. He looked like he'd seen a ghost. He pulled out a set of keys with his trembling hand, and fumbled in an attempt to press the unlock button on the key chain. Before he could try again, I tackled him to the sidewalk. The keys bounced out of his hand and slid under a nearby Dumpster.

I put one hand on his chest to hold him down, his heart jackhammering under my palm. I tucked my gun into the back of my pants and patted Bennett down. I found a small, snub-nosed revolver in a shoulder holster and tucked that into my pants, too. Bennett stared at the bullet hole in my shirt.

"You're dead," he said in a hoarse whisper. "I *saw* you die!"

I retrieved a pair of plastic wrist ties from my pocket. I rolled Bennett onto his stomach and started binding his wrists together behind his back.

He didn't put up a fight, only craned his neck around to stare at me with a combination of horror and awe. "How are you still alive?"

If he wanted an answer, he was asking the wrong guy. I didn't know any more than he did. I pulled Bennett onto his feet and dragged him toward where I'd parked.

Two

The night-black Ford Explorer was a gift from some rich businessman Underwood pulled a job for, back before my time. I didn't know the details. Underwood said it was better that way. But the Explorer was perfect for collection jobs. It was big enough to be imposing, the kind of car you didn't want to get in the way of, and had enough room in the back to hold whatever Underwood sent me to collect—computer equipment, works of art, briefcases full of money. Collector, I thought. It was a fancy name for a thief.

But this was the first time I'd ever been sent to collect a *person*. What was Underwood planning to do with Bennett once I brought him in? I thought of Underwood's black door again and shuddered. I put it from my mind. I was hired muscle, paid to *do*, not think.

I took the BQE back to Brooklyn. The traffic wasn't too bad this late at night. Bennett sat in the backseat with his hands tied behind his back. He stared out the window like he was trying to put two and two together but kept coming up with the wrong number. When I exited the expressway and steered the Explorer onto Flatbush Avenue, he finally found his tongue.

"Maddock," he said. "I left him behind to dispose of your body. What happened to him?"

I glanced at him in the rearview mirror. "He's dead." I didn't fill him in on the details, but it was the same every time, for all nine of my deaths. The thing inside me, whatever it was that brought me back time and again, did so by siphoning the life out of whoever was unfortunate enough to be closest to me. It was like there was only so much life to go around, and every new life it gave me had to be taken from someone else. I didn't know why, but for some reason I wasn't allowed to stay dead. Then again, after surviving nine different deaths, maybe it wasn't smart to start looking a gift horse in the mouth.

Bennett was quiet a moment. "Maddock had a wife and kids."

"Maybe he should have gone into a different line of work," I said.

Bennett kept talking. "The girl's going to grow up to be a real heartbreaker, but the boy?" He shook his head. "Dumb as a rock, just like his dad. Like his dad *was,* anyway. Before you killed him."

Probably, he was lying about the wife and kids. I said, "Nice try. Underwood wants to see you, and I'm not going back empty-handed."

Bennett smirked and looked out the window again. "Why not? I think we both know there's nothing he could do to you. How do you punish a man who walks away from a gunshot to the chest?"

Suddenly I wished the radio in the dashboard worked. At least then I could ignore Bennett instead of letting his words get under my skin. He was right, Underwood couldn't kill me any more than Maddock could, or any of the others who'd tried, but I wasn't working for Underwood because I was afraid of him. I was working for him because he was the best chance I had of finding the answers I was looking for: Who was I? Why couldn't I remember anything before a year ago? Why didn't I stay dead? Underwood had connections all over New York City, criminals and crooked cops alike. If anyone could turn over the right stones to find the truth it was him. All he asked in return was that I run some odd jobs for him. Be his collector. I owed him for everything I had. Even my name. It was Underwood who'd given me the name Trent to tide me over until we found my real one. *It's a Celtic name,* he'd said. *It means prosperous. And you, my friend, with your special gift, are definitely going to help me prosper.*

I looked at Bennett in the rearview. "So what did you do?"

"What do you mean?" he asked.

"You must have done something pretty bad if Underwood sent me to bring you in," I said, though I wondered why I was bothering. Not that long ago, Bennett had ordered his enforcer to kill me. The odds of him wanting to play Confession were pretty damn slim. Still, I was curious, and the worst that could happen was he'd tell me to go fuck myself. "What was it? Did you steal from him?"

Bennett barked out a laugh. "Like that son of a bitch has anything I want."

"What, then?" I pressed.

"Jesus, you don't even know the man you're working for, do you? Underwood's a collector, like you, only he sends his errand boy to do it for him. Art, rare books, gemstones—the weirder and uglier the better. Stuff the real nut jobs in Park Avenue penthouses pay top dollar for. With all the weird shit he specializes in, I guess it was only a matter of time before he started collecting freaks like you, too."

I tensed at the word. I wanted to shove it back into Bennett's mouth with my fist, but I let it slide. "So what does Underwood want from you?"

"Information," Bennett said. "But we've got history, him and me, bad history. He knows no amount of money is going to buy my good graces. Not anymore. The only way I'm going to give it up to a bastard like him is if he forces it out of me, and he knows that. As soon as I caught wind he was on my tail I thought he would come for me himself. I thought he would at least show me that much respect, but instead he sends you. Fucking *Night of the Living Dead*."

That was the second time Bennett had poked at me about it. He was fishing for information, but I wasn't about to give him any. The way I saw it, if I couldn't die, it was no one's damn business but my own.

"You sound like you've never seen someone wear a bulletproof vest before," I said. It was a stupid lie. It sounded ridiculous the minute I said it.

Bennett's eyes flashed from the backseat. He saw through the lie instantly. "You could use some lessons in the art of bullshit. No, you were dead, pal. As dead as can be. Maddock felt for a pulse. I trained him to be thorough like that, but I didn't need the confirmation. I've seen enough dead bodies to know what they look like. And you, errand boy, were a fucking corpse."

I shook my head. I'd started the lie, as unconvincing as it was, and now I had to stick with it. "You're wrong. It was a vest."

"One that stops bullets and also prevents anyone from finding a pulse? Must be a hell of a vest. Wish we'd had those when I was in the Army."

I gritted my teeth and kept my eyes on the road. What did I care what Bennett thought? It wasn't like he could hold it over me. I'd probably never see him again after this anyway. Most likely, no one would. He would disappear behind the black door like the others.

"Don't know why I was so surprised anyway," Bennett continued. "It's not like you're the first man I've seen come back from the dead."

I glanced into the rearview to meet Bennett's eyes.

"Oh, that got your attention, did it?"

I scowled. "If you've got something to say, Bennett, just say it."

"I was in Kuwait in 'ninety-one," he said. "My unit was working with some Brits to breach one of the minefields the Iraqis had planted all over the southern part of the country. We could only work during the day, though. It was too dangerous at night, so we spent the nights handing out candy to the local kids. You know, trying to win hearts and minds, all that bullshit. One day, when we were about halfway through the minefield, this orphan boy, just a little thing dressed all in rags, came running out toward us. Guess he thought we had candy for him. This one Brit, Sully, was the first to see him. He broke away from the rest of us and ran for the kid to try to warn him away, but I guess Sully forgot where to step. He triggered a land mine and got blown fifty feet across the sand. We all rushed over to help him, but we knew it was too late. No one could survive a blast like that.

"Except when we got there, Sully wasn't dead anymore. He didn't even look banged up. He was just lying there on the sand, staring up at the sun, as surprised as we were that he was in one piece. He told us later he didn't remember the explosion, that everything just went black and he saw a tunnel and a bright light, the whole shebang like right out of the fucking Bible. Then he was back on the sand like nothing had happened. None of us could explain it, least of all him."

My mouth went dry. My palms felt clammy on the steering wheel. Another man who couldn't die? Did that mean there were others like me out there? If there were, it was possible they had answers. They might even know my real name.

Bennett kept talking. "A couple of weeks later we were doing recon in some godforsaken, bombed-to-hell village outside Kuwait City when a sniper got him. Hit him right between the eyes. Sully was dead before he hit the ground. This time he stayed dead."

My shoulders slumped. Sully wasn't like me after all. I should have known—Sully had seen a bright light, but I never saw anything when I died, only an unending darkness. Maybe there wasn't anyone else like me. Maybe I was unique, some kind of mutation, an accident of nature, and there were no answers. That was the way the world worked, wasn't it? It didn't give a damn about anyone, it just kept turning like some inexorable machine.

Bennett leaned forward from the backseat until his face filled the rearview mirror. "Maybe you've got a lucky streak going, just like Sully did. But you gotta ask yourself, errand boy, when's your luck going to run out? You can only cheat death for so long before it comes to collect."

I ignored him, turning the car onto Empire Boulevard. Normally a major thoroughfare jammed with traffic, it was deserted at this hour—3:21 a.m. by the clock on the dashboard. I was able to drive the length of the boulevard quickly, passing darkened storefront churches, closed beauty salons, and West Indian restaurants with their gates down. When I saw the gas station coming up, I slowed the car.

The Shell station was a derelict from another decade, shuttered for going on twenty years. The pumps were dry, and the only things on the shelves inside the convenience mart were cobwebs and rat droppings. It was what was under the station that mattered. Back in the 1960s, the original owner had bought into the Red Scare so fully that he'd built a fallout shelter beneath it. It made the perfect base of operations for someone like Underwood who didn't want to be found. I pulled up to the chain-link fence and got out of the car to unlock the gate. I glanced up at the sign that towered over me. The *S* had fallen off years ago, leaving the word HELL written across the sign's faded yellow clamshell shape in enormous red letters. Underwood got a big kick out of that.

I drove around the back of the station, locked the gate again behind us, and then opened the back door of the car. I grabbed Bennett's shoulders and hefted him out.

He squirmed out of my grasp. "Get your hands off me, you freak." He took a deep breath and held his chin high. His attempt at dignity would have been a lot more impressive if we hadn't been standing in an abandoned gas station parking lot. "Which way?"

"This way," I said. I guided Bennett around the back of the station to the storm doors at the base of the rear wall, keeping one hand on the plastic tie between his wrists in case he tried to run. Then I said, "I'm going to let go for a second. You're not going to try anything, are you?"

"What if I did?" he asked. "Would you kill me like Maddock?"

Not like Maddock, I thought.

I let go of the plastic tie and pulled open the storm doors. Below, cement steps descended into a murky darkness. I guided Bennett down the steps until we reached the dirt floor at the bottom. Before us was a metal door embedded in a cement wall. The old fallout sign was still bolted next to the door, three yellow triangles inside a black circle, faded and dented with age. I gave the special knock Underwood had taught me, then heard the sound of a bolt being pulled back. The door swung inward. A hulking shape stood in the doorway—Big Joe, one of Underwood's enforcers. He was six foot five with shoulders that looked broad enough to scrape the walls of the narrow hallway behind him.

Big Joe sized up Bennett, then turned to me with an all-too-familiar glare of hostility. "Took you long enough, T-Bag." There's a cliché about organized crime henchmen being men of few words. It's a cliché for a reason. We're not exactly eloquent. "Underwood was expectin' your sorry ass half an hour ago."

"There were some complications," I said.

"Big surprise. There's always complications with you." Big Joe stepped aside to let us in, then closed and locked the door. "He's waitin' for you inside."

I escorted Bennett past Big Joe and into the hallway.

Bennett snickered. "T-Bag? Really?"

Annoyed, I kept my mouth shut and pushed him forward.

"Do you even know what tea bag means?" Bennett pressed. "He must really hate you."

Hate wasn't a strong enough word for the way Big Joe felt about me. He blamed me for the death of Ford, Underwood's collector before me. Ford and Big Joe had been tight. If Big Joe thought he could get away with it, he would slit my throat as payback in a heartbeat. Not that I would stay dead, but he was the kind of guy who'd do it anyway just to blow off steam.

A string of work lamps lit the hallway, clamped along the seams between the walls and ceiling. As we walked deeper, the constant hum of the portable generator grew more audible. Bennett shivered and hugged himself for warmth. Our breath clouded in front of us. For some reason, Underwood kept it freezing cold in the fallout shelter, using the generator to power several portable air-conditioning units set up throughout the space. Just one of his many peculiar eccentricities. The hallway emptied out into a large, cement-walled room that was lit by bright standing lamps and a ceiling fixture. The walls were stained with a brownish-yellow tinge from cigarette smoke. Dark circles from extinguished butts spotted the red and tan Oriental rug on the floor. There were two gray metal doors in the right wall and another door in the left. The black door. I averted my eyes from it. In the middle of the room, a wide table stood cluttered with empty pizza boxes, drained liquor bottles, and a couple of small crates of stolen goods. Directly under the table was a big steel lockbox containing a cache of handguns.

Underwood's second enforcer, a muscular, neckless bull of a man who went by the name Tomo, was sitting on a folding metal chair. He stood up as soon as he saw us enter. He straightened his shirt's hem over the butt of the gun tucked into his pants.

Underwood himself sat on a reclining easy chair on the far side of the table. He had his legs up and his arms folded behind his head like he was enjoying a lazy afternoon in his backyard. Dark black sunglasses masked his eyes. He was never without them, even inside or at night. When I first met him, I thought he might be blind. He wasn't. He was just the kind of guy who always wore sunglasses because he thought it made him look intimidating, imposing. In the Brooklyn crime world, appearances were everything.

"There he is, the man of the hour," Underwood said, getting up and coming around the table. As he came closer, the smell of his cologne was overwhelming. Underwood practically bathed in Obsession for Men, another of his eccentricities, but of course no one dared tell him to dial it down. "Did our friend here give you any trouble, Trent?"

"Nothing I couldn't handle," I replied.

Underwood turned to Bennett. "So glad you could join us, Mr. Bennett. I've been waiting a long time for this."

"Go fuck yourself, Underwood," Bennett spat.

Underwood smiled a thin, closed-mouth grin. "Tomo, would you take our guest in back, please?"

Tomo stepped forward. He grabbed Bennett by the arm and dragged him toward the black door.

"You're not going to get what you want, Underwood," Bennett shouted. "I don't care what you do to me." Tomo opened the door and pulled Bennett inside. Before the door slammed shut again, I caught a glimpse of a single wooden chair in the middle of a bare room. The chair had straps across the armrests and on the two front legs. There was a drain in the cement floor beneath it. I felt cold all over.

Underwood turned back to me and noticed the bullet hole in my shirt. "So it happened again," he said. I nodded. "And it was just like before? You're okay?"

"I'm not dead yet," I said, and handed him Bennett's snub-nosed revolver.

Underwood pocketed the gun. Then he laughed and tapped me lightly on the cheek with his open palm. The potent, musky scent of his cologne tickled my nose. "Good dog. See, what did I tell you? You're a miracle, Trent. We're going to do amazing things together, you and me. So do me a favor and lose the long face, okay?" He pulled a wad of bills out of his pocket, peeled off a few, and handed them to me. "Get some rest, you've earned it. Once I get what I need from Bennett, I'm going to have a big job for you. Your biggest yet. There's a lot riding on this one, and I'll need my best man on it. You're my best man, aren't you, Trent?"

"Sure," I said. I pocketed the money. The black door glared at me like the eye of the devil.

Underwood made guns out of his fingers and pointed them at me. "I knew I could count on you. You're my go-to guy!" He opened the black door and went inside, blocking my view of whatever was happening in there. When the door slammed shut again I was left standing alone in the room.

I sighed and approached the first of the gray doors in the opposite wall, the one that led to my room. With no home of my own, Underwood had given me the room rent-free. At the start it had struck me as a generous act of friendship, but now, suddenly, I wondered if it was something else. If maybe he wanted me close so he could keep an eye on me, like a pet you don't quite trust.

From the corner of my eye I saw the second gray door swing silently open. I turned. Peeking out from behind the door was a woman. She had a thin face, big eyes so dark they almost looked black, and long, ragged black hair that fell in slender wisps across her features. She was Underwood's wife, or girlfriend. To be honest, I wasn't really sure what the status of their relationship was. Underwood never talked about his personal life, only business. But she was never far from his side. She never spoke a word to me, or to anyone as far as I knew. In the year I'd been here I had yet to hear Underwood address her by name. Maybe she didn't have one.

She glared at me, her eyes narrowing. I hated when she did that, which was all the time. I got the feeling she was scared of me, or disgusted by me. Maybe both.

She disappeared behind the door again, and I went into my room. The cement walls there were just as bare as in the main room, but unlike the main room there was no rug, just more cement that felt cold and hard against my feet when I took off my shoes. I'd never bothered to decorate the room in any way. It would have been like admitting this was where I would always live, that I'd never find my real home, and I refused to accept that.

A twin-sized bed, rescued from a garbage dump, rested along one wall, its metal frame speckled with rust, the mattress moldy and stained. I sat down on the bed. I wondered what was happening to Bennett on the other side of the black door. I expected to hear the sounds of torture coming through the walls, the high-pitched whir of a drill or the meaty slap of fists hitting flesh. I expected to hear Bennett scream. I waited a long time, but the sounds never came.

In a way, the silence was worse.

Three

I don't sleep. I can't, my body won't let me. I learned pretty fast that it's one of the side effects of not being able to die, like there's some kind of battery inside me that won't turn off. I feel tired sometimes, but never sleepy. That makes my downtime boring, frustrating, or both.

But that night I had a special ritual to perform. One I didn't enjoy but felt compelled to do.

I lifted the mattress. On one side was a small tear in the fabric. I reached inside and pulled out the pen and sheet of paper hidden inside the stuffing. There was a list written on the paper, a list I'd been keeping—and adding to—for the past year. I kept it hidden in the mattress because I didn't want anyone else seeing it. It felt sacred to me in ways I didn't fully understand. No one else would understand it, either. I sat down on the bed and read over the list:

1. *Ford*
2. *Wellington*
3. *Braum*
4. *Langan*
5. *Francisco*
6. *Perry*
7. *Petrucha*
8. *the boy*

Then I took the pen and added another name to it.

9. *Maddock*

All the lives I'd stolen, reduced to the equivalent of a shopping list. Writing down their names was a compulsion. It helped me remember them, and that seemed like the right thing to do. I could recite the list forward and backward by now, knew their names by heart, all except one. Number eight, "the boy." The only one who didn't belong. The others were killers, racketeers, and thieves, but not him. He hadn't done anything to anyone. He hadn't tried to kill me first the way the others had. The boy had simply been in the wrong place at the wrong time.

I thought of the crack house on Fourth Avenue again, and had to forcefully push it from my mind. The memory of the boy had been lurking in the back of my head like a ghost ever since. I didn't want to think about it. One night off, that was all I wanted. A way to forget, even if only for a few hours.

There was an old TV set in the corner of the room, rescued from the same garbage dump as my bed. It barely worked, and when it did its rabbit ears only picked up a single station, a local-access channel that showed old movies. I watched whenever I could. It was more than a pastime—it was my teacher. Everything I learned about the world that didn't come from Underwood came from watching Humphrey Bogart, Cary Grant, Lon Chaney Jr., and Boris Karloff.

I turned it on and watched for a couple of hours, taking in all of *Werewolf of London* and part of *The Maltese Falcon* before I realized I was too distracted to pay attention. I kept thinking about the boy, and God-knows-what happening to Bennett behind the black door. I needed something stronger than the TV. I turned it off and pulled out the other item I'd hidden inside the mattress. It was a paperback book I'd found one rainy day on the stoop of a brownstone in Park Slope after running a collection for Underwood. Something about the sight of the book lying there, discarded, unwanted, and alone, pelted mercilessly by the rain, had filled me with an unexpected sadness. I pitied it, felt almost a kinship with it, so I stuffed it inside my coat to keep it safe from the storm, and brought it back with me.

It seemed so small in my hands now, a fragile thing. Its rain-battered pages had dried, but they'd also become swollen and brittle from the moisture they'd absorbed. The cover art was a painting of a flat blue sea with a big white castle on the far shore. A ship with tall sails floated upon the waves. Standing on its deck was a woman in a white dress with long, flowing auburn hair. She held a sword in her hands. Above her, a winged horse and a flying lizard faced off. The title was printed along the top in a curled script: *The Ragana's Revenge* by Elena De Voe. I opened the book carefully so the damaged pages wouldn't tear.

At the front was a detailed map of a land called Kallamathus, charting regions with names like the Cliffs of Treachery, the Forest of Dark Secrets, and the Sea of Miseries. I thought it was ridiculous and chuckled at the idea of New York City's geography named in a similar, absurdly specific manner. The Street of Forgotten Trash Bags. The Avenue of Impossibly Expensive Restaurants. I turned the page to a foreword by the author explaining how the magical kingdom of Kallamathus was based on an alternate version of Eastern Europe, and in fact the word *ragana* was Lithuanian for *witch*. Then, finally, the story began, describing the adventures of a dirt-poor peasant girl named Armelle who lived in a realm of magic and strange creatures, and discovered her world was far more dangerous, yet far more richly rewarding, than she ever knew. At the back of the book was a lengthy glossary of invented words that I found myself consulting regularly as I read, just to figure out what the hell the characters were talking about, and who was who. It didn't help that most of the characters had unpronounceable names comprised of strings of consonants broken by random apostrophes—all except for the heroine, Armelle, and the villain, the Ragana. Armelle befriended a magical, telepathic horse (or rather, a Q'horse, only the Q and the apostrophe were silent), fell in love with the pointy-eared elf prince Ch'aqrath, and discovered she wasn't a peasant at all but an orphaned princess who was prophesied to save the kingdom from the Ragana.

"There are worlds within worlds," Ch'aqrath declared, petting the Q'horse's soft, snowy mane. "The Ragana plans to tear this world asunder and reveal the true world that lies beneath its mask."

"And what world would that be?" Armelle queried bravely, though her full, rosy lips quivered with the foreboding fear that overcame her.

Ch'aqrath set his handsome jaw, alerting her that what he was about to tell her was knowledge known only to Elfkind. "It is a world of wonders and terrors the likes of which you could never believe," he replied. "Your kind is so fragile, my beautiful companion. Were they to behold the truth, they would surely fall into fits of madness."

I grunted, annoyed. Elena De Voe had gotten it wrong. You didn't need a secret, hidden world to scare people. The real world was awful enough. I continued reading, but by then the spell the story had cast over me was broken. As the Ragana unleashed an army of dragons upon the royal palace, I stopped, closed the book, and put it aside.

Dragons, magic, worlds within worlds—it was all preposterous. There was no magic to protect you from the rich and powerful; if you didn't learn to lie, cheat, and steal, you were ground down. There were no ancient prophecies that guided people toward their destiny; everyone just muddled along as best they could. There were no poor peasants who were secretly wealthy royalty; the poor stayed poor under the heels of the rich, and they always would. It was the way of the world. In this world, the *real* world, there were only cold cement walls and dangerous men who patted you on the cheek and smiled as they called you a dog.

And there was death. Death was everywhere. It lurked in the barrels of the countless guns that had been pointed in my direction, and behind black doors in rooms with drains in their floors. Death was a constant, the *only* constant—and yet even death had rejected me. For reasons it refused to explain, death didn't want me any more than the world of the living did.

It brought me back to the same question I asked myself every day: Who was I? Like Armelle, did I have a family somewhere I didn't know about? Parents, siblings, a wife and kids? If I did, then why was no one looking for me? I'd walked every inch of this city on jobs for Underwood and hadn't seen a single missing-person flyer with my picture. Why had no one ever recognized me on the street, stopped me, called me by my real name?

Maybe I was more like the Ragana, who rose fully formed from the Sea of Miseries, a self-contained force that existed only to bring evil and suffering. A freak, just like Bennett had called me.

Or maybe there were no answers.

No, I couldn't accept that. There *had* to be answers. They were waiting for me in a past I couldn't remember. But every time I tried, every time I forced my mind to reach back beyond the previous year, I came up empty.

I lay back on the bed, folding my arms under my head. I stared at the cracks in the ceiling and the cobwebs that gathered in the corners. I tried to put my thoughts in order so I could make sense out of them. So much was lost to me, but these, at least, were the things I knew to be true:

One. I was a man. Okay, that one wasn't too hard to figure out, but it was as good a place to start as any. Judging by my reflection, I was in my mid to late thirties, with dark eyes and dark hair, though that wasn't much to go on. I'd spent hours memorizing my features, studying my hairline, the cut of my jaw and shape of my nose, every crease around my eyes and fold in my ears, but the truth was there was nothing distinctive about my appearance. I'd scoured my body for scars, tattoos, anything that might help someone identify me, but there weren't any. It was frustrating, but not entirely surprising. If my body could heal bullet wounds then surgery scars, tattoos, or marks from childhood accidents weren't likely to stick around either.

Two. My amnesia was retrograde, a word I'd learned when I researched my condition on the free computers at the Brooklyn Public Library. It meant that I couldn't remember who I was or where I lived, but I could still talk, tie my shoes, drive a car, feed myself. I also learned that the condition most likely stemmed from one of two possible causes, either brain damage or a mental defense mechanism against a traumatic event. So had I suffered a brain injury or seen something my mind couldn't accept? There was no way to know. My memory, up until a year ago, was like a frustratingly blank piece of paper. Which brought me to the final item on the checklist of what I knew.

Three. The brick wall. My earliest memory, and only a vague one at that. I remembered regaining consciousness lying on my back in front of a brick wall. I wasn't sure how much I could trust that memory, since my mind was constantly trying to fill in the blanks with fabricated stories, but this one at least *felt* true. The wall in question seemed average, but there was something about it I still wasn't sure if I'd really seen or only imagined. One of the bricks had a symbol scratched into it. In the fuzziness of my memory I thought it looked like an eye inside a circle. I remembered sparkles of light dancing along the wall and fading away like dying embers as I opened my eyes. I remembered a small, swirling wisp of smoke, as if someone had just put out a cigarette.

I figured the brick wall probably belonged to an alley somewhere in the city, only I had no idea where. My next memory was of running down an empty street at night, lost and confused. I found a hospital, but without any ID and with no signs of physical trauma they turned me away. After that I camped on park benches and under bridges, rummaging through garbage cans for food and shooing away the rats that came too close at night. In the mornings I would move on, hoping to find someone or something that would remind me who I was. But all I found was Underwood.

He'd been in one of his stash houses, off of an alley in Harlem, a small, concrete hut with a counterfeit Con Edison sign on the door to keep people out. I was ravenously hungry, and the smell of food lured me down the alley. The lights coming out of the hut's windows had looked so warm that I couldn't help myself. When I saw the door was slightly ajar I didn't bother knocking, my hunger was too great. I just walked right in. They were all there, Tomo, Big Joe, Ford, Underwood, and the dark-haired woman, standing around a table loaded with stacks of cash and empty fast-food wrappers. The woman saw me first, her dark eyes widening with alarm. She didn't say a word, but the look on her face was enough to alert the others. Tomo, Big Joe, and Ford turned on me with their guns drawn. Then I felt something hit me in the chest. That was the first time I died. The next thing I knew I was waking up in a Dumpster, my shirt riddled with bullet holes. Only I didn't have any bullet holes in *me* anymore. As I crawled out, I stepped on something that crunched underfoot. I looked down and saw a shriveled, desiccated corpse lying beside the Dumpster. Ford. He'd been unlucky enough to get the order to carry my body out to the Dumpster, and being the closest living person had paid the price for it. Ford's was the first life I stole. The first name on my list, and the reason Tomo and Big Joe wanted me dead. The three of them had been like brothers.

After that, Underwood knew someone like me could be useful. He took me off the streets, put a roof over my head, and filled my pockets with enough money to clothe myself and keep my belly full. He promised to help me find the answers if I worked for him in the meantime. He gave me hope. He gave me a purpose.

The hope remained. But lately, ever since the crack house, I'd been wondering if the purpose was the right one.

Four

"Bennett's people have control of a number of properties around the city, mostly warehouses and shipping piers. Whatever they can rent out fast and cheap or use for themselves as stash houses," Underwood said. It was the next night, and we were sitting at the table in the main room of the fallout shelter. I'd changed into a fresh new shirt and burned the one Maddock had put a bullet hole in. I'd burned nine ruined shirts so far. I hoped I could get through tonight, at least, without ruining another one. When your life is this messed up, you keep your goals simple.

The black door was closed. I wondered if Bennett had been released alive or if his bruised and beaten corpse lay on the other side of the door even now. I pictured the drain in the floor painted red with blood. I felt cold then, and turned away.

The second gray door was open, revealing a small room that was the mirror image of my own, except without a bed. Instead, there was a couch, a couple of chairs, and a floor lamp. The dark-haired woman sat on the couch, staring blankly into space while Tomo sat on a chair across from her, keeping an eye on her. She would go catatonic like this on occasion. More than once I'd seen her sitting with her eyes open but completely unresponsive—lights on but nobody home. Sometimes it only lasted a few minutes, other times she didn't seem to come back to herself for hours. I wondered if she was a junkie and Underwood was selling stolen goods on the black market to feed her habit. It didn't strike me as a good use of his time or money, but maybe that was what love did to people. I wouldn't know.

Underwood continued talking, pulling my attention back to him. "Sometimes, when these properties sit empty, they get squatters. A certain object I'm looking for recently made an appearance at one of these properties, in the hands of some people who aren't supposed to be there. I just didn't know which property until I got it out of our good friend Bennett. This is where you need to go."

He pulled a piece of paper from his pocket and passed it to me. Even his hand reeked of cologne. He'd written down an address, *49th and West Side Highway*, and beneath it he'd scrawled a name, *Balakier*.

"It's a warehouse that used to belong to an import company, but it's been abandoned for a few years now. The people who are squatting there have a wooden box in their possession. I'm told the box has an old metal crest on its lid. A couple of lions and a shield. That's how you'll recognize it. Get the box and bring it to me."

"How big is it?" I asked.

"About the size of a suitcase, two feet long, a foot wide. It's big, but it won't be too heavy for you to carry."

"What's in it?" I asked.

"Just bring it to me. This one's a game-changer, Trent. I already have a buyer lined up for it, one who's willing to drop so much cash for it that I could *own* this town. So don't worry about what's in it, don't open it, don't mess with it, I don't want you fucking it up. Don't do anything with the box except bring it straight back here. Got it?"

"Got it." I put the paper with the address in my pocket and stood.

"One more thing," he added. "This won't be a simple in-and-out job like the others. Whoever has the box won't be stupid enough to leave it unguarded, and they're not going to give it up without a fight. Things might get hairy, but if anyone can handle it, it's you. That's why I wanted you on this. You're my go-to guy. I'm counting on you."

I nodded and pulled on my leather jacket. "Anything else I need to know?"

"Yes," Underwood said. He picked casually at his teeth with a fingernail. "Once you've taken the box from them, kill them. No survivors. I don't want anyone left alive who can trace this back to me. There's too much at stake."

My throat went tight.

"Something wrong?" he asked. He must have noticed me tense up.

"It's just that you've never asked me to kill anyone before," I said.

He raised an eyebrow. "I don't like having my orders questioned," he said. "And I don't like doing favors for someone who questions them. Is there going to be a problem?"

In the reflection of his black sunglasses, I saw myself shake my head.

"Good. Now go bring me that box." Underwood stood up from the table and started toward the other room, where the dark-haired woman sat staring into space.

I rose and followed him. "Underwood, wait."

He turned to face me, impatient. "What is it now?"

"Have you found anything new? About me, I mean?"

His scowl became a grin. "You better believe it. And it's big. All those inquiries I've been making have paid off in spades. Believe me, you're going to be very happy with what I found."

"What is it? Tell me."

"All in due time," he said. I stared eagerly at him, waiting for more, but he just smiled. "When the box is in my hands, and the ones you've taken it from are dead, then I'll tell you everything you want to know." He nodded toward the corridor that led to the exit. "Better get a move on, Trent. I don't like to be kept waiting."

I felt like I was going to explode. I wanted to know *now,* but Underwood was already walking away. I wouldn't get any more out of him. Biting back my frustration, I walked to the fallout shelter door. Big Joe was there, waiting like a doorman. He sneered at me. "What's eating you?"

"Nothing."

Big Joe pulled back the bolt on the door, unlocking it. "You be careful out there, T-Bag. Nobody lives forever. Not even a freakshow like you."

I parked the Explorer on 49th Street between 11th Avenue and the West Side Highway, then walked the rest of the way. The nighttime chill had settled over the city, and I pulled my leather jacket close around me for warmth. The address Underwood had given me was a two-story brick building in an enclosed cul-de-sac on the other side of the highway, flanked on either side by piers that stretched out into the dark waters of the Hudson

River. The walls of the cul-de-sac hid it from the streetlamps and the blinking lights of the piers' freight cranes. And from witnesses. A faded sign on the building's façade read BALAKIER IMPORT & EXPORT. I waited for a break in the West Side Highway's traffic, then hurried across.

The closer I got to the warehouse, the less I wanted to go inside. It felt like hundreds of tiny, imaginary hands pushing me back, trying to stop me. I didn't like this job. A simple in-and-out collection was something I was used to, but this was a whole other ball game. It was enough to make me want to turn back. But Underwood had answers, finally. Answers I'd waited a year for, and if I wanted them I didn't have a choice. I had to see this through.

I crept around to the side of the building, keeping to the shadows as I slid my back along the graffiti-covered wall. There were four big windows on the first floor. Their glass panes had been smashed long ago. Now the windows were boarded from the inside with sheets of plywood. Light bled out through the corners of the boards and from under the wooden double doors in the middle of the wall. I pulled my gun. A muffled voice came from inside. I couldn't tell what it was saying, but one thing was unmistakable. It was a woman's voice.

Damn. Underwood hadn't told me who would be inside. On the drive over I'd imagined it would be men like Tomo and Big Joe, thugs who wouldn't hesitate to shoot me dead if I didn't shoot them first. But a woman?

No survivors, that was what Underwood said. So be it, then. Whoever was in there probably had it coming anyway. I wasn't about to let my first shot at getting some concrete answers slip through my fingers.

I gripped the gun tighter and tried the handle on one of the doors. It was unlocked. I pushed it open and stepped through.

Inside, the warehouse was a single enormous open space. The hardwood floor was bare and scuffed. Two rows of thick, wooden floor-to-ceiling support beams spanned the room like carefully arranged dominoes. Saucer-shaped metal light fixtures hung on long chains from the ceiling—or what was left of the ceiling. There was a wide, gaping hole in it that looked like something heavy had broken through, and recently. The floor below was littered with debris, chunks of cement, and large pieces of wood and tar from the roof. Old wooden crates and heaps of broken, waterlogged furniture had been pushed against the walls in stacks, forming a makeshift circle around the center of the room. What I saw within that circle stopped me in my tracks.

I noticed the woman first. She was short, not more than five feet tall, with long, thick black hair. She wore jeans and a bulky cargo vest over a plain long-sleeved shirt. She held a wooden staff horizontally in front of her with both hands in a defensive stance. Mounted at the end of the staff was what looked like a small black ball. Whoever she was, she didn't see me. She was too focused on the six men in front of her.

They had their backs to me so that all I saw was their long, slate-gray trench coats. They didn't have any weapons that I could see. They advanced on the woman, forcing her back toward the crates behind her, penning her in. Six big men against one small woman. I didn't know what the hell was going on, but I didn't like those odds. It was clear from the look on her face that she didn't either.

I raised my gun and took a cautious step closer. My foot accidentally kicked a small chip of fallen cement and sent it skittering loudly across the floor.

Shit.

The six men stopped moving. Their trench coats split apart down the middle and blossomed out to their sides. Too late I realized they weren't trench coats at all.

They were wings.

All six of them spun on me. I'd expected to see the scowling, beefy faces of mob enforcers, but these weren't men. They weren't even human. Their faces were gray, craggy, and elongated like the snouts of hairless dogs. They had long pointed ears, short stubby horns that sprouted from their brows, and black, deep-set eyes that fixed me with a glare that said I was about to become dinner. One look at their wide, tusked mouths and ivory dagger teeth and I was sure there was room enough on the menu for me and the woman both.

Too shocked to move, I blinked instead, which wasn't much help.

The woman saw me then, and shouted, "Run!"

The winged creatures shrieked, a sound as loud and piercing as a siren. They launched themselves into the air, wings flapping, and as they came at me I had just enough time to wonder what the hell I'd walked in on.

Five

I forced my arms to lift the gun and take aim at the flying creatures. I was still stunned at the impossibility of what I was seeing, but somehow I managed to pull the trigger four times in rapid succession. The nine-millimeter slugs slammed into the chest and face of the creature at the head of the pack, only to ricochet off its skin. It paused in midair, surprised but not hurt, then continued toward me with the others. The beat of their huge, gray, batlike wings created drafts strong enough to stir the dust and debris on the floor.

Whatever these things were, bullets couldn't kill them. And bullets were all I had. I was screwed.

I ran for the warehouse door, but one of them dropped down in front of it, blocking my exit. It had a withered yellow eye that looked like an old wound from some long-ago fight. I skidded to a halt, pointing the gun at it out of blind instinct, but Yellow Eye just chittered at me. These things weren't scared of guns.

While I was distracted, another one rammed me from behind, knocking me to the floor. Its claws felt like razors slashing through the back of my leather coat, through my shirt, and into my skin. I gritted my teeth against the pain and rolled over. The flayed, bleeding skin on my back burned where it touched the hard, filthy warehouse floor.

The creature landed on me with its full weight, pinning me to the floor. It brought its face closer, near enough for me to see the Y-shaped scar on its cheek, and to get a whiff of its earthy, abattoir odor. Scarface sniffed me like it was checking the bouquet of a vintage wine. Then it recoiled, not liking what it smelled.

"You don't smell so great yourself, you ugly son of a bitch," I said.

Scarface opened its wide, toothy maw in an angry roar. I swung my gun up, jammed the barrel between its jaws, and pulled the trigger. The muzzle flash lit up the cavernous interior of its mouth, illuminating a field of small, nubby teeth that lined the inside of its cheeks. Scarface unfurled its wings and flew back up to the ceiling, coughing and gagging on the gunsmoke but otherwise unharmed. Damn, what did it take to kill these things?

More to the point, what the hell *were* they?

I wondered for a moment if this might all just be in my head. As an explanation, it wasn't beyond the realm of possibility. I'd read somewhere that if the human brain went without sleep for ten days it started to hallucinate. Twenty days and it bordered on insanity. I hadn't slept in a year. Prior to that I couldn't be sure, but it was possible I'd never slept in my entire life. Maybe it was finally catching up with me. How insane would a man have to be after a lifetime of sleep deprivation?

But the scratches in my back felt real enough. No hallucination could be that excruciating. As impossible as it seemed, this was really happening.

I got back on my feet and tucked my gun into my pants. It was useless against the creatures, but I knew better than to toss it. It was Underwood's Golden Rule, drilled into my head since day one: Never, ever lose your gun. You never know when you're going to need it.

Across the room, the short woman was swinging her staff at the creatures. They hung in the air above her, bobbing and feinting just out of reach. She grunted and bit her lip in frustration. Scarface had rejoined the pack, and together the creatures trilled and clucked. The sound was alien but unmistakable. They were laughing at her. Toying with her before moving in for the kill.

I glanced at the open door. Yellow Eye had gone to join in the fun, too, leaving the door unguarded. Just outside, I could see the brick wall that sheltered the warehouse from the surrounding piers. The low, distant hum of West Side Highway traffic floated to me. It would be easy to escape, to leave this insanity while the creatures were distracted and run back to the safety of the world I knew. Getting out while I still could was the smart choice.

The short woman grunted as she swung her staff at the five chittering things flapping in the air above her. I looked at her, then back at the exit. Screw this. I took a quick step toward the door. Then I stopped.

Five. There were only five of those things toying with the woman. Where was the sixth?

I turned around just as the sixth creature came winging out of the shadows in the corner of the ceiling and rammed into the woman from behind. She fell. The staff flew out of her hands, clattering to the floor and rolling until it came to a stop at the base of a stack of crates on the opposite side of the room. All six of the creatures descended toward her like a pack of wild dogs on a wounded animal.

Scarface got to her first, wrapping long talons over the top of her head. Her eyes—a clear, astonishing blue, I noticed for the first time, and as bright as the noontime sky—widened in terror. She scrabbled against the floor, trying to pull away, reaching desperately for the staff that was dozens of feet too far from her fingers. The creatures swarmed around her.

She didn't look like she could put up much of a fight against the six of them, especially without her staff. They would make short work of her, but it might give me enough time to get away. The open doorway was right behind me.

So why weren't my stupid feet moving?

Ah shit, I thought, and ran toward the pack. Even with amnesia, I had no doubt this was the dumbest thing I'd ever done in my life.

When I reached them, I grabbed the nearest creature around the neck and tried to pull it away from her. It didn't even turn to look at me, it just swung its arm into my face. It felt like getting hit with a wrecking ball. I was thrown clear across the room. I landed on my back, sliding across the floor until I slammed into one of the thick wooden support beams. A sudden, searing pain raged in my shoulder.

I struggled to sit up, but I could tell right away my shoulder had been dislocated. Across the warehouse from me, Scarface yanked the woman's head back, exposing her throat. The others gnashed their teeth in anticipation. The woman's face was a mask of defiance. She slipped one hand into a pocket of her cargo vest and pulled out a small, round, reflective object. A mirror of some kind, I thought. She held it out toward Scarface, muttered something, and a bright light burst out of the mirror. Scarface shrieked and let go of her, backing up a step and covering its eyes. The woman scrambled to her feet and started to run.

I admired her courage, but she didn't get far. The other five creatures tackled her, bringing her down to the floor again. They trilled in laughter and drew back their claws to strike. I tried to stand, but the sharp pain in my shoulder was too much and I fell again. Like a fool, I'd gotten involved, stuck around to try to save this woman when I could have gotten away, and now, for my trouble, I would get to watch these creatures tear her to pieces. Lesson learned.

With a loud crash, a window in the wall behind me exploded inward, and what looked very much to my startled eyes like an enormous gray timber wolf came rocketing through in a shower of broken plywood. It landed on the floor, then bounded again, pouncing on Scarface. The two fell in a tangled mess. The other creatures took to the air again. The wolf got its jaws around Scarface's neck and clamped down, shaking it violently even as the creature scratched and raked at the wolf's flanks. There was a snap, loud enough that I heard it from the other side of the warehouse, and Scarface went limp in the wolf's jaws. Its wings twitched and then fell still.

Wincing in pain, I got to my feet. I steadied myself against the support beam, then slammed my shoulder into it, knocking the joint back into its socket. The pain was staggering. Bursts of light flared behind my eyes. A moment later the pain subsided to a dull throb. I looked up. The five remaining creatures were winging toward me. Apparently they had decided I was an easier target than the wolf. Lucky me.

"The staff!" the woman shouted at me. "Use the staff!"

It was on the floor by my feet. I picked it up. The wood felt thick and heavy, as solid as a Louisville Slugger. Then I nearly dropped it again in disgust. Up close, I saw that what I'd originally mistaken for a black ball at the end of the staff was actually a mummified human fist. A real one.

But the winged creatures were streaming toward me and I didn't have time to think about why there was a dead human hand attached to the staff. I swung the wooden end of the staff at the creatures, trying to bat them away.

"You're holding it the wrong way!" the woman shouted. "Turn it over! Hit them with the fist!"

Right. Sure. The fist. I tried to turn the staff around again, but one of the creatures grabbed the other end and wouldn't let go. It sneered at me with a grotesquely scarred mouth. I tug-of-warred with Harelip while the others circled. My injured shoulder throbbed.

"Use the fist!" the woman yelled again. She sounded annoyed.

"What do you think I'm trying to do?" I yelled back.

But it was too much. My shoulder was still too weak after its disloca-tion. The staff slipped from my hands. Without the counter-tension of my tug-of-war partner, I fell on my ass. Harelip bobbed in the air with the staff in its hands, laughing at me. The others joined in. Assholes.

The wolf sprang again, bounding over my head. I caught a glimpse of a leather cuff fastened around its right front leg. The wolf clamped its jaws through Harelip's leathery wing and dragged it back down to the floor. The other creatures bobbed and shrieked in the air, eyeing the wolf warily. The wolf snapped its massive jaws at Harelip, who dropped the staff and grabbed the wolf's snout, batting at the animal's head and haunches with its wings. It got its legs up under the wolf and raked its sharp nails along the wolf's belly, tracing deep red lines through the fur.

"Thornton!" the woman cried out in anguish.

The wolf whimpered in pain. It tried to get its jaws around Harelip's neck, but it was already too weak. The wolf's hind legs buckled. Harelip flipped it over, straddling it and scratching more deep gashes into its belly. The wolf whimpered again and squirmed to get away. Harelip grabbed it and stood, lifting the wolf over its head and effortlessly tossing it across the room. The wolf struck the far wall, leaving a red spatter of blood where it hit. Then it dropped, crashing through a pile of old crates and furniture that tumbled down on top of it.

"No!" the woman yelled. She ran toward where the wolf had landed. The creatures in the air flew after her, chittering.

Except for Harelip. Harelip stayed where it was, facing away from me as it licked wolf blood from its fingers. I picked up the staff, gripping it toward the bottom like a baseball bat, the blackened fist at its top.

Harelip sensed me coming. It spun around, fixing me with its jet-black eyes. It opened its wide, tusked mouth in a bloodcurdling hiss.

"You picked the wrong night to fuck with me," I said, and swung the staff like I was batting for the outfield. The human fist at the tip struck Harelip square in the chest.

Bullets bounced off these creatures' skin, so in truth I didn't expect any better results from the staff, despite the short woman's insistence that I use it. But the moment the fist connected there was a bright explosion of light and fire. Harelip was knocked backward through the air. A glowing, orange spiderweb of fire spread across its skin. Harelip tumbled through the air trailing embers and char, and hit the wall on the opposite side of the warehouse so hard that the bricks cracked and buckled. Harelip exploded into a chunky cloud of burning ash.

I blinked dumbly at the staff in my hands. What the hell just happened?

Six

The four remaining creatures hovered in the air above the short woman. They glanced at the charred remains of their companion at the foot of the wall, then glared at me. They looked pissed, but they also looked wary of the staff in my hands.

I shook it at them threateningly. "Anyone else want a piece of this?"

Yellow Eye shrieked angrily at me, then flew up through the gaping hole in the ceiling. The other three followed, and they disappeared into the dark night sky.

"Yeah, I didn't think so," I said.

Now that the creatures were gone, I went to see if the woman was all right. If she was injured, she didn't show it. She began frantically tossing aside the old crates and debris that stood between her and the wolf that had come out of nowhere.

"They're gone," I told her.

She glanced over her shoulder at me. "Help me. I can't leave Thornton here."

"Look, lady, I'm sorry about your dog, but those things could come back at any moment," I said. "We have to get out of here."

"He's not a dog," she said. She gritted her teeth as she pushed a half-smashed crate out of her way. "Just help me."

If she wanted to stay here to find her pet, she was crazy. Which probably meant I was, too. We'd both seen the same impossible things, fought off the same creatures that couldn't be real. And yet, she didn't seem fazed by it at all. Maybe she was used to being crazy. I could always ask her for tips.

With a heavy sigh, I put down the staff and helped her lift away the heavier bits of furniture and junk. "What were those things?"

"Gargoyles," she said, grunting as she pulled another crate clear of the mess. "They must have followed us here from the cathedral. I cast a ward around this place, but I guess it was too late. They must have already seen us come here."

I didn't understand half of what she said. I looked up at the gaping hole in the ceiling again. "Gargoyles? For real? Like, off of buildings . . . ?"

She glared at me. "Do they *look* like they came off of buildings?" She sighed and gazed up at the hole. "They waited until I was alone, and then they broke through." I understood that part, at least. It was the gargoyles who'd put the hole in the roof. "I should have known better. This is all my fault." She picked up an old metal folding chair from the pile and threw it aside in frustration. It clattered loudly on the floor. I decided to hold off on any more questions for a while.

Between the two of us the job went quickly. A few minutes later we finally cleared away the last of the debris.

"Thornton!" she said.

But the body on the floor wasn't Thornton. Thornton was a big gray timber wolf, but what lay on the floor was a naked man, curled on his side in the fetal position. He wasn't breathing. The floor around his body was slick with blood from the long, deep scratches in his chest and stomach. Bits of something red and meaty poked out of the wounds.

Then I noticed a leather bracelet around his right wrist, in the same place I'd seen it on the wolf's leg. It had the same intricate, interwoven design in the leather and thin strands of gold. How was that possible? I was sure I'd seen a wolf.

I thought of the old movies I'd seen on the TV in the fallout shelter, ones where Henry Hull and Lon Chaney Jr. played men who became wolves. There was a word for it, but it was impossible. I didn't even want to think it.

She knelt beside the naked man and felt his neck for a pulse. "Oh no," she said.

"He's dead," I said. It wasn't a question so much as confirmation. There was no way Thornton *couldn't* be dead with his body torn open like that, but sometimes people didn't believe it until they saw for themselves. They had to touch the body with their own hands because the enormity of it was too much to process otherwise. The mother of the little boy, number eight on my list, had done that. She'd put her hands on the boy's cheeks like she was checking him for a fever. The memory turned into a rock in my stomach. Suddenly I felt useless and stupid standing there watching yet another woman mourn her loss.

She leaned back on her haunches and shook her head. "Oh, Thornton."

"We should go," I said. I took her arm to help her up, but she yanked it away.

"I told you, I'm not leaving him here."

I knelt down across the body from her. "Look, those things, those *gargoyles* aren't going to stay away for long. We need to move now, before this place is crawling with them."

She looked over her shoulder at the empty warehouse. "They've gone to get help. I'd say we've got about fifteen minutes before they come back with twice their number. That should give us plenty of time."

"Plenty of time for what?"

She didn't answer. She reached into another pocket of her cargo vest and pulled out a long, thick, golden chain. Dangling from its end was a pendant in the shape of a starburst. Four small red gems were arranged in a diamond formation at its center.

I looked up at the hole in the ceiling. We didn't have time to play with jewelry. The sooner I left, the better. But I couldn't leave her behind. If those creatures came back and caught her alone, she was as good as dead.

She rolled Thornton gently onto his back. Then she depressed the center of the starburst pendant with her thumbs. A long, sharp spike popped out of its back with a metallic *snik*. She held it over Thornton and chanted some words I didn't understand. They were in some other language, one I'd never heard before, but there was something eerie about it that drew a shiver down my spine.

"What are you doing?"

She ignored me. When she was done chanting, she took a deep breath and slammed the pendant down on Thornton's chest, driving the spike into his heart like a dagger blade.

"No!" I shouted, reaching to stop her, but it was already too late. "What the hell is wrong with you?"

She lifted Thornton's head gently and slid the chain around his neck. "Now we just have to wait and give the Breath of Itzamna time to work."

I stared at her, wondering if I ought to leave her behind after all. She was clearly out of her mind. Or maybe the whole damn world had gone mad. After all, I'd died nine times already but was still here, alive and kicking. In what kind of sane world did *that* happen?

She saw the confusion in my face and said, "That's what the amulet's called, the Breath of Itzamna. It was given to me by a nine-hundred-year-old Mayan shaman in a tattoo parlor in Los Angeles. Let's hope it works as well as he said it would."

Ridiculously, I felt a pang of disappointment that someone so beautiful and brave could also be batshit crazy.

Against my better judgment, I asked, "Do you really expect me to believe there are nine-hundred-year-old Mayan shamans living in L.A.?"

"Just one," she corrected me. "The others are in San Diego these days, mostly. They share an apartment complex near the zoo."

Of course. I should have guessed as much. "That's insane," I told her.

"Not really," she said. "It's nice there and the rents are cheap." She turned to me, her brow knitting with sudden confusion, as if it had only just occurred to her that I was a complete stranger. "Who are you?"

"My name's Trent."

"Trent." She shook my hand. Hers was so small it practically disappeared in my grip. "I'm Bethany. Thank you, Trent. If you hadn't come along when you did, I don't know what would have happened. I guess I owe you my life. I don't think I could have held off six gargoyles on my own, even with the Anubis Hand."

I raised my eyebrows. "The what now?"

Bethany nodded at the staff on the floor with the mummified human fist. "Only two things in the world can hurt a gargoyle. Sunlight—or any bright light, really—and the Anubis Hand." She looked at the pile of ashes by the wall that had once been Harelip. "But maybe you can help me out, Trent, because the thing is, I've never seen the Anubis Hand do that before. It can hurt gargoyles, it can knock them unconscious, but it's never burned them to cinders before."

I shrugged. "Maybe *you* can only knock them out, but I'm, what, three times your body mass? No disrespect, but I gave that gargoyle a pretty good smack."

She looked at me skeptically. "Well, whatever you did, it saved my life. Probably yours, too."

Not likely, I thought. I turned away from her, and Bethany gasped in alarm. "Trent, you're injured!"

The adrenaline from the fight had numbed the pain so much that I'd forgotten about the wounds on my back. So much for getting through the night without ruining another shirt. "I'll be okay," I told her. "I'm tougher than I look."

"It's not every day someone walks away from a gargoyle attack," she said. "You should count yourself lucky."

"I guess so." I still didn't fully understand what had happened. Gargoyles, a staff called the Anubis Hand, an amulet named the Breath of Itzamna, a man who just a few minutes before had been a wolf . . . If the door had opened just then and a magical, telepathic Q'horse had trotted in, I wouldn't have been surprised.

"Come on, Thornton," Bethany whispered.

"What exactly are you expecting to happen here?" I pressed.

She ignored me and continued talking to the dead body. "We need you. You're the only one who knows where it is now."

"Where what is?"

Finally, she acknowledged my presence again. She shook her head and said, "A box. It's nothing you need to concern yourself with."

Oh God. In all the chaos, I'd forgotten about the box. My stomach dropped. Bethany was one of the squatters Underwood had mentioned. I'd made a serious mistake. I saw that now. I'd gotten carried away in the moment and let my guard down. I never should have told her my name, or found out hers. That was only going to make it harder to do my job.

"Tell me about the box," I said. She didn't answer. She kept her eyes on Thornton.

I'd saved her life, only to have to kill her myself. Because she didn't just know my name, she'd seen my face. She could identify me, trace me right back to Underwood, which was exactly what he didn't want. I reached behind my back for the gun in my waistband. My mouth went as dry as sand. My heart lurched into my throat. My fingers grazed the gun's handle. This was important, I told myself. There was too much riding on this.

When the box is in my hands, and the ones you've taken it from are dead, then I'll tell you everything you want to know.

I wrapped my fingers around the grip of the gun. My index finger touched the trigger guard.

"Bethany, where is the box?"

I started to pull the gun free.

Between us, Thornton sat up suddenly, gasping air into his lungs.

Seven

There was no doubt in my mind that Thornton had been dead. Well and truly dead. I'd seen the body with my own eyes, clear as day, and they didn't come any deader. And yet, one minute he was lying motionless on the floor with his guts practically falling out of his stomach, and the next he was sitting up and hyperventilating like he'd just surfaced from a deep-sea dive.

Startled, I let go of my gun, leaving it tucked in the back of my pants. Adrenaline surged through me, my muscles coiling, ready to spring away if he made any sudden moves. In the back of my mind, I wondered if this was how Bennett had felt when he saw me coming for him after I died.

The thought blossomed into another, more earth-shaking one. Was it possible Thornton was like me?

"Thornton?" Bethany said.

He stared at her, gasping and choking, still trying to catch his breath. "Bethany? What happened to me? I—I can't breathe."

"Take it slow," she said. "Don't force it. Just stop trying to breathe and you'll be okay." She turned to me. "Help me get him up."

I closed my mouth, suddenly aware that it had been hanging open this whole time. Bethany took one of Thornton's arms. I reached for the other, then paused. I didn't want to touch him. I didn't want to be anywhere near him. I had the sudden and inexplicable urge to beat him with a shovel until he stayed down for good.

"Please, I can't do this alone," she said.

We didn't have a lot of time before the gargoyles came back, so I reluctantly took Thornton's other arm. His skin felt cool and clammy, like a slab of raw meat. I didn't like it, it didn't feel right, but I helped him get to his feet. He was heavy, cumbersome, awkward. In that moment, I finally understood the term dead weight.

Thornton wobbled unsteadily on his feet. He tried to walk, but his knees buckled under him and he stumbled. Bethany and I kept him upright. "I can't feel my legs," he said.

"Just take it slow," Bethany repeated.

I glanced at the hole in the warehouse ceiling and wondered just how slow we could really take it. Bethany had said the gargoyles would be back soon, and with help. Where did they fit into all this? Was their attack on Bethany purely random? Somehow I doubted it. It wasn't like the *New York Post* was running articles on random gargoyle violence in the daily police blotter. So what had they been doing here?

"Something's wrong, I—I can't feel *anything*." Thornton looked down at himself and noticed, for the first time, the amulet at his chest. The small red gems at its center pulsed with a subtle, rhythmic glow, almost like a heartbeat. "Is this . . . ?"

"The Breath of Itzamna," she said.

"Why am I wearing it?" He paused, then looked up at Bethany. "Oh, no. I'm dead? I'm fucking *dead*?"

"Try to stay calm, Thornton," she said. "The Breath of Itzamna worked. It brought you back."

"No, I—I don't feel right," he said. "I'm cold. Numb. I can't even feel my heartbeat. The only time I'm breathing is when I talk."

"That's because technically you're not alive," she explained. "Just . . . back."

I bit back a swell of disappointment. Thornton wasn't like me any more than Bennett's fellow soldier Sully was. He was only up and moving because of the amulet. Somehow it had the power to bring him back. An amulet that could reanimate the dead. My brain tried to wrap itself around that but only wound up hurting.

"Christ, I'm a fucking zombie," Thornton groaned.

"We have to keep moving," Bethany told him. "Can you walk?"

He took a wobbly step forward. A rope of something thick and gray almost fell out of an open gash in his stomach before he pushed it back in with his hands. "Oh my God, I'm disgusting!"

We helped Thornton toward the door, his feet sliding stiffly along the warehouse floor. "Help me get to my clothes. They're right outside." He glanced at Bethany sheepishly. "Sorry about all the man flesh on display. It's hard to make the change while I'm wearing clothes."

She grinned at him. "Please, like I've never seen you change before? I'm used to you letting it all hang out."

Thornton groaned. "That's not a nice thing to say to someone who's been disemboweled."

Bethany stopped to pick up the Anubis Hand from the floor. I took the opportunity for one last glance around the room. She'd said Thornton was the only one who knew where the box was, which meant it wasn't in the warehouse anymore. A moment ago I'd been ready to use my gun to get her talking, but now a new strategy occurred to me. If I stuck with these two, they would lead me to the box. I was sure of it.

We carried Thornton through the door. Outside, the familiar sights and sounds of the West Side Highway had a surprisingly calming effect on me. Maybe the entire world hadn't been turned on its head after all.

A pile of discarded clothing sat under the broken warehouse window: jeans, boxer shorts, black sneakers, socks, a dark blue button-up shirt, and a long coat. Bethany handed me the staff and helped Thornton get dressed. Once he had his shirt buttoned up and felt more confident that his insides wouldn't fall out again, he insisted on finishing the job himself.

He put on the rest of his clothes with the speed of someone who was used to constantly shedding his garments and then donning them again. Of course, he had a good reason for it. *Change,* they'd called it. Such a simple word, as if turning into a wolf was an everyday thing. When he was finished, he gingerly adjusted his shirtsleeve to accommodate the leather bracelet around his wrist, and said, "Much better. I almost feel like my old self again." A dark stain spread across the shirt where his stomach had been torn open. "Well, I did say almost." He drew his long coat closed around him.

A familiar shriek sounded from somewhere in the dark night sky. I couldn't see anything up there, but it was close enough to draw a chill on the back of my neck. "They're coming. We have to go now."

"There's no way we can outrun them," Bethany said, her eyes frantically searching the sky. "They're faster than we are. We need to take cover."

"The subway," Thornton said.

"It's too far," I said. "But I've got a car parked across the street."

Thornton nodded. Bethany said, "Lead the way."

There was no time to wait for a break in the traffic, so we hurried across the West Side Highway like suicidal fools. Bethany and I supported Thornton between us as cars screeched to a halt and honked angrily. A cabbie yelled, "Get out of the fucking road, ya morons!" I smiled to myself. The world almost felt normal again, predictable, a place where everything made sense and angry cab drivers yelled obscenities at pedestrians.

When we reached the other side of the highway, I brought them to where I'd parked the Explorer and opened the back door. Bethany got in first, then helped me load Thornton in beside her. I gave them the Anubis Hand to lay across their laps, and slammed the door closed. I quickly checked the sky for gargoyles, then got in the driver's seat and started the car.

"Where to?" I asked.

"Just drive," Bethany insisted, so I did.

Forty-Ninth Street, like so many of the streets in New York City, only went one way. It took us back to the West Side Highway. I made a quick right onto the highway, then another onto Fiftieth Street, speeding east across town to put as much of the city between us and the warehouse as I could. I worked the gas pedal, maneuvering the car through the narrow passage between the double-parked U-Haul and Con Edison trucks that lined the street. I hated driving in this part of town, especially when I was in a hurry. I expected gargoyles to fly out from the shadows at any moment. I glanced nervously at everything we passed—empty shuttered storefronts, a rental-car lot, a twenty-four-hour parking sign, the small, leafless, sickly trees that lined the sidewalks—but the coast was clear. So far, anyway. When I reached the corner of Eleventh Avenue, the traffic light turned red and I braked to a stop, trying to calm down. I looked in the rearview mirror. In the backseat, Thornton was clutching his stomach and gritting his teeth.

"I feel like I swallowed a block of ice," he groaned.

"Your body is adjusting," Bethany told him. "Your muscles are trying to go into rigor mortis, but the amulet won't let them."

"Wonderful," he muttered.

The light turned green, and I hit the gas. The next block was lined with three- and four-story tenement buildings. A dark shape stood on a street-side fire escape. I stared at it as we passed, expecting it to spread its wings and leap down at us, but up close I saw it was just a man out for a smoke.

Thornton said, "By the way, I didn't catch your name, friend."

"Trent," I answered, trying not to think about the fact that there was a talking corpse in the backseat of my car.

"Trent, you look like you've seen a ghost," Thornton said. He chuckled.

"That's not funny," Bethany said.

Thornton ignored her. "You have a last name?"

"Just Trent," I said. Underwood hadn't seen fit to give me a last name along with the first. Honestly, I didn't want one, not yet. A last name implied family, history, whole generations of people I belonged with. The only last name I wanted was my real one, when I found it.

"Okay, that's cool," he said. "Nice to meet you, Trent. I'm Thornton Redler. I take it you've already met the always-charming Bethany Savory. And yes, that is her real name. Thanks for your help back there. So where'd you come from? I haven't seen you before. Did Isaac send you?"

I weighed my options carefully before answering. If I lied and said Isaac sent me—whoever that was—my cover would be blown the minute they tried to verify it. That would be disastrous. If they were going to lead me to the box, I needed them to trust me. So I shrugged like I didn't know what he was talking about, which wasn't a stretch. I said, "I don't know any Isaac. I was just walking by the warehouse when I heard a scream. I thought someone was in trouble, so I went inside to investigate. The next thing I knew, I was being attacked by those things—those gargoyles."

"Do you always rush into abandoned warehouses when you hear someone scream?" Thornton asked. "That's a good way to get yourself killed. Take it from me, getting killed is no fun. I don't recommend it."

Been there way more times than you, buddy, I thought.

The block between Ninth and Tenth Avenues was lined with more trees. Even without their full foliage, they were perfect hiding places for something with wings. I scanned the treetops cautiously as I drove, but the farther we got from the warehouse without incident, the better I felt our chances were.

In the backseat, Thornton convulsed suddenly. He doubled over, groaning, and hit the button on the door handle that lowered the window. He leaned his head out of the Explorer, opened his mouth, and regurgitated a spray of dark red liquid that splashed to the street below in a viscous puddle. I glanced at the sidewalks, hoping no one was around to notice. I needed us to stay inconspicuous. There were a few nighttime pedestrians on the block, but they continued on their way, dutifully ignoring the zombie vomiting blood out of the back of my car. Good old New Yorkers. They really couldn't care less.

Thornton reeled back into the car and raised the window. He collapsed against the seat. "What's happening to me?"

"Don't worry," Bethany explained. "You had blood in your lungs and stomach from your injuries. The amulet was helping you clear it out, that's all."

"Don't worry?" Thornton's pale lips glistened a dark red. He wiped his sleeve across his mouth. "I'm dead and vomiting blood, Bethany. I think that's pretty fucking worrisome."

She sighed and shook her head. "I'm sorry, I didn't know what else to do. I couldn't just leave you there."

Thornton calmed down. "Sorry. I'm just freaked out. I can't help it. I'm not like you, I can't always be so in control. So is there anything else I should know about being a zombie? Am I going to start craving brains next?"

She blew out her breath. "There *is* something."

"I knew it. Might as well sign me up for the next Romero movie."

"Thornton, listen to me, this is important. The amulet's effects are only temporary."

He was silent a moment, then asked, "How long have I got?"

"It's not an exact science, but . . . twenty-four hours, give or take."

In the rearview, I saw him wipe his hands over his face. "God. I need to see Gabrielle. Right now."

Bethany shook her head slowly. "I'm sorry, Thornton, we can't go back yet. If we do, we'll lead the gargoyles right to Citadel."

"Bethany, for Christ's sake, I *have* to see her."

"You will, I promise," she said. "Tomorrow, when the sun is up and it's safe, we can go back, but right now we can't. I need you to understand that."

Thornton chewed his thumbnail worriedly. "You promised, Bethany. I'm going to hold you to that."

I didn't know who Gabrielle was, but judging from the way Thornton was so desperate to see her before his time ran out, I figured she was important to him. His girlfriend, maybe. So what did that make Bethany?

In the backseat, she said, "Now we just need to get the box back, before . . ." She trailed off self-consciously.

"Before I die, you mean. Permanently this time." Thornton leaned his head back against the top of the seat. "Shit, Bethany. You always figure you're going to die sometime, but it always seems so far away. Though, on the plus side, I'm *already* dead, so I guess I don't have to worry about it anymore."

"Thornton, I'm serious about the box," she said. "You know how important it is we get it back to Citadel safely. It's why we split up in the first place, so you could find someplace to hide it."

Thornton sat up. "That's why you brought me back, isn't it? It wasn't because you couldn't leave me there, it wasn't sentimental, it was because I know where the box is and you don't. Jesus, Bethany. I'm right, aren't I?"

She didn't answer. Her silence did it for her.

I slowed behind a car that was taking a right turn onto Ninth Avenue and did my best not to look like I was eavesdropping.

Thornton glared icily at Bethany. "You don't have to worry about it. The box is safe."

"You're sure?" she pressed.

He nodded. "I left it in the safest place I could think of, with someone even the gargoyles wouldn't dare mess with."

Her eyes widened. "Oh no, you don't mean—?"

"I gave it to Gregor."

"Tell me you didn't," she said. "Gregor's a compulsive hoarder. He keeps everything."

"Just another reason it'll be safe with him."

She groaned. "There's no guarantee we'll ever get it back now. Not from him."

"He owes me a favor. A *lot* of favors, actually. He'll give it back. Trust me, I know what I'm doing."

Bethany sighed and crossed her arms. It was evident she was someone who hated not being in complete control of a situation.

"Who's Gregor?" I asked.

"An old friend," Thornton said.

"Very old," Bethany added, like that cleared things up.

Apparently that was all they were willing to tell me. I pressed a little harder. "Is that where we're going now, to get this box back from Gregor?"

Bethany shook her head. "Just keep driving. Right now, our priority is to make sure we've lost the gargoyles."

I maneuvered the car across the intersection at Eighth Avenue, still heading east. I checked the side mirrors. The buildings in this part of town were too tall for me to see anything but walls and windows, but we were moving at a pretty good clip, especially by Midtown standards. "I think we've shaken them off."

"It won't be that easy," she said. "They've got our scent. I wouldn't be surprised if they were still tracking us but hanging back, waiting to see where we go."

"What's their beef with you anyway?" I asked.

"They want the box," Bethany said.

That made two of us. "Okay," I said, "but why?"

"It's complicated."

Why wasn't I surprised? Everything had gotten a lot more complicated when I walked into that damn warehouse. "News flash, sweetheart, I'm the guy who saved your ass back there by turning a gargoyle into a pile of ashes, so maybe you can clue me in on what this is all about."

Bethany turned to Thornton. "Did this asshole just call me *sweetheart*?"

Thornton leaned forward in his seat. "Wait, what are you talking about, turning a gargoyle into ashes?" I told him what had happened when I used the staff. His eyes bugged. "But that's impossible, the Anubis Hand isn't supposed to—"

"I'd really like to be the one asking the questions right now," I snapped.

I drove across Broadway, staying on Fiftieth Street. On the next block, a short one between Broadway and Seventh Avenue, the traffic was backed up to a standstill. I reluctantly slowed to a stop behind a fresh-produce delivery truck. Its big, boxy semitrailer blocked my view of the street ahead. I realized then that I'd made the wrong choice. This close to Times Square, I should have known the traffic would back up. Considering what might be following us, I didn't like having to slow down, not even for a moment. I threw the Explorer into reverse and checked the mirrors, but I was already too late. Cars were filing in behind us, boxing us in place. Damn. If the gargoyles found us now, there was no place for us to go. Our only escape route would be on foot, out in the open.

"What do the gargoyles want with the box?" I pressed. "What's so special about it?"

"It's theirs, kind of," Thornton said.

I met his eyes in the rearview. "What?"

"It doesn't belong to them," Bethany interjected quickly. "It doesn't belong to anyone. Look, what's important is that we can't let them get their hands on it. There's a good reason it was kept hidden for so many years. The safest place for it now is locked away where no one can get to it."

"What is it, some kind of weapon?" I asked.

"Not exactly," Bethany said. "But in the wrong hands, it would be extremely dangerous."

"Not to be a stickler," I said, "but isn't that the definition of a weapon?"

Outside, a chorus of angry honking began. Traffic inched forward, then stopped again.

Thornton looked out the window, lost in his thoughts. "We should have left the box where it was."

"You know we couldn't," Bethany told him.

"Where was it?" I asked. "You said it was hidden."

"Have you heard about the renovations they're doing at St. John the Divine uptown?" she asked. I shrugged. I didn't keep up with current events much. "Well, the construction workers were repairing the foundation and found a secret chamber under the cathedral. A chamber older than the cathedral itself. The only thing inside it was the box. They probably would have sent it somewhere to be examined. They might have even tried to open it themselves. Anyone could have gotten their hands on what's inside. We couldn't take that risk. We didn't have a choice, we had to go in there when no one was around and take the box."

"Wait, wait, wait," I said, turning around in the seat to gape at them. "You stole it?"

"We *secured* it," Bethany corrected me. "I told you, what's in that box is too dangerous."

I chuckled and shook my head. They were thieves, just like me. Sure, I called it *collecting* and they called it *securing,* but whichever word you used, and whatever rationale you gave for doing it, it was the same damn thing.

"But we were sloppy," Thornton said. "We should have realized there was a ward around the chamber. As soon as we took the box out, that was it. It was like every gargoyle just *knew.* Within minutes, they stormed the cathedral. We barely got out of there alive. That was last night, and we've been running ever since. This mission has been screwed from the start."

"I don't understand it," she said. "We did everything the way we were supposed to. We did it by the book."

"And look where it got us," Thornton said. "You've always been a stickler for protocol, Bethany, but sometimes you've got to throw the book out the window and listen to your gut."

She frowned, clamming up. She also wasn't the type who liked being told she'd gotten it wrong.

The honking up ahead grew louder. Drivers started yelling. More car horns blared, loud and long. The traffic inched forward again. Whoever said getting there is half the fun wasn't from New York City.

"This would be a lot easier if you just told me where we're going," I said.

"There is no *we,*" Bethany insisted. "I'll let you know where to drop us off. It isn't far now. After that, just go home and forget you saw us. Forget about all of this."

Damn. I still needed them to lead me to the box. I couldn't find Gregor on my own. I thought about the gun in my waistband, but threatening them wouldn't work. Thornton was already dead; a gun wouldn't intimidate him. God, how crazy had my life become that I was wondering what it would take to intimidate a dead man? I shook it off and forced myself to focus. What I needed was a way in, a way to convince them they needed me.

"Are you sure going off on your own is such a good idea?" I asked.

"Look, Trent, I'm grateful for everything you've done, but we've put you in too much danger already," she said. "It's us the gargoyles want, not you. You'll be safer if we go our separate ways."

"It's not me I'm worried about," I said. "Who's going to protect *you*? You'll be out there on your own, and those things almost killed you once already."

"They did kill me, remember?" Thornton said.

"My point is, if they're as tenacious as you say they are, they're not going to stop trying until they've finished the job."

"You don't have to worry about us," she said. "We know how to take care of ourselves."

"Didn't look like it back there," I said.

"Well now you're just being rude," Thornton said. "Didn't anyone tell you it's not nice to speak ill of the dead?"

The truck ahead moved forward a few feet. I inched the Explorer along behind it until it stopped again. We were close to the intersection now. The honking and yelling got louder.

"Look, you're in no shape to take on the gargoyles alone," I said. "There were only six of them in the warehouse and look how that went. What happens if there are ten next time, or twenty?"

"Forget it," she said. "I'm not about to let you get yourself killed. This isn't your fight. You're not going to talk me out of this, Trent. My mind is made up. I'm just going to ask you to drop us off and that'll be the end of it."

Damn. She was adamant. I didn't see a way in.

The truck in front of us started rolling forward again, its right turn signal flashing. "Looks like we're moving now," I said, and eased my foot onto the gas pedal.

The truck turned right onto Seventh Avenue, its big white body moving away like a curtain being pulled aside, and I finally saw what had caused the traffic jam. My eyes widened in alarm. My foot instinctively stomped on the brake.

A jet-black horse stood in the center of the intersection, half shrouded in the steam that billowed from a manhole in the street beneath it. Armored metal plates covered its flanks, shoulders, and neck, and sheathed its head, nose, and muzzle. Seated atop the horse was a man wearing a full suit of coal-black armor. A tattered black cape hung from the spiked paul-drons on his shoulders and fluttered behind him in the breeze. His head was completely encased in a black helmet capped by two long, black, branching stag's horns. He sat facing the Explorer. I couldn't see his face beneath the helmet's visor, but the shiver along my spine told me he was looking right through the windshield at me.

"What the hell is that?" I said.

Thornton and Bethany leaned forward in the backseat at the same time.

"Oh, fuck," Thornton said.

"Drive!" Bethany yelled.

The horse snorted and scraped at the blacktop with one hoof, its black tail twitching. The man astride it kept one gauntleted hand on the thick black chain that doubled as the horse's reins. With the other, he un-sheathed the sword at his side. The blade was long, as dark as onyx, and curved like a scimitar. It was sharp along the front edge and serrated with nasty-looking hooked barbs on the back.

Bethany dove forward and grabbed the steering wheel, yanking it to the right. She screamed in my ear, "Go! Now! God damn it, Trent, drive!"

I hit the gas. The tires squealed against the pavement as we turned onto Seventh Avenue.

In the rearview, I saw the horse rear and gallop after us, the man in the black suit of armor holding his sword high.

Eight

I spun the Explorer wildly onto Seventh Avenue. The tires screamed in protest, the smell of burning rubber coming through the window. Bethany yelled in my ear, "Go, go, go," and I stomped the gas pedal to the floor and nearly torpedoed right into the back of the produce truck in front of us. I gritted my teeth and spun the wheel frantically, every muscle in my body tensing in anticipation of the collision. We just missed the truck, though the front of the Explorer clipped it. The right headlight shattered and flickered out. I pulled into one of the middle lanes and hit the gas again while my heart tried to pound its way out of my rib cage.

The bright lights of retail signs and enormous video billboards lit Seventh Avenue like it was daytime, illuminating the sea of shining yellow metal ahead of us. Taxicabs, a whole fleet of them, spread out over the road like an obstacle course. I cursed under my breath. Why did it have to be Times Square? Even at this time of night, the traffic was so thick it moved at a snail's pace. I kept my foot on the gas, drove right up behind one of the taxis, then switched lanes and did it again. It was the only way to keep moving. The street was six lanes wide, though the far left lane was taken up with parked cars. Five lanes, then. Not good. Eventually I'd run out of room to maneuver, especially once we got closer to the intersection where Seventh Avenue merged with Broadway and the traffic of two major arteries was funneled into one. Then what the hell was I going to do?

I glanced at the side mirror. The man in black armor wasn't far behind, maybe seventy yards but gaining fast as his horse galloped through the narrow aisle between cars. Weren't horses supposed to be spooked by traffic and blaring horns? This one wasn't. It wasn't even wearing blinders. The drivers, on the other hand, were plenty spooked. They swerved and collided in the horse's wake, metal grinding against metal, glass popping. On the sidewalk, pedestrians gawked, their well-honed New York apathy momentarily shattered. Slowly, inevitably, the camera phones came out and flashes burst along the sidewalk like a chain of supernovas. I kept my focus on the road. In the backseat, Bethany and Thornton twisted around and stared through the rear window.

"We're screwed," Thornton said.

"I knew the gargoyles were going for help, but I didn't think it would be *him*," Bethany said.

I swerved around a cab, then another, ignoring their angry honks. "Who the hell is that?" I demanded.

"The Black Knight," she said. "He's their king."

I glowered at her in the rearview. "The gargoyles have a *king*?"

"You definitely don't want to mess with him," Thornton said.

I shifted my gaze to the side mirror. The Black Knight was still there, closing the gap between us. The neon lights glinted off his black sword, limning the sharp edge in red, blue, and green.

"He mustn't catch us, Trent!" Bethany said. "Do you understand me? If the Black Knight catches us, we're dead!"

"Speak for yourself," Thornton muttered.

Bethany ignored him. The look on her face was one of desperate terror. This was a woman who was brave enough to take on six gargoyles with what was essentially a long stick, yet just the sight of the Black Knight had terrified her. I didn't want to find out why. I swerved to change lanes again, hoping to put more cars between us and the Black Knight. I glanced at the speedometer: fifty-nine miles per hour. And yet somehow, maddeningly, the horse was still gaining on us.

A police siren cut the air, sharp and loud, but I couldn't see the cruiser yet, couldn't even figure out where it was. Ahead, the light at Forty-Ninth Street turned yellow, then red. I stomped on the gas pedal and blew through the intersection just as the cross street's traffic started to flow. Cars swerved to avoid hitting us, honking and shouting. One was the NYPD cruiser with the shrieking siren, the red and whites flashing on its roof. It skidded to a halt behind us, directly in the Black Knight's path. I figured that ought to slow the armored bastard down. Maybe even give us enough time to shake him.

"Jesus Christ, get out of there!" Thornton shouted from the backseat. He was twisted around, staring anxiously through the back window at the police cruiser.

I checked the mirror and saw the Black Knight's horse run straight into the cruiser. But instead of hurting the horse, the cruiser, a couple thousand pounds of metal and glass, slid sideways across the blacktop like it was made of cardboard. It collided with the rear of a delivery truck, and its windshield and the red and white lights on its roof shattered in a rain of glass. The horse barely noticed as it continued galloping after us. The cruiser stayed put. I couldn't tell if the cops inside were alive or dead.

"Trent, look out!" Bethany cried.

I tore my gaze away from the mirror and back to the road. In front of us, a city bus pulled away from the bus stop at the curb, directly into our path. The glowing M20 on the digital display window on the back of the bus looked so big and close through the windshield that I gasped. I jerked the wheel to the left and stamped down on the gas, trying to get ahead of the bus, but it was too late. It slammed into the side of the Explorer, sending us skidding diagonally across the lanes.

"Hang on!" I shouted. I stepped on the brakes with my full weight, nearly lifting myself out of the seat. The tires locked and squealed against the road. In the backseat, Bethany and Thornton were thrown to one side as they scrabbled for something to hold on to. The Explorer rocked, threatening to tip over, then settled to a stop straddling two lanes. I looked through the passenger side window, which now faced oncoming traffic. I caught a glimpse of the Black Knight riding toward us. Then suddenly all I could see was a monster Suburban bearing down on us, its driver leaning on the horn. The Suburban's wheels screamed as it braked, but the momentum kept it sliding forward. I stepped on the gas again and twisted the steering wheel, edging forward, but it was too late. The Suburban struck the rear of the Explorer. I heard shouts of alarm from the people on the sidewalk as our back wheels slid ninety degrees across the blacktop. Bethany and Thornton cried out, clutching the safety grips on the ceiling above the doors. We came to an uneasy stop rocking back and forth on the suspension. I held onto the steering wheel with white knuckles. My heart squeezed into my throat like it wanted to make a break for it.

Down the street, the Black Knight's horse knocked aside a station wagon like it was a Matchbox car, and kept coming. I ignored the honks and the angry cries of the Suburban's driver, turned to my two shaken but unharmed passengers in the back and barked, "Seat belts! Now!" Bethany and Thornton buckled themselves in without a word. I did the same and hit the gas again. The engine chugged and wheezed in protest, but thankfully the car moved. I continued down Seventh Avenue, but this time the speedometer stayed at forty-five no matter how hard I stepped on the pedal.

Thornton twisted to look out the rear window again. "He's gaining on us!"

"Can't you make this thing go any faster?" Bethany demanded.

"I'm trying!" I yelled back. I glanced in the side mirror. The Black Knight was shadowing us, relentless. "What does he want from us?"

"The box," Bethany said. "He's the one who sent the gargoyles after it in the first place."

Everyone wanted the box, it seemed. It was bringing the freaks out of the woodwork. What was so special about the damn thing?

Another siren pierced the night. A second NYPD cruiser came rocketing down Seventh Avenue to pull up alongside the horse. It tried turning toward the horse to nudge it toward the side of the road, but the horse ignored it. The Black Knight swiped at the cruiser with his sword. There was a sudden eruption of sparks, and the police cruiser wobbled, lost control, and veered into a street-side lamppost. People scattered on the sidewalks. The Black Knight kept coming.

We shot across Forty-Eighth Street. I glanced at the side mirror. The Black Knight was so close I could almost make out each individual hooked barb on his sword. The horse's enormous nostrils flared just above the stenciled words OBJECTS IN MIRROR ARE CLOSER THAN THEY APPEAR. I ground the accelerator into the floor. The engine wheezed and coughed. Wisps of smoke billowed out from under the hood. The speedometer dropped to forty.

I cursed and hit the steering wheel. It didn't make the Explorer go any faster.

The Black Knight rode up alongside us. Holding tight to the metal reins with his free hand, he tipped himself toward the Explorer and slashed with his sword. The blade tore effortlessly through the metal chassis, trailing sparks that rained onto the street. Bethany and Thornton gasped and cringed away from it. The edge missed them by inches.

I turned the wheel, trying to ram the horse, but it galloped easily out of reach. As soon as I righted the car, the Black Knight rode back to us. The curved, black blade of his sword came through the roof at an angle, jabbing into the narrow space between me and the steering wheel. I cried out and pushed myself back in my seat so hard I thought I'd break all the way through it. The Black Knight yanked his sword free again, its hooked barbs tearing chunks of metal from the roof and leaving a jagged hole.

The Black Knight swung again, this time smashing the window beside me. Tiny cubes of safety glass spilled across my lap. I changed lanes, pulling away from him. The traffic had thinned, most of the drivers had turned off of Seventh Avenue to avoid the chaos. The good news was that the mostly empty street allowed me to maneuver more easily. The bad news was that it let the Black Knight do the same.

He kept pace with the Explorer, the jabs and swipes of his sword continually forcing me to change lanes and move farther to the right. Up ahead, I saw Times Square's triangular pedestrian mall approaching on the right side of Forty-Seventh Street, marking where Seventh Avenue and Broadway intersected at a sharp angle. Only then did I realize that the Black Knight was trying to force me off the road. I tried to edge my way left again, but the sword came slicing toward the driver's side door. I instinctively yanked the wheel to the right to avoid the razor-sharp blade and realized, too late, that was exactly what the Black Knight had wanted me to do.

We jumped the curb onto the mall, narrowly avoiding the tall stand of bleachers that angled above the *TKTS* windows at the north end, where theater buffs normally stood in long lines to buy cheap Broadway tickets. Luckily, at this hour there were no customers lined up there or I would have plowed right through them. Past the bleachers there were dozens of tables and chairs arranged along the pedestrian mall. They were all empty, the tourists and transients who normally sat there must have seen us coming and took off. It sounded like the *rat-a-tat* of a machine gun as the

Explorer plowed through the tables. Plastic chairs, abandoned Styrofoam coffee cups, fast-food wrappers, and empty plastic shopping bags bounced and slid off the hood and windshield.

I hit the brakes and spun the wheel, but we were going too fast to come to anything resembling a controlled stop. The Explorer struck a cement barricade at the far end of the mall. The next thing I knew we were off the ground and tilting sideways, then upside down. The cubes of safety glass from the broken window jumped off my lap and out of the leg well, raining up to the ceiling. I felt the seat belt strain under my weight, the strap cutting into my shoulder and chest. The Explorer came down on its roof, skating across the section of Broadway that was closed to traffic, and crashed into the side of a clothing store, shattering the store's floor-to-ceiling display window. Only then, finally, did we stop.

My head, neck, and shoulders throbbed. The wounds on my back flared with new pain. I reached for the seat belt and, bracing myself, released the buckle. I tumbled upside down from my seat, bumping my neck and shoulders against the ceiling. I winced and tried to get my feet under me again. I had to scrape my knees and shins past the steering wheel, but finally I lay on my side and did a quick check of my limbs. No broken bones. I was lucky. "Are you okay?" I called back to Bethany and Thornton.

They lay in a tangled heap below the overturned backseat, caught like flies in the web of their seat belts.

"I have some exciting new wounds and my right arm seems to be bent the wrong way, but otherwise I still feel dead," Thornton replied. "Thanks for asking."

"My leg," Bethany groaned, her voice laced with pain. "I'm jammed in."

From the way the car was lying, I couldn't see the Black Knight, but I knew he wasn't far. If he found us like this, it would be like shooting fish in a barrel. I thought about how easily that sword of his had cut through metal. I didn't want to know what it would do to us.

"Thornton, help Bethany," I said. I crawled through the hole where the driver's side window used to be and out onto the sidewalk. I stood up, but I was still dizzy from the accident. I steadied myself against the side of the car. People on the sidewalks in the distance still had their cell phone cameras raised, flashes popping. Damn. If any of them got a clear picture of my face, not only would I have botched this job, I would have blown any chance of getting information out of Underwood. My only hope was that the cameras were too far away to capture any detail.

Then, slowly, it dawned on me that I wasn't the one they were taking pictures of. The Black Knight trotted up and slowed his horse to a stop. He dismounted. He didn't pay any attention to the crowd across the street. His attention was fixed on me.

I tried to tug open the car's back door, but it was wedged stuck. I dug in against the sidewalk and gave it another yank, a hard one. With the loud groan of metal scraping against metal it opened, but only halfway. "Can you move?"

Bethany looked up at me, her teeth clenched against the pain. "I don't know, but I'll damn well try."

I looked over the top of the overturned car. The Black Knight was striding toward me, holding his sword low.

"If you're going to try, you better do it now," I said. I pulled my gun from the back of my pants and aimed down the barrel at the Black Knight. "Back it up," I shouted. The Black Knight ignored me, continuing toward us. I cocked the gun. "Back the *fuck* up." He drew closer, lifting his sword. "Fine. I warned you," I said, and squeezed off two shots in quick succession.

Both of them ricocheted off his armored breastplate. It didn't even slow him down.

"You gotta be kidding me," I said. I put the gun away and squatted down by the open door again. "Can one of you tell me why everyone is immune to bullets all of a sudden?"

They'd gotten free of their seat belts, and now Thornton was trying to push Bethany toward the door with his left arm. It wasn't working. "See if you can pull her out," he urged me. His right arm hung limply at his side.

I took both of Bethany's hands and pulled, but she gritted her teeth in pain and didn't budge. "Get out of here, Trent," she said. "There's no point in all three of us dying."

"When are you going to stop trying to get rid of me?" I said.

I spotted the Anubis Hand lying near her. If the Black Knight was the king of the gargoyles, did that mean the Anubis Hand would have the same effect on him that it did on the gargoyles in the warehouse? There was only way to find out. I pulled the staff out of the car.

"Just run, Trent, before you get yourself killed!" Bethany yelled.

I walked around to the front of the car and faced the Black Knight, holding the staff in both hands. "We don't have the box you're looking for," I said.

The Black Knight lifted the heavy, angry-looking sword over his head and brought it down toward me. I swung the staff, knocking his blade aside. I followed through with the momentum, spinning around and ramming into him with my back. I brought one elbow up hard into the Black Knight's breastplate. The metal felt as hard as rock. Pain surged up my arm. The Black Knight didn't so much as stumble.

Still, he moved slowly in all that armor. I could use that to my advantage. Before he had a chance to get his sword up, I spun again, and this time I swung the staff up and out. The Anubis Hand struck the Black Knight's helmet full on.

I waited for the flash of light, for the Black Knight to be thrown backward in a blazing inferno, but nothing happened. Instead, he shrugged off the blow and came at me again.

Shit. I backed away, holding the staff defensively in front of me. I risked a quick look over my shoulder. Thornton was out of the car and helping Bethany through the door. His limp right arm was crooked at the elbow in a way that looked painful. The leather bracelet hung cockeyed at his wrist. Bethany had an angry cut on her right knee that dripped trails of blood down her jeans leg. I turned back to the Black Knight just in time to see him raise his sword, preparing to strike.

As the blade came down, I brought the staff up to block it. The sword cleaved the staff in two, and suddenly I was holding two useless pieces of wood, one with a mummified fist attached to it. Damn, I thought, now what?

"Run, Trent!" Bethany shouted. "You can't win! He'll kill you!"

Maybe I couldn't win, but I sure as hell wasn't going to leave them here for the Black Knight to cut to pieces. I held the two halves of the broken staff like clubs and took a deep breath. I didn't have a plan, let alone a strategy for fighting him, but there was no way I was going to let this asshole get past me.

I ran at him and got past his sword before he could swing it. The Black Knight pivoted, and hit me across the face with his armored forearm. It felt like getting hit by a steel girder. I fell onto my back. The two pieces of the staff fell out of my hands.

The Black Knight loomed over me. He lifted his black-bladed sword high, its sharp point gleaming above my face.

"Fuck you," I said, "and the horse you—"

Before I could finish, the Black Knight drove his sword down toward me.

Nine

I rolled aside. The Black Knight's sword clanged against the pavement where my head had been only a moment ago. He raised his sword and brought it down again. This time I rolled in the opposite direction, narrowly avoiding the sharp edge of the blade as it buried itself deep in the concrete. As the Black Knight struggled to pull the sword free, I got back on my feet.

There wasn't enough time to run. The Black Knight yanked the sword free, sending tiny bits of concrete showering through the air. He advanced on me again and swung the sword. I jumped back, feeling how close the point came to my chest as it cut past me. I took another step back and bumped up against the Explorer. The Black Knight kept coming. With nowhere else to go, I climbed on top of the overturned vehicle.

On the sidewalk, Bethany sat leaning against the wall of the clothing store. She grimaced in pain and rubbed her injured leg. Thornton stood feebly beside her, his broken arm preventing him from carrying her to safety. In this condition, they were helpless. It was up to me to keep the Black Knight away. Unfortunately, I didn't know how I was going to accomplish that. Bullets didn't hurt him. Neither did the Anubis Hand. I needed a weapon of some kind, but I didn't have anything.

The Black Knight started toward Bethany and Thornton, the metal of his armored feet hammering the sidewalk. Desperate to draw the Black Knight's attention away, I shouted, "Hey!" The Black Knight stopped and looked up at me. I was surprised it worked.

The Black Knight remained as stoic and silent as ever, staring up at me through his visor. I grinned back at him. I didn't know what the hell I was doing, but at least I had his full attention. He kept looking up at me, not making any attempt to climb up onto the car after me. I wondered if his armor was too heavy to let him.

"What's the matter, are you too lazy to climb up here, or are you just afraid of heights?" I taunted. "How many fights has the mighty Black Knight lost because someone got up on a chair? Are you always this pathetic, or is this a special show just for me?"

The Black Knight rose straight up off the ground, levitating like a circus trick until he hovered at the same height as me.

Shit. I backed away. Hanging in midair, the Black Knight took a step forward, placing one armored boot onto the Explorer, then the other. Balanced on its roof, the Explorer tipped forward under the Black Knight's weight. He stomped toward me, the tip of his blade pointed at my chest. I backed up the incline of the overturned vehicle, raising my hands defensively.

"I told you, we don't have the box," I said.

He took another step forward. I got the feeling he didn't care whether we had the box or not. He just wanted us dead. I took another step back.

"Trent, get away from him!" Bethany shouted from the sidewalk.

I reached the end of the Explorer, and stopped. There was nowhere left to go. Below, it was only a short drop to the street. I could easily make the jump if it weren't for the fact that it would lead the Black Knight directly to Bethany and Thornton.

The Black Knight took another step forward. Standing at the center of the vehicle now, his weight shifted the balance again. As the Explorer tilted, it threw both of us off our footing. I wobbled and steadied myself, but the Black Knight was wearing heavy, cumbersome armor. It took longer for him to regain his equilibrium. I wouldn't have another chance to catch him off guard, I realized. It was only when I was already barreling toward him and saw the Black Knight lift his sword to skewer me that I realized I'd done something stupid again.

I was close enough to grab the wrist of his sword hand before he struck. I struggled to keep the sharp edge of the blade away from me, not to mention the hooked barbs on the other side. This close to the Black Knight, I could see through the slits in the visor of his helmet, but I didn't see anything inside, not even streetlight reflecting off his eyes. There was nothing on the other side of that visor but darkness.

"Don't let him touch you!" Bethany shouted.

But it was already too late. The Black Knight wrapped the hard fingers of his gauntlet around my neck. The metal felt unnaturally cold against my skin. To my surprise, the fingers of his gauntlet grew even colder, burning my skin like frostbite as they squeezed. I struggled to catch my breath.

Something wormed its way into me then, something dark and icy that flowed from the Black Knight and hollowed me out inside. It sapped my energy. I felt sluggish all of a sudden, exhausted. I had to force myself to stay upright. Desperate, I moved one hand away from the Black Knight's wrist and clutched the metal gorget over his neck. We wrestled, locked in our awkward embrace as we tried to overpower each other.

The Black Knight's sword inched closer. I gritted my teeth and pushed harder against him. The icy metal fingers sank deeper into my neck. The frozen blackness inside me continued its work, draining my energy. In a few moments I would either black out or my windpipe would be crushed. Probably both. I pushed as hard as I could, every muscle in my body tensing to the breaking point. My head throbbed. It felt like I was going to explode.

Suddenly, a bright, bluish-white light poured out of my hands and spread like lightning across the Black Knight's armor. He released me, and the cold darkness that had been spreading through me dissipated instantly. He stumbled back and staggered from side to side, rocking the overturned car precariously. Then he doubled over like a drunk in pain.

I stared, my mouth hanging open. What the *fuck* . . . ?

I didn't have time to think about it. The web of bluish-white light around the Black Knight sizzled out. He started to straighten, already recovering. I rushed him, ready to put my hands on him again and hoping that whatever had just happened would repeat itself. He didn't give me the chance. Before I reached him, the Black Knight burst apart. His body separated into a dozen big, black crows. They scattered, cawing, and flew up into the night sky. Stunned, I watched them fly away until I couldn't see them against the dark anymore. The Black Knight's horse was gone, too, I saw. Vanished like it had never been there.

This night was getting crazier. Or maybe I was. Either way, it looked like I'd won. Even if nothing else made sense, I knew that this, at the very least, was a good thing.

I hopped off the overturned car. I collected the two halves of the staff and brought them over to Bethany and Thornton. "Sorry," I said. "I guess a staff isn't so great against a sword."

They stared at me with their mouths agape. "It doesn't matter," Bethany finally said. "The staff is just a piece of wood. The power is in the hand itself."

I supposed that made sense for something called the Anubis Hand.

Sirens blared suddenly in the distance. Not just one or two cruisers this time. It sounded like dozens. After all the damage the Black Knight had caused, including two demolished police vehicles, the NYPD clearly wasn't taking any more chances. From the sound of it, they'd called in every cop they could find.

"We have to get out of here," Thornton said, before I could. "The last thing we need is the police getting involved. Bethany, can you walk?"

The gash in her leg looked pretty painful, but she used the wall behind her to push herself up from the sidewalk. Then she winced and groaned and slid back down onto her backside. "Damn it. I—I don't know if I can."

"You're going to have to," I said. I handed the pieces of the staff to Thornton so I could help her up. With his good arm he tossed one segment of the staff aside and kept the segment with the fist. He put it in the pocket of his long coat, fist first.

I held out my hands, and she put hers in mine. They looked so small and delicate that they reminded me of doll's hands. I helped her to her feet. "Thanks, I think I've got it," she said. I let go. She stayed upright.

The sirens grew louder. We ducked around the corner, with no choice but to head back toward Eighth Avenue. We moved too slowly for my liking, with Bethany limping and Thornton still not fully mastering the art of walking on dead legs. We only made it half a block before Bethany had to stop. The three of us piled into the shadowy, recessed doorway of a Broadway theater that was locked up for the night.

I poked my head out and watched the cops pull up to the overturned Explorer. They'd brought the riot van with them. I took that as a good sign. It meant they didn't know what to expect when they got here, they'd only gotten reports of a disturbance in Times Square. They weren't looking for anyone in particular. More to the point, they weren't looking for me.

The Explorer's plates were fake. They couldn't be traced back to me or Underwood. But my fingerprints were all over the car, a cinch to dust and lift. I had no idea if my prints were in AFIS. Certainly the people Underwood sent me to steal from weren't the type to call the cops, but there were thirty-odd years I couldn't account for. But even if my prints weren't in the system, what about Bethany's and Thornton's? They were thieves too, even if they refused to call themselves that. Did they have records? Their prints and DNA were all over the inside of the car. They could lead the cops right to me.

"Tell me the truth," I said. "Just how many item have you 'secured' before now?"

"Lots," Thornton said. "We've been doing this for years."

I watched some of the cops inspect the car while others interviewed people in the crowd. Cell phones changed hands, pictures and videos being replayed for the authorities. I wished I knew what was on those videos, or how clear they were.

"Do the cops know who you are? Do they know your faces? Have your fingerprints?"

"No," Bethany said. "We're careful. Always. We don't leave a trail."

"You left enough of a trail for the gargoyles to find you," I said. "The Black Knight, too."

"There's a world of difference between the Black Knight and the NYPD," she insisted.

That didn't make me feel any better, but it would have to do. "Can you walk?" I asked.

"I'm going to need a minute." She bent over to inspect the gash in her leg.

I was antsy and wanted to keep moving. The more sidewalk we could put between us and the cops, the better. I turned to Thornton and for the first time noticed a long strip of skin had been scraped off his cheek in the car crash and was now dangling from his cheek. I could see the striations of the pale, bloodless muscle beneath. "You should fix your face. It'll attract attention like that."

Thornton frowned like he thought I'd just insulted him. Then he raised a hand to his cheek and felt the flap of skin hanging loose there. "Ew." He pressed the skin back into place until it stuck. Now it just looked like he had two big, ugly scars on his cheek that came to a point under his eye. "Better?"

I shrugged. "I'm not sure *better* is the right word, but it's good enough." I turned back to Bethany. She was still bent over, carefully removing bits of dirt and gravel from her wound. Her thick, dark hair fell forward to reveal one ear. My breath caught in my throat. Her ear came to a point at the top. It reminded me of Ch'aqrath, the elf prince in *The Ragana's Revenge.*

"Are you—are you an elf?" I blurted. Hearing it out loud like that, I immediately cringed at how stupid I sounded.

She looked up at me, her sky-blue eyes flashing with indignation. Then she straightened up and quickly brushed her hair over her ear again. "Don't be absurd," she snapped. "No one's even seen an elf since World War Two." She said it as if I should have known something so obvious.

"Oh," I said.

"Trent, what was that back there?" she asked. "That energy that came out of you, how did you do that?"

I looked at my hands. I wasn't sure what I expected to see, but they didn't look any different to me. "I don't know. It just sort of happened."

"Bullshit," Thornton said. "You did magic, Trent. Magic doesn't just *happen.*"

"What?" I scoffed. "Come on, give me a break. There's no such thing as magic."

Thornton rolled his eyes. "No such thing as magic, he says. You might as well say there's no such thing as gravity."

Granted, there shouldn't have been any such thing as gargoyles, werewolves, amulets that raised the dead, or knights who turned into crows, either. Maybe Thornton was right and magic was real after all. Hell, maybe *The Ragana's Revenge* was nonfiction. Who was I to say? I was an amnesiac. Everything I knew about the world I'd learned from a Brooklyn crime boss and old black-and-white movies on a half-busted TV.

"No one has ever fought the Black Knight and survived," Bethany said. "Not until you."

"Fess up, Trent," Thornton said. "First you turn the Anubis Hand into a freaking cannon, then you zap the Black Knight back to whatever hole he crawled out of. You've been holding out on us. What are you? A magician? Thaumaturge? No, let me guess, a mage?"

I shook my head. "I have no idea what you're talking about. I honestly don't know what happened back there. All I did was touch him." A noise from the street caught my attention. The cops were trying to get the Explorer's doors open. "We don't have time for this. We have to keep moving or they'll find us."

"Fine," Bethany said. She took my hand and started limping determinedly up the street, leading me like a dog on a leash toward Eighth Avenue. Thornton followed with his broken arm swinging loosely at his side. "Come on, magician," she said. "Forget what I said about going our separate ways. I'm not letting you out of my sight."

And just like that, I was in.

Ten

We continued making our way toward Eighth Avenue, but we moved maddeningly slowly. The cut on Bethany's knee had stopped bleeding, but her jeans leg was slick with blood and she was still limping. Thornton walked stiffly, hugging his broken arm close to his side. The car crash had done a number on me, too, reopening the scratches on my back and adding new, small ones on my face that itched more than they hurt. I was pretty sure the Black Knight had left finger-shaped bruises on my neck, too. We were a sorry bunch. As we hobbled our way up the sidewalk, I glanced back every few steps, hoping the cops hadn't noticed us. So far, they hadn't.

"It's not the police we need to worry about," Bethany said, huffing with exertion. "Ten to one the gargoyles are still on our trail. We might have gotten away, but that's only a temporary setback for them. They won't stop until they get what they want."

"Shh," Thornton hissed, stopping. Bethany and I stopped too. Thornton scanned the sky quickly. "I thought I heard something."

I looked up, glancing at the rooftops and fire escapes. There were no gargoyles in sight, but that didn't mean they weren't close by.

"Keep moving," Bethany said.

We rounded the corner onto Eighth Avenue. The sidewalks were busy with pedestrians and people milling outside the bars smoking cigarettes. I felt myself relax a bit. Maybe there was safety in numbers. But then, gargoyles didn't seem like the type to care if any innocent bystanders got between them and their prey.

Bethany finally released my hand. She'd been keeping a tight grip on it the whole way up the block from Seventh Avenue, as if she were worried I'd run away. Her palm had felt warm against mine, much warmer than I'd expected it to, like there was a tiny furnace burning inside her. Probably it was just adrenaline, or maybe women with pointy, elflike ears ran naturally higher body temperatures. When she let go, I felt a confusing mix of relief and disappointment not to be holding her hand anymore. I reminded myself it was better not to think of her as a person. She was a mark, someone I intended to steal from at the soonest opportunity, nothing more. I couldn't afford to slip up again, not when so much was riding on delivering that box to Underwood.

Bethany slowed down to catch her breath. She turned to Thornton. "Do you still have your phone? I have to call Isaac and let him know what happened."

There was that name again: Isaac. Who was he? Their boss, it sounded like. If they were thieves like me, Isaac was their version of Underwood.

With his good arm, Thornton pulled a cell phone out of his pants pocket, but the crash had turned it into junk. Its casing was broken open and a deep crack bisected its blank screen. He fiddled with the power key, but the screen stayed dark. "This phone's deader than I am," he said and stuffed it back into his pocket.

Bethany turned to me. "What about you? Have you got a phone?"

"Sorry, no." Underwood didn't let me carry a cell phone. The calls were too easy to intercept, he said, even from the anonymous pay-as-you-go phones. Even worse, the authorities could use the array of cell towers all over the city to triangulate your physical location in seconds. When I was out on a job, like now, I was on my own. Sink or swim. "You don't carry one?" I asked her.

She shook her head. "I can't. There's too much interference from all the charms in my vest. Every cell phone I've ever owned has gotten fried." She took a deep breath. "Okay, what we need is to get out of the open and find someplace where we can think, preferably someplace with a public phone."

A public phone was a tall order in this day and age, but Thornton spotted a neighborhood bar up the block. A sign above the door read CELTIC PUB in big white letters and a neon four-leaf clover lit up the window.

"Bars usually have phones. I don't know about you two, but I could use a drink anyway."

"I wouldn't say no to that," I said. After everything that had happened, a drink to take the edge off was just what I needed.

Walking into the bar in our torn and bloody clothes, we were quite the sight. If we wanted to look inconspicuous enough to blend casually into the crowd, we failed miserably. But then again, this was New York City. No one even looked up from their drinks when we entered. It was like a bad joke: An elf, a zombie, and a man who can't die walk into a bar, and no one cares.

There were only a dozen customers inside, all of them sitting along the length of the bar. The cushioned booths on the other side of the room were empty. The air smelled of greasy food and spilled beer. A jukebox in the corner played the Drifters at high volume: *"They say the neon lights are bright on Broadway, they say there's always magic in the air . . ."*

Magic. God, Thornton said I'd done magic. I'd *seen* magic, too, hadn't I? Or was there some other explanation for an amulet resurrecting a dead man, or a man in black armor turning into a flock of crows and flying away? I didn't want to think about it. I just wanted a drink.

Two big flat-screen TVs hung on the wall above the bar, one showing the tail end of a baseball game and the other tuned to the local twenty-four-hour cable news channel, NY1. The sound was off on both, but the closed captioning had been turned on, white subtitles scrolling across blocky black backgrounds at the bottom of the screens. The bar's overhead fixtures were turned down low and supplemented by multicolored chili pepper lights that had been strung up along the walls. A woman stood in the short, narrow hallway at the back of the bar, talking on a pay phone. I pointed out the phone to Bethany.

"You guys sit tight, I'm going to call Isaac," she said. She seemed calmer. She was in her element now, taking charge of a situation.

"Wait, let me," Thornton said. "Gabrielle's there, too. I have to talk to her."

Bethany shook her head. "Sorry, no. I need you to lay low right now and not draw attention."

"How am I going to draw attention while I'm on the phone? Besides, have you seen your leg? It's like something out of a horror movie. You're going to draw a lot more attention than I am."

"Unfortunately, that's not true," she said. "You have to trust me. There's something that happens to people when they're around the undead." She paused and glanced around to make sure no one could hear her over the music. "They may not know what it is, but they'll sense something's wrong. Their instincts will tell them. The more they're aware of you, the more on edge they'll be. I need both of you to just take a seat and keep your heads down, all right?"

I remembered the feeling I'd had when Thornton sprang back to life, that urge to make him properly dead again, even if it meant caving in his skull. Bethany was right, that had come from somewhere deep inside, some primal instinct.

Thornton frowned. "Great, so I'm not just dead, I'm a pariah, too?"

"Thornton, I promise you I'll put you on the phone with Gabrielle if I can, but first I need to report back to Isaac. It's protocol, and we haven't had a chance to check in since last night. He needs to know things have escalated."

Thornton nodded, but he didn't look happy about it. "Everything has to be by the book with you, doesn't it," he said bitterly. "Protocol above all else. Christ, you don't have a heart in your chest, you've got fucking *Robert's Rules of Order*. Just remember I don't have a lot of time left, and right now I could not give less of a rat's ass if everyone in this bar gets a funny feeling off me. I *have* to talk to Gabrielle."

If his insult stung her, she didn't show it. "I know you do. I'll be quick, I promise." She made her way to the back and stood behind the woman on the phone. I watched her ask the woman to hurry, but the woman turned her back and kept gabbing. She ignored Bethany and tapped the small, yellow garbage can under the phone with the toe of her shoe.

"I need a drink," Thornton said. "Like, now." He leaned against the end of the bar and flagged down the bartender.

He was a beefy, bald man with a salt-and-pepper goatee and a tight black T-shirt. He did a double take when he saw Thornton. He frowned, narrowed his eyes, and said, "Look, buddy, we don't want any trouble here."

Thornton raised a confused eyebrow. "No trouble, I just wanted to get some drinks for me and my friend here."

The bartender's eyes dropped to something behind the bar. I figured it was either a baseball bat or a shotgun. I tensed, but then the bartender said, "Yeah, sure. Just keep it cool."

"Always. So, one Guinness and . . ." He turned to me. "What'll you have?"

"A shot of Jameson," I said.

The bartender nodded, and with one last wary glance at Thornton went off to get our drinks. Thornton turned to me. "What's his problem?"

"Bethany said this would happen," I said.

"Yeah, well, he's just going to have to deal. They all are. I didn't exactly ask for this."

The bartender came back a moment later with our drinks. He didn't look Thornton in the eye when he set the glasses down on the bar. Thornton struggled to reach into his right pants pocket, but his broken right arm wasn't cooperating. He tried again with his left hand but the angle was wrong. "Damn it," he muttered. He turned to me and jutted his hip forward. "Can you just reach in there and grab my wallet?"

"Uh, that's okay, I got it." I pulled out my own wallet and threw some of the bills Underwood gave me onto the bar. The bartender scooped them up and left. He couldn't get away from Thornton fast enough.

Thornton took the pint of Guinness with his left hand and started walking toward one of the booths near the back. I picked up my shot of Jameson and noticed my hand was shaking. The amber liquid threatened to spill over the rim of the shot glass. I put it down again and took a deep breath, trying to calm myself.

Something had come through me back in Times Square, something powerful that I didn't understand. It had been strong enough to send the Black Knight packing and yet, like the nine times I'd come back from the dead, it was something I couldn't control. The energy that came out of my hands—nothing like that had ever happened before. Suddenly the question of who I was took a backseat to the question of *what* I was. That frightened me. I wasn't so sure I wanted to know. What if I didn't like the answer?

I picked up the shot glass again and downed the Jameson in a single gulp. It burned on the way down and warmed my stomach. This, at least, was something familiar, something I could control. I tapped the empty shot glass and asked the bartender for another.

He filled it for me. "There's something strange about your friend," he said. "Something I don't care for."

"Don't worry, he won't make any trouble."

My hand didn't tremble as much when I picked up the second shot and carried it to the booth Thornton had chosen. In back, Bethany was standing at the phone now, cradling the handset between her ear and shoulder. The woman who'd been hogging it all this time was sitting on the bench behind her, doubled over and vomiting into the same small, yellow garbage can. She looked surprised and embarrassed, as if the sickness had come over her from out of nowhere. I wondered what Bethany had done to her to get her off the phone.

Bethany reached into a pocket of her cargo vest. At first I thought she was fishing for money to put in the coin slot, but instead she pulled out a small object that looked like scrimshaw, a fragile, round latticework of bone or ivory. She touched it to the side of the pay phone and kept her hand over it, hiding it from sight. A brief flash of blue light appeared between her fingers. Then she put the object back in its pocket and started dialing. Apparently Bethany had something in her vest for every occasion, including making a public phone work without paying. Once a thief . . .

I sat down across from Thornton. He was staring in frustration at the pint of Guinness on the table in front of him. He tried to reach for it with his broken right arm, but his arm wasn't responding properly. His face looked paler, and though I couldn't be sure in the dim light, I thought I noticed a slight green tinge to his skin that made the dark scar on his cheek even more prominent. The lights from the amulet on his chest pulsed through his shirt. He reached for his beer with his broken arm again and failed.

"Just use your other damn hand," I said, losing patience.

"Screw that," Thornton replied. "Now it's the principle of the thing. Anyway, I don't even think my arm is fully broken, just knocked out of whack. If I can just push this bone back into place . . ." He put his left hand on his right elbow, where it bent the wrong way. He bit his lip and pushed. I heard a loud crack that made me wince. Thornton lifted his right arm and wiggled his fingers experimentally. "There. I'd say as good as new, but we both know that would be a joke."

As he reached for his pint glass, I noticed that the leather bracelet on his wrist had twisted. The clasp had caught his skin and was starting to tear it.

"Whoa, let me help you with that," I said. I reached for the bracelet. Thornton yanked his arm back.

"Don't touch it," he snapped. "It was a gift from Gabrielle. No one touches it but me."

I put up my hands in a gesture of surrender. "Sorry, I was just trying to help. It looked like it hurt."

Thornton adjusted the bracelet and released the caught flap of skin. "It doesn't. Nothing hurts. I can't feel a thing. I didn't even feel anything when the car flipped over. It was like I was watching it on TV instead of actually being there." He lifted his pint glass and took a deep gulp. Then he grimaced and slammed the glass down on the table. A dollop of foamy stout sloshed over the side and ran down the glass. He pushed the beer away in frustration. "And I can't taste anything, either. I should have known. Even in human form I normally have a heightened sense of smell, but that's gone now. Makes sense I wouldn't be able to taste anything, either. That only leaves me with two senses, and who knows how long those are going to stick around?"

In human form? Damn, I'd nearly forgotten he was a wolf when I first saw him. I turned the shot glass around and around between my thumb and forefinger. "Can I ask you something?"

"Shoot."

"You're—you're a werewolf." It didn't come out as a question, though I meant it to.

He smiled. His lips looked so pale I almost couldn't tell where they ended and his teeth began. "Werewolf is such a vulgar term. It makes me think of Lon Chaney Jr. in an Afro wig and big plastic teeth. Not to get all formal on you, but lycanthrope is the proper term for what we are."

I picked up the glass and downed the second shot a little too fast. I had to suck air into my mouth to dull the burn. "We? There are more of you?"

He shrugged. "Of course. There are hundreds of us in the U.S. alone, thousands around the world. We're as thriving and vibrant a culture as any other. You should see our holiday parties. Or on second thought, scratch that. Lycanthropes aren't exactly known for their table manners, and most of the time we don't bother cooking the meat. Now that I'm thinking about it, it's actually kind of a disaster."

"Is Bethany a were—a lycanthrope, too?"

"Oh God, no," he said. "Though sometimes I wish she was. She could stand to ease up a bit, lose that stick up her butt and get in touch with her wild side. But no, she's human, I guess. Though sometimes I wonder."

"The ears," I said.

"Yeah. That and the fact that I don't think I've ever seen her laugh," Thornton said. "So, quid pro quo time. Now I get to ask you something."

I squirmed in my seat, uncomfortable with the spotlight suddenly being turned on me. It wasn't that I wasn't used to lying, I lied all the time on these collection jobs; it was that for some reason, just then, I didn't want to. Against my better judgment, I was starting to like Thornton. "Shoot," I said.

"The Black Knight," he said. Funny, his question didn't come out as one, either.

"I don't know what to tell you," I said. "I'm not a magician or a mage or . . . whatever that other word was."

"Thaumaturge," he said. "Someone who works miracles."

"Yeah, well, I'm definitely not that. I can't explain what happened. As soon as the Black Knight touched me it felt like my strength was draining right out of me. I felt tired, weak, and cold, like the temperature dropped thirty degrees in a second."

Thornton nodded. "That's what he does. One touch and the Black Knight sucks the life right out of you. It's why no one has ever survived a fight with him. No one until you. I'm sure you can understand why I'm interested in how you managed that, exactly."

I shrugged. "Your guess is as good as mine. Probably better, actually. Right now, nothing is making any sense. I didn't do anything, it just . . . happened."

He looked skeptical. "You really don't know?"

"It feels like this is all a practical joke and I'm still waiting for the punch line."

"Huh," Thornton said. "I wouldn't have pegged you for a newbie. The way you handled yourself, I would have thought you'd been working magic for a long time."

"Magic." I shook my head. "I'm losing my damn mind."

"It's not so bad," Thornton said. "The first time I got my wolf on, I felt pretty much the same way you do now. I almost lost my shit."

"Did you get bitten?" I asked.

He rolled his eyes. "Please. Forget all that bullshit from the movies. You're born into lycanthropy. You don't need to get bitten, and you sure as hell don't need a full moon to change. My first time happened in ninth grade when the school bullies decided to chase me home from school. I was terrified. I thought they were going to kill me. The next thing I knew, I was running on all fours. Maybe it's the same for you. Your life was in danger back there, and you tapped into a power you didn't know you had. A survival mechanism. But it's nothing to worry about. Take it from me, these things get easier to control after the first time."

"You're saying what happened back there could happen *again*?" I looked at my shot glass and wished it weren't empty.

"You'll get used to it. People get used to all kinds of weird stuff."

He had a point there, said the man who kept coming back from the dead. But I was barely used to *that*, how was I supposed to get used to this new ability, too? What other surprises were lurking beneath the surface, waiting to show themselves? It felt like too much to think about.

I glanced at the TV showing NY1, and my heart jumped. On the screen, a reporter in Times Square was standing in front of my upside-down Explorer, which was walled off by yellow police tape. Thornton caught my expression and turned to see for himself. The reporter's lips moved in a silent pantomime of speech while the closed-captioning subtitles scrolled across the bottom of the screen.

... *LEFT THREE OFFICERS INJURED, ONE CRITICALLY, IN WHAT WITNESSES ARE CALLING A YOUTUBE STUNT GONE DISASTROUSLY WRONG* ...

"I don't get it," I said. "How can they just brush it off like that? Those witnesses saw the Black Knight. They saw us fighting."

Thornton shrugged. "People see what they want to see. It's human nature. They barely glance at strangers' faces. Their minds fill in the blanks, and unless they know differently they just see what they expect. It's the same when it comes to magic or the supernatural. People just see what they want to see." I threw him a skeptical look. "You don't believe me?

Okay, tell me then, what did you see when you first went into the warehouse? Was it gargoyles?"

I thought back. I had entered the warehouse with my gun drawn, seen the hole in the ceiling first, and then Bethany, and facing off against her—

I'd seen exactly what I expected to see.

"Men in trench coats," I answered. Thornton nodded as if he'd proven his case. "Did the gargoyles *make* me see that?"

"Nope, that was all you. But don't feel bad about it, it could have been worse. A lot of people don't see gargoyles coming until it's too late. All those stories you hear about people disappearing off of cruise ships or kids vanishing from school trips without a trace . . ."

"That's gargoyles, too?"

"Sometimes. Sometimes it's other things. Gargoyles aren't the worst of what's out there."

There were *worse* things? I wasn't sure I wanted to know. "Okay, but what about the Black Knight? Everyone saw him. How can they just explain him away as some lunatic making a YouTube video?"

Thornton leaned forward and lowered his voice. "Most people think that all they see is all there is. Sometimes they don't even know what they're really seeing. Look around, look at the people in this bar. Any one of them could be a lycanthrope, or a vampire, or a shape-shifting demon in human form. If you didn't know those things were real, how could you tell?"

I looked at the drinkers lined up at the bar, studied their faces, but everyone looked normal to me. "I can't," I conceded.

"Exactly," Thornton said. "Magic exists, but it's a shadow world. It flourishes in the places people don't look, the streets they don't go down at night. Sometimes it's right under your nose, and if you don't know what you're looking for, you're not going to see it."

I kept looking at the drinkers. A few must have felt my eyes on them because they turned in my direction. But it wasn't me they were looking at, I realized quickly. It was Thornton. They leaned toward each other, murmuring something under the jukebox music and glaring at him with the intensity of a hawk hunting a mouse.

Thornton, oblivious to the men staring at him, kept talking. "Trust me, it's better this way. If people knew the truth about what's really out there, they'd go looking for it and get themselves killed. Or worse."

I turned back to him. "Worse? What would be worse?"

He ignored my question. "It's not safe out there, and it's getting worse by the day. There are forces at work that are supposed to keep everything in balance, but I'll be damned if they're doing their job anymore. Sure, once upon a time everything was supposedly in perfect balance, the light and the dark. Then the Shift happened, and everything went to hell."

"The Shift?"

"Something happened that tipped the balance. The darkness got stronger, and the light got weaker. Over time, magic grew darker and darker. You can't carry it inside you anymore the way magicians used to. If magic gets inside you it infects you, corrupts you, turns you dark. It changes you into something *wrong*. The only safe way to handle magic now is with artifacts, objects that are infused with spells. Charms, amulets, weapons."

"Like the Anubis Hand," I said.

Thornton tapped a finger against the amulet on his chest. "And this."

I thought of the energy that had come out of my hands, and all the times I'd woken up from being dead. Did I have magic inside me? Was that what gave me these abilities? If I did, would it corrupt me, turn me into something wrong?

Had it already?

"There are hundreds of the Infected out there," Thornton continued. "They've either embraced the darkness inside them or been subsumed by it, and their numbers are growing every day. The things that thrive in the dark have crept into the abandoned and forgotten places of the world and spread like a disease. It's an avalanche, growing stronger from its own momentum. I don't even know if it can be stopped anymore, or if things can be put back to rights. We do what we can. We secure magical artifacts before they can do any harm or fall into the wrong hands, but we keep our heads down. We don't draw attention to ourselves, and we don't take anyone on outright." He reached into his coat and pulled out a lighter and a pack of Marlboro reds. He stuck a cigarette between his lips and lit it. "Maybe you think we're cowards, but it's the only way we can survive when we're this outnumbered."

"I don't think you're cowards," I said. "But I think you're a fool if you think you can change the world. It is what it is. It's never going to change."

"Maybe. Maybe not." He took a drag off his cigarette. He couldn't taste it any more than he could the Guinness, but it seemed to calm him. He let the smoke out in a long, leisurely exhalation, a gray cloud that swirled up toward the light fixture above the table. More smoke wafted out from between the buttons of his shirt, exiting his body through the deep gashes in his torso. I decided it was better not to mention it to him.

"Oi, you can't smoke in here!" the bartender shouted over the music. "Take it outside!"

The men at the bar who'd stared at Thornton earlier turned to glare at him again. A grizzled old man in a porkpie hat added, "You shouldn't smoke anyway. Bloody things'll kill you."

"Too late for that," Thornton muttered. He dropped the cigarette into his beer, where it sizzled out.

I watched Thornton closely. "Are you scared?" I asked.

"Scared of what?"

"Dying."

"Nah, dying's easy," he said. "Comedy is hard."

"I'm serious."

His gaze was steady as it met mine. "I'm already dead, Trent. What's there to be scared of?"

I shrugged. "What comes after."

"Ah." He thought about it a moment, then said, "You know, I've seen filthy, abandoned subway platforms turned into beautiful, ornate goblin temples. I've seen creatures that live at the bottom of the Central Park Reservoir that would make you scream in terror if you caught even a glimpse of them, only they're the most peaceful beings I've ever met. They spend all day preparing elaborate meals of algae and phytoplankton, and then at night they put on puppet shows for their young. The universe never stops surprising us, Trent. Nothing is ever what it seems. The way I figure it, death is no different. It's just another kind of existence, another plane of reality."

It sounded nice, and I hoped he was right. I didn't tell him that my own experiences with death were very different. I never saw another plane of existence. I never saw anything at all.

"It's not what comes next that scares me, Trent," Thornton continued. "What scares me is leaving Gabrielle. I can't even imagine not having her by my side. It's funny, all the little things in a relationship that can bug you, like your girlfriend's mad that you left hair in the shower drain, or you're mad that she turned off the cable box when you wanted to DVR your favorite show, and then suddenly . . ." He paused a moment, staring at the soggy cigarette floating in his Guinness. "Suddenly there's an expiration date, and you realize how much time you wasted on stuff that doesn't matter. You realize love is a lot bigger and a lot more important than you ever thought it was."

I was going to have to take his word on that, though I often wondered if there was someone I'd loved, or who'd loved me, before my past was stripped away. My guess was no. If someone loved me, wouldn't they try to find me?

"Thornton!" Bethany shouted over the music. She held the phone out for him. Thornton leapt out of the booth and took it from her. He put the phone to his ear and leaned against the wall with his back to the bar. I couldn't see his expression, but I could guess what it was.

The bartender, Porkpie Hat, and the rest of the men at the bar watched Thornton at the public phone. They glared at him and muttered to each other. They looked nervous, on edge.

Bethany came to the booth and sat in Thornton's seat. She scowled at the pint glass with the cigarette in it and pushed it away. "Ugh, what have you two been doing?"

"So what's the plan?" I asked.

"Just like I said, it's not safe to meet up with Isaac yet, not with the gargoyles still out there. We can't risk leading them right to him. But he told me about a safe house that's just a few blocks from here. We're supposed to meet a woman there named Ingrid Bannion. Isaac is calling her now to let her know we're coming. We'll stay at the safe house until the sun's up. The gargoyles won't risk being out in the daylight, it hurts them too much."

"But you said it doesn't kill them?"

"Not much does." She leaned closer, her hair falling over her eyes in a way that made her look a lot younger than she was. "I told Isaac about what happened with the Anubis Hand, and what you did to the Black Knight. He's very interested in meeting you."

"Who *is* Isaac?" I asked. "You've been talking about him all night but I have no idea who he is."

"He's the man we work for."

I nodded. I'd thought as much. "The one who sends you out to secure magical artifacts before any of the Infected get them."

She arched an eyebrow at me in surprise, the corners of her lips curling up in a half-smile. "I see you and Thornton have been talking. Good. I bet Isaac could use someone like you."

I liked the fact that I'd impressed her. I liked even more that I'd made her smile.

I pushed the thought away. It was dangerous to get attached. I knew that. What was I, some goddamn amateur?

"Right now Isaac, Gabrielle, and Philip are back at Citadel, tracking the gargoyles' movements," she said. "They can keep the gargoyles occupied with some spells to misdirect them, but until the sun is up he wants us to wait it out somewhere safe. That's the best he can do for us."

Citadel. She'd mentioned that name before, back in the Explorer. Isaac's base of operations. I still didn't know where it was. Citadel was another word for castle or fortress, but where was there any such thing in New York City? It had to be close enough that Thornton had considered going right back there from the warehouse. I also made a mental note that there were five people involved in Isaac's operation, including Bethany and Thornton. That complicated things. Two people I could steal from without breaking a sweat. Five was a lot harder.

And then there was the second part of Underwood's orders, the part about not leaving any survivors. My stomach felt sour thinking about it. I pushed it aside. It was a bridge I'd cross later. First things first. I didn't have the box yet. I didn't even know where it was, other than that someone named Gregor was holding onto it for them.

"Something on your mind?" she asked. "You've got that look in your eye again."

"I have a look?" I asked.

"You've got a lot of looks, actually, but I call this one the *I'm about to punch someone* look."

She smiled again. I forced myself to look away before it sucked me in. I said, "I don't get it. Isaac is here in the city, right?" She nodded. "Then why doesn't he come help you? Why hasn't he picked you up yet? You've been on the run since last night."

"It's policy," she explained. "Once we're out in the field, we're on our own."

That sounded uncomfortably familiar. "So he just hangs you out to dry?"

"It's not like that. Isaac knows what he's doing. But if we're going to do any good, none of this can be traced back to him."

That, too, sounded familiar. I found myself growing unexpectedly angry. "Why? What makes him so special that he needs protecting?"

"It's not who he is, it's what he's got."

Before I could ask anything else, the scuff of somebody's shoe against the floor made me turn. The people at the bar were off their stools and on their feet, milling about restlessly. They were focused like a laser on Thornton, who was too busy talking to Gabrielle on the phone to notice them. They looked like animals that had been backed into a corner, shifting their weight nervously back and forth, from foot to foot. They didn't approach Thornton, but it was only a matter of time. I could feel the violence brewing. It thickened the air.

Thornton hung up the phone and came back to the booth, grinning from ear to ear. His smile made the scar on his cheek look even worse. The torn flap of skin wobbled like it was going to come loose again.

"See? I told you I'd make sure you got to talk to her," Bethany said.

Thornton nodded, still beaming. "She's sure there's something that can help me. She told me she's going to read every spell book she can get her hands on to find a way to circumvent the amulet's time limit. She thinks she might be able to make its effects permanent."

"That's good news," I said.

"If anyone can do it, Gabrielle can. I know she can," he said.

Bethany looked down, avoiding his eyes. It looked like she had something to say but had chosen to keep her mouth shut instead.

"Hey!" someone called. Thornton didn't turn to see who it was, but I did. It was one of the guys at the bar, a man in his thirties with the sloppy, red-splotched features of someone who'd been drinking since he was old enough to lift a glass. He and the others had clustered together in a tight pack, giving themselves over to a primal herd instinct. Behind them, the bartender had his hand on whatever was under the bar. I was curious about what it was, but not enough to want him to pull it out.

"Hey," the man called again.

Under the table, I pulled my Bersa semiautomatic out of the back of my pants and transferred it to the pocket of my leather jacket, just in case.

"Hey, you!" the man called.

This time Thornton turned around. "Jesus Christ, *what?*"

They came forward hesitantly, taking half-steps but keeping their pack positions. Their fear of Thornton was so strong it had turned into a seething hatred. It was like watching a herd of gazelles muster up the courage to attack a lion.

The bartender finally lifted the object from behind the bar. A wooden Louisville Slugger. I let out a small breath of relief. It was better than a shotgun, and it meant as long as these guys didn't start with the pitchforks-and-torches routine I could leave my gun in my pocket.

I slid out of my seat and showed them my empty hands. "Is there a problem?"

Porkpie Hat jutted his chin at Thornton. "He's the problem. What does he want? Why is he here?"

Thornton opened his mouth to answer. I knew he was going to say something smart-assed that would only make things worse, so I jumped in fast and said, "We're not looking for trouble."

"Then why don't you just get the hell out," the bartender said. Then, to emphasize his point, he hit the countertop with his baseball bat a couple of times, like he was shooing away a raccoon.

"We were just leaving," I said.

"See to it, then," the splotchy-faced man said.

We left the booth and left the bar, exiting back out onto Eighth Avenue. I hoped Isaac and the others were doing their job keeping the gargoyles distracted, because now that we were outside again we were exposed and vulnerable.

Bethany led the way downtown. I kept an eye on the sky, but so far so good. No gargoyles, at least none that I could see against the dark.

"What the hell was their problem?" Thornton demanded.

"Sorry, but I told you," Bethany said. "It's a survival instinct left over from primitive times. People can sense the undead, but only on a purely subconscious level. If you asked any of them back there why they were so on edge, they wouldn't be able to tell you. They couldn't help themselves."

"That's me, always bringing out the best in people." He sighed. "So I really am a pariah, then."

"Not to us," she said. She took him by the good arm as we crossed Eighth Avenue. It struck me as a rare moment of warmth from her, the first time I'd seen her act like Thornton's friend instead of his supervisor.

We cut through one of the side streets. We were in the theater district, but it was already late enough that the restaurants and piano bars were closed. The sidewalks were deserted. I didn't like being this out in the open.

We passed an alley between buildings. Instinct made me turn and look inside. I didn't see anything but a thick cloud of steam. It roiled and twisted, and then something broke through it. A gargoyle. It crawled sideways along the brick wall like a bug. I froze.

The gargoyle lifted its head to look at me. I recognized it from the warehouse. Yellow Eye. But then it did something I didn't expect. Without making a sound, Yellow Eye retreated back into the steam and vanished. I didn't understand. The gargoyle had seen me. There was no way it couldn't have. So why didn't it attack?

Bethany stopped walking. She came back to see what I was looking at, but by then it was just an empty alley. "What is it?"

"I thought I saw—" I started to say.

The chilling shriek of a gargoyle sounded somewhere above us. I looked up and saw a winged shape moving along the rooftops.

"Run," I said, but the gargoyle was already swooping down toward us.

Eleven

The gargoyle soared over the awnings and curbside trees, tracing our route down the sidewalk. We were injured and slow, but even if we'd been able to run quickly the gargoyle could have overtaken us without much effort. As it was, it must have thought we were child's play. It swooped into Bethany from behind, knocking her to the sidewalk. She tried to get back on her feet, but the gargoyle landed on top of her. It straddled her back and pinned her down.

I skidded to a halt. My hand was on my gun before I remembered bullets were useless against these things. Damn it, weren't Isaac and the others supposed to be drawing the gargoyles away?

Bethany struggled to get free, but the gargoyle was too heavy. She tried to reach into her vest for a charm, but her arms were pinned the wrong way for that. Perched on her back, the gargoyle drew back one claw, preparing to strike.

"Get off of her!" Thornton yelled. He ran at it, brandishing the broken half of the Anubis Hand. He swung it before the gargoyle could react. The mummified fist connected with the gargoyle's snout. There was a much smaller flash this time, and no web of fire, but the gargoyle still tumbled off of Bethany, stunned. Thornton helped her up, and together they started running. The gargoyle stumbled side to side on its feet for a moment, its wings twitching, then shook its head clear. It saw Thornton taking its prey away and released an angry shriek.

"Thornton, the staff!" I shouted. He tossed it to me. I caught it and ran at the gargoyle, noticing for the first time that it wasn't Yellow Eye.

Strange, Yellow Eye hadn't come back after mysteriously retreating into the alleyway. I swung the staff, and the Anubis Hand connected with the gargoyle's jaw. There was a much brighter flash now. The gargoyle was knocked backward, burning as it rolled across the street, giving off sparks and embers until it finally exploded in a burst of blackened ash. I turned back to the others. "Now *that's* how you hit a gargoyle," I said.

Bethany was pale and out of breath. Her spill on the sidewalk had opened the cut in her knee again, and she was leaning against Thornton for support. "Save the gloating," she said. "We have to get to the safe house before more of them come. It isn't far now."

"Can you walk?" I asked.

Instead of answering, she let go of Thornton, turned around, and started limping quickly up the block toward Ninth Avenue.

"Okay then," I said, and followed.

We turned downtown on Ninth, moving as quickly as we could. I kept a tight grip on the Anubis Hand, just in case. A nearby shriek, like the hunting call of a bird of prey, froze us in our tracks. A dark, man-sized shape moved across the night sky. It was little more than a shadow against the darkness, but the silhouette of its wings was unmistakable.

"Your boss isn't doing his job," I said.

"You're wrong about that," Bethany replied. "If he wasn't, we'd already be dead."

We turned west onto Forty-Third Street, a quiet, sleepy block. A gargoyle landed on top of one of the buildings along the street. It crouched on its haunches and folded its wings onto its back until it looked every bit the twin of its architectural namesake. From its high perch, it scanned the street below.

Bethany grabbed Thornton and me, and pushed us into a dark doorway across the street. She put her hand on my chest, pushing me as far back against the door as she could. I felt the heat of her skin through my shirt.

"Don't move," she whispered. "Stay quiet. Don't even breathe."

"Not a problem," Thornton whispered back.

The gargoyle's head whipped in our direction, as if it had heard us. I felt its icy gaze narrowing in on us like a rifle sight. It launched itself into the air toward us.

"Run!" Bethany said.

We took off down the street. The gargoyle came after us, chittering and shrieking. I took a swipe at it with the Anubis Hand, but the staff was half the length it used to be. The gargoyle easily maneuvered away from it. Without a weapon, the only thing to do was run, so we ran like mad.

Up ahead, in the middle of the block, a figure stepped out into the street. She was an older, slender woman in her late sixties or early seventies, wearing a billowy red blouse and black cotton pants. Strands of long gray hair blew back from her face in the breeze. She saw us, there was no way she couldn't have, but she didn't move, she just stood there in the middle of the street like a lunatic.

"Get away!" I shouted, waving. "Get inside!"

She stood her ground. I looked back, saw the gargoyle was gaining on us, then looked at the woman again. She didn't look remotely frightened.

She extended her left arm. Her hand and forearm were sheathed in a long white glove, the kind someone might wear to a fancy ball, except she was only wearing one of them. Her right hand was bare. Something sparked in the palm of her glove, and then a column of fire exploded out of it. It arced through the air toward the gargoyle. As the flames passed over my head, I dropped to the pavement and looked up in time to see them envelop the gargoyle. The creature fell out of the sky like a burning comet. By the time it hit the street, there was nothing left but a few smoldering bones that looked like blackened twigs.

The woman lowered her arm. A thin wisp of smoke wafted from her glove.

My eyes were so wide I thought they might pop out. "That was amazing," I said.

The woman nodded. "It was, wasn't it?"

Before I could ask her who she was, a dozen big black crows swooped down from the night sky behind her. A moment later, they came together to form the Black Knight astride his armored horse.

Bethany shouted, "Behind you!"

The woman spun around. The jet-black horse snorted and hoofed the pavement.

"You," she said. There was so much anger dripping from that one word it was immediately clear to me these two had met before. The woman raised her white-gloved hand again. Fire spat from her palm to wash over the Black Knight. But when the flames dissipated, he was unharmed.

The Black Knight reached for his sword. I pushed myself off the sidewalk and onto my feet. As soon as the Black Knight saw me, he froze, his sword halfway out of its scabbard. Then he pulled it the rest of the way out, leveled it in my direction, and urged his steed forward, the woman now all but forgotten. He wanted a rematch.

The Black Knight galloped toward me. I threw myself aside a second before his blade would have run me through, hitting the concrete with my shoulder. I rolled to a stop at the edge of the street, wincing with pain, and saw the Black Knight and his horse break apart. A dozen crows flapped their way into the night sky and didn't come back. I stood up, rubbing my sore shoulder.

"That's strange. I've never seen the Black Knight retreat like that," the woman said. She studied our faces, then smiled. Deep dimples appeared in the shallow wrinkles of her cheeks. Her brown eyes twinkled as she smoothed down the sides of her blouse. "You must be Isaac's friends."

"Are you Ingrid Bannion?" Bethany asked.

"I am." She looked up at the sky. "Maybe we should take this inside, where it's safer." She started walking toward an abandoned lot between two town houses in the middle of the block. A chain-link fence separated us from the patch of overgrown grass beyond it, but for some reason I had trouble focusing on it. It was like the empty lot didn't want me to look too closely. I blinked and squinted, but the strange feeling didn't pass. I wondered if I'd hit my head on the pavement without realizing it.

"Is the safe house close by?" I asked.

"Oh yes, it's quite close," Ingrid replied. She stepped up onto the sidewalk in front of the empty lot—and then kept stepping up right into the air. White-painted cement stairs appeared beneath her feet with each step she took, until finally she stood on the landing at the top of what appeared to be a freestanding stoop.

There was a house there, I realized, but somehow I couldn't see it. The moment the thought struck me, the empty lot wavered like a mirage and a white, stucco-walled town house appeared in its place. It stood three stories tall and twice as wide as the town houses that flanked it, as if someone had bought two neighboring buildings and fused them together seamlessly.

At the top of the steps, Ingrid stood before double doors that were crowned with a peaked, stone cornice. Both doors were decorated with holly wreaths sporting red plastic berries, though Christmas was still three months away. Lights glowed warmly through the thin white curtains in the windows. A collection of small Hummel figurines had been arranged on the inside of the windowsill next to the doors, all of them dressed like little ceramic shepherds with various musical instruments in their hands or pressed to their cherubic lips.

This was the safe house? I'd pictured something a little more formidable. Less Hummel and more iron bars.

Ingrid opened the front door and motioned for us to follow her inside. I climbed up the stoop behind Bethany and Thornton, hesitant to put my full weight on steps that had appeared out of nowhere. But when I put my foot down it was solid. At the same time, I felt something pushing against me. It came in waves, reminding me on some level of the tiny, imaginary hands I'd felt trying to push me away from the warehouse.

A few steps above me, Bethany spread her fingers as if she were letting a breeze run through them. "Ingrid, I can feel the ward around this place. It's incredible. The strongest I've ever felt."

"Oh, thank you, dear," Ingrid said, holding the door open for us. "But I can't take the credit. I'm about as good at casting wards as I am at programming my cell phone. No, it was put there by a dear friend."

Was the ward what I was feeling pushing against me? Bethany had used the word before, but I still had no real idea what it meant.

The entrance hallway of Ingrid's town house was narrow and smelled of lavender and Murphy's Oil. A vase of dried flowers stood on the credenza along the wall, and arranged around its base were more Hummel figurines set on doilies. I took it all in, the quaint umbrella stand by the door, the wooden shoe rack beside it with the words GOD BLESS THIS MESS carved across the top. The outside was nothing like I'd expected for a safe house, but the inside made me downright uneasy. There were no guards, no weapons, nothing that made me feel safe.

Ingrid closed the front door, then locked the dead bolt above the knob. "This house may be protected by a ward, but there's no harm in being careful." She turned to us, rubbing her hands together to warm them after the cool autumn night air. "There now. You must be Bethany?" She extended her right hand, the one without a glove, and Bethany shook it.

"Yes, I'm Bethany Savory. This is Thornton Redler."

Ingrid shook Thornton's hand next, and the happy smile faded from her face. "Oh, dear. Oh, I'm so sorry, young man. What did those awful creatures do to you?"

He touched the scar on his face with his other hand. "It's okay."

"I don't mean the scar," Ingrid said. "When I touch someone I can see their aura. It's a gift I've had all my life. A person's aura shows me everything I need to know about them. For instance, Bethany's aura is a bright yellow, almost lemon. That tells me she's a woman of purpose, that getting the job done right is important to her. It also tells me she's someone who doesn't like it when things are unpredictable or out of her control. Not when it comes to her duties, or her personal life."

A slight blush colored Bethany's cheeks. I chuckled, and she shot me an annoyed look. Clearly, Ingrid had pegged her to a tee.

"Every living thing has an aura, from simple houseplants to the most evolved creatures," Ingrid continued. "But not you, Thornton Redler. You don't have any aura at all."

Thornton pulled his hand out of her grasp. "Well, this day just keeps getting better."

"I'm sorry, I didn't mean to embarrass you," Ingrid said. "You don't look half bad for someone who's," she paused to choose her words carefully, "passed on."

"I haven't passed on yet," he insisted.

"No. No, I suppose you haven't," she said. She turned to me next and stuck out her hand. "And you are . . . ?"

I looked at her hand. If I took it, would she see too much? What if she saw that I was a thief? Or worse, saw the thing inside me? What if she didn't see my aura, but instead saw nine of them—nine stolen auras stacked on top of each other like anonymous bodies in a mass grave? I wasn't willing to risk it.

I stuck my hands in my pockets and said, "I'm Trent."

Ingrid let her hand drop to her side. "Nice to meet all of you. Any friend of Isaac's is a friend of mine. I just wish our meeting were under better circumstances. Please, come inside." She escorted us down the entrance hall toward the flight of wooden stairs that led to the second floor. As we passed the kitchen, I smelled traces of pork chops and a hint of sautéed greens with garlic and lemon. My stomach growled. I hadn't eaten in several hours, and now the hunger was catching up with me.

Bethany limped up the steps ahead of me, favoring her hurt leg. Thornton moved stiffly, as if his limbs refused to bend properly anymore. At the top of the stairs, an elaborately decorated living room ran the entire width of the extra-wide town house, its walls lined with overflowing bookcases. A set of eight upholstered, high-backed wooden chairs had been loosely arranged around the room, some against the wall and some in a semicircle around a coffee table with a wrought-iron base and a marble top. A long couch sat in the middle of the room with embroidered throw pillows at either arm. On the wall past the couch I noticed an old, blocked-off fireplace, a decorative remnant of a time when the buildings in this part of town didn't have radiators or central heating. Its mantel was cluttered with framed pictures and Hummel figures. Above it, bolted to the wall, was a glass case containing six ornate, antique swords, their hilts together and their blades radiating out in a sunburst formation. In the far corner, near the stairs that led up to the third floor, an antique grandfather clock ticked loudly, its baroque, arrow-shaped hands showing the time as 1:30 a.m. I hadn't realized how late it was. I'd left the fallout shelter a little past ten.

I crossed the room to the tall, narrow windows and pulled aside the thick white curtain. The street below was empty. Nothing moved along the rooftops.

"Make yourselves comfortable, I'll be right back," Ingrid said. She went downstairs again, the wooden steps creaking under her feet.

I took off my coat and inspected the damage. The leather on the back was ruined, shredded beyond repair. It was a shame, I liked that coat, though by now I knew better than to get attached to anything I wore. I hung it over the back of one of the upholstered chairs, and sat down. The chair's high back rubbed against me, irritating the scratches on my back. I winced and leaned forward to take pressure off the wounds.

Bethany and Thornton sat on the couch, facing me. In the bright lights of the living room, the wound on her leg looked terrible, even through the hole in her jeans. Thornton's skin was definitely turning from gray to a pale shade of green, especially around his eyes, his mouth, and the scar on his cheek. The three of us looked like we'd been to Hell and back. Maybe minus the back part.

"You're sure we'll be safe here?" I asked Bethany.

She nodded. "The ward around this house will keep anyone from finding it."

"I didn't even see this place until . . ." I paused, unsure how to describe what I saw. "Is that what a ward does?"

"It's a spell that hides things," Bethany said. "But it can't hide what you've already seen, or what you already know is there. That's why none of us saw the house until Ingrid showed us where it was."

I nodded. I was starting to understand, albeit just barely. "So if the Black Knight saw it, too . . ."

"He didn't," she assured me. "He was already gone."

I hoped she was right about that. Ward or no, I'd feel safer if we had a cache of weapons, at least.

"I don't like just sitting here," Thornton said. He rubbed his hands along his thighs restlessly. "I should be with Gabrielle."

"You'll be with her soon," Bethany said.

"Right, once the sun comes up," he said. He glanced at the clock. "That'll be in, what, four hours? That's four hours we're wasting here. Four hours I could be spending with her, either looking for a spell to keep this amulet from shutting itself off or . . . or saying goodbye."

"If Gabrielle and Isaac both think it's best that we stay here, that's good enough for me," Bethany said. "It should be good enough for you, too."

Thornton turned away from her and gnawed at his thumbnail. The nail fell off. He watched it tumble into his lap, and said, "I just don't want to waste any time."

Bethany didn't answer. For what felt like a very long time, none of us spoke. The air prickled with tension. I glanced at the staircase and wondered when Ingrid was going to come back. Finally, Bethany said, "I'm sorry, Thornton. If I'd known about this place, we could have come here sooner. Maybe even avoided the warehouse altogether. Then things might have been different."

Thornton shook his head. "No, I'm the one who's sorry. I've been acting like an asshole because I don't know how to cope with this. You can stop beating yourself up, Bethany. It wasn't your fault."

"Isaac put me in charge of this mission, remember? That means I'm responsible for everything that happens, including what happened to you. It's as much my fault as anyone else's."

He tapped the amulet under his shirt. "You're also the one who gave me my second chance. Don't forget that."

The steps creaked as Ingrid came back upstairs. She was carrying a silver tray laden with a ceramic teapot, four teacups, a heaping plate of cookies, and a first-aid kit. She set it down on the coffee table. "I thought you might be hungry. If you don't mind my saying so, you all look a little worse for wear, so I brought bandages, rubbing alcohol, and a needle and thread if anyone needs stitching up. I'm not a doctor, but I know a thing or two about fixing people up after they get into scrapes."

"Thanks," Bethany said. "I think we can use a little of everything."

The cookies on the table made my mouth water. I took one off the plate and bit into it, tasting oatmeal and cinnamon. It was good, really good. I finished it quickly, grabbed a handful more, and began stuffing them in my mouth.

Thornton stared at me. "My God, were you raised by wolves? Because I was, and even they didn't eat like that."

I looked up at him, crumbs dropping from my lips, my mouth too full to answer.

Ingrid laughed. "Leave him be, he's hungry." She picked up the first-aid kit and opened the lid. "So, which one of you poor, battered souls wants to be first?"

Thornton needed her attention the most. Even if he wasn't in danger of dying from his wounds, being dead already, his shirt could only do so much to hold his insides in place. He needed to be stitched up. Thornton struggled to remove his shirt. His arms worked stiffly, especially the broken one he'd hastily reset at the bar, but he refused Bethany's help. Once his shirt was off, he lay back on the couch and put his hands over his wounds as if he were ashamed of them. His skin had turned a sickly gray all over. An angry purple bruise painted his side where the blood had first settled when he died. Bethany got up from the couch to give him room to stretch out.

"Let me see," Ingrid said, gently taking Thornton's wrists. He resisted for a moment, then allowed her to move his arms away from his wounds. They resembled deep black chasms in his torso, rimmed with a coppery crust where the blood had dried, and tinged with green along their edges. The Breath of Itzamna remained spiked into the center of his chest, pulsing with its artificial heartbeat.

Ingrid touched the amulet gingerly with her white-gloved hand. Thornton explained, "It's what brought me back. After I died."

She nodded as if it were no more unusual than a scar or tattoo. Thornton's eyes filled with gratitude that she wasn't making a big deal out of it. She took a set of reading glasses from the coffee table, put them on, and took a closer look at his wounds. "This isn't so bad," she lied. "Nothing a little needle and thread can't fix. I'll have you right as rain in no time."

Thornton beamed at her. "I think I love you, Ingrid Bannion."

"Handsomer men than you have told me that. You'll have to try harder." She retrieved a needle and a spool of black thread from the first-aid kit.

Thornton looked at her white glove. "What happened to your hand?"

Ingrid blanched. "It's nothing. Don't worry, I can still stitch with the best of them."

Thornton sat up a little. "I'm sure you can, but unless the single-glove look is suddenly all the rage, I'm guessing it's not nothing."

Ingrid sighed. She put the needle and thread down, her face reddening with embarrassment. "It was a long time ago. I was young and brash. I thought I could just take in a little magic and it wouldn't affect me. I was wrong."

"Is that how you're able to read auras?" Bethany asked.

"No," Ingrid said. "That's something I was born with. What I took into me, and still carry inside me, is the fire magic you saw outside. It was a mistake I'll have to live with for the rest of my life. Like I said, I was young. I thought it would be different for me. I thought I was invulnerable, the way the young always think they're invulnerable." She looked at the glove. "Turns out I wasn't anything but a fool."

"May I see it?" Thornton asked.

She shook her head vehemently. "Trust me, it's better if you don't."

"Ingrid," he said, flashing a charming smile. "I'm sure you've played this game before with lots of lucky guys. I showed you mine. Now you show me yours."

"Thornton, please, just leave it alone," she said.

"You're worried I'll judge you," Thornton said. "I won't. You can trust me on that."

Ingrid looked at him a long time, then finally nodded. "Just remember, it's not as bad as it looks, and it doesn't hurt. It's under control."

She unrolled the white glove slowly, grimacing as she pulled it up from her elbow to her fingers. Finally, she pulled it free. The extent of what the infection had done to her hand and forearm was astonishing. Aside from the five fingerlike appendages at the end, the misshapen, squamous limb didn't look like anything human.

Twelve

"It doesn't look so bad," Thornton said.

Ingrid smiled warmly. She pulled the long white glove back over her arm. "You're a bad liar, Thornton, but a good man. I bet your aura was a beautiful color. Probably a bright royal blue." She put her hand in her lap, as if to hide it. "You know how it is when you carry magic inside you. This is what it did to me. Morbius managed to contain the infection before it got worse, and before it could corrupt my mind, but the damage had already been done."

"Who is Morbius?" Bethany asked. "The name sounds familiar."

"A powerful mage, and a dear friend," Ingrid said. "He's the one who put the ward around this house. He's no longer with us." For a moment she was quiet, lost in her own memories. I got the sense that she'd seen more and experienced more than anyone I knew, and not all of it was good.

"I want to show you something, Ingrid," Thornton said. He began unbuckling his leather bracelet. His stiff fingers made it difficult.

"Do you need help?" Ingrid asked. She reached for the bracelet.

Just as he'd done with me, Thornton jerked his arm away from her. "Don't. Sorry, I don't mean any offense, but I don't let anyone touch this bracelet."

"It must be very important to you," Ingrid said.

Thornton managed to unbuckle the clasp and remove the bracelet. There, on the inside of his wrist, was a patch of skin that was marbled and glassy like an opal. He tapped it with a fingernail. It made the same sound as tapping a stone. "Once upon a time, I was young and foolish, too. Back then I had trouble accepting what I was, and like a fool I thought magic could cure me. It didn't. It didn't do anything but infect me, though it was several years before any symptoms manifested. Isaac contained it before it spread, but it left me with this souvenir." He buckled the bracelet around his wrist again. "See, Ingrid? If I judged you, I'd only be judging myself, too."

Ingrid looked at him a long moment. "I think I love you back, Thornton Redler."

She stitched him up as best she could, a job made easier by the fact that he couldn't feel any pain. While she worked, Bethany took a handful of bandages from the first-aid kit and came over to me. "Take off your shirt," she said.

"Excuse me?" I said.

"That gargoyle got your back pretty good," she said. "We should take care of it before it gets worse."

"I'm fine. Really." I gestured at her injured leg. "You should probably tend to that knee instead."

"It can wait," she insisted. "I'm serious, Trent. Between getting mauled by a gargoyle and being in a car crash, you're not fine. That's the adrenaline talking. After everything that's happened, your wounds might be a lot worse than you think they are. So, the shirt."

She was determined, which meant nothing I said was going to change her mind. I knew that much about her already. There was no way to explain to her that no matter how bad my wounds were they weren't life threatening, not to me; no way to explain that the thing inside me always brought me back from the dead fully healed, which included wounds both old and new. I wondered sometimes what would happen if I lost an eye or a hand, if they would grow back too, but it wasn't something I ever hoped to put to the test.

"Have it your way," I said, "but I'm telling you I'm okay." I unbuttoned my shirt, pulled it off, and tossed it on the carpet. I turned my chair around and leaned forward with my back exposed. "You should save the bandages for yourself. You'll just be wasting them on me."

"You don't have a very high opinion of yourself, do you?" Bethany asked. She circled around behind me, and a moment later I felt her unusually warm hands on my back as she inspected my wounds. Her touch on my bare skin made me uneasy. I felt vulnerable, like I'd left myself open to a knife between the ribs. I was pretty sure Bethany wasn't the knifing type, but after a year among the criminals of Brooklyn, old habits were hard to shake.

Her hands felt good on me. Too good. I didn't like that, either.

"You're tense," she said.

I grunted in reply, which only proved her right.

"Looks like the gargoyle didn't cut you too deep. The bleeding's not too bad," Bethany said. "You got lucky. One good swipe from a gargoyle can cut clean through bone. About an inch to the right and an ounce more force and it would have severed your spinal column."

"Told you I was fine," I said.

"You've been mauled by a gargoyle," she said. "I think we have different definitions of fine."

"I've had worse."

"Funny, you don't have any scars to show for it."

Of course I didn't. "They're on the inside," I quipped.

"I'm going to have to clean out your wounds." Bethany retrieved a bottle of rubbing alcohol and a few cotton balls from the first-aid kit. "This might sting a bit."

"I think I'll be okay."

"Your tough-guy act isn't as convincing as you think it is." She dabbed an alcohol-soaked cotton ball against my back. I bucked in the chair, loudly sucking air through my teeth. "See? Not so convincing."

"It was just cold," I insisted, clenching my jaw as the burning alcohol cleansed my wounds.

Ingrid laughed. "I never thought I'd say it, but I kind of miss this. Being part of a team, I mean, like you three and Isaac."

"We're not exactly a team," Bethany said. "We're more like freelancers. Isaac hires us when he needs us to secure an artifact."

"It's a living," Thornton said. "When Isaac found me and offered me a job, I jumped at it. I was at a low point in my life, probably the lowest I've ever been. I felt like I had nothing to live for back then. Now I do." He looked down at the amulet on his chest. "How's that for irony?"

Ingrid *tsked* and shook her head as she continued her stitch work.

"Freelancers. It was different back in my day. We were together all the time. We would eat together, drink together, and on occasion we even lived together, right here in this house. It was a bond that lasted a lifetime."

"Who's we?" Thornton asked.

"There were five of us back then, fighting the good fight," she said. "We called ourselves the Five-Pointed Star."

Bethany froze in the middle of attaching a self-adhesive bandage to my back. "Wait, *you* were part of the Five-Pointed Star?"

"Oh yes," Ingrid said with a grin. "You wouldn't think it to look at me now, but I could mix it up in my day."

"I thought I recognized the name Morbius," Bethany said. "He was the Five-Pointed Star's leader, wasn't he? I've heard stories about them—about you, the things you did back in the day. You were legendary."

Ingrid blushed and shook her head. "Sometimes I forget four decades have passed since Morbius brought us together. Time has a way of sneaking up on you. The others are all gone now. I'm the only one left to remember it all, and there's so much to remember. Fighting trolls under the Kosciusko Bridge. Vampires in the Brooklyn-Battery Tunnel. Sirens off the coast of Coney Island . . ."

As she spoke, I noticed a framed photograph on the end table near my chair. I picked it up for a closer look. Five people stood in the same room we were in now, three men and two women. This was the Five-Pointed Star, I realized. I almost didn't recognize the woman on the far right in the batik-print caftan dress until I noticed the white glove on her left hand. Ingrid, some forty years younger. She'd been strikingly beautiful back then, with long, chestnut-brown hair parted in the middle, and sharp, chiseled features that hadn't yet softened with age. The other woman in the photo wore a long, black, wool knit dress, a small star tattoo at the center of her forehead peeking out from beneath her black bangs. Her skin was as red as brick, and her eyes burned yellow like two miniature suns. Two men stood side by side between the women, both with long stringy gray hair, lengthy knotted beards, and matching dark blue robes embroidered with strange gold symbols. They looked like twin wizards right out of a storybook; all they were missing were big pointed caps on their heads. And standing at the center of the group was the man I figured had to be Morbius, their leader. He stood tall in a wide-lapelled herringbone jacket, black iridescent necktie, and bell-bottomed trousers. His arms were crossed in front of his chest. His square, lightly stubbled jaw jutted forward as if he were daring the world to take a swing.

They were freaks, just like me, each with their own strange abilities. But more than that, they'd found a place where they belonged. With each other.

I put the picture back on the end table. It was a lot to take in at once. The world was nothing like I'd imagined all those times I lay awake in my room in the fallout shelter. It was so much bigger. Worlds within worlds, just like Elena De Voe had written in *The Ragana's Revenge*. There was so much I didn't know, so much more I needed to learn. The weight of it felt staggering.

"Back then, you couldn't walk two feet in Bushwick without tripping over a portal to some other dimension," Ingrid was saying. "That was how Maalrok, the war god of the Pharrenim, found his way into our world. Oh, he was a nasty one, let me tell you. Half man, half lizard, ten feet tall with six arms." She gestured at the glass case over the mantelpiece, where the six antique swords were displayed. "Those were his. I kept them as a souvenir. Of course, we never could have stopped him and closed off the portal to his world without the help of a talented young man from the neighborhood by the name of Isaac Keene."

"So *that's* how you know Isaac," Bethany said. "He talks about the Five-Pointed Star a lot. They were his inspiration."

Ingrid nodded, but the smile faded from her face. "I remember the way he looked at us that day. His eyes were so wide. There was such innocence in them. Such wonder."

Bethany dabbed an alcohol-soaked cotton ball on a small cut on my forehead, but I waved her away. "I'm fine, really. You've done enough."

"Suit yourself. You can put your shirt back on." She sat down on a nearby chair and began cleaning her wounded knee through the hole in her jeans leg.

I bent to pick my shirt up off the floor, half expecting the pain in my back to flare up. It didn't. Bethany had fixed me up like an expert. Somehow that didn't surprise me. She struck me as the kind of person who strived to be an expert at everything.

"After Morbius died, Isaac wanted to take his place on the team," Ingrid continued. "I wouldn't let him. It was too dangerous. You don't need me to tell you what it's like out there, and it's only getting worse, not better. I told him the best thing he could do was keep his head down and not draw attention to himself. I made him promise—no, I made him *swear* to leave it alone, but it wasn't easy. Morbius had filled that boy's head with the same grandiose nonsense he put in mine back when he first asked me to join his grand experiment. Morbius believed that burying your head in the sand wasn't the answer. It didn't make you any safer. He said there comes a time when you have to take a stand, even if no one stands with you. He knew damn well there was no safe way to fight the darkness that's spreading through the world, but he was convinced it had to be done no matter what the risk. And it cost him his life."

"What happened?" I asked.

She frowned, her lips pressed tight. "The Black Knight happened. With a touch, he sucked the life right out of Morbius. That's all it took, just one touch. It was so fast, it was horrible. After Morbius died, we couldn't go on without him. He was the glue that held us together, he and his dream of a better world. The darkness was too strong for us to fight. If it could kill Morbius, it could kill anyone." She looked down at her hands. "I didn't want that to happen to Isaac, so I told him to do exactly what Morbius said *not* to. I told him to hide."

"I'm sorry," Bethany said.

Ingrid took a deep breath, collecting herself. "It was a long time ago. But now it seems the Black Knight is after *you,* and I can guess why. Isaac told me what you found. I'm begging you to be careful. I don't know what happened just now, why the Black Knight flew off like that, but we got lucky. He'll keep coming for you. I wish I knew how to stop him, but don't I think he *can* be stopped."

"Trent did a pretty good job of it earlier tonight when he kicked the Black Knight's ass," Thornton said.

"What?" Ingrid looked at me, surprised. "You fought the Black Knight and *survived*?"

I took another cookie off the plate and bit smugly into it. "I didn't just survive, I sent him packing."

Ingrid's mouth fell open. Unexpectedly, her face reddened with anger. "You should have killed him when you had the chance."

There was so much fury in her voice, a fury that had built up for decades, that my smugness wilted. She peppered me with question after question about my encounter with the Black Knight. I told her everything I knew. When I was finished, she nodded to herself like something finally made sense. "*You're* the reason he backed off outside. You hurt him once. He doesn't know what else you're capable of."

"That makes two of us," I said.

"But you *hurt* him," Ingrid repeated. "He may find you unpredictable, but he'll be back. You can count on it. You've got his attention now. You're going to need help, and I think I have just the thing." She walked over to the bookshelves and started scanning the spines, tapping her finger against her chin. "Unfortunately, there isn't a lot of information available about the Black Knight. No one knows where he came from or the extent of his powers. Just about all anyone knows is that he's the king of the gargoyles, though he wasn't their first king, and he's not a gargoyle himself."

So that was why the Anubis Hand hadn't worked on him, I thought. It only worked on gargoyles. Good to know. "So what is he then?" I asked.

Ingrid ran her finger along the hardcovers crammed into the shelves. "Good question. I've been researching the Black Knight for years, ever since he killed Morbius. I tried to find out anything I could—where he came from, what he is, if he has a base of operations, any weaknesses or vulnerabilities, *anything*—but I hit dead end after dead end. And then I found something interesting in Bankoff's annotated *Libri Arcanum*. A connection I hadn't noticed before. Ah, here it is." She pulled a thick, hide-bound tome off the shelf, put her reading glasses on again, and flipped through the pages until she found what she was looking for. "There's a story of an alchemist who came to the New World from Europe in the middle of the seventeenth century. His name and likeness have been lost to time, but he's widely considered to be the first known European magician to come over. Supposedly, he lived for a few months in a Dutch trading settlement called Fort Verhulst on the southern tip of Manhattan. Then one day, for reasons unknown, he ventured out into the wilderness and was never seen again. Everyone figured he was either killed by the Lenape Indians who lived in the area and weren't exactly friendly with the Dutch, or that he died from starvation or exposure." She flipped ahead again, moving whole chunks of pages until she stopped near the end of the book. "Now, listen to this. The first known sighting of the Black Knight was in the mid-seventeenth century, shortly after Minuit bought the island of Manhattan from the Lenape Indians. That was around the same time that Stryge, the first king of the gargoyles, died. No one knows where the Black Knight came from or how he became the gargoyles' king, but here's where things get *really* interesting. The very first sighting of the Black Knight was at Fort Verhulst, the same settlement the alchemist used to live in."

"What happened?" Bethany asked.

"He came with gargoyles. They killed fourteen people that night. Fourteen seemingly random people—shopkeepers, traders, trappers, farmers, a bartender. The strange thing is that according to firsthand accounts, the gargoyles left Fort Verhulst long before sunrise, and they left the rest of the settlers alive." She looked up from the book, peering at us over the reading glasses perched on the end of her nose. "You know how bloodthirsty gargoyles are. They revel in violence and carnage. For them to leave the other settlers alive, to show that kind of restraint, just doesn't make sense. So it got me thinking. If this was the same settlement the alchemist lived in, maybe the victims weren't chosen at random. Maybe they had a connection after all, one no one thought to look into."

"The alchemist himself," Bethany said.

Ingrid nodded. "Precisely. Look at the timeline. The alchemist disappears from Fort Verhulst. Not long after, the Black Knight makes his first appearance at the same fort, and orders the gargoyles to kill fourteen specific people. It can't just be a coincidence. I think the alchemist and the Black Knight are the same person."

"But that would make him over four hundred years old," I said.

"Obviously he's not human anymore," Ingrid explained. "But what if he was once? And what if the first thing he did after becoming the . . . the *thing* he is now was to eliminate everyone in the settlement who knew his true identity?"

"But why bother?" I asked. "What would be the point? They already thought he was dead and probably would have gone on thinking it."

"Exactly. Why bother? Unless those fourteen people knew something about him that he didn't want them knowing. Something that was dangerous to him, that would leave him vulnerable."

"But even if that's the case, everyone who knew the Black Knight's secret died four hundred years ago," Bethany said.

Ingrid closed the book. "True. It's just a theory I'm working on. I hadn't given it much weight before because I assumed, as everyone did, that the Black Knight was simply invulnerable. But then Trent came along, and now more than ever I'm convinced."

"Convinced of what?" I asked.

She leveled her gaze at me. "If we discover what the Black Knight's secret is, we can kill the son of a bitch."

Thirteen

As the clock ticked toward 2:30 a.m., Ingrid led us upstairs, to the top floor of the safe house. There, we found a long hallway lined with doors, two on each side and two in the far wall.

"I've got plenty of room for all of you," she said. "There are more bedrooms up here than I know what to do with."

"You live alone?" Bethany asked. She was walking better, no longer favoring her right leg now that her knee was bandaged and wrapped tight with gauze. Unfortunately, the same couldn't be said of Thornton, who was supporting himself against the roof access ladder in the corner of the landing. I'd assumed he would walk better now that he'd been stitched up and didn't have to worry about his insides spilling out, but instead his movements had become even stiffer than before. The greenish discoloration of his skin had spread, and he'd started to give off a pungent, sickly sweet odor. I'd been around enough dead bodies to recognize the smell.

"I've got the whole place to myself, I have for years," Ingrid was saying. "I suppose if I had one regret about my time with the Five-Pointed Star, it's that I never had time for anything else. After Morbius died and the team broke up, I kept the house. I thought I'd just live a quiet, normal life like everyone else, but by then it was too late to start a family."

She pointed to one of the doors at the end of the hall and told us it was the bathroom, but I wasn't listening anymore. An old-fashioned black Bakelite telephone sat atop a small round table against the wall. As soon as I saw it, I thought of Underwood. Since I hadn't come straight back with the box, he would be waiting for my call.

A thousand-pound weight pressed on my shoulders. The truth was, I liked Bethany, Thornton, and Ingrid. They were good people. They didn't slap my cheek and call me a dog the way Underwood did. They hadn't tried to kill me or lie to me. They welcomed me, took me in, fed me, and tended to my wounds. They treated me as an equal, as a friend.

But Underwood was waiting, and so were the answers he'd promised. I felt like I was standing on thin ice, only I didn't know which side of it I wanted to be on.

Once you've taken the box from them, kill them. No survivors.

I could feel the heft of the gun in the pocket of my leather jacket. My blood felt like ice water.

I turned away from the phone and everything it was making me think about, and let my eyes wander over the framed photographs that hung in clusters on the wall. A lifetime's worth of memories were on display, each photograph hanging so close to the next that there was hardly any bare space between them. I looked at the closest one, a snapshot of Morbius and Ingrid standing in front of the Statue of Liberty. His arm was around her shoulder. They were smiling so wide it was like they didn't have a care in the world. I noticed dozens more photos of the two of them, and suddenly I understood the root of her anger, why she was so eager to see the Black Knight dead. The Black Knight hadn't just killed her colleague; he'd killed the man she loved. It wasn't that she hadn't had time to start a family, it was that she'd never stopped mourning.

Ingrid opened one of the doors along the wall, revealing a small bedroom. "Thornton, I think you'll be comfortable here. This bed is nice and soft."

Thornton walked stiffly past me to the doorway, trailing his foul odor. He bumped clumsily into the door frame, then leaned casually against it like he'd meant to do that. He stuck his head into the room and gave it a quick, dismissive look. "I'm not tired," he said. "There are other things I'd rather be doing right now than sleeping."

"You need to rest, Thornton," Bethany told him. "You've been though a lot today. Your body is still adjusting."

"There's no way I'm going to be able to sleep," he said.

"You have to try, for your own sake," she said. "The more active you are, the more energy the amulet expends. If you don't rest, it'll burn out even faster."

Thornton sighed and crossed his arms. The green patches of skin around the protruding bones of his wrists looked darker now, fading toward an ugly purple. "Fine. Just promise me we're out of here at the crack of dawn. I mean it, Bethany. I'm not hanging around. The minute, the *second* the sun is up and the gargoyles hightail it back home, I'm on my way back to Gabrielle, with or without you."

"That's the plan," Bethany said. "Now get some rest. I just need to talk to Trent, and then I'm turning in, too."

Thornton turned to enter his room, wobbling momentarily on his feet. If I didn't know better, I would have thought he was drunk. "If you two are going to make out all night, try to keep it down."

"Bite me, werewolf," Bethany said.

Thornton slammed the door in her face.

"Poor thing," Ingrid said. "He may not feel pain, but he's hurting inside."

Bethany didn't answer. Her face was long and weary, the face of someone whose decisions were weighing on her.

Ingrid continued the tour, opening the bedroom next to Thornton's for Bethany. For me she opened the door across the hall. "This was Morbius's room," she told me.

I was surprised Ingrid and Morbius hadn't shared a bedroom. I thought they'd been lovers. Maybe they never got the chance. I saw regret etch itself deeper into the lines of Ingrid's face as she took in the room. I got the feeling she stood in this doorway a lot and reminisced.

She came back to herself, and looked at me. "You're about Morbius's size, give or take. There should be something in the closet that'll fit you if you want to change out of those clothes." She turned to Bethany and sized up her diminutive frame. "I'm sorry, but I don't think I have anything that will fit you."

Bethany shrugged. "You and every clothing store in New York. Trust me, I'm used to it. I'll be okay with what I've got."

Ingrid bid us good night and disappeared into her bedroom at the end of the hall. I went into my room. It was bigger than the other two, with a queen-sized bed against one wall, a small desk and chair, a love seat, and in front of the curtained window a tall dresser topped with more photos of the Five-Pointed Star. I wondered if Ingrid had kept this room exactly as it was when Morbius died.

Bethany followed me inside. I heard her quietly close the door behind her. I didn't turn around.

"It's not going to work," I said.

"What's not going to work?" she asked.

I draped my ruined leather coat over the desk chair and sat down on the love seat, facing her. She stayed standing in front of the door.

"Whatever spell Gabrielle comes up with," I said. "It won't work, will it? I saw it in your face as soon as Thornton mentioned she was trying to find a way to help him. He saw it, too, I think, but he doesn't want to hear it. He wants to believe there's a way to keep the amulet going indefinitely."

She nodded, her face clouding. "There's a good reason the Breath of Itzamna isn't permanent. I'm sure you've noticed how bad Thornton's muscle functions are now, the discoloration of his skin, the smell."

"The smell is hard to miss," I said.

"His body is decomposing at an accelerated rate. It's a side effect of the amulet. His body will keep decomposing faster and faster as long as the amulet is functioning." Her eyes wavered and broke contact with mine. "I had to do it. I had to bring him back. But there's no magic in the world that can bring the dead back to life. Not fully, not the way you and I are alive."

Her words struck me with an unexpected force. After everything I'd learned tonight about magic, I was convinced my ability to come back from the dead was magical in nature—a spell some magician had put on me, or a spell of my own that I no longer remembered. But if Bethany was right, then even now, even in a world where magic existed, I was no closer to the truth than I'd been yesterday, or the day before that, or any of the days since I'd woken up in front of that brick wall.

"There's nothing?" I pressed.

She shook her head sadly. "There are some things even magic can't do. But trust me, it's better this way. Even if Gabrielle *could* find a way to keep the amulet functioning, Thornton's body is still dead. It'll keep decaying. He would be stuck in a rotting shell until there's nothing left but dust. That's not something I would wish on my worst enemy. No, for Thornton's sake, the best thing we can do is just let it run its course."

"So you lied to him," I said. She stayed quiet. "You told him he could go back to Gabrielle in the morning, but that's not your plan at all, is it? You still need him to get the box."

She looked away, refusing to meet my eye. "I don't like it any more than you do. He's my friend. But when things go wrong, someone has to keep a clear head. Someone has to keep their eyes on the goal so things don't get worse."

"And that would be you," I said. "Even if it means letting your friend die."

She glared at me, her face setting hard as stone. "You need to wrap your head around this, Trent. Thornton is already dead. There's nothing anyone can do for him now. Not me, not you, not Gabrielle. Dead is dead, and no one can change that."

But someone *had* changed it. I'd come back from the dead more than once, and fully back, not trapped inside a rotting corpse like Thornton was. I just wished I knew how or why. If I did, I could help him.

I caught myself. Help him? Wouldn't it be easier to let him die? That way, his blood wouldn't be on my hands when the time came.

Bethany sighed. "Let's just drop it, okay? This isn't what I came here to talk about."

"So what did you come here to talk about?"

She looked at me like I ought to know. Suddenly I wasn't happy to be alone with her. I felt like she could see right through me. At that moment I was very glad to be sitting on the love seat, because it was about as far from those probing eyes as I could get without actually leaving the room.

Finally, she crossed her arms over her bulky cargo vest. "I think I've been more than patient with you, Trent. I figured you would tell us the truth when you were ready, but I don't think we can afford to wait anymore."

I looked up at her sharply. "What are you talking about?"

"It's obvious you haven't been honest with us," she said. "It's time to come clean."

My heart thumped like a tin drum in my chest. How much had she figured out? I glanced at the closed door directly behind her. Standing between it and me, her message was clear. There was no way out, not until she got an answer.

"The Anubis Hand, the Black Knight," she continued. "The things you did shouldn't have been possible."

I very nearly sighed with relief. She didn't know anything. "I told you before, Bethany, I don't know how I did those things. I was as surprised as you were."

"Huh," she said. The word dripped with skepticism. "See, I keep going over it in my head, but your story doesn't add up. You weren't just passing by that warehouse tonight, were you? You said you heard me scream and came looking, only I didn't scream. I don't scream, Trent. Ever."

"I don't know, maybe it was a gargoyle I heard," I said. "Whatever it was, it was enough that I thought I should investigate. Anyway, what's with the third degree? If I'd decided to ignore it and keep moving, you'd be dead right now."

"But you weren't just investigating, you were expecting trouble. You walked into that warehouse with your gun already drawn."

"I always carry a gun," I said. "New York's a dangerous city."

She arched an eyebrow, not buying it. "Enough games. I want the truth. Who are you? For real?"

"Bethany, come on." I shook my head.

"Because here's the thing, Trent," she said. "The reason your story doesn't add up? I put a ward around that warehouse. It didn't work on the gargoyles because they already knew we were there, but the ward was still active. That means even if it couldn't stop the gargoyles, it still should have kept the warehouse hidden from everyone else. It should have been hidden from *you*, Trent. Unless you already knew it was there. Unless you *meant* to come to the warehouse. So do you still want to insist you were just passing by, or do you want to tell me the truth?"

I remembered the peculiar feeling of the little hands pushing me back as I drew closer to the warehouse. At the time, I thought it was just a manifestation of my own reluctance about the job, but now I understood it was more than that. Without knowing it, I'd walked right through Bethany's ward. No wonder I'd felt the same thing on the front steps of the safe house.

Bethany's sky-blue eyes bore into me. I looked away. She had me dead to rights, and like a cornered animal I felt the need to protect myself. My leather jacket was still draped over the desk chair. The grip of my Bersa semiautomatic peeked out from the pocket. It was so close I could draw it in a second. Less than a second.

But if I did, there would be no going back. I would cross the threshold to cold-blooded killer. Was that what I was? Or was that what Underwood wanted to turn me into?

I hated this tug-of-war inside me. How could I know what kind of a man I was when I didn't even know *who* I was?

"Everyone has their secrets, Trent," Bethany said. "I get that. But if I'm going to keep you around, I need to know if I can trust you. So I'll ask you again, who are you really?"

I blew out my breath and whispered, "I don't know." I said it so softly I didn't know if Bethany could even hear me.

"I don't believe that for a second," she said. I should have known nothing got past those pointed ears of hers. "I have charms in my vest that can make you tell the truth, but they'll also cause you a lot of pain. I don't want to have to use them, but I will if you keep lying to me."

"I'm not lying," I said. "I don't know who I am."

She furrowed her brow. "What do you mean? How can you not know?"

"For the past year, I've been living without any memories. Who I am, where I'm from, everything about myself, it's all just a big blank." I fidgeted in my seat, wondering if I was doing the right thing. Aside from Underwood, I'd never told my story to anyone. There hadn't been anyone else to tell, frankly, and keeping it to myself for so long had buried it deep enough that after a while it felt like something that needed to be protected. Trusting Bethany with the truth made me uncomfortably vulnerable, but it also felt oddly freeing, like shrugging off heavy chains.

She narrowed her eyes, wondering whether to believe me or not. "You're talking about amnesia?"

I nodded. "I can't remember anything before a year ago. Not my friends, my family, my job. It's like I didn't exist at all before then. As far as I can tell, no one's even looking for me. Amnesia is supposed to be temporary. I hoped I would remember eventually—hell, I try to *make* myself remember all the time—but it's been a year and the memories haven't come back." I looked up into her eyes. "Bethany, I know I shouldn't be able to do the things I did. I don't know how I did them. I didn't have any control over it, I swear. They just *happened*."

She shook her head. "People can't cast spells without knowing how, Trent. There's no such thing as involuntary magic."

I shrugged. "There is now."

She crossed the room so quickly that I froze in surprise when she pulled open my collar and put her hand down the back of my shirt.

"What the hell are you doing?" I demanded.

I tried to get up from the sofa, but she pushed me back down. "Sit!" I felt something sticky peel off my back and thought she'd removed one of the bandages. But when she pulled away from me, I caught a glimpse of what was in her hand. My skin crawled. It wasn't a bandage. It was moving. Alive.

I leapt off the sofa for a closer look. At first I mistook it for a spider, but then I saw there were no legs attached to its fat, ridged thorax, only round, slimy, saucerlike suction cups. Whatever it was, it was small, roughly the size of a nickel. It fit snugly in the center of her palm and glowed a bright neon green.

I shivered. How long had that thing been stuck on my skin? "What is that?"

She studied the creature. "It's green."

"I can see it's green, Bethany, but what the hell *is* it?"

"A Collodi tick," she explained. "It's a rare interdimensional insect that feeds by absorbing a harmless amount of its host's psychic energy. But they're also remarkably sensitive to their host's psychological state. They actually change colors when exposed to different psychic stimuli. It makes them the perfect lie detector. They turn yellow if the subject is lying, and green if the subject is telling the truth. Yours is green. That's good."

My jaw dropped. "Wait a minute. *You* put it on me? Downstairs, when you were bandaging me up, you put that *thing* on me?"

"I'm sorry," she said. "I had to be sure."

I stared at her, taken aback not just by what she'd done, but also by what a close call it'd been. More than anything else, it drove home the fact that I was walking a very thin line. "You had no right, Bethany!"

She pulled a small, clear plastic box from a pocket in her cargo vest, dropped the Collodi tick into it, and replaced it in the pocket. "Try to see it from my perspective, Trent. You come out of nowhere, a complete stranger who claims to have no knowledge of magic whatsoever, and then you start killing gargoyles like a pro and fending off the Black Knight with powers no one else possesses. You can see how that might make me suspicious. I had to be sure I could trust you."

"And what if that thing was yellow instead? What would you have done?"

"This." She extended her arm. A wooden wand shot out of her sleeve and into her hand.

I blinked. "A magic wand? Seriously?"

"Scoff all you want, but the Endymion wand is stronger than you think," she said. "It would put you into a deep sleep before you knew what hit you."

I doubted that. I don't sleep, and I was pretty sure no wand would change that. "You had that thing all along but you didn't think to use it on the gargoyles, or the Black Knight?"

"It only works on humans. Against anything else it's just a pointy stick." She tucked the wand back into her sleeve. "Look, I don't expect you to understand, but this mission Thornton and I are on is too important. If the box falls into the wrong hands, a lot of people will die. I can't let anything get in our way, or anyone."

I sighed and sat down on the love seat again. "The box. Everything comes back to that damn box. What's in it that's so important?"

"Something ancient, and powerful, and extremely dangerous under the right conditions. You're safer not knowing any more than that. Anyway, right now I'm a lot more interested in talking about you. A man with no memory of who he is. It takes a lot to surprise me, but I honestly didn't see that one coming. It could explain a few things, though."

"Like what?"

"Why the ward around the warehouse didn't affect you, for one," she said. "There are a small handful of immensely powerful magicians in the world called mages. They're the only ones who can carry magic inside themselves without becoming infected. They're powerful enough that certain spells don't work on them—illusion spells mostly, like wards. They can see right through them. Given the things I've seen you do, it makes me wonder. What if you were a mage before you lost your memories? If you were that powerful, there might be some kind of subconscious connection with the magic inside you, almost like muscle memory or a survival instinct that kicks in when it's needed." She sighed then and shook her head. "But no, mages are much older. You can't be a mage without decades of advanced study. Frankly, you don't look old enough to be one."

"Maybe I'm older than I look," I said. "I could have lived a healthy lifestyle. Lots of vegetables and jogging."

Bethany smirked. "Somehow I doubt that's the answer. But when this is all done and we've got the box back safe and sound, I can ask Isaac to look into any reports of magicians or mages who went missing a year ago. Who knows, maybe he'll find something."

I stared at her dumbly for a moment, not sure what to say. I hadn't expected her to want to help, especially without asking for something in return. I wasn't used to anyone giving a damn. When I finally found my tongue, I said, "You'd do that for me?"

"We're not so different," she said. "I don't know much about myself, either. I never knew my parents, or where I came from. I spent my whole childhood being passed from one foster home to another, waiting to be adopted, but it never happened . . ." She paused, absently touching the thick hair over her pointed ear. I could only imagine what it must have been like for her, passed over time and again for adoption because she was different. She must have felt like as much of a freak as I did. When she spoke again, she wouldn't meet my eye. I could tell she wasn't used to opening up like this. "I learned pretty fast not to get attached to anyone. Either they'd get adopted away or I'd get shipped off to another home. I spent a lot of time alone, looking for ways to pass the time. That's how I discovered I had a natural aptitude for engineering charms. It's funny how boredom and self-preservation can bring out your hidden talents, isn't it?"

"It's not everyone who would help out someone they don't know," I said. "Thank you."

She opened the door and smiled at me. "You saved my life twice now, Trent. The least I can do is help you get yours back."

I watched her walk out of the room and close the door behind her. Bethany kept surprising me. One minute she was an icy battle-axe, interrogating me like a cop and hiding gross, lie-detecting bugs on my body, and the next she acted like a friend, like she actually cared and wanted to help.

The former I could handle, I was used to adversity, but the latter left me feeling conflicted and unsure of myself. I didn't know how to deal with the sudden surge of warmth I felt toward her.

I looked at the photos on the dresser again. Morbius stared back at me through unknown years, strong, sure of himself, a natural-born leader. Ingrid had referred to him as mage. Could I be a mage, too, I wondered? Was it possible I was a mage so powerful I'd found a way to cheat death? But then, what had happened to me? How had I lost my memories? Bethany didn't think being a mage was the answer, but I held onto it like a drowning man. Because if I was a mage it meant I wasn't a freak of nature. It meant I wasn't alone.

I felt like I was soaring inside. There was so much more to tell Bethany. So much more I hoped she could help me discover. For the first time I could remember, I felt like I'd found a place where I belonged, where I could be happy. For the first time, I felt truly alive, which was an odd thought for a man who can't die. I felt like I was a part of the world around me. A world that suddenly felt wide open.

The grip of my gun peeked out at me from the pocket of my leather jacket. Damn. How was I going to tell her about Underwood? If I told her the truth about why I came to the warehouse, there was no way she'd still want to help me. Worse, I would be drawing her deeper into my own mess, putting her in more danger than she already was. There were consequences to knowing about men like Underwood.

He was still waiting for me to come back with the box. Probably, he was already wondering what was taking so long. It was only a matter of time before he sent Tomo and Big Joe to come looking.

What the hell was I going to do?

Fourteen

The bathroom at the end of the hallway was filled with pink bottles of hand lotion, baby-blue tubes of facial cleansers, and hanging sponges that looked like great puffs of lace webbing on a string. As I washed the last of the blood and dirt from my hands and face, I noticed the shower curtain was decorated with images of giant sunflowers. The whole room smelled of perfume and powder. It was hard for me to imagine it belonged to the same woman who had once fought and defeated a giant six-armed lizard-man from another dimension. And yet, despite the strangeness of it, it was also oddly comforting. This was a home, a *real* home, and a far cry from the cold cement walls of the fallout shelter. This was how people were supposed to live.

Walking back to my bedroom, a flash of light in the darkened hallway caught my eye. I glanced over my shoulder and saw that the door to Bethany's room was slightly ajar. Through the sliver of open space between the door and the frame, I caught a glimpse of her moving through the room. She'd taken off her cargo vest. I'd grown so used to seeing its bulky form covering her that I was surprised at how slim she was without it.

She turned her back to me and pulled her shirt off over her head, revealing a tattoo of a fiery bird that covered her entire back. Its burning wings reached across her shoulder blades, its talons framed the base of her spine. Was this the work of the nine-hundred-year-old shaman with the L.A. tattoo parlor, I wondered? The ink work was so vivid that even from where I stood I thought I could make out the shape of each feather.

I caught myself staring and continued the rest of the way into my room. I closed the door as quietly as I could behind me.

As the hours passed and the moon traveled across the night sky, I lay alone in my room and tried not to think about her. I didn't know many women. It wasn't like I had the opportunity to meet them through work like a normal person. The criminal underworld was still mostly a man's world, and the few women I'd crossed paths with would just as soon stick a knife between your ribs as look at you. The only woman I saw with any regularity was the creepy, dark-haired woman who was always with Underwood, and I really, really didn't want to think about her just then.

Bethany was different. I'd felt a connection with her from the moment we met, and yet we came from completely different worlds. Bethany risked her life on a regular basis trying to do good. Me, I was a thief. I stole things. Sometimes I stole lives. She was about rules and protocol. I was dumb muscle, paid to do, not think. We couldn't be more different if we tried.

In my mind's eye, I saw her pull her shirt up over her head again, saw the fiery bird inked on her back . . .

Annoyed at where my thoughts were headed, I got up from the bed. The night was creeping by at a snail's pace and I needed something to distract myself. Things were complicated enough as it was, I didn't need to add any more wrinkles by wondering what other parts of Bethany's body might be covered in tattoos.

I didn't have *The Ragana's Revenge* with me to read, so I decided to rummage through the wall closet instead, hoping I'd find some clothes to replace my ruined shirt and jeans. Like most New York City closets, this one seemed to have been added as an afterthought to the already cramped living quarters. It was just a foot and a half deep. The shelf up top was cluttered with dusty old hats, a stack of ashtrays, a battered suitcase, and an awkwardly shaped object I couldn't make out at first. I pulled it off the shelf for a closer look. It was a primitive wooden idol shaped like a man, but with hundreds of iron nails hammered into it from top to bottom. I shuddered and put it back on the shelf quickly. I didn't know what it was. With some things, I figured it was just as well not to know.

Hanging from the wooden bar under the shelf were Morbius's old clothes. I tried on a variety of the shirts and pants, but he must have been more broadly muscled than I was. They were all slightly too big for me. I was about to give up when I finally found a shirt that fit, and shortly after, a pair of pants. Hidden under some folded bedsheets I found a box containing a pair of black leather boots. I grabbed a coat as a replacement for my ruined leather jacket. Once I had them all on, I looked at myself in the mirror on the back of the closet door.

Black linen shirt. Black jeans. Leather boots. Long brown trench coat. Now *that's* more like it, I thought, beaming at my reflection.

A sudden creak of the floorboards outside my door made me freeze. Dim light from the hallway spilled through the crack under the door, along with the shadows of two legs. Someone was standing right outside my room.

Bethany? No, my instincts told me right away it wasn't her, or any of the others. But that was impossible. No one else—*nothing* else—could get into the safe house. I kept my eyes on the shadows under the door and didn't make a sound.

Then came the faint but persistent scratching of what sounded like a single fingernail on the door.

Scritch. Scritch. Scritch.

A chill crawled up my spine. Slowly, quietly, I pulled my gun out of the leather jacket on the chair and crept toward the door. In the light underneath, the shadow legs moved off. Footsteps traced the floor outside, heading away from my room.

I opened the door slowly. In the hallway, the overhead lights were still out, but now there was some kind of faintly glowing ball hovering low on the floor by the baseboard. The magic version of a night-light, I supposed. Across the hall Bethany's door was still ajar, a strip of pitch black space showing between the door and the jamb. My gut clenched. Had whoever was out here gone into her room? I heard the wooden steps creak under someone's weight. I looked quickly and thought I saw a shape on the stairs that led down to the second floor, just a brief flash of silhouette, no more discernible in the dark than a shadow. I would have thought it was my eyes playing tricks on me if it weren't for the odor lingering in the air. It was sickly sweet, like rotting meat. My first thought was Thornton, but this scent was different. It wasn't him.

I reached the landing and looked down into the living room. The lights were off, but the bright glare of the streetlights bled through the curtained windows. It gave me just enough light to see a dark shape move across the living room floor in silhouette. It was a man, short and wearing a blazer that looked ragged around the shoulders.

I lifted my gun and hurried down the steps, but when I got to the bottom he was gone. No, there he was, descending the flight of stairs at the other end of the room, the black blob of his head and shoulders disappearing into the dark stairwell. Holding the gun in front of me, I crossed the living room and risked a quick glance down the stairs. Below was only an inky pool of darkness. I couldn't see a thing.

The stairs creaked under the intruder's weight, and then stopped. He'd reached the bottom. I strained to listen, trying to discern which direction he was moving in now, but I didn't hear anything.

I started down the stairs slowly. I tried to be quiet but the steps creaked under my feet. I might as well have used an air horn to announce my approach. As I descended, the darkness swallowed me. I hoped if I couldn't see the intruder, he couldn't see me, either.

When I reached the bottom, I stayed by the stairs, listening for any movement. My eyes adjusted slowly to the dark, helped by the diffused haze coming through the curtained window near the front door, but I didn't see anyone.

The doorway to the kitchen was on my right. It was the only place the intruder could have gone. Holding my gun with both hands, I crept into the room.

The stench of decay was stronger here. I felt along the kitchen wall for the light switch, and flipped it. The overhead snapped on and flooded the room with light.

I didn't see anyone.

Just as I began to wonder if I was imagining things, he rushed me from my blind spot, little more than the dark blur. He slammed me up against the kitchen wall and put one forearm across my throat. He used his other hand to push my gun hand to the wall and pin it there.

When I finally had a chance to focus on his face, I gasped in surprise.

"Hello, errand boy. Long time no see," Bennett said. His skin was pale and waxy. His lips and eyelids had darkened to a bruised purple. He was wearing the same blue pinstriped suit he'd worn last night, though now it was stained and torn. There was a long, straight gash across his neck. Beneath it, dried blood painted a trail down the front of his shirt. I stared at the wound in horror. God, was that what Underwood had done to him behind the black door? Slit his throat?

Except, now Bennett was here in Ingrid's kitchen. Did nothing stay dead the way it was supposed to in this damn world? Was the barrier between life and death really so weak that anyone could just come and go as they pleased? He wasn't wearing an amulet like Thornton, so what was he doing walking and talking when he ought to be six feet under? How the hell had he even gotten inside? Bennett wasn't a ghost. He felt solid, real. Wasn't there supposed to be a ward around the safe house to keep everyone out? If Bennett was here, it meant either the ward had stopped working or he'd walked right through it like it wasn't there. Neither answer was comforting. But then, there was nothing comforting about being held against the wall by a walking corpse, either.

"You're dead," I managed to croak, like it would be a news flash for him.

"As a doornail. You should try it sometime." His cracked, dry lips spread in a grin, and for the first time I noticed pinpoints of brilliant red light shining inside the pupils of his eyes like finely focused lasers. "It's not like you think. Death is so different from what I expected. No pearly gates. No light at the end of the tunnel. Sully was full of shit about all of that."

I struggled to free my gun arm, but he was strong, even stronger than he'd been when he was alive. He banged my wrist against the kitchen wall until the gun slipped from my hand and dropped to the floor. He kicked it to the other side of the room.

"You made a big mistake, errand boy," he said. "You pissed off the wrong people. Now something's coming for you, something real bad. When they get here, everyone in this house will die. Even you. Do you understand? This isn't like getting shot in a playground in Queens. This is a whole new ball game. They will take you apart in ways you can't come back from. So listen good: You can't stop them. Don't even try. If you fight them, you'll lose."

He let go of me. I doubled over, holding my throat and coughing. "Why are you telling me this?"

"Consider it professional courtesy, one dead man to another." Bennett looked over his shoulder at the kitchen window. Outside, the sky was growing lighter. "The sun will be up soon. They're coming at dawn, which means you're running out of time. If you want to live, you better start running now."

"I have to warn the others," I said. "I have to get them out of here."

I turned to the door, but he was already there, blocking my path. I glanced over my shoulder at the empty spot where he'd been standing. I hadn't even seen him move.

"Fuck the others, they're irrelevant," Bennett said. Before I could protest, he pulled a small object out of the inside pocket of his blazer and put it in my hand. "Here, take this."

It was a small cloth pod, curved like a kidney bean and rough like burlap. Its surface was speckled with tiny dots of metal. It felt warm, and something thrummed inside it like the gears of a machine.

"What is it?" I asked.

Bennett ignored me. He picked my gun up off the floor and handed it to me. "You'd better take this with you, too. You're going to need it."

"Take it with me? I'm not going anywhere until—"

White light burst out of the object in my hand. It was blinding, filling the room until everything—the walls, the floor, the kitchen table, even Bennett himself—was obliterated from view. A moment later the light faded.

The kitchen was gone. So was Bennett. In fact, Ingrid's whole house was gone. I was standing alone on a circular patch of cement and grass in the middle of a big, empty traffic circle. I glanced around in a desperate panic, trying to get my bearings, but saw only empty sidewalks, shuttered storefronts, and darkened windows.

I looked at the strange little object still in my hand, and understood then what it was. A magic charm, like the ones Bethany carried in her vest. Bennett had tricked me. The son of a bitch had used a charm to transport me away from the house against my will.

I looked up at the tall granite column that rose out of a dry fountain bed beside me. Perched seventy feet atop it and lit by floodlights against the night sky was the unmistakable marble statue of Christopher Columbus.

Shit. I was in Columbus Circle, nearly a mile from the safe house, and from whatever was heading there now to kill everyone inside.

"Send me back!" I shouted into the empty street. "Damn it, Bennett, send me back!"

Fifteen

Down the canyon of Central Park South, bookended on one side by the edge of the park and on the other by skyscrapers, the sky was already fading from black to gray. In the distance, a violent slash of pink tore at the eastern horizon.

They're coming at dawn.

How much time did I have left? Half an hour? Less? I cursed under my breath. Wherever he was now, Bennett obviously had no intention of sending me back to the safe house. That left me with precious little time to cover roughly a mile's distance and get the others out of the house before it was too late. I looked at the strange burlap charm he'd given me, but I didn't have the first clue how to make it transport me back. I stuffed it in my pants pocket. The only way I was going to get back to the safe house was on my feet.

I put my back to the impending dawn and darted across Columbus Circle, up the sidewalk to Ninth Avenue, then swung left to bolt downtown. An empty cab drifted along the street beside me, but when I tried to hail it the cab sped by, its off-duty light shimmering in the predawn gray.

I kept running, trying to outrace the rising sun and wishing Bennett had just stayed dead where he belonged. Why had he come back to warn me? He certainly didn't owe me any favors after I'd handed him over to Underwood.

I pushed the question from my mind and tried to focus on just getting back to the safe house, but the void it left was instantly filled by more questions: Without an amulet like the one Thornton wore, how had Bennett come back from the dead? When he said I pissed off the wrong people, who did he mean? Who was coming to the house at dawn, and why couldn't I stop them?

I barreled down empty sidewalks and through intersections, the gun in my trench coat pocket banging against my hip, and all the while the sky kept brightening. I crossed Ninth Avenue against the traffic light, barely avoided getting hit by a speeding *Daily News* delivery truck, and ran up a side street toward Tenth. How much time was left? How soon before dawn?

Farther up the block, I noticed a figure walking toward me. From a distance the man was just a shadowy silhouette, but as I drew closer his features clarified, sharpened. My heart jumped into my throat. I skidded to a halt, breathing hard.

It couldn't be.

Tomo.

Where the hell had he come from?

I turned to run back the way I came and slammed into a wide wall of a man coming up behind me. "Whoa, where you goin', T-Bag?" Big Joe asked with a sneer. "Been lookin' for you."

His fist connected with my jaw. I fell, the back of my head hitting the sidewalk and flaring with pain. I tasted blood and wiped it from the corner of my mouth. "How did you . . . ?"

"Find you?" Big Joe finished for me. He grabbed the lapels of my trench coat and hauled me onto my feet. "Underwood's got eyes everywhere. You know that."

He dragged me across the sidewalk to a run-down building whose glass front door was propped open with a brick. He yanked the door open all the way and pulled me into the vestibule inside. The stench of urine was overpowering. Two homeless drunks lay curled against the walls, sleeping off the effects of the empty bottles scattered around them. Tomo followed us in, pulling his gun and using the butt to smash out the single lightbulb that hung from the ceiling. Big Joe kicked the drunks awake and told them to clear out. They didn't wait to be told twice.

Big Joe slammed my back into the wall. I groaned as pain flared through my wounds.

Tomo put his gun away, which was a relief, but the grin of sick satisfaction on his face told me not to get too comfortable. "I think it's time to teach this piece of shit a lesson," he said.

Big Joe brought his face up close to mine, his breath hot on my cheek. "We oughta kill you now while we have the chance."

"We've been waiting for the right time ever since you wasted Ford," Tomo added.

"And we'd do it, too, if we thought it would take," Big Joe said. "But I know you, freakshow. You wouldn't even have the decency to stay dead. Though that could be kind of fun, too, killing you as many times as we like. We could take turns, try out interesting and exciting new ways of making you die."

I reached for my gun, but Big Joe grabbed my arm before I got it. "Nice try." He twisted my arm away, took the gun out of my pocket, and put it in his own. Then he punched me in the stomach.

I doubled over, gasping. He'd knocked the air right out of my lungs. Big Joe grabbed a fistful of my hair and pulled me upright again. "You're lucky Underwood wants to see you, T-Bag. Otherwise me and Tomo could do this all day."

I bristled at the nickname T-Bag. I'd always hated it. He knew it, too, which is why he kept using it. I spat in his face and said, "Go fuck yourself."

He punched me again, in the kidney this time. It hurt like hell. "Keep giving me attitude and next time I'll use a knife instead of my fists," Big Joe said. He shook his head in disgust. "I told Underwood from the start you'd be trouble, but he didn't listen. He shoulda found a way to bag-and-tag you the minute you iced Ford, only Underwood thought a freak like you might be useful. There's a fuckin' joke if I ever heard one."

Outside, the sky kept brightening in its unstoppable march toward dawn. I thought of Bethany and the others, still asleep, not knowing what was coming. I struggled to get free, but Big Joe's grip was like a vise. "I didn't kill Ford," I insisted. "Not on purpose. I can't control it when it happens."

"Keep talkin', T-Bag," he said. "Give me a reason to see if you can come back from a bullet in the brain."

"That'll do," a familiar voice said from somewhere behind Big Joe.

Big Joe released me and took a step back. Tomo took a step back, too, and between them I saw Underwood standing in the vestibule doorway. He came forward until he was standing right in front of me, the overwhelming stench of Obsession for Men inundating my nostrils. He looked me up and down.

"Nice outfit," he said. "You been shopping?"

I wiped my bleeding mouth with the back of my hand. "Underwood—"

"Where's the box?" he said. It came out less like a question than the verbal cocking of a gun.

I saw him then for what he was, no longer blinded by the things he'd done for me. This was the true Underwood; he was a burning coal, a coiled viper ready to strike. It was why so many people were afraid of him. It was why I should have been from the start.

Through the glass door, I saw the gray murk outside grow less murky. I was running out of time. I had to get out of here fast, but there was no way Underwood was going to let that happen. He searched my face, waiting for an answer, his eyes hidden behind his black sunglasses. I had a feeling if I ever saw his eyes, they would be as empty and merciless as a shark's.

"I don't have it," I told him.

"How much longer until you do?"

"I'm working on it."

Underwood shook his head. "I asked you a question."

"Today," I lied. "I'll have the box for you today. Just let me go get it. Let me do my job."

Underwood's mouth tightened into a hard line. "What did I say when I sent you out last night? Didn't I tell you there was a lot riding on this? Didn't I tell you I had a buyer waiting to dump fucking *truckloads* of money on me for that box? I told you I needed it ASAP, and yet here you stand, empty-handed and coughing up excuses like some fucking chump. Only you're dressed in brand new clothes like you spent all night picking through the racks at Barney's instead of doing what I asked. Do you know what that makes me wonder? It makes me wonder if I can trust you. And if I can't trust you, something drastic needs to happen." He flicked a speck of dust off the shoulder of his coat. "Here's a little something for you to keep in mind, Trent. I may not be able to kill you, but that doesn't mean I can't make you hurt. It doesn't mean I can't make you *wish* you could die."

I remembered the chair behind the black door, the drain at its feet. As if on cue, Tomo pulled a straight razor from his pocket and flicked it open. I saw the sharp edge of the blade and thought of the gaping slit in Bennett's throat. "Let me give him a taste, boss," Tomo said.

He and Big Joe both took a step toward me, but I put up my hands. "Wait! Just wait!"

Underwood glanced wordlessly at his two enforcers. They stepped back.

I let out my breath slowly. "It's not what you think, Underwood. It's this job. There are complications."

"You and your fucking complications," Big Joe spat.

Underwood lifted a hand. "Now, now, let's hear him out."

"The box wasn't at the warehouse. They hid it because there are others looking for it."

He frowned. "Who?"

"That's the thing," I said. "They're . . . gargoyles."

"Gargoyles?" he said. "Never heard of them. Who are they, a street gang?"

"They're not a gang, Underwood, they're gargoyles. *Actual* gargoyles, with wings and claws and teeth—"

He burst out laughing. "Christ, Trent. When did you start hitting the pipe?"

"You've got to listen to me," I said. "This isn't like the jobs you've sent me on before. Things are happening that I can't explain. Impossible things."

"Oh yeah? Like what?" He looked at Tomo and Big Joe, then back at me, a half-grin on his face. I got the sense he was only tolerating this because he found it amusing.

I took a deep breath. I knew how crazy I sounded already, and I was about to sound even crazier. "Just a few minutes ago, Bennett came to see me."

Underwood laughed again, and Big Joe and Tomo joined him. They laughed like they'd never heard something so funny. "Now I know you've lost it," Underwood said. "Trust me, Bennett's not going to be paying any visits to anyone."

"But I saw him," I insisted. "That's what I'm trying to tell you. It's the box, Underwood. Everything connected to it is royally fucked up. It's dangerous. You may think you can handle it, but you're in way over your head."

I felt Big Joe's fist hit my cheek before I even saw him swing. I fell to my hands and knees on the thinly carpeted floor of the vestibule. "Know your fucking place, T-Bag!"

Underwood crouched down next to me. "Trent, Trent, Trent. When did you become such a disappointment? How did a simple job like this become too much for you to handle?"

I spat on the floor, my saliva tinged with blood. "Walk away from this one, Underwood. Whatever's in that box, it's not worth what'll come after you once you've got it."

"Walk away? Do you know how much money is on the line? Come on, Trent, enough with the bullshit. I'll tell you what, just bring me the box and all will be forgiven. We can pretend we never had this conversation. I want it in my hands by tonight. Don't make me come looking for you again. Am I clear?"

I shook my head. "It's not just gargoyles, man, there's this *thing* in black armor."

"Okay. Give us a minute, guys," Underwood said. Tomo and Big Joe left the vestibule to stand guard outside the door, leaving us alone. Underwood held his hand out to me. I looked at it like it was a dog ready to bite me. Finally, I took it and he helped me to my feet. His hand was ice cold, as though he'd absorbed all the air-conditioning from the fallout shelter. "I've always tried to do right by you, haven't I, Trent? I gave you a job and a place to sleep. I made certain inquiries into your past, like I promised. Do you remember what I told you last night? I think you're going to be very happy with what I found. *Very* happy."

I studied Underwood's face, but behind his sunglasses his expression was inscrutable.

"My name?" I whispered.

He nodded. My chest went tight. Underwood knew my name. He knew it and I didn't. It was almost too much to handle.

"Tell me," I begged. "Just tell me my name. Please. Just tell me that one thing."

"I'm wondering if you're ready," he said. "Maybe you don't want it as badly as I thought. After all, I told you what you had to do first and you still haven't done it."

"Please," I said again.

"The terms of our deal are quite clear," he said. "Bring me the box. Leave no witnesses. Hold up your end of the bargain and I'll hold up mine."

I swallowed hard. I was so close to the truth I could almost taste it, but what Underwood was asking me to do . . .

I'd made a terrible mistake, aligning myself with this monster. I knew that now. Hell, I'd known it ever since the little boy in the crack house, only I hadn't done a thing about it, hadn't even tried, and now it was coming back to bite me.

Underwood sighed. "I blame myself. This is my fault. I thought you could handle this one on your own, but I see now I was wrong. That's why I'm sending Tomo and Big Joe with you."

My chest squeezed tight. "What? No, Underwood—"

He raised a hand to shush me. "No, it's okay, it's good that they'll go with you. The job will go a lot faster." He turned to call Tomo and Big Joe back in.

"Wait," I said quickly. Underwood faced me again. "There's no need to get them involved. I can do this."

"Are you sure?" Underwood asked. "They could be a big help. They're not squeamish about torture, or killing. To tell you the truth, I think the crazy bastards actually get a kick out of it. I once saw Tomo gun down a man's grandmother just to get him talking."

"I'll handle it myself," I insisted.

Underwood bared his teeth. It took me a moment to understand that he was smiling. "There's the Trent I know. Good dog."

He clapped me on the cheek, harder than usual. There was nothing remotely friendly about it.

In that moment, I knew he was lying. He hadn't found anything, and he never intended to. He'd lied to me from the start, used me, manipulated me into doing terrible things while he filled my head with empty promises. I'd wanted so badly to believe he would help me find the answers that I'd gone along with it willingly, ignoring any second thoughts. What a fool I was. What a goddamn fool.

Outside, sunlight swept down the street from where the sun crested the horizon. Dawn. Time had run out. I had to go *now*.

"I'll have it for you by tonight," I said again, hoping he wouldn't see through the lie. I moved to get past him. "But I have to go—"

"Stay a moment," Underwood said.

Damn. Why wouldn't he let me go? "If you want the box, I have to go now."

"Stay," Underwood repeated. The tone of his voice told me I didn't have a choice. "Did I ever tell you about Gibbons?"

"No," I said quickly. The street continued to brighten. I wiped my sweaty palms on my jeans. Each beat of my heart felt like the ticking of a clock.

"Gibbons was my collector, like you, only way back in the day," Underwood said. "I sent him to collect a diamond shipment headed for a Diamond Row merchant who'd crossed me. Only Gibbons never came back from the job. See, he thought he could just take the diamonds and run. He forgot who he was messing with. He forgot I've got eyes and ears all over this city. I caught up with him in a bar in Harlem, some cheap, off-the-grid joint where he thought he'd be safe. I walked out of that bar half an hour later, but he didn't. Neither did his girlfriend, or his brother, or any of the others who helped him take what was rightfully mine. The dumb son of a bitch honestly thought he could run from me. But nobody can run from me, Trent. Nobody can be protected from me. I always get what I want. I always take what's mine. I always win. Funny I never told you that story. It's one of my favorites." He grinned the way I imagined a mad dog did when it was about to take a chunk out of you. "*Now* you can go."

We walked out of the vestibule together. As Tomo and Big Joe stepped aside to let us through, a sleek black sedan pulled up to the curb and idled there, engine purring.

Underwood took my gun back from Big Joe. "You remember how to use this, right?" He tossed me the gun. I thought about putting a bullet in him and just ending the charade right then and there, but it would only bring Tomo and Big Joe down on me and I didn't have time for that. Instead, I slipped the gun into the pocket of my trench coat. Underwood winked at me and said, "I knew you were my go-to guy."

From behind the steering wheel, the black-haired woman stared at me the way she always did. Her dark eyes looked like bottomless black pits.

It seemed to take forever for Underwood, Tomo, and Big Joe to get in the car. As soon as they drove away, I took off down the block, running as fast as I could. My shadow grew with each passing moment as the sun inched its way up. I tried not to think about what might be happening back at the safe house. Were they fighting for their lives? Were they already dead?

I thought of the list of names, crumpled and hidden inside my mattress. In my mind, I saw the little dead boy in the crack house again, his tiny, shriveled corpse cradled by his shrieking, grieving mother. I squeezed my eyes shut and tried to make the image go away, but it stayed, stuck there like glue. What if I was already in too deep to ever get out? Some people didn't deserve redemption. It terrified me to think I might be one of them.

I turned onto Ingrid's block and crashed directly into a man walking toward me. I tripped, but the man reached out and steadied me.

"Yo, I got you, pal," he said. He looked homeless, dirty and foul-smelling with long hair and a knotted beard. His fingernails were rimmed with dirt. The words CHILD OF FIRE were written across the chest of his stained, ratty T-shirt in flaming letters. "Spare some change, pal? Can you help me get something to eat?"

I shook him off without a word and kept running. In the middle of the block I spotted the safe house and prayed I wasn't too late. When I ran up the stoop, I could still feel the powerful ward pushing against me. For a moment I thought that meant everything was okay, that they'd fixed the ward and were still safe inside—until I reached the double doors at the top of the steps.

The right-hand door was open a crack. That was wrong. Ingrid wouldn't have left it open. Even with the ward protecting the house, she'd still locked the doors last night. I'd seen her do it. It's something ingrained in all New Yorkers, as deep as any primal instinct. No matter how safe your neighborhood is, you always lock your door.

I pulled out my gun and carefully pushed the door open. The entrance hallway was in shambles. The umbrella stand and shoe rack had been overturned. The Hummel figurines had been knocked off the top of the credenza and lay broken in dusty shards on the floor.

I looked to the staircase at the far end of the hallway, and my heart dropped into my gut like a chunk of ice.

Halfway up the steps, Ingrid Bannion lay on her back in a pool of her own blood.

Sixteen

I put my gun away and ran to the stairs. Judging by the defensive wounds on Ingrid's arms and the smoking black scorch marks on the wall, she hadn't gone down without a fight. She was bleeding heavily from multiple stab wounds, but she was still breathing. She was still alive. I knelt over her. Whoever did this had come looking for me. This was my fault. I should have been here.

"Ingrid," I said.

Her eyelids fluttered at the sound of her name. "Trent?" She opened her eyes, focusing on me. She winced in pain. "They came right through the ward . . . I couldn't stop them . . ."

"Who were they?" I said.

"Shadowborn," she said.

I shook my head. "I don't know who that is."

"Trent, listen to me." She sounded winded, a wet rattle at the end of each breath. "Something's wrong. They never should have found us . . . not with the ward up . . . they must have had help . . . someone told them . . . someone betrayed us. . . ."

"I have to get you to a hospital." I started to slip my hands under her as gently as I could, but she stopped me.

"No. Leave me . . . there's nothing you can do. Find the others. Help them." Ingrid coughed, and blood sluiced out from between her lips. "I was wrong, Trent. You have to tell Isaac—tell him I was wrong. It can't end like this . . . everything Morbius believed in . . . everything the Five-Pointed Star stood for. Promise me you'll tell Isaac to keep fighting . . .

keep fighting the darkness . . . Promise me." She touched my face with her bare right hand. Her fingers were sticky with blood. And then her eyes filled with sudden terror, and she shook her head violently. "Oh God, Trent, your aura . . . it can't be . . ."

She looked so frightened of me, of what she saw in me, that I felt a sudden surge of shame, like a monster confronted with its own reflection. But I had to know. I had to. I put my hand over hers, pressing her palm to my cheek. "What do you see? Who am I?"

Her voice wavered. "No. Your aura . . . it's—it's not human . . . Oh God . . ." She coughed blood again, her whole body racking with the effort. She turned away, as if she couldn't bear to look at me any more.

A chill went up my spine. "Ingrid, please tell me. Tell me what I am. Ingrid . . ." She didn't answer. It was only when her hand slipped limply off my cheek that I realized she was dead. I reached down and closed her eyes.

What had she seen that terrified her so much?

What the hell was I?

A sudden crash from upstairs startled me. I reached for my gun. Whoever the shadowborn were, they were still in the house. I raced up the steps. On the second floor, I found the living room in shambles. Furniture had been overturned, and more broken figurines littered the floor. The glass display case above the mantelpiece had been smashed, leaving a heap of fallen antique swords beneath it. A round, silver object was half-buried in the wall at shoulder height. It took me a moment to realize it was the serving tray Ingrid had used last night. Someone had thrown it with such force that it had embedded itself in the plaster.

But the room was empty, the only movement the motes of dust swirling in the columns of morning light from the windows.

Another crash came from overhead, the sound of a door being kicked open. Shit, the bedrooms. I hurried up the steps to the third floor, my finger on the trigger of the gun, but when I reached the top, the hallway was empty. All the doors were closed except one. The door to Bethany's bedroom. From where I stood on the landing I couldn't see inside, but a sliver of the wall was visible. So were the shadows that moved across it. Someone was in there—multiple someones, it looked like—and from the sound of it they were tossing the room. Why? Wasn't it me they were after?

Did they really think I'd be hiding under a bed? I inched toward the open doorway, keeping my finger on the trigger.

I only made it a couple of steps before a figure walked out of the room and into the hall. It wore a sleek, black leather jumpsuit that extended up over its neck to form a tight, seamless hood around its head. Its face was hidden behind an oval steel mask, plain and featureless. There weren't even any eyeholes, though apparently it didn't need any to know I was there. It turned to face me right away.

So this was a shadowborn. It didn't look so tough. In fact, it looked pretty scrawny under all that leather.

I leveled the Bersa semiautomatic at it, but had to stop myself from emptying the clip into its chest. This thing had killed Ingrid and I wanted it dead for that—hell, I wanted it to *suffer* for that—but I needed information first. "Where are the others? What have you done with them?"

By way of an answer, the shadowborn drew a katana from the sheath on its back. The sword's long, thin, single-edged blade glinted in the light of the hallway.

"I was kind of hoping you'd say that." I pulled the trigger, but as soon as the shot rang out the shadowborn was gone. The bullet punched a hole in the wall on the far side of the hallway. A moment later, the shadowborn reappeared in the same spot, blinking back into existence as quickly as it had vanished.

I lowered my gun. "What the hell . . . ?"

It occurred to me this was why Ingrid hadn't been able to stop them downstairs, not even with her fire magic. If they could vanish into thin air like that, faster than a bullet, then Bennett was right. They really were unstoppable.

Keeping Underwood's Golden Rule in mind, I dropped the gun into my coat pocket. I wanted my hands free.

The shadowborn's katana cut through the air with a high-pitched whistle. I jumped back, narrowly avoiding the blade. No way was I going to let *this* shirt get ruined, too. Or anything worse. Bennett had said they could take me apart in ways I couldn't come back from. I didn't want to find out what that meant.

Just then, two more shadowborn, identical to the first, walked into the hallway from the bedroom. They drew their katanas in unison.

Three against one. The odds had already been pretty bad, but they'd just gotten worse. I backed up, keeping my eyes on the shadowborn. All three of them winked out of sight. A moment later, they reappeared right in front of me. Startled, I fell backward, landing on the floor in front of one of the closed bedroom doors. The shadowborn raised their katanas. I closed my eyes, waiting to be skewered like shish kabob.

The bedroom door burst open, and an enormous timber wolf bounded out. Two of the shadowborn above me disappeared just as Thornton was about to pounce on them. He crashed into the wall instead. The third shadowborn stayed where it was, bringing its katana down toward me in a swift chop.

With a loud *clang,* the blade stopped an inch from my chest, blocked by a thick steel sword that had come out of nowhere. I looked up and saw Bethany standing above me, holding one of the swords from the smashed display case downstairs.

"Where the hell have you been?" she asked.

I grinned, relieved to see her. "It's a long story."

But the shadowborn had no intention of giving us time to catch up. It swung its katana at Bethany, and she parried the blow. They fought, their blades clashing and ringing. I got back on my feet. On the floor of the bedroom Bethany had come out of, I saw another sword identical to hers lying beside a pile of Thornton's discarded clothing. I scrambled into the room and picked up the sword. It was heavier than I expected, its handle slightly too long for my hand. But then, it had been crafted for the six-armed war god of the Pharrenim, not for me. I hoped I'd be able to handle it. There was no guarantee a sword would be any better than a gun against the shadowborn, but at least it would give me something to defend myself with.

I rushed back into the hallway. Bethany was still fighting, wielding her sword like someone who'd been in her share of swordfights before. But every time she managed a thrust or jab that should have crippled her opponent, the shadowborn simply disappeared to avoid her blade, then reappeared and attacked again.

Down the hall, Thornton was keeping the other two shadowborn busy. Every time he lunged at them, snapping his massive lupine jaws, they winked out of sight and reappeared nearby. They tried to stick him with their katanas, but on four legs he was too fast for them.

One of them noticed me. It vanished and reappeared right in front of me. Its sword was already coming my way by the time I realized what was happening. I brought my own sword up and blocked its attack. It lunged. I blocked its blade again, and again after that, marveling at how well I was doing. As far as I knew, this was the first time I'd ever held a sword, and yet my hands were acting like they knew exactly what to do with it.

It wasn't the first time I'd been surprised by how well I could fight, though before now it had always been hand-to-hand combat. Somehow, I could fight like I'd been trained by the best. It was something that came over me, like instinct or muscle memory, and more than once I'd wondered if I was a boxer in my previous life.

Now this. Who the hell was I that I knew how to handle a fucking *sword*?

But in my excitement I got cocky, and the shadowborn managed to get the tip of its katana under my cross guard. With a flick of its wrist, it sent the sword flying out of my hand and clattering to the floor.

The shadowborn came at me quickly. I grabbed both its arms, trying to force the katana blade back as it inched closer to my neck. The shadowborn pushed forward with a strength that belied its slender frame, forcing me back against the wall and pinning me there. I struggled to hold the blade at bay, my own warped reflection staring back at me from the shadowborn's blank steel mask.

How hard was that steel, I wondered? Only one way to find out. I snapped my head forward, butting the hard bone of my forehead against the mask. It hurt like hell, but I hoped the blow would stun the shadowborn long enough for me slip out of its grasp.

It didn't work. The shadowborn didn't seem affected at all, though its mask loosened, slipped off, and fell to the floor.

What lay beneath the mask wasn't a face, at least not anymore. It was a skull, mossy and brown and caked with dirt. Indistinct fleshy masses wriggled in the empty eye sockets. It took me a moment to recognize them as worms.

I got my boot up against the shadowborn's stomach and shoved it back. It bent to pick up its mask, and I took the opportunity to grab my sword again. Not that there was much I could do with it. Even if I got lucky and landed a blow, I couldn't kill what was obviously already dead.

The odds just kept getting worse.

The wolf bolted past me. Thornton was making a break for the stairs. Bethany broke away from the shadowborn she was fighting and ran with him. "Trent, let's go!" she shouted.

I followed them, risking a glance back over my shoulder. All three shadowborn vanished. They reappeared on the landing before us, cutting us off from the staircase.

We were trapped.

The shadowborn lifted their katanas, the sharp edges of their blades gleaming like razors.

Seventeen

The shadowborn advanced on us, blocking our one exit. I grabbed Bethany by the hand and pulled her into the nearest bedroom. Thornton bounded in after us. Inside, I let go of Bethany and kicked the door shut. Then I hit the lock button in the center of the doorknob, more from habit than because I thought it would actually help. There was no way that flimsy lock would stop the shadowborn. Neither would the door for that matter, not if they could pop up wherever they wanted. We needed a better way to keep them out.

I turned from the door and saw that we were in the room I'd stayed in last night, Morbius's room. It, too, had been searched by the shadowborn. The bed was overturned, the love seat smashed to pieces, the dresser drawers dumped, clothes from the closet torn off their hangers and heaped on the floor. What the hell had they been looking for?

Bethany pulled a small object out of her vest and slapped it onto the wall next to the door. It stuck in place, a wooden disc with a round, obsidian stone at its center. As the stone gave a brief flash, the charm sent a glowing latticework of light across the entire wall and door before it faded.

"What is that thing?" I asked.

"An Avasthi phalanx," she said. "It'll keep the shadowborn from phasing through the wall, but it won't hold them for long. It's only a matter of time before they just break down the door instead. But I have no intention of making it easy for them." She glanced quickly around the room. Her gaze settled on the dresser near the window on the far side of the room. Its drawers had been pulled out and the pictures of Morbius and the Five-

Pointed Star had been swept off it onto the carpet. "Trent, bring that dresser over here."

I hurried to it, kicking the empty drawers and their contents out of my way. I grabbed the top corners of the dresser, but a sudden movement outside the window caught my eye. A sliver of the street below was visible through a gap in the curtains. On the sidewalk across from the house, a shape in a hooded, blood-red cloak moved toward the mouth of an alley between two buildings, an alley that glowed with a flickering blue light. The shape stopped and turned toward me, as if somehow it knew I was watching. Inside the hood was a skull, not of bone but of polished, gleaming gold. The flickering light from the alley reflected off its hollow eyes and rictus grin.

The shadowborn thumped angrily on the other side of the door, and Bethany shouted, "Trent, the dresser!" I turned to look at her, then the door, then back to the window. Below, the sidewalk was empty. The shape was gone. So was the strange flickering light.

"I thought I saw . . ." I started to say, then stopped. What did I think I'd seen? The Grim Reaper? Death finally coming for me? Had someone really been there, or was I seeing things?

I slid the dresser across the floor and propped it in front of the door as a barricade. The shadowborn continued banging from the other side. It sounded like they were throwing their shoulders into it, trying to force it open. The dresser rocked away from the door. Without its drawers, it wasn't heavy enough to do the job, but there was no time to gather them and put them back in. Instead, I put my back to the dresser and dug my boots into the carpet.

Another heavy thump. The door rattled in its frame and the dresser bucked behind me. "We need to get out of here, fast," I said. "It's too far down to jump out the window. We'd never make it without breaking our legs on the sidewalk, and then we'd be sitting ducks. You got anything else in that vest of yours that can help? Like maybe a rope ladder?"

Bethany shook her head. "Besides, we can't leave without Ingrid."

"Ingrid's dead," I said. It came out with all the delicacy of a blunt object to the head, but I had to break the news to her and we didn't exactly have time for tact.

Bethany's shoulders slumped. "Oh God. She insisted on staying downstairs and holding them off so we could find a place to hide. I told her it was too dangerous, but . . ."

The shadowborn battered the door. The dresser lurched against my back. I dug my boots deeper into the carpet and hoped the door would hold.

Thornton paced back and forth across the floor, limping on stiff legs. The decomposition that plagued him in his human form had transferred to his wolf form as well. His gray pelt was mangy, knotted, and in places thin enough to show the discolored, rotting skin beneath. The stench of decay came off him even more pungently than before, caught and amplified by all the hair. The amulet's lights pulsed rhythmically from where it sat embedded in the fur of his chest, above the dark zigzag of stitches along his underbelly.

"I don't understand," Bethany said, pulling my attention back to her. "This house was supposed to be safe. How did the shadowborn get in? Did the ward fail?"

"No," I said, "the ward is still up. I felt it downstairs, just as strong as before."

"Then how the hell did they find us?" she demanded.

"They're not the only ones," I said. "Someone else got inside. Last night, when you were asleep."

Her eyebrows shot up in surprise. "What? Who?"

"His name is Bennett. *Was* Bennett. He's dead now."

She blinked. "You killed him?"

"Complicated question, but no, when he stopped by he was already dead. He was all . . . messed up."

"You should have told me someone got in," Bethany said angrily.

"I didn't have a chance. He gave me something, a charm I think, and the next thing I knew it zapped me across town to Columbus Circle. But first Bennett warned me. He said something was coming for me. Bethany, this is all my fault. It's me they're looking for."

"Don't be an idiot," she said. "They're not looking for you, they've been turning this place upside down looking for the box. That's the only reason Thornton and I are still in one piece. They were too busy trying to find the box to look for us."

"That doesn't make sense. The box isn't even here. You said it was with Gregor."

"*They* don't know that." She chewed her bottom lip as she thought. "Whoever summoned them gave them the wrong information. But it still doesn't explain how they got past the ward."

Ingrid had wondered the same thing. She'd said someone had betrayed us.

And then it hit me. God, how could I have been so stupid? I'd wondered why Bennett was bothering to help me, but I should have trusted my instincts. When I'd come back to the house, the front door was unlocked. Someone had to have done that from the inside, and there was only one person who would have.

Bennett. He'd led the shadowborn right into the safe house.

If I saw that dead son of a bitch again, I would put a stake through his fucking heart.

"It was Bennett," I told Bethany. "He lied to me. He played me like a damn fool." But if Bennett and the shadowborn were working together, why give me advance warning? Why get me out of the house before they came? What was he up to?

The dresser bucked hard against me, as if all three shadowborn had thrown themselves against the door at once.

"You said he gave you a charm?" Bethany asked. "Let me see it."

Bracing my legs, I pulled the small, bean-shaped object out of my pocket and tossed it to her quickly.

Bethany studied the charm a moment, turning it over in her hand. "It's a displacer, a limited range teleportation charm. They're almost impossible to come by and extremely difficult to engineer. Dead or not, this Bennett has some impressive skills."

"I doubt he made that thing," I said. "That's what keeps sticking in my head. If Bennett had access to something like this, he would still be alive."

She frowned. "You should have told me. It's never a good sign when the dead are up and walking."

Thornton growled at her.

"Present company excluded," she added.

"But that's the weird thing, he wasn't like Thornton," I said. "He didn't have an amulet. He was just . . . walking and talking."

"That's impossible," she said. "Spirits of the dead can only possess the living, they can't possess dead bodies, not even their own. At least, not without the help of a charm like the Breath of Itzamna. And to even get a dead body to rise at all is . . ." She paused. "Wait. Did you see anything in his eyes, like a light that didn't belong there?"

I nodded, gritting my teeth as I pushed back against the lurching dresser. "A red light."

Thornton stopped pacing. He turned to Bethany and whined.

"Trent, that wasn't the man you knew," she said. "That was a revenant, a dead body controlled by magic. It's a puppet, nothing more."

"But he *knew* me," I said. "He mentioned things only he would know."

"Whoever created the revenant would have access to his memories as long as his brain was still fresh enough. But to even create a revenant, you'd have to be an extremely powerful necromancer . . ." She trailed off, chewing her lip again. "I don't like this. Something's going on. Revenants, the shadowborn . . . this is much bigger than we thought."

There was another thump on the door. This time, the sharp tip of a katana broke through the wood. I flinched away from the blade but kept my back against the dresser.

"We're running out of time," I said. "Tell me you've figured out a way to get past the three zombie musketeers out there."

She sighed. "We can't, that's the problem. We're trapped here. The Avasthi phalanx is the only thing keeping us safe. The minute we leave this room, we're dead."

"There's got to be a way," I said. "We fought off the gargoyles, we'll fight these guys off, too."

She shook her head the way you do when a small child says things that are funny and sad at the same time. "We don't stand a chance. The shadowborn are trained assassins. They don't leave survivors."

"We're not dead yet," I told her. "We've still got Bennett's charm, the whatever you call it, the displacer. Do you know how to make it work?"

Her grim expression told me it wasn't going to be as easy as that. "I do, but displacers are designed to teleport a single individual, not three. It won't get us all out." She held the charm out to me. "You should take it. I can get you away from here. This was never your fight to begin with."

The shadowborn pushed against the door. I strained against the dresser to keep the door from breaking. "Forget it. We'll find another way."

"No one's asking you to be a hero," she insisted. "This might be your only chance to get out of here alive. Please, just take it. I don't think I can handle another death on my conscience." Her bright blue eyes were big and shimmering. It would have broken my heart if there weren't three moldering corpses on the other side of the door trying to kill us.

"I'm not leaving you here," I said.

She stared at me, then sighed and dropped the displacer into a pocket in her vest. "I don't get you, Trent. I can't figure you out."

"Join the club," I said. "Look, last night I told you I don't know who I am, but the truth is, I'm starting to think maybe I do. And right now, I'm the guy who gets you out of here."

Thornton gave a short warning bark as two more katana blades broke through. The shadowborn were focusing their efforts on one part of the door, trying to chop a hole in the wood.

Bethany sat down on the floor, dropped her sword, and put her head in her hands. She was panicking, giving up, but I couldn't let that happen, not if we were going to survive this. I had to keep her focused.

"If I'm going to get us out of here, I need you to tell me everything you know about the shadowborn. You said spirits can't possess dead bodies, but I saw what's under their masks. They look pretty damn dead to me."

There was another loud thump against the door. The dresser rocked precariously, almost knocking me away. Bethany flinched. It unnerved me to see her this frightened. If someone like her could come undone, it meant none of us were safe.

"Bethany, I can't do this without you," I said.

Finally, she looked up at me. "Right, the shadowborn. Okay. Legend has it they were heroes once, defenders of the weak and vulnerable. Some well-meaning magician put a spell on them, an immortality spell, to thank them. This was in the early days after the Shift, when no one knew yet just how dangerous magic had become. The spell twisted their minds. They became thieves, mercenaries, assassins for hire. Only, the immortality spell worked, or at least it half-worked. They were granted eternal life, just not eternal youth to go with it. They never stopped aging. The shadowborn aren't spirits who've returned to their dead bodies. Their spirits never *left* their bodies, not even after those bodies withered and rotted. That's why there's nothing we can do. That's why we can't kill them. There's nothing left to kill."

Thieves, killers, unable to die—it occurred to me I had more in common with the shadowborn than I did with Bethany or Thornton. It made me wonder if my fate would be the same as theirs. I'd never given any thought to whether I was aging normally. If I was, if I kept growing older but couldn't die, would I end up like them, a shambling undead thing?

The door jolted behind me. It wasn't going to hold much longer. We were running out of time. "Okay, so if we can't kill them, how do we get out of here?"

She shrugged. "We don't. That's what I'm trying to tell you. You saw what they did out there. The shadowborn can phase out of the material plane at will. When they do, you can't touch them, you can't even see them. They can walk right past you, right *through* you, and you wouldn't even know it. They can pass through walls or doors like they're not there. They can attack from any direction, from out of the shadows. It's how they got their name. It's what makes them such perfect assassins."

There was another loud thump on the door, followed by the *chuk* of a katana blade cutting into the wood. Bethany's face went the color of ash.

"Fine, if we can't attack them and we can't get out, how do we at least even the odds?"

Bethany opened her mouth to speak. Her expression informed me I was about to be called an idiot again, but then she stopped. She reached into her cargo vest, pulled out the displacer charm, and started scraping at it with her thumbnail.

Another thump. The wood splintered behind me. "Put that thing away, Bethany. I told you I'm not leaving without you."

"I know, and that was sweet of you." She glanced up at me, but as soon as our eyes met she looked back down at the charm quickly, as if suddenly embarrassed. "Anyway, that's not what I'm doing. Basically, charms are a way to carry magic safely. Every charm has a spell inside it that gives it its power. I just need to find a way to reverse the spell inside this one."

"What will that do?"

"Think about it," she said. "It's a teleportation charm, right? What's the opposite of teleportation?"

"I don't know, staying where you are?"

"Being *stuck* where you are," she said. "What you said got me thinking. Even the odds. If I can change the spell inside this charm from a displacement spell to a *containment* spell, the shadowborn won't be able to phase anymore. We might actually stand a chance of fighting our way out of here." She inspected the displacer closely, turning it over and over. "This would be a lot easier if I'd engineered the charm myself. Whoever made it could have used any of a hundred different spells, and without knowing exactly which one I don't know how to properly reverse it. It's a crap-shoot."

Sword points pierced the door behind me. "We don't have a lot of time," I said. "They're going to break through any minute. You'll only have one shot at this."

"Then I'm going to have to try to force the spell to reverse itself," she said. She glanced around the room. "I need a talisman, an object to act as a focal point for the spell. It has to be something symbolic of being stuck in place. It could be anything, but it would be best if it were metal, like a pin or—"

"A nail?" I asked.

"A nail would be perfect," she said.

I turned to Thornton. "In the closet, on the top shelf, you'll find a wooden idol. I saw it there last night."

Thornton loped to the closet and rose up on his hind legs. Standing like that in wolf form, he was tall enough to reach the top shelf easily. He nosed his way in and knocked the idol to the floor. The hundreds of nails that had been hammered into it thudded against the carpet.

"That thing got enough nails for you?" I asked.

Bethany picked it up and inspected it. "A West African *nkisi*. It's tourist-grade magic, nothing with any real power. No wonder they stuck it in a closet. But the nails are real enough."

She twisted one of the nails in the idol's head, gritting her teeth with the effort until it slid out of the wood. She held onto the nail and dropped the idol.

"Now what?" I asked.

"Now you cross your fingers while I try to reverse the charm," she said.

I crossed my fingers. "Does this really do anything? Like, magically?"

She sighed. "It's a figure of speech. I meant you should hope this works, because if it doesn't, we're dead." She looked up at me from the displacer, her eyes grimly serious. "Trent, I'm going to have to open the charm. When I do, the magic is going to try to get inside you. You can't let it. If it does, there's no telling what it'll do to you. I need you to look away from it. That's the only way to be sure. Okay?"

I nodded. "What about you?"

"It can't get inside me. I've got the sigil of the phoenix on me. Magic can't get through that. It'll protect me." I remembered the tattoo of the fiery bird on her back. I should have known it was something more than a trendy style choice. "Don't worry about me, you just remember to look away. You too, Thornton. Ready?"

The door cracked behind me. It wasn't going to hold much longer. "Do it," I said.

She wedged her thumbnail into a seam on the side of the displacer and worked it until the charm split open on tiny hinges. A bright white light glowed from within it like a miniature, trapped star. I looked away quickly. A second later, a wall of sound hit me. It was like a hundred voices shouting wordlessly in my ear, and beneath it, a thousand more singing tunelessly. I saw my shadow jumping all over the wall as the spell inside the charm flickered and danced. I felt light-headed and dizzy. My skin burned like it was on fire. Was that the magic trying to get inside me? I thought of Ingrid's grotesquely mutated arm and the living corpses on the other side of the door. I didn't want to end up like either of them. I squeezed my eyes shut. That seemed to help.

Somehow I was able to hear Bethany's voice over the noise. She was muttering in the same weird language I'd heard her use back at the warehouse. Once again the eerie tone of the words gave me goose bumps. Magic—it wasn't all sweetness and light, Q'horses and elf princes the way Elena De Voe had written about it in *The Ragana's Revenge*. I saw now, firsthand, there was a darkness to it, something as old and bleak as an ancient tomb.

Through my eyelids I noticed the light change, dimming from bright white to a pale, rosy red. I heard chunks of wood break away from the door but I didn't dare open my eyes to see what was happening. "Bethany, hurry!"

Something shoved the dresser hard, knocking it away from the door. It tumbled forward, taking me with it. When I hit the floor, I rolled away to keep the dresser from landing on top of me. "Bethany!" I couldn't keep my eyes closed anymore, not if the shadowborn had gotten through. I opened my eyes, and just then the screaming in my ear stopped, the bright light went away, and the dizziness passed. Bethany had closed the charm again, I saw, only now the nail was driven through its center.

Portions of the door splintered and broke as the shadowborn punched and kicked their way through. A moment later, the door came out of its frame and toppled to the floor. Thornton backed away with his hackles up, a long, low growl emanating from his throat. I ran for my sword and picked it up off the floor.

Bethany bit one end off the altered charm and spat it onto the floor. Then she held the charm out in front of her like a weapon, aiming it at the shadowborn in the doorway. "The good thing about nails," she said, "is that they're not just the perfect talismans for containment spells. They also make damn good triggers." She pressed the nail's head with her thumb. A shower of dim, rosy sparks sputtered from the open end of the charm—

And then nothing.

The color drained Bethany's face. "I'm sorry," she said. "We're dead."

Eighteen

In a blink, the shadowborn were gone, and just as quickly, they appeared directly in front of us. They lifted their swords, ready to strike. On instinct I pushed Bethany behind me, and accidentally touched the retooled charm she was still holding. A blast of light—a fuller, darker red this time—erupted from the end of the charm and filled the whole room, tinting everything crimson. When I yanked my hand back, the blast faded.

The shadowborn retreated, reeling and swaying as if they were dizzy. Somehow, I'd done this. I looked at my hand in shock.

Bethany stared at me. "How did you . . . ?"

There was no time to figure it out. The shadowborn were already recovering. But had the containment spell worked? There was only one way to find out. I kicked the wooden idol off the floor and watched it sail toward them. The shadowborn, used to phasing out of the material plane whenever they felt threatened, didn't bother moving out of the way. They tried to phase instead. The idol thumped against the chest of the closest shadowborn, then fell to the floor. In unison, the three of them looked down at it, then back up at me. Alarmed, they backed away from us and grouped together by the door, holding their katanas up defensively.

"It worked!" Bethany cried, laughing with relief. "It actually worked! They can't phase anymore!"

"Great," I said. "Now all we have to do is not get killed."

Bethany pocketed the charm and grabbed her sword off the floor. "Go for their heads," she said. "I don't know if it will kill them, but it's our best bet to keep them from coming after us. Thornton, you take the one on the left. Trent, the right. I'll take the one in the mid—"

Before she finished, Thornton sprang at the shadowborn. He bowled right through them, knocking them back onto the hallway floor outside.

"That works, too," Bethany said.

Without their ability to phase, the shadowborn were clumsy and disoriented, trying to untangle from each other and get back on their feet. Thornton didn't give them a chance to recover. He latched his strong, lupine jaws around one shadowborn's neck and dragged him off down the hallway.

Bethany and I charged at the remaining two while they were still down. I drove my sword straight into the first shadowborn's chest, but my excitement at landing a blow was short lived. The shadowborn were immortal, in their own way. A sword through the chest wasn't much more than a mild annoyance to them. Still, this one fixated on the sword piercing its chest for a moment. It had probably been centuries since the undead assassin felt anything like fear. I hoped it was feeling it now.

I pulled my sword out. The shadowborn leaped to its feet. It held its katana in front of it and backed down the hall toward Ingrid's bedroom. It knew it no longer had the advantage.

I spun, eyeing the staircase at the far end of the hallway. On the landing, Thornton still had his jaws around his shadowborn's neck. Then his jaws closed with a loud, grisly snap. The shadowborn went slack as its head rolled away from its body and bounced down the steps.

Bethany bumped me as she ran past, heading for the stairs. Smart woman.

I followed her, glancing quickly over my shoulder. The second shadowborn was sprinting like a flash behind us. In a single smooth, quick motion, it jumped, somersaulting through the air, and landed gracefully on its feet halfway down the stairs. It started climbing toward us. Bethany and I backed away. Thornton stood his ground, snarling.

I looked around frantically, searching for another way out, but all there was on the third floor were bedrooms. At the far end of the hall, the first shadowborn edged toward us. Shit. The stairs were the only way down, and trying to fight past the shadowborn on a narrow staircase would be suicide. So would staying put, but with one shadowborn coming up the stairs and another approaching from the opposite end of the hall, we were penned in. Then I saw the roof access ladder in the corner of the landing.

It was our only chance. I ran for the ladder and started climbing. Bethany and Thornton guarded the ladder, her sword raised, his teeth bared, ready to fend off the two remaining shadowborn and give me enough time to get the trapdoor to the roof open.

The trapdoor was secured with a simple sliding lock. I slid the small metal bar back from its housing, then shoved the trapdoor open. Bright morning sunlight poured in from above. I pulled myself up onto the tar and cement surface of the roof.

Bethany started up the ladder next, climbing fast. As soon as she was high enough, I grabbed her wrist and quickly pulled her the rest of the way up. When she was safely on the roof, I looked down through the opening again. Thornton was still on the floor below, snarling at the shadowborn. They were keeping their distance from him for now, but they wouldn't for much longer.

"Thornton, come on!" I called, though I wondered how he was going to join us on the roof. A wolf couldn't exactly climb a ladder, and Thornton wouldn't risk changing back to his human form while the shadowborn had him surrounded.

In a moment, I had my answer. With a mighty leap, Thornton was halfway through the trapdoor, his front paws on the roof, his hind legs dangling below him. He pushed and scrabbled against the ladder until he was all the way through. Below, the shadowborn gathered at the base of the ladder and looked up with their featureless steel masks. I kicked the trapdoor closed. It didn't lock from the outside, which meant it couldn't keep the shadowborn from following us, but hopefully it would buy us a few extra seconds.

I glanced around, trying to get my bearings. A cement wall as high as my knee traced the perimeter of the roof, separating it from the roofs of the neighboring town houses. It also fenced off the steep drop to the street at the front of the building. I moved to the back and saw an interior court-yard below, walled in by the backs of the buildings that abutted it. There was no fire escape, and despite the heaps of big black trash bags and bundled cardboard along the walls, the courtyard was definitely too far down to jump safely.

Bethany was breathing hard, still catching her breath. She had a cut on her cheek from a shadowborn's sword. "What happened down there? How did you get the charm to do that?"

"I don't know," I said tersely. I scanned the rooftops for the fastest way to get back to the street.

Bethany grabbed my arm and looked at me angrily. "Well, you better start figuring it out. A displacer can only move one person at a time. Reverse it to a containment spell and the same principle should apply, only when you touched it the spell was a hell of a lot stronger than it should have been. It affected *all* of them. So tell me what the hell is going on!"

Through the closed trapdoor came the sounds of the shadowborn climbing the ladder. "They're coming. We have to keep moving," I said.

Bethany cursed, annoyed that I hadn't answered her question, but when I ran, she ran too. We headed away from the trapdoor and across the roof, skirting around a big metal air-conditioning vent and satellite dish in our path. We jumped over the low wall to the adjacent roof and kept running, moving from rooftop to rooftop. On each one I searched for a door that could lead us inside, but they all had trapdoors like the safe house, locked from below with no way for us to pry them open. I slowed down to look back and saw that the shadowborn had smashed through the trapdoor and were pulling themselves up onto the roof. I turned and kept running. Up ahead, Bethany and Thornton had come to a stop. Directly in front of them, the wall of a tall apartment building towered into the sky like a windowless brick cliff face. There was nowhere left to run.

I saw the top of a fire escape ladder hanging off the back edge of the roof we were on, leading down to the interior courtyard. "There!" I said, pointing.

We ran for the ladder. The shadowborn had almost caught up already, sprinting unbelievably quickly across the rooftops. For what were essentially corpses in leather jumpsuits, they were a hell of a lot more agile than they had any right to be. At this rate, we'd never make it down the fire escape in time.

I stood in front of the ladder and held my sword ready. Beside me, Bethany did the same. "Go," I said. "I'll hold them off."

"Forget it. You can't handle both of them on your own."

"Bethany, go!" I said, but she didn't budge. I shook my head. "You are infuriating."

"So are you," she said.

The two shadowborn leapt nimbly over the last low wall and landed a few yards away from us. Thornton sprang at them. They split up, and Thornton landed in the empty spot between them. They were already running past him as he skidded to a halt, lost his footing, and fell over. The shadowborn advanced on Bethany and me.

I intercepted the first one, while the second went for Bethany. Free from the narrow confines of the hallway, I found myself better able to use a sword. Unfortunately, so did the shadowborn, who attacked so viciously and swiftly that it was all I could do to make sure I didn't get cut to ribbons. I backed up. The shadowborn attacked again and again so fast that its blade would have been invisible if the metal hadn't flashed in the sunlight.

The relentless onslaught forced me back against the top of the fire escape ladder. I tried to push my way forward again, but the shadowborn didn't yield. Neither did I. I couldn't. There was no place to go but the four-story fall to the courtyard below.

The first shadowborn swung its katana in a swift arc. The blow knocked the sword out of my hand. The shadowborn swung the katana back again quickly, and sliced open my throat.

The skin of my neck felt like it was on fire. I couldn't breathe. My throat, mouth, and lungs filled with blood. I put my hands over my neck, trying to stanch the bleeding, but it didn't help. The blood kept flowing out over my fingers. I wobbled on my feet, light-headed. My vision grew gray and fuzzy around the edges.

"Trent!" Bethany shouted. She sounded a thousand miles away, but I saw her, a blurry, Bethany-shaped blob running toward me. Behind her, the wolf was tearing the second shadowborn to pieces.

The first shadowborn was still standing in front of me, taking satisfaction in watching me die. I heard the *swish* of a sword cutting the air, saw the shadowborn's head fly off its shoulders, and then there was only Bethany and the wolf staring at me. Bethany said, "Oh God, Trent, your throat . . ."

She reached for me, but my legs buckled and I fell backward. Then everything tipped away and I was falling.

I twisted my head to look down. The hard concrete floor of the courtyard rushed up to meet me. This one was going to suck.

When I hit, the impact broke my back, both legs, and one arm. Maybe my neck, too. It was hard to tell because I couldn't feel anything anymore. But I knew from the impossibly odd angles in which my limbs were arranged and the glistening pool of blood spreading out from my head that it was bad. I heard a deep, echoing thunderclap in the distance, followed by another and another, growing softer and further apart each time, and realized it was my own heartbeat.

My vision clouded and blurred for a moment, and suddenly Bethany was crouching over me, her hands on my neck, trying to stop the bleeding. It was futile. Even if the blood loss didn't kill me, my other injuries would. Bethany's lips were moving, she was saying something, but I couldn't hear her over the slowing thunder of my heart.

The familiar feeling of dying came over me—the cold emptiness, the sense of falling without movement. I had only a few seconds left. I had to warn Bethany. If she was this close to me when I died—

Get away! I shouted, or thought I did, but the shadowborn's blade had taken my voice from me.

You have to run, Bethany! You have to get away from me! I tried again, but all that came out of my mouth was a wet gurgle. The gray at the edges of my vision turned black and crept across my eyes, slowly dimming everything around me to nothing. *Please . . .*

The last thing I saw before the darkness swallowed me whole was Bethany's face, too close, still too close . . .

Nineteen

What do you care who dies, as long as you get to keep living?

They were Underwood's words, spoken some two months before. The day things started to change.

My mark was a crooked antiquities dealer called Naschy. It was supposed to be an easy job, at least according to Underwood, but I'd already been his collector long enough to know things were never really that easy. There were always complications. In this case, the complication took the form of Naschy seeing me coming and gaining a few minutes' head start. By the time I followed him into a crack house on a desolate stretch of Fourth Avenue in Brooklyn, he could have already been anywhere inside. With no electricity in the old, abandoned building, the darkness only helped him hide.

I moved through the rooms with my gun out. Skinny, hollow-eyed crackheads sat on filthy mattresses along the walls, taking drags off their glass pipes and picking at their soiled rags. Some of them bolted when they saw my gun. Some didn't bother.

In a nearly lightless hallway deep inside the house, a shape came out of the darkness in front of me. I raised my gun, but it wasn't Naschy, it was a young boy dressed in filthy clothes, with his hair all tangled in knots. He couldn't have been more than ten years old.

I lowered my gun and asked him if he'd seen anyone matching Naschy's description. The boy pointed at a closed door at the far end of the hall. I walked cautiously toward it. The boy followed me. "Beat it, kid," I whispered. The boy just stared. "Go on, get out of here. Go home."

The boy didn't move. He gave me a confused look, and I realized my mistake. This *was* his home.

"You don't want be anywhere near here, kid." I gave him a hard shove. The boy ran off, ducking around the far corner of the hallway. I watched him go, then kicked open the door. Naschy was waiting inside, a briefcase in one hand, a gun in the other.

"Back off," he snarled.

"That's not going to happen," I told him. "Hand over the briefcase and we can both walk out of here, Naschy. This doesn't have to end badly. Underwood just wants what's his."

Naschy shook his head. "This isn't his to take."

"I'm told otherwise."

"You have no idea what kind of man Underwood is, what he's capable of," Naschy said. Sweat dotted his brow. "Whatever he told you about me, about what's in this briefcase, it's a lie."

"I don't particularly care," I said.

Naschy fired, cutting our conversation short. The bullet hit me in the chest and I dropped like a sack of bricks. Naschy ran out of the room, his footsteps tracing a path toward the front door.

As I lay bleeding, cold and numb with shock, I heard the scuff of sneakers in the doorway. It was the boy, staring at me from just outside the threshold. A creeping blackness filled the corners of my vision as the boy took a few tentative steps toward me, and then the blackness swallowed the world.

When I opened my eyes again, I didn't know where I was, or why I was lying on a bare, filthy floor. I didn't know why there was a woman weeping in the corner. She was kneeling and cradling something in her arms. I lifted my head and saw what it was—the withered remains of a little boy. Her son, I figured, and then it all came back, slamming into me with the force of a stone. I'd cheated death again, but this time the thing inside me hadn't stolen some thief or murderer's life. It had stolen a little boy's. An innocent's.

The woman's hair was as knotted and dirty as her son's. Her nose ran as she wailed. Her lips were pale from the drug. She said, "You come in here with a gun, big man shooting up the place. It should be you who dead, not him, not my boy. He never hurt no one. He a good boy. But not you. What kind of monster steal from a child? Steal his *soul?*"

I stared at the dead boy in her arms. The walls felt like they were crushing me, the whole world coming down on my head.

She fixed me with a cold, hateful glare. "You gonna burn for this."

Afterward, deep beneath the abandoned gas station with its broken HELL sign, I sat trembling in my room. Tomo had picked up where I left off and gotten the briefcase from Naschy. He didn't say how, but if I were a betting man I'd wager the cops would find Naschy in an alley somewhere with two in the back of the head.

The others were still celebrating their score with shots of Black Label in the main room of the fallout shelter, but I didn't feel like joining them. I didn't see the point. I wondered if there'd ever been one.

Underwood appeared, leaning casually against the door frame of my room. "What's the matter, Trent? You worried I'm angry because Naschy got away from you? Don't sweat it. We got what we wanted. You're still my go-to guy."

"It's not that," I said. I told Underwood what happened with the boy. "It shouldn't have gone down like that. He was just a kid."

Underwood shrugged. "He lived in a fucking crack house. You really think he had a future? If he wasn't hitting the pipe already, it was only a matter of time. So he's dead, big whoop. You're alive, that's all that matters."

"It's not right," I said. I didn't feel cold, but for some reason I couldn't stop trembling. "That kid didn't have it coming. He didn't deserve it."

"The fuck do you care? It's the law of the jungle. The lion eats the monkey, or whatever the fuck lions eat. He doesn't do it because the monkey had it coming, he doesn't give a fuck about the monkey. He does it because that's what he has to do to stay alive. Just like everyone else. Just like you."

I couldn't shake the woman's words. *You gonna burn for this.*

"Don't go soft on me now," Underwood said. "This is who you are. It's your gift. This city, Trent, it's a jungle too, and the same laws apply. Kill or be killed. So you gotta ask yourself, when the shit goes down who would you rather be, the lion or the monkey?"

————

I gasped air into my lungs and opened my eyes. The sunlight stung like needles. I was lying on the hard concrete floor of an outdoor courtyard, but I couldn't remember why. Had I died again? How? Where was I?

A moment later it came rushing back, the fight, the fall, and the last thing I'd seen—

Oh God. Bethany.

I turned, expecting the worst, but she was there, kneeling beside me, looking down at me with a shocked expression on her face.

I was just as shocked as she was. "You're alive!"

"More to the point, so are you," she said. She stared at me like she didn't know what she was looking at. "Except you died right in front of me. I saw it. I *know* you were dead." She showed me her palms, red and wet. "Your blood is still on my hands, only you're not even bleeding anymore. What the hell is going on here?"

I ran a hand across my throat. The cut from the shadowborn's katana was gone, healed over. She stared at me expectantly. "I don't stay dead," I told her. "I couldn't even if I wanted to. I don't know how or why. It's just the way I am."

She wiped the blood off her hands on the cement. I stood up. She didn't help me. I got the sense she didn't want to touch me. "You're going to have to do better than that, Trent. Coming back from the dead? That's not supposed to happen. But that's not even the worst of it." Her eyes studied me like I was a specimen in a petri dish. "Something came out of you. When you were lying there, dead, that same energy that attacked the Black Knight came out of you again. Tendrils of it, snaking out of you like it was looking for something."

I blinked, surprised. The power that had zapped the Black Knight was the same that kept bringing me back from the dead?

"It came right at me," she continued. "It felt like I'd stuck my finger in an electric outlet. It tried to get inside me, the way magic does, only the sigil of the phoenix couldn't stop it. It felt like it was draining me. I think it was trying to kill me."

"God, Bethany . . ." I reached out, but she backed away. Damn. I was a monster to her now.

"When you opened your eyes, you said you were surprised to see me alive." Her gaze bored into me, as though if she looked hard enough she could figure it all out. "You knew this would happen, didn't you? It's not the first time."

"I tried to warn you, but . . ." I hung my head, knowing how foolish I sounded. I should have told her the truth from the start. "You stopped it," I said finally. "How?"

"I almost didn't," she said. "It was strong, and it was relentless. I could barely move. It took my last ounce of strength to pull this out of my vest and put it on." I hadn't noticed the object dangling from a string around her neck until she lifted it to show me. It was a small, pearl-like sphere veined with a sparkling blue ore. "The charm deflected it away from me. Another second and I would have been dead."

"I'm sorry," I said. "I don't know how to control it. I wish I could. I wish I knew what it was, or why it keeps happening."

I was relieved that Bethany had survived, but I'd also learned something important. She'd deflected it with a charm. That meant the thing inside me wasn't an unstoppable force. It meant there was a chance it could be contained or controlled, if only I could figure out what the hell it was.

A chill crept over me then. It meant something else, too, I realized. Something horrible.

"Oh, no. Bethany, if you deflected it, where did it go?" I spun in a circle, looking at all the buildings that enclosed the courtyard. There were dozens of apartments nearby. Inside any one of them could be a body crumpled lifelessly on the floor, another innocent victim.

Bethany grabbed me by the arm and turned me to face her. "Trent, stop it. I need to know if it's going to happen again. I need to know if we're safe."

My heart pounded in my chest, each beat a reminder of the stolen life that surged inside me. My limbs and back weren't broken anymore. The ache of my dislocated shoulder was gone. So was the dull throb where the gargoyle had lacerated my back. There was blood from my no-longer-slit throat on my shirt and trench coat, but other than that everything was back to normal, reset to zero, and all because someone else had died in my place.

Back to normal. That was a joke. There was nothing normal about me. According to Ingrid, I wasn't even human.

The woman in the crack house had been right about me. I was a monster, and I would burn for this.

Bethany wanted to know if she was safe, but the truth was, no one was safe. Not from this. Not from me. She stared at me, and in her eyes I saw such fear, such disgust, that I wished I'd stayed dead this time.

Thornton's voice called out suddenly from a distance, interrupting us. "Bethany! Bethany, you need to see this!"

She held my gaze for another second. "Don't go anywhere," she said, then broke away and ran to the corner of the courtyard, where an alleyway connected it to the street. I followed her. When I got to the alley, I saw Thornton standing about halfway down. He was back in human form, fully dressed again, and as unharmed by the thing inside me as Bethany was. Of course, he technically wasn't alive anymore, so he had no life force to steal, but the sight of him upright and functioning came as a relief all the same.

When he saw me, though, it wasn't relief that showed in his face. It was shock. "What . . . I thought . . . how . . . ?" he stammered.

They both stared at me, waiting for an explanation, but I didn't have one.

"Trent, how did you do it?" Thornton pressed. "You were dead. I saw you die."

"I don't know how it happens," I said. "It just does."

Thornton's gaze fixed me with the intensity of a laser sight. A flood of emotions washed across his features—confusion, resentment, anger. Finally, he snapped out of it and stepped aside, revealing a shape down by his feet. "There's something you should see."

A skeletal figure sat slumped against the alley wall, papery and withered. Damn. Another one.

"It looks like he's been dead a long time," Thornton said.

I squatted down beside the corpse. "No. Only a few minutes."

"But look at him," Thornton said.

"Trust me. I know what I'm talking about." A T-shirt hung loosely off the corpse's rib cage. I read the words printed in flaming letters on the shirt and realized I'd met this man before. I hadn't helped him when he'd asked, hadn't even spoken a word to him, just ran right past him like he didn't matter. Now he was dead because of me, another innocent bystander, another name to add to the list. The tenth. I didn't have the list with me, but it didn't matter. I'd committed it to memory. I didn't know this man's name any more than I knew the name of the boy in the crack house, so I mentally added him to my list with the only information I had, the words on his T-shirt.

10. *Child of Fire*

I looked up at Bethany. "This is where it went. When you deflected it away from you, it found him instead."

"*What* found him?" Thornton demanded. "What are you talking about?"

"There's something inside me that won't let me stay dead," I said. "It steals the life from whoever's close by and gives it to me. That's what it was trying to do to you, Bethany. You were right, it was trying to kill you." I stood and looked down at the body again. "Trying to do *this* to you."

Bethany stooped down to touch the corpse's neck, as if she were feeling for a pulse. "Fascinating. Complete energy transference from one body to another. Only, that's not supposed to happen, ever. It shouldn't be possible."

"But the Black Knight does the same thing, doesn't he? Sucks the life out of his victims?"

"That's different. The Black Knight can kill with a touch, but he doesn't absorb his victim's life force. He doesn't use it as his own."

"How do you know?"

She straightened up again. "Because magic is a natural element. There are immutable laws that govern it, just like there are laws that govern physics or chemistry. Certain things just aren't possible, and in just the past few minutes you've already done two of them."

I looked down at the body again. "That's why I believed Bennett when he said it was me the shadowborn wanted. Because of what I am."

She studied my face. "And what are you, Trent?"

"I don't know."

She crossed her arms and arched an eyebrow at me. "You answer every question with 'I don't know.' You don't know who you are, you don't know what you are, you don't know how you do the things you do."

"What do you want me to say?" I snapped. "I could make something up if you want. I've made up a hundred stories already trying to explain this to myself, but none of them are the truth. Do you have any idea what it feels like, not knowing what you are? Not even knowing if you're human?"

"I remember feeling that way quite a bit before I accepted what I am," Thornton said.

"I still feel that way," Bethany said. "But there's a world of difference between my not knowing who my parents are and you not knowing how you're able to come back from being dead."

"You said you could help me find out," I pressed. "Last night you said I could be a mage."

She shook her head. "I was wrong. You're not a mage. Mages can't do what you do. The energy that came out of you . . . I've never felt anything like it before. There's nothing in any spellbook that can do that. Even the sigil of the phoenix couldn't protect me."

"What does that mean?" I asked.

She frowned at me. "It means this goes way beyond magic, Trent. This is something entirely new."

Thornton winced suddenly and doubled over. He put a hand on the alley wall to steady himself. "Guys, something's wrong," he said. "I'm getting weaker."

I helped him upright again. His skin looked waxy, the discoloration darkening to a purplish black. Through the material of Thornton's shirt, the amulet's lights pulsed much more dimly than before.

He gripped the lapels of my trench coat until he was steady, but when I let go of him he kept holding on. He pulled me closer. "Trent, you've got to help me. However you brought yourself back, you've got to do it for me too. Please."

"It doesn't work that way," I said. "I wish it did."

"You got back up like it was nothing," Thornton insisted. "Trent, please, I'm begging you."

He searched my eyes desperately, but there was nothing I could do. "I'm sorry, I can't. Whatever this thing is inside me, it only takes life. It doesn't give it."

He let go and glared at me. "You mean it doesn't give it to anyone but you."

"Thornton, that's not fair. You can see for yourself how it works." I gestured at the dead body at our feet. "There are others just like him. They're all dead because of me. I'd give you this power in a heartbeat if I could, just to be rid of it."

Thornton scowled. "Don't talk to me about what's fair. Don't *ever* talk to me about what's fair. You don't have that right." He turned to Bethany. "I'm going now, just like I said. I'm going to see Gabrielle before it's too late. You're on your own." And with that, he walked quickly out of the alley, his anger and determination keeping him upright.

Bethany followed after him. "Thornton, wait!"

I hung back, looking down at the dead body slumped against the wall. Who was he, I wondered? Would anyone miss him? Or was he like me, a man with no past, no family, no ties to the world?

I left the alley and hurried to catch up with the others. I reached them just as Bethany was saying, "Thornton, you can't go back yet. I'm sorry, but you can't."

"It's not up for debate," he said. He kept walking, barreling past the early morning commuters emptying out of their apartments buildings. "You gave me your word, Bethany. You said I could go back in the morning. Well, it's fucking morning, so I'm going back."

At the corner, he stopped, looking like he was about to fall over. He leaned against a lamppost. Above his head, the crosswalk signal changed from the little walking person to the don't-walk hand.

"Please, Thornton, listen to me," Bethany insisted.

"Why?"

She gave a frustrated little groan. "Because Trent had a visit from a dead man who was carrying a charm he couldn't have made himself. You know as well as I do spells don't cast themselves. Someone turned Bennett into a revenant and gave him the displacer. Someone who wanted Trent out of the way. Someone who knew exactly where to find us."

"It has to be the same person who sent the shadowborn," I added. "I think Bennett led them to the safe house."

"I told you, it's not Bennett, it's just his body. A puppet," she corrected me.

"Okay, so the Black Knight's still pissed off about last night, big surprise," Thornton said. "We'll be safer back at Citadel anyway."

She shook her head. "The Black Knight is powerful, but he's not a necromancer. He can't make revenants from the dead. There's only a small handful who can do that, and an even smaller number who would dare summon the shadowborn. Don't you get it? It's not just the Black Knight who's after the box anymore. Word must have spread that the box has been found. For all I know, every Infected in the city is coming out of the woodwork trying to find it. That's why you can't go back yet. It's why none of us can. Because even worse than the fact that they knew where to find us is the fact that they know *we're* the ones with the box."

"But they made a mistake," I said. "They assumed we had the box with us at the house. That should buy us some time."

"Not a lot," Bethany said. "As soon as they realize their mistake, they're going to come after us again. If they found us once, they can do it again. We have to get the box back from Gregor *now*."

The light changed. Thornton started across the street. "We can leave it there, it'll be safe with him."

Bethany hurried to keep pace with him. "There *is* no safe place for it. The Autumnal Equinox is tomorrow. You *know* that. We don't know what's going to happen."

"Wait, what does the equinox have to do with anything?" I asked.

She ignored me, still trying to convince Thornton to listen to her. "The safest place for it is in Isaac's vault, where we can keep an eye on it. As soon as we get the box I promise you we'll go back, but right now we need you. I don't know how to find Gregor, but you do. And even if I knew the way, he wouldn't give it to me. He doesn't trust topsiders, but he trusts you, Thornton. You're the only one he'll give it to. We can't do this without you."

Topsiders? The equinox? Just when I thought I was getting a decent handle on things, I was confused again. I felt like a preschooler sitting in on a Ph.D.-level class.

Thornton stopped in the middle of the sidewalk and turned to Bethany. Pedestrians, annoyed to find someone standing in their way, mumbled to themselves about stupid tourists, but when they looked up and saw his face they blanched and skirted around him quickly. "I have to see Gabrielle," he said. "Bethany, I'm fucking *dying*!"

"You're already dead," she said. He winced at the harshness of her words. "If we don't secure that box, there's a damn good chance everyone else is going to die, too. I can't let that happen, even if it means not getting you back in time. This is bigger than you, Thornton. It's bigger than all of us."

He glared at her, his eyes like steel. I saw the muscles of his jaw clench under his waxy, pale skin. "You really are a bitch, Bethany. Do you know that?"

"Yes," she said.

He sighed. "Fine, I'll take you there. Let's just get this over with." He walked back in the direction we'd come from, purposely knocking into Bethany's shoulder as he passed. The pearl-like charm around her neck jangled.

She shook her head. "I don't have a choice," she said, but I didn't know if she was talking to me or herself.

"You can take off that charm now," I said. "The danger's passed."

She glared me. "I'm not taking any chances," she said.

I followed then as they walked single file down the sidewalk. They didn't speak or look at each other. Silence filled the space between us like poison gas. I didn't like it. For a while there, being with Bethany and Thornton had felt like the closest thing to friendship I'd ever known, but whatever bond of trust and camaraderie that had developed between us was broken now, maybe irreparably.

One thing still nagged at me, something Bethany had brought up but couldn't answer. Whoever had sent Bennett and the shadowborn knew where we were. But there was a ward around the safe house, and Bethany had told me how wards worked. Nobody should have been able to find us unless they already knew our location.

Ingrid was right. Someone had betrayed us. Someone who knew exactly where we would be last night.

Someone had turned Bennett's corpse into a revenant in order to get me out of the way before the shadowborn came. Why? And why use Bennett, of all people? That was no accident. It implied that whoever was behind it knew me—or at least enough about me to know Bennett and I had crossed paths before. There were very few people with that kind of information.

Put together, all the clues pointed to someone on the inside.

But who? It couldn't be Bethany or Thornton. Fear wasn't something you could fake, and they'd both been genuinely frightened of the shadow-born. What about the colleagues Bethany and Thornton had mentioned—Isaac, Gabrielle, and Philip? Any one of them could have sold us out to get the box for themselves.

All roads led back to that fucking box. Underwood was holding it over my head as leverage and forcing me into an impossible position. It was putting Bethany and Thornton in constant danger. It was getting people killed, good people like Ingrid. I was starting to hate the damn thing.

And just like that, I knew what I had to do about it.

I quickened my pace to catch up to Bethany. Thornton continued walking briskly ahead of us, not looking back and doing his best to stay upright.

"You mentioned the equinox before," I said. "What does that have to do with the box?"

"The equinox is when what's inside the box becomes incredibly powerful," she said. "More powerful than you can imagine."

"It still sounds like some kind of weapon to me," I said. She didn't answer. "I guess I'm finally going to see it for myself, huh?"

"I guess so," she said, "provided Gregor gives it back to us. He's a hoarder. He's not exactly known for sharing."

"He'll give it back. We'll make him if we have to."

She arched an eyebrow at me. I still hadn't decided if I found it endearing or annoying. "Good luck with that," she said.

"Trust me, I can be very persuasive when I want to be," I told her. "So how far away is Gregor's apartment?"

"He doesn't live in an apartment."

"House, then. Whatever."

She smirked and shook her head. She pointed at the street corner, where a sewer grate sat at the curb. "He lives down there somewhere. Through the sewers."

"Seriously?" I asked. "Thornton gave the box to a homeless man?"

"Gregor's not a man, Trent," she said. "Gregor's a dragon."

I stopped, staring slack jawed at her as she walked ahead. "He's a what now?"

Twenty

The ruins stood on the far side of the West Side Highway, directly across from the lush greenery of DeWitt Clinton Park, with its manicured grass and impeccable swing set. The ruins looked out of place, a reminder of a much older New York City, before the relentless tentacles of gentrification had strangled it. Once an apartment building, time and decay had turned it into little more than an empty, crumbling, graffiti-covered façade. With no walls and no roof, it stood open to the elements.

Thornton led us through the hole where the front door should have been. Beyond it, where the interior of the building once stood, was a field of overgrown grass and weeds. He led the way through the field and past a low, broken brick wall that marked the rear corner of the building. There, he cleared away some trash and twigs to reveal a thick metal door in the ground, inscribed with the words N.Y.C. SEWER. A padlock sat hooked, but not locked, through the door's latch. Thornton removed the lock and pulled the handle, but the door slipped from his fingers and clanged shut again. He stared at it as if he couldn't understand what had just happened.

I pulled the door open for him. Beneath it was a hole in the ground— dark, rectangular, and lined with concrete. A ladder stood bolted to the side, running deep into the darkness below. Behind me, Thornton was still staring at his hands.

"You okay?" I asked.

He looked up at me, and said only, "We should hurry." They were the first words he'd spoken to either of us in nearly half an hour.

Bethany started down the ladder first. When she'd descended a dozen feet or so, I went next. It grew darker the deeper down I went. The sunlight from the doorway above me dissipated in the murk. After a moment Thornton began his descent, closing the door above him and casting us in complete darkness. With no way to see how far down the ladder went, I couldn't tell where I was on the rungs. I felt like I was floating in outer space. By the time I reached the bottom, I figured we had to be a good forty or fifty feet down. I expected to step off the ladder into a knee-deep river of sewage. The idea of walking through human excrement wasn't the most enticing prospect, but walking through New York City's seemed exponentially worse somehow. I was happily surprised when my boots hit dry metal instead. In the darkness I heard Bethany digging around in her vest. She mumbled a creepy incantation, and a moment later there was light, emanating from the same round, mirrored charm I'd seen at the warehouse. She held it in front of her like a flashlight to illuminate the cement tunnel around us.

I wiped the grime from the ladder off my hands. "You can't seriously tell me there's a dragon living under New York City."

"Is it really so hard to believe?" she asked. "You've probably heard him moving underground at night, or seen the smoke of his breath coming up through manholes all over the city."

"I thought that was just the subway, and steam," I said.

"Sometimes. Other times it's Gregor, out looking for more treasure to hoard."

Treasure? My mind swelled with images of a room full of gold, and chests overflowing with silver and jewels. It made my fingers tingle. I could buy my freedom from Underwood with that kind of money. Grease enough palms to get the answers I needed. How much would it take? I wondered. How much could I carry?

Once Thornton reached the bottom of the ladder, he held onto the rungs an extra moment for balance. He didn't make eye contact with either of us. Bethany shone the light one way, then the other. The tunnel extended deep into the distance on either side. The walls and ceiling were curved to form an almost perfectly round tube, arcing down to meet the flat metal platform of the floor.

"Which way?" she asked.

Thornton didn't reply. He just started walking, following the thick iron pipes that snaked along the ceiling.

"I guess we're going this way," Bethany said. We started walking after him.

"There's something I don't get," I said. "There must be sewer workers down here all the time, Con Ed guys fixing the underground transformers, phone company workers checking the lines. You're telling me in all this time no one has noticed a dragon living down here?"

"Maybe they just don't know where to look," she said. "Gregor has lived down here a long time. My guess is, he knows how to stay out of sight."

"How long is a long time?"

She shrugged. "Who can say? Gregor is an Ancient, one of the first creatures to walk the Earth. Before civilization, before recorded history, before there was anyone or anything else here, this world belonged to them."

"You're fucking with me," I said, but her expression was serious. "That would make him *millions* of years old."

"Plenty of time to learn how not to get caught," she said.

"How can anything live that long?"

"If I knew the answer to that," she said, "I'd be a very rich woman."

The air grew more humid the farther we went. I heard the faint trickling of water up ahead. The tunnel opened out onto another that ran perpendicular to it, an older tunnel whose walls and ceiling were fashioned from stone bricks instead of cement. A stream of something pungent ran through a narrow trench at the center of the floor. Suddenly I envied Thornton the loss of his sense of smell.

The farther we walked the more I sensed we were descending deeper beneath the city. I heard the flow of water through tunnels above us, the distant sound of subway wheels far overhead, and wondered just how deep we were. I wasn't sure how long we'd been walking, and after turning down numerous branching tunnels I was pretty sure I was lost. Thornton knew where he was going, but if something happened to him, or if his amulet ran out of juice before we got back to the surface, we were screwed. There was no way we'd find our way out again.

Thornton stopped halfway down a tunnel and ran his hands over the bricks in the wall. "There's a door here. It'll open if you push."

I inspected the wall. It looked solid, without any seams to indicate where a door might be hidden. "Are you sure this is the right spot?" Thornton gave me an impatient look. "Okay, I believe you, I just don't see any door."

"Just push," Thornton insisted.

I braced my legs and pushed against the wall. The bricks were slick with condensation, which made it hard to grip, but surprisingly, they gave a little under my weight. I pushed harder, and a large, square slab of the wall slid inward. After a moment a hidden mechanism took over, and the slab withdrew on its own, pulling in and sliding aside until there was an enormous opening in the tunnel wall. Big enough, I noticed, for something much, much larger than us to pass through.

Beyond the doorway was another tunnel, this one illuminated by burning torches set in iron sconces along the walls. Bethany extinguished the glowing charm with another muttered incantation, and put it away in her vest. We stepped through the doorway and started walking. The wall slid back into place behind us.

I watched the flames gutter on the torches. Torches didn't just light themselves, which meant *someone* had to have lit them. But a dragon? Was I really supposed to swallow that?

This tunnel was much taller and wider than the others. The walls were hewn from a peculiar reddish-brown rock that had been worn smooth over time, as though it had been eroded by an underground river that long since dried up. Every inch of the walls and ceiling was decorated with carved symbols—pictographs, sigils, emblems, and figures, all flickering in the guttering torchlight. Whatever they were, they looked old. Really old. How long had this tunnel been hidden down here?

Abruptly, the tunnel came to a dead end where a massive, round stone slab had been set into the center of the wall. It was carved in bas-relief with eight human-shaped figures, as featureless as silhouettes, except for the chiseled auroras of light around each of them and the strange symbols etched on their torsos.

"What is it?" I asked.

Thornton studied the figures. "A puzzle. We can't go any farther until we solve it."

"You've been down here before, you must know the answer," Bethany said.

"It's different each time," he said. "That's how Gregor keeps everyone out. Especially thieves."

"So what are we supposed to do?" I asked. "It doesn't even look like a puzzle."

"I think we're supposed to choose one of these eight figures," he said. "But what's the criteria here? Why select one over the others? Who are they supposed to be?"

"It must have something to do with those symbols," Bethany said. "If we can decipher what they are, maybe we can figure out the rest."

Thornton moved closer to study the designs etched onto the figures. "They're not symbols," he said. "They're pictograms. Runes. It's Ehrlendarr, the language of the Ancients."

"Can you read it?" I asked.

Thornton sighed. "Gregor taught me to how to speak it a little, but reading it was never my forte. This first one looks like it means breath. Wind? Damn, I'm just not sure."

I examined the figures. Other than the different runes on each one, they were identical. I didn't see any other clues as to who they might represent. I reached out to touch one of them, but Thornton batted my hand away. It felt like being hit with a slab of cold meat.

"Don't," he snapped. "Not until we're sure. If you choose the wrong one, valves open in the walls and this whole chamber gets flooded with fire."

I pulled my hand back. Apparently Gregor took his security seriously. Anyone who made the wrong choice was toast. Literally.

I studied the figures again, making sure to keep a safe distance. "If the first word is breath, or wind, maybe they're not people. What else comes in groups of eight?"

Thornton hung his head and chuckled to himself. "I'm an idiot. I was so focused on the runes it didn't even occur to me to wonder why there were eight of them. Bethany, look at these other markings around them, like each one is giving off energy or power."

Bethany's whole face lit up. "It's *them*."

"It's got to be," Thornton agreed. "That first word isn't breath or wind, it's air. These runes represent the eight elements."

"Eight? Aren't there only four?" I asked.

"No, there are eight," he said. He pointed to each one of the figures. "Air, earth, water, fire, metal, wood, time, and magic."

"So these figures are the elements," I said.

"No," Bethany said. "They're the Guardians."

"The who now?" I felt like I was lagging about a hundred miles behind them.

"They have other names you may have heard of," she explained. "The Athanasians. The Everlasting. Those Who Dwell Between. They're ageless and omniscient beings who live at the center of all things, in a place called the Radiant Lands. It's said that at the dawn of time, these eight beings were granted eternal life and dominion over the elements, one for each of them. They've always been there, watching over the world, maintaining the balance. Some say they're gods and that they created the Ancients, and from the Ancients came the mortals and all life on Earth."

"You buy any of that?" I asked. It sounded pretty crazy to me. But then, *everything* was sounding crazy to me.

She shrugged. "I don't know. I've never been very religious."

"If they're supposed to be watching over us and maintaining the balance, they're doing a piss-poor job of it," Thornton said. "All the suffering and misery in the world, all the darkness and evil, and the Guardians don't do a damn thing. It's like they're above it all, happy to just sit back and watch while everything falls to shit."

Something occurred to me. I turned to Thornton. "In the bar last night, you told me there were forces that were supposed to keep everything in balance. You meant them, didn't you? The Guardians?" He nodded. "But you also said something went wrong."

"It did," he said. "Centuries ago, one of the Guardians disappeared. Left. Just gave the world the finger and took off to who knows where. It threw off the balance, and everything changed. Guess which element this Guardian had dominion over."

That one was easy. "Magic," I said, and a piece of the puzzle slid into place. "That's what caused the Shift."

"You got it in one," Thornton said.

"So when Morbius created the Five-Pointed Star, he was trying to restore the balance that had been changed by the Shift."

"Except it got him killed, and the balance is still screwed up," Thornton said. "I'm not surprised no one took up the mantle after him. Who's going to risk their lives to put things right when even the Guardians don't have your back? When they can just leave their posts whenever they want and let everything come crashing down?"

I looked at the figures again. "So if there are only seven Guardians left," I asked, "how come there are eight of them here?"

Bethany's eyes grew big, and she turned to me with a wide grin. "Trent, there might be hope for you yet. I think you just gave us our answer. If solving this puzzle depends on us choosing one of the Guardians over the others, it makes sense it would be the one who's not there anymore."

She pointed at the eighth figure, all the way at the end. I'd thought the rune on that figure looked like a simple circle, but now, as I looked closer, my heart lurched in my chest. It was an eye inside a circle—the same symbol on the brick wall in my earliest memory. The rune for magic? How could that be? What did it mean?

Thornton moved his hand to the figure Bethany had indicated. He cast a quick, uncertain glance at her. "You're sure? I told you what happens if we're wrong."

"Do it," she said, nodding gravely.

He smirked. "That's so you, Bethany. Possibly your last words before dying and they're a direct order." He pressed his palm against the figure, and it sank an inch into the surrounding rock. A loud grinding noise echoed through the tunnel, followed by the sharp, metallic *clank* of a lock giving way on the other side of the wall. The slab rolled aside on a hidden track, disappearing into the wall and leaving a huge, round doorway before us.

Bethany let out the breath she'd been nervously holding, and went through first. Thornton and I went after her, and once we were through, the slab rolled back into place behind us. Before us sprawled an enormous, vaulted tunnel, much wider and longer than the last one.

It was like walking into a museum of New York City history—that is, if museums were filled with mountains of garbage. Lit by more torches along the walls, the tunnel was so cluttered with junk that there was only a narrow path down the middle for us to walk on. The junk had been sorted into piles: broken TVs of every make and model, from early 1950's tubes to high-definition flat screens; discarded dressers and chests of drawers; mounds of old mattresses; a towering pyramid of aged air-conditioning units; a teetering, almost sculptural heap of garbage cans, both old-time aluminum receptacles and modern polyethylene bins. Bethany was right about Gregor being a hoarder, only I hadn't expected his treasure chamber to be filled with the things most New Yorkers left out on the curb for garbage pickup. It was a far cry from the piles of gold and jewels I'd imagined.

Something glittered by the side of the path, catching my eye. It was a tall pile of subway tokens. The Transit Authority didn't use tokens anymore, I knew. They'd been replaced years ago by prepaid swipe cards that were a lot cheaper to manufacture. I'd never seen a token before. Curious, I reached for one, but Thornton shot me a warning glance.

"Don't touch anything, don't take anything," he said.

I pulled my hand back. "I was just—"

"Trust me, he'll know," Thornton interrupted. He didn't mention what the consequences of touching Gregor's "treasure" were, but after learning what would happen if we chose the wrong answer to the puzzle, it was a fair guess that the punishment would be gruesome and permanent.

Thornton turned to continue walking, but his legs suddenly gave out from under him and he fell. I heard the distinctive snap of bone, but I couldn't tell what had fractured. His limbs looked all right, even the mangled arm he'd reset. A rib, maybe? Dead and decaying at an accelerated rate, he'd become as fragile as porcelain.

Thornton squeezed his eyes shut and gritted his teeth, pushing himself up onto his hands and knees. He punched the floor angrily. "Damn it, come on!"

I took him by the shoulders to help him up.

"Don't," he said. He didn't look at me, just shrugged my hands off. With a groan, he sat back on his haunches, wrapping his arms around his stomach as if he were in pain. In the guttering torchlight I saw his hands were marbled with black necrotic tissue. The lights from the amulet on his chest pulsed even more weakly than before. "I was supposed to have twenty-four hours," he said. "You told me I had twenty-four hours."

Bethany moved toward him. "Thornton, what's happening? Talk to me."

He turned his face away from her. When he spoke his voice sounded hollow. "I can see myself rotting. I can *feel* it from the inside. It's horrible. You should have left me dead, Bethany. I didn't ask for this. I didn't ask you to bring me back."

"I didn't know what else to do," she said. She knelt down in front of him. "I'm sorry, Thornton. I know you're worried, and I know you're scared, but I won't let anything happen before we get you back to Gabrielle. I promise."

He turned to her, finally. His eyes were dry, but I thought he would have been crying if he could have. "You can't promise that, Bethany. No one can."

Silently, she stood, offered him her hands, and helped him back to his feet.

We continued down the tunnel. Ahead of us was another titanic doorway, this time filled with bright light pouring through from the other side. The air grew colder as we approached it. I closed my trench coat around me, my breath steaming in front of my face, and followed Bethany and Thornton through it into the light.

On the other side, I paused and blinked, certain what I was seeing couldn't be real. I'd expected another chamber or tunnel, but what spread out before us now as far as the eye could see was a vista more suited to the Himalayas than a cavern beneath the streets of New York City. We were standing on a stone bridge, long and wide and rimmed with ice. In the distance a range of snow-capped mountains rose out of a shroud of white mist. I walked to the edge of the bridge and looked over, past the enormous icicles that dangled beneath us, but the mist hid the ground below. It was impossible to tell how far down it went. There was no visible light source in this place, and yet light permeated the landscape from all directions. It looked like sunlight, but it couldn't be. We were still underground. How could there be sunlight beneath the city? How could *any* of this be here?

"Where are we?" I asked, my breath forming a cloud.

"Tsotha Zin, also known as the Nethercity," Thornton said. "It's a safe haven, a place where many of those who believe it's become too dangerous on the surface choose to live, under Gregor's protection. They don't trust anyone who's still on the surface—topsiders, they call them—but Gregor and I have an understanding."

I stared out at the mountain peaks in awe, and noticed tiny shapes along the slopes that resembled houses. "You're telling me someone built a city under New York?"

"No," he said. "I'm telling you someone built New York over a city." He cupped his hands by his mouth and shouted, "Gregor!" His voice echoed across the mountaintops. He called it again. I thought, skeptically, that Gregor was an odd name for a dragon.

As the echoes died away, the mist below the bridge roiled and broke. A massive shape reared up before us like a mountain in its own right, only it was alive and moving, an enormous, reptilian head at the end of a long, sinuous neck.

I gasped and took a nervous step back. Gregor bore only a passing re-semblance to the dragon on the cover of *The Ragana's Revenge*. His hide was shingled with thick, stone-gray scales, not green ones. Where his eyes should have been there burned two cold, white fires. His head was encir-cled with yellowing ivory horns that swept back like a crown from his serpentine face. There was something that seemed almost prehistoric about him, an air of such immense age that suddenly I had no trouble believing he was as old as Bethany claimed.

The nostrils at the end of his long snout flared as big as windows as he inhaled a deep breath. The massive suction nearly pulled me off my feet. Bethany held onto my arm to keep from falling over. Then the dragon opened his titanic jaws and let loose an angry, deafening roar. The heat of his breath blasted me like a furnace. I couldn't help noticing that his teeth were bigger than I was. He could swallow me with a single bite.

"It's okay, Gregor, they're with me!" Thornton shouted.

The dragon closed his jaws, the echo of his roar bouncing across the mountains and dying away. He lifted his head high, exhaling plumes of steam from his nostrils, then lowered himself to the bridge again. Once more, the dragon inhaled mightily. I braced my legs to keep from being vacu-umed into Gregor's nostrils. Bethany clung to me again until it was over.

"The tiny female is unknown to me. You know strangers are not welcome here," Gregor said. The long spiky bristles that dangled like a beard from his chin quivered as he spoke. His voice boomed across the mountain range like thunder.

If my jaw could have dropped any farther than it already had, it would have landed at my feet. Not only was the dragon talking, he could speak English. I turned to Bethany, but she put a finger to her lips before I could say anything. I turned back to the dragon. He was studying me with his burning eyes. Somewhere in that white fire I sensed a vast intelligence.

"This one, the male," Gregor continued. "The stench of death clings to him. He is not what he seems."

I stiffened. Just how much could Gregor tell about me with a sniff?

"Yeah, he's all kinds of wrong," Thornton agreed. "But even so, I can vouch for him. I can vouch for them both."

"Very well." Gregor swiveled on his long neck to face Thornton. "I see you have returned with the Breath of Itzamna upon your chest, old friend, and the scent of the dead. I regret that your fate has found you so soon. I will miss your companionship."

Clearly uncomfortable, Thornton changed the subject quickly. "Please tell me you still have the box I left with you."

"Of course," the dragon said. A gigantic hand rose from beneath the bridge, its scaly claws balled in a fist. All three of us backed up to give the hand room as it came to rest before us. "I promised you I would keep it safe, and I have done no less. I would give it to none but you."

Thornton nodded. "I know. Believe me, just this once I wish that weren't the case." He looked at the dragon's massive fist. "Thank you, I'll take it now."

"However," the dragon said, "it is such a *pretty* box."

Thornton rolled his eyes. "Gregor . . ."

"I would hate to lose such a beautiful item from my collection," the dragon continued. "It brings me such pleasure to look at."

I glanced at Bethany. Once again she gestured for me not to say or do anything to interfere.

"Gregor, I'm running out of time," Thornton said. "The Breath of Itzamna won't last much longer. Please, I need the box."

"I propose a barter, then. A fair trade," Gregor said.

Thornton frowned and shook his head. "What do we have that you could possibly want?"

"Something of equal beauty that I may keep," Gregor said. He swiveled his massive head until he loomed over Bethany, and my blood went cold. The dragon wanted *her*? For what, a snack? I moved to get between them, but she warned me to stay back with a quick shake of her head. Gregor continued, "The bauble that hangs around the female's neck has caught my eye. I would have it in exchange for the box."

I breathed a sigh of relief, but Bethany didn't. "Now just a minute," she said, putting her hands on her hips.

The dragon lowered his head to regard her more closely. His burning eyes narrowed with contempt. "Thornton, inform this tiny topsider that she is not to address me unless I require it."

Thornton put his head in his hands. "Oh God, that's not going to go over well."

"I'll address you as I see fit!" Bethany shouted back at Gregor. The sight of a five-foot-tall woman bellowing indignantly at a titanic, eons-old dragon would have been funny if I weren't so worried that Gregor would respond by squashing us all with one gigantic hand. "And furthermore," she continued, lifting the charm on the string around her neck, the blue veins in the little pearl-like sphere sparkling like glitter, "do you have any idea how hard it is to engineer a personal energy-barrier charm? This *bauble*, as you call it, isn't for sale!"

"A shame. Its colors please me," Gregor said. "I am afraid we have no deal, old friend."

Thornton looked up at the dragon sharply. "Gregor, *please*."

"I have given you my terms," the dragon said.

Thornton looked at Bethany. Bethany looked at me—the real reason she was reluctant to part with it. "I told you, you're safe now. It's over," I said. She looked skeptical. "Bethany, I know I kept something from you, something bad, but sooner or later you're going to have to start trusting me again."

She took a deep breath, lifted the charm from around her neck, and held it up by the string. "Don't make me regret this," she said to me.

A second enormous hand appeared from below the bridge, one long talon extended. Bethany hooked the charm's string over the tip of the nail. The hand receded back into the mist with her charm.

Gregor's other hand opened, and something tumbled out of his enormous, scaled palm to land at Thornton's feet. My breath caught in my throat.

The box.

It was just as Underwood had described it, a foot wide by two feet long, and fashioned from a dark, weathered wood. The corners were cased in brass. A brass handle was hinged on one side so it could be carried. A trunk lock, also brass, was bolted to the wood and kept it securely closed. On the lid was the crest Underwood had said would be there, an iron-stamped coat of arms featuring two lions standing on their hind legs, their mouths open in pantomime roars. Between them, their forelegs supported a shield topped with a bejeweled crown. Unfurled across the face of the shield was a banner with words written in a language I didn't know: *IN DE EENHEID, STERKTE.*

After everything we'd been through, the creatures we'd fought, and the lives that had been lost, the box looked crushingly ordinary. But then, boxes didn't have to be special. It was what they contained that mattered, and what was inside this one had left a trail of blood, death, and betrayal behind it.

I'd known this moment would come eventually. I'd been anticipating it, even dreading it. But I already knew what had to be done.

Thornton took the box by its handle, but he was too weak to lift it.

"Let me," I said, moving toward him.

Bethany got there first. She lifted the heavy box with a grunt and held it like a suitcase at her side. "No offense, Trent, but I'm not letting this box out of my sight again."

Damn. I nodded and smiled like it was no big deal. I would have another chance.

Gregor began to descend back into the mist. "Guard that box well, old friend, and beware. What sleeps inside it must not be allowed to awaken. There are whispers. The oracles warn of an immortal storm, a gathering force so powerful it threatens all existence."

"I don't understand," Thornton said. "An immortal storm? What does that mean? What does it have to do with what's in the box?"

"Warn the others who dwell topside. The immortal storm must not come, or it will seal the doom of all—mortals, Ancients, and Guardians alike."

Gregor disappeared into the mist and was gone. Thornton ran to the edge of the bridge and looked over. "Wait!" But there was no sign of the dragon.

As we walked back toward the tunnels, I kept my eyes on the box. I'd looked at the situation from every angle. There was only one way to throw off Underwood's yoke from around my neck and send the message that he couldn't manipulate me anymore. Only one way to keep Bethany and Thornton safe from the dangerous forces that wanted the box for themselves. Only one way to bring to an end all the suffering and death the box brought with it.

I had to destroy it.

Twenty-one

By the time we climbed out of the sewers and emerged from the field behind the brick ruins by the West Side Highway, storm clouds had rolled in to give the sky a gray, swollen overcast. Rain was coming. I could feel it in the soupy humidity that drew sweat from my pores. Was this the immortal storm Gregor had warned us about? Nothing about the dark clouds overhead seemed different from any I'd seen before. Whatever an immortal storm was, and whatever dangers it brought with it, I was pretty sure this wasn't what the dragon had meant.

A dragon. I'd seen a living, breathing *dragon* under New York City. Yesterday I would have scoffed at the idea of dragons—*had* scoffed at it while reading *The Ragana's Revenge*—yet everything that happened since then had been a crash course in just what was and wasn't possible. It was as if I'd fallen through the rabbit hole directly into Elena De Voe's head. Even the name of the Nethercity, Tsotha Zin, was like something out of her book, though I supposed even in the real world an ancient, magical city underneath New York wasn't going to be named Boise. I promised myself that if I ever met Elena De Voe, I'd ask how much of her novel was fictional and how much was true.

We traveled east, trying to hail passing cabs, but with the sky threatening rain all the cabs were already taken. Bethany cursed and kept walking, keeping a tight grip on the box. Thornton limped stiffly beside her. The pedestrians on the sidewalk, instinctively sensing a wrongness about him, gave him a wide berth, even if they didn't understand why. I was starting to envy them their blissful ignorance.

But I had my own situation to worry about. How was I going to convince Bethany and Thornton to give me the box? After everything they'd been through to keep it safe, would they give it up without a fight if they knew what I planned to do with it? However it happened, I was going to have to do it soon. Much sooner than I'd thought.

Because a sleek black sedan had been following us for blocks now, ever since we left the ruins. It hung back in traffic, trying to stay inconspicuous as it shadowed us around corners and down side streets, but my instincts knew when I was being followed. Worse, I recognized the car. I'd seen it before, just this morning, with a dark-eyed woman at the wheel.

How the hell did Underwood keep finding me? One time I could chalk up to bad luck, but this? This was the universe laughing at me, telling me that no matter how hard I tried, no matter what I did, I'd never be out from under the man's heel. I'd made a deal with the devil, and if there was one thing I knew from watching old horror movies, it was that no one ever walked away from a deal with the devil.

Two men dressed in black appeared at the far end of the block, rounding the corner and walking toward us. They were too far away to see clearly, but from their size and the way they walked I recognized them right away: Tomo and Big Joe. I should have been surprised, but I wasn't. Their appearance had the inevitability of clockwork. Maddening, infuriating clockwork.

"Shit," I said, stopping.

Bethany and Thornton stopped, too. "What is it?" she asked.

"We're being followed."

"What?" Bethany looked up and down the street, but she didn't know what to look for, not the way I did.

There was no way to retreat with Underwood in the car behind us, and no way forward with his two enforcers heading our way. I hoped Tomo and Big Joe hadn't seen me yet, but that was unlikely. They were professionals. They knew exactly who they were looking for. Probably, they'd spotted me the moment they turned the corner. We had to get off the street. I needed someplace close to duck into. I glanced around desperately and spotted an auto body shop twenty feet away, its retractable garage door open to reveal an enclosed workspace that stretched deep into the building. I took Bethany and Thornton by the arm and pushed them toward the shop. "This way. Quickly."

"Trent, who's following us?" Bethany demanded.

"Someone dangerous," I said. "Now move."

Inside, the auto body shop was wide enough to hold three cars side by side, though there was only one there at the moment, its hood up and its deconstructed engine exposed like entrails. Next to it, a young man in his early twenties sat on a folding metal chair, eating his lunch out of a Chinese restaurant's Styrofoam container. It wasn't the perfect hiding place, it would have been better if no one saw us at all, but it would have to do. We were running out of time.

The young man looked up from his meal as we entered the auto body shop, noisily sucking a lo mein noodle into his mouth. He was scrawny, with an unruly mess of dirty-blond hair and a sleeve of tattoos down each arm. His ears were pierced with open metal spools that stretched his earlobes into big fleshy hoops. The patch on his shirt was embroidered with the name Chaz. We only had his attention for a moment before he dismissed us by looking down at his noodles again. "If you need your car worked on, come back in half an hour. Everyone's out to lunch."

"Is there a back door to this place?" I asked

That caught his attention. He looked up again, confused. "Huh?"

"A back door, Chaz," I repeated, annoyed. I scanned the shop. It was small and cluttered. I didn't see any doors in back. "Or how about another room, the office, anything that's away from the street?"

He put his Styrofoam container on the floor under his chair and stood up slowly. "Who are you? What are you talking about?"

We were getting nowhere fast. I glanced through the open garage door at the sidewalk outside. How far away were Tomo and Big Joe now? What about Underwood? I waved Bethany and Thornton to the back of the shop, and they retreated to the far wall. It would have to be enough.

"Sorry, Chaz, but if you know what's good for you, you're going to have to go." I nodded toward the open door. "Trust me, in a couple of minutes you're going to wish you weren't here anyway."

"The fuck are you talking about?" Chaz demanded. His confusion was making him angry. He puffed up his chest like a frog trying to look bigger than it was. "You think you're gonna rob this place? Well, think again, motherfucker!" He started to reach for a metal lug wrench sitting on the car engine.

I didn't have time for this. I got to him before he reached the lug wrench. I hooked two fingers through the large, stretched hoop of his earlobe and pulled, dragging him toward the doorway.

"Ow! Ow! What the fuck, man?"

I pushed him out onto the sidewalk. "If you want to keep living, Chaz, you'll walk away from here and won't stop until you hit the river."

"Yo, back it the fuck up!" he raged, rubbing his sore ear. "You pull that shit again and I'll beat your punk ass down!" It was empty bluster, I could tell from the way he tilted on his feet, ready to move away from me, not toward me. I'd spooked him. Now he was more bark than bite.

"Chaz," I said calmly, making sure to call him by his name again. It was an old con-man trick, or so I'd been told. Keep using the mark's name and they lower their guard. "Chaz, I don't have time to tell you how much danger you're in. You just need to run." I pulled the gun halfway out of my coat pocket, just enough to give him a peek at it. "So run."

He stared at the gun. Apparently that was all he needed to finally send him sprinting down the sidewalk.

There was a key box on the wall next to the doorway, the key still in it. I turned the key, and the garage door motor on the ceiling groaned to life. The door rolled down and hit the sidewalk with a solid, comforting *clang*.

"Tell me what's going on," Bethany demanded. "Who's out there?"

"How many are there?" Thornton asked.

I walked toward the back of the auto body shop, where they were waiting. "Bethany, I'm going to need you to give me the box."

"Forget it. I already told you I'm not letting this thing out of my sight again," she said. "What's this about? What's happening?"

"We don't have a lot of time," I said. "The people who are coming are much, much worse than you can imagine. They're going to take the box from you by force if they have the chance. But if you give it to me, I can do something about it."

"Who are they? How do you know them?"

"Bethany—"

"Damn it, Trent, tell me what's going on!"

A tension headache stabbed my temples like a knife. Why did she have to be so damn infuriating? We didn't have time for this. It wouldn't take long for Tomo and Big Joe to figure out where we were. That was their job, what they were good at. They hunted people on Underwood's orders, and when they found them, they did terrible things to them. "Just give me the damn box," I said, and tried to grab it out of her hand.

She jumped back, dropping the box on the floor behind her. In a flash, the Endymion wand shot out of her sleeve and into her hand. At the same time, instinctively, I pulled my gun out of my coat. We stood in a silent standoff for a moment, Bethany aiming her wand at me, me aiming my gun at her.

Thornton's eyes went wide. "Whoa, whoa, what the hell?"

I ignored him. "Drop the wand, Bethany."

"Sooner or later I'm going to have to trust you again. That's what you said," she said bitterly. "I should have trusted my instincts. It was no accident you were at that warehouse."

"Guys, come on," Thornton pleaded. "We're on the same side, here."

"No, we're not," Bethany said. "It was all a lie, wasn't it, Trent? You were after the box all along."

Thornton turned to me, shocked. "Is that true?"

I swallowed. It went down like broken glass. "Yes," I said, "but it's not the whole—"

Bethany snapped her wrist. A jagged, white arc of energy burst out of the Endymion wand's tip and instantly struck my forehead. It felt like a slight electric shock, the kind you get when you touch metal on a cold day, and then . . . nothing happened.

"The sleep spell won't work on me," I said. "I don't sleep."

Her face fell. I expected anger, or defiance, but mostly what I saw was disappointment. Somehow that was worse. It stung me deep in my chest. I clamped down on it, forced myself to stay cold and focused. I'd gotten pretty good at that over the past year, so how come it was so damn hard to do now?

She lowered the wand and let it fall to the floor. "Why are you doing this?"

"I've got something hanging over my head, something bad, and the box is the only leverage I've got," I said. "Please, just step away from it so I can pick it up. You too, Thornton."

Thornton didn't move an inch. His face was stony, defiant. "Make me, asshole."

Bethany didn't move, either. "What happens once you have the box? You kill us?"

"Good luck trying," Thornton said.

"Once I have it, I'll leave, I promise. I don't want to hurt anyone." I lowered the gun to show them I meant what I said.

It was a mistake. Thornton immediately changed into wolf form, and this time I saw it happen. In an instant, his human form melted like water and re-formed itself as the timber wolf. But because he acted so quickly, he hadn't taken off his coat and clothes first. The material stretched and tore around him, dangling in strips off his back and clinging tightly to his haunches and hind legs. He let out an angry growl, but he was too weak and too tangled in his clothes to do anything but limp over and nudge at me feebly with his snout in an attempt to knock me over. He bit my leg, but his jaws were too frail to give the bite any power and his teeth didn't even penetrate my jeans. I sighed. Seeing the once formidable wolf reduced to this was heartbreaking.

"Stop," I said softly. "Thornton, just stop."

The wolf backed away, growling hoarsely. He stumbled, fell onto his side in the shadow of the car, and remained there, drained and depleted, his eyes still fixed angrily on me. The lights on the amulet pulsed weakly.

Bethany reached for her cargo vest, but I lifted the gun again and she stopped.

"Bethany, please," I said. "Just step away from the box. I don't want to hurt you."

She moved to stand in front of the box, squaring her shoulders and lifting her chin defiantly. "That's funny, coming from someone pointing a gun in my face. No, if you want the box, this time you're going to have to pull the trigger."

She wasn't bluffing. Bethany wasn't the bluffing kind. She would die to protect that goddamn box. She was brave and dedicated, I'd give her that. She had been since the moment I'd met her. I respected her for it. In another world, one that was more just, we could have been good friends. I would have liked that, but there was no hope of it now, not after this.

I thought about all the terrible things Underwood had manipulated me into doing, and all the while I'd naively believed he'd get the answers I wanted in return. I thought about the chair with the straps, and the drain in the floor, and the monster I worked for, and knew it couldn't go on like this. I had to get out, and the box was my only ticket. I swallowed, my throat dry as sandpaper. My palms were sweaty against the grip of the gun. My finger trembled on the trigger. I'd been so sure about what I had to do, but now that the moment was here it felt like everything was unraveling, spinning out of control. It shouldn't have come to this. There should have been another way, but I was so used to acting alone, so used to relying on the intimidating power of a gun to get what I wanted, that, ironically, I'd fallen back on what I'd learned from Underwood. But my training hadn't prepared me for this, for pointing a gun at the only people who'd ever treated me with kindness.

I guess you can only wonder if you're a monster so many times before you become one.

Bethany must have read the conflicting emotions in my face because her tone softened. "Whatever's going on, whatever's hanging over your head, this isn't the way."

But it was too late now. After you pull your gun on someone, there's no going back. "Just hand over the box, okay?"

"Why?" she demanded, incredulous. "What could you possibly want with it?"

"I'm going to destroy it," I said. "It's the only way out for me, and believe it or not, for you, too. Destroying that thing is the only way any of us will be safe."

Her reaction surprised me. She shook her head. She looked almost sorry for me. "You can't."

"Watch me," I told her.

"Trent, just put the gun down and we can talk about this. Don't you think others have tried to destroy what's in this box? Hell, I would destroy it myself if I could, but it can't *be* destroyed. It just heals itself, puts itself back together again. It's like you that way."

I stared at the box on the floor by her feet. "It's *alive*?"

At that moment, the garage door motor roared, startling me. The door rolled up, revealing Chaz standing on the sidewalk outside. He grimaced at us as he pulled his key out of a key box on the outside wall.

He wasn't alone. Big Joe held Chaz tightly by the arm. Beside him, Tomo flashed me a malicious, triumphant grin, and said, "Why are you always runnin' away from us, T-Bag? Don't you wanna play with your friends no more?"

Twenty-two

Keeping a tight grip on Chaz's tattooed arm, Big Joe pushed him forward into the auto body shop. "Thanks for unlocking the door, kid. Remember when I said we'd let you go afterward? I lied." In one swift motion, he grabbed Chaz's head with both hands and twisted. Chaz's neck snapped with a muffled crack.

"No!" I shouted, but it was too late. He shoved Chaz's limp body into the corner of the shop.

Big Joe sneered at me. "You're not gonna act all holier-than-thou, are you, T-Bag? You know you've got just as much blood on your hands as I do."

"You know these men?" Bethany demanded.

"They're the ones I warned you about," I said. I looked at Chaz's body. The kid was dead and I might as well have painted a target on him. They must have caught him running away from the auto shop. I glared at Big Joe and Tomo. My jaw went tight. My finger twitched on the trigger, but as much as I wanted to take them down, I kept the gun pointed down at the floor. I didn't want things to get any more out of hand than they already were.

Tomo nudged Big Joe with his elbow, chuckling and pointing at Thornton. "Dude, that's gotta be the most fucked-up dog I've ever seen."

Thornton growled and pushed himself up onto his feet. His legs trembled under his weight.

Bethany reached for her vest, but I held up a hand to stop her. Tomo and Big Joe hadn't drawn their weapons yet, but there wasn't a doubt in my mind they were armed. They always were, and they were quick on the draw. Bethany would be dead before she could pull out a charm.

"So, you got the box or what?" Tomo demanded. "Underwood's waitin'."

"The girl's got it," Big Joe said, nodding his chin toward Bethany and the box at her feet. "Yo, T-Bag, you gonna introduce us to your friend? She's smokin' hot."

"Short as hell, though," Tomo said. "What is she, a kid? You bangin' her, you fuckin' perv?" He and Big Joe laughed, and my temper flared.

"Come on, T-Bag," Big Joe said. "Grab the box, waste the girl, and let's get out of here. Unless you think we should take turns with her first. Share and share alike, right, T-Bag?"

"Charming," Bethany said.

I'd had enough. "Back off," I said, and lifted my gun, pointing it at them.

"Whoa, what the fuck are you doing?" Big Joe demanded. He stared at the barrel of the Bersa semiautomatic for a moment, then grinned. "Look, if this is about before, I'm sorry we kicked your ass, but you had it coming." When I didn't say anything or put the gun down, he sighed. "Ah, I see. You're making a big mistake. A big fucking mistake." He and Tomo reluctantly put their hands up.

"Tell Underwood he's not getting the box," I said. "Tell him I'm done being manipulated and lied to. If he comes after me it's his own funeral."

Big Joe shook his head. "Keep dreaming. Underwood wants that box. One way or another, we're not leaving here without it."

I kept my gun trained on them but glanced over my shoulder at Bethany. "Bethany, give me the box. It's the only way I can be sure."

"Not on your life," she said.

The moment I took my eyes off them, Big Joe and Tomo moved like lightning, reaching into their jackets and pulling out their guns. I cocked my gun. "Don't," I warned.

Big Joe kept his gun trained on me. Tomo drew a bead on Bethany. Thornton growled louder, his hackles rising. Somehow he found the strength to lope toward them, but he was slow and his whole body shook from the exertion.

Tomo kept his eyes on the wolf's approach. He swallowed nervously, his instinctual aversion to the undead kicking in. "Call this fucking thing off," he yelled, his voice wavering.

"Thornton, get back," I said, but the wolf ignored me. He inched closer to Tomo, snarling and baring his fangs. Then, without warning, one of his front legs gave out and he tipped forward, off-balance. Tomo kicked him hard across the snout. Thornton skittered backward, tripping over his tangled clothes and collapsing to the floor.

Big Joe locked eyes with me and spat on the floor. "You dumb piece of shit. You're fucking with the wrong people."

A voice from behind him said, "No, gentlemen. *You* are."

Tomo and Big Joe turned.

Standing in the doorway of the auto body shop was a man in his late fifties with a mane of coppery red hair on his head and a neatly trimmed beard that matched it. He wore a long, hunter-green duster that flapped behind him in the breeze. He wasn't alone. To one side of him stood a tall, statuesque woman in a black leather jacket, her skin as smooth and dark as onyx. She had black, braided dreadlocks tied back behind her head. On his other side stood a lean, sinewy Asian man in a black turtleneck and mirrored sunglasses.

"Who the fuck are you clowns?" Tomo demanded. He and Big Joe turned their guns on the newcomers.

The red-bearded man grinned. "The name's Isaac Keene. These are my associates Gabrielle Duchamp and Philip Chen. Commit those names to memory, gentlemen. The next time you hear them, you're going to want to run."

The two enforcers cocked their guns. Big Joe said, "Sorry to break it to you, pal, but there ain't gonna be a next time."

They both pulled the triggers in quick succession. At the same time, Isaac waved a hand in the air before him as if he were tracing a giant circle. The bullets hung in midair, frozen just a few inches away from Isaac. He thrust his arm out in front of him, palm forward. There was a quick, bright flash, and suddenly Tomo and Big Joe were off their feet and hurtling back toward the shop wall as if a wrecking ball had hit them.

But Isaac's hand was empty. He wasn't holding a charm or artifact the way Bethany and Thornton did when they worked magic. The flash—the *spell*—had come directly from the palm of his hand. Isaac, I realized, was carrying magic inside him.

Tomo and Big Joe crashed hard into the wall, their guns flying from their hands, and then fell in a heap on the floor, unconscious. The suspended bullets fell harmlessly at Isaac's feet, tinkling like wind chimes.

A loud squeal of tires came from the street outside. Underwood's black sedan pulled away from the curb and sped past the auto body shop. He would be back, though. I was sure of it. He wanted the box too badly to let it go.

The man in the black turtleneck and mirrored shades, Philip Chen, moved away from Isaac's side so fast he was little more than a blur. In a second he was in front of me, grabbing the front of my shirt in his fist and slamming me back against the wall. He wrenched the gun out of my hand, his grip so strong I thought my fingers would break under the pressure. Philip pocketed my gun. Then he *smelled* me. He brought his face right up to the bloodstains on my collar and shirt and sniffed me like I was a bouquet of flowers.

"I can smell your blood," he said, his face close enough for me to feel hot breath on my throat. Where he gripped my shirt, his stone-like fist pressed so hard into my chest it felt like my ribs were going to crack. I couldn't breathe. In the reflection of Philip's mirrored sunglasses, I saw my own face turn red with asphyxiation. "Your fear and confusion make your blood smell like candy to me," he said.

"Philip, don't," Bethany said.

Philip scowled. "I saw him through the wall when we were coming up on this place, Bethany. He was holding a gun on you. Give me a reason not to open him up."

"Believe me, I'd love to see him get what's coming to him, but we need him," she insisted. "Someone named Underwood is after the box. Trent's the only one who can tell us who he is and what kind of threat he poses."

Philip seemed unconvinced, continuing to press me against the wall with his face inching closer to my neck. I glanced down and saw my boots were dangling several inches above the floor. Philip wasn't just holding me against the wall, he was holding me *up,* and effortlessly. His strength was staggering.

"Philip, that's enough," Isaac said.

Bethany had been unsuccessful, but apparently two words from Isaac were all it took to make Philip back down. He lowered me to the floor, relaxing the pressure on my chest, but he kept a tight grip on my shirt. I coughed and gasped air into my lungs. Philip's lips peeled back from his teeth in a grin. His canines were long and pointed, sharp enough to pierce flesh. "I guess it's your lucky day," he said, "but you so much as breathe wrong, I'll tear out your throat."

Given those sharp teeth, I had no doubt Philip could do just that if he had a mind to. I looked into his mirrored shades, wishing I could see his eyes to get a better read on him. I realized with a jolt that I could see my whole torso in the reflection, but I couldn't see Philip's arm holding my shirt. The front of my shirt was bunched and twisted, but there was no hand gripping it, just the knot of fabric.

"You don't have a reflection," I said. Apparently, I'd developed a knack for stating the obvious.

Philip grinned, showing his fangs again. "When you look this good all the time, you don't need one. Now just stay put, or I'll show you what kind of damage a vampire can really do."

I figured it wouldn't be smart to put that to the test. Across the shop, I watched Bethany approach Isaac.

"You shouldn't have come," she said. "You know it's against protocol. It's your own rule."

"You can blame Gabrielle," he said. "She wouldn't take no for an answer. It was hard enough getting her to stay at Citadel last night when she knew Thornton was in trouble, but she threatened to go to him as soon as the sun came up, with or without me. Since I couldn't talk her out of it, I thought it would be safer if I came with her. As for Philip, well, you know what he's like. He won't let me out of his sight. So, the gang's all here."

The woman with the dreadlocks and leather jacket knelt beside Thornton. She cradled him gently in her arms, and suddenly I put two and two together. Gabrielle Duchamp was the one Thornton kept talking about. The love of his life.

Thornton had changed back to human form, but he looked worse than ever. He was wasting away, his emaciated body nearly lost in the folds of his tattered clothes. The lights on the amulet pulsed so dimly I could barely see them.

Gabrielle kissed Thornton's face and mouth. "I'm here, baby. I've got you."

His discolored, necrotic hand reached up to stroke her hair and touch her face. He winced in frustration and pulled his hand away. "I—I can't feel you."

"How is he?" Isaac asked, putting a hand on Gabrielle's shoulder.

She scooped Thornton up in her arms, lifting him off the floor as though he weighed nothing at all. "There isn't much time," she said. "We have to get him back to Citadel."

"Bring Thornton to the car. We'll follow," Isaac said. Gabrielle carried Thornton out of the shop. Isaac turned back to Bethany. "I only wish we'd found you sooner. We thought you were still at the safe house. When we got there, we found Ingrid. . . ." He paused a moment, then continued, "After that, I remembered that you'd used the Breath of Itzamna on Thornton. The amulet gives off a distinct arcane signature that I was able to track down."

"I'm so sorry about Ingrid," Bethany said. "She was an amazing woman. She died protecting us."

"And protecting this." Isaac crouched over the box and brushed his fingers along the lid. "The Van Lente Box. I've heard stories all my life, but I never thought I'd see it with my own eyes. It's like seeing history itself."

I blinked. The Van Lente Box? The damn thing had a *name*?

Isaac picked the box up by its handle. Bethany didn't stop him. She hadn't let me hold the box, hadn't trusted me enough even before I pulled a gun on her, but she let Isaac take it without protest. I wondered if there was something between them, if they were more than employer and employee. The thought put a sudden, unexpected pang of jealousy in my chest.

"The sooner we get it into the vault the better," Isaac said. He carried the box toward the doorway, and pointed at me. "Bring him."

Philip yanked me away from the wall and pulled me forcefully toward the door.

Bethany collected Tomo and Big Joe's guns from the floor and tucked them into her pants. "What about these two?"

"Leave them here. By the time they wake up, we'll be long gone. But him," Isaac nodded at me, "him I want."

Philip kept a bone-crushing grip on my arm, guiding me out onto the sidewalk. A gleaming black juggernaut of an Escalade was parked at the curb, its windows tinted dark as ink. The rear hatch was open, and Gabrielle was laying Thornton gently on the carpeted floor of the cargo area, making sure he was as comfortable as possible.

I listened as Bethany brought Isaac up to speed on everything that happened at the safe house. Isaac confirmed that he and the others had found the shadowborn's bodies there. They were still alive, he said, even with their heads separated from their bodies, just immobilized. He'd burned them to ashes with something he called a flaming dervish—a spell, I guessed—then scattered the ashes to the wind just to be sure.

"What I don't understand is what the shadowborn were doing there in the first place," he said. "They shouldn't have been able to find the safe house. The ward was still active when we got there."

"I've been asking myself the same thing," Bethany replied. "The shadowborn were looking for the box, which means whoever sent them not only knew we had it, they knew exactly where to find us. I don't like it, Isaac. It's like they know our every move."

That's because they do, I thought. Ingrid had said we'd been betrayed, and the only ones who knew we were at the safe house were here now—Isaac, Gabrielle, and Philip. One of them had to be the traitor. One of them had sent the shadowborn to kill Bethany, Thornton, and Ingrid, and to steal the box.

But it still didn't explain Bennett. His presence had been a personal touch. Very, very personal.

Isaac put the box in the rear cargo area with Thornton and Gabrielle, then came back around to where I was being held. Philip released me, but I'd seen how fast the vampire could move. I knew better than to try to make a break for it.

"Trent, look at me," Isaac said.

I did, noticing for the first time that Isaac's eyes were blue like Bethany's, though not as bright as hers. There was a wariness that darkened them. They were the guarded eyes of a man who'd seen more terror and wonder in his years than most people did in a lifetime. Maybe two lifetimes.

"I can't risk you knowing where we're taking you," Isaac said, "so I'm going to have to put you to sleep."

I smirked. "Good luck with that. Ask Bethany, she already tried. I don't sleep."

Isaac's eyes seemed to fill my field of vision, though he hadn't moved any closer. Everything else receded, fading into a dim, murky twilight.

"I'm a mage, Trent," Isaac said. "Do you know what that means?"

"You're smarter than the average bear?" I said, but my words were slurred. There was nothing before me now but Isaac's eyes. The street, the others, everything else was gone.

"It means this time you'll sleep."

I blinked. My eyelids felt heavy, my limbs weak and relaxed. "It won't . . . work . . ."

I fell limply back against the car. I slid off and felt someone catch me before I hit the sidewalk. Then I was gone.

Twenty-three

An unfamiliar weightlessness buoyed me. I was numb, my senses completely cut off from the outside world, but it wasn't the same kind of numbness I knew, the kind that came with cold or shock. This was something altogether different, something I'd never experienced before, as if I were no longer inside my own body. Was this sleep?

If it was, I was surprised that my mind was still active. The darkness that had enveloped me as soon as I closed my eyes was gone, and I found myself standing before a brick wall. I recognized it immediately, even before I saw the brick with the eye-like symbol carved into it. The Ehrlendarr rune for magic. It was the wall from my earliest memory, and yet, something wasn't quite right. The sparkles of light that had played across the bricks, the curling wisp of smoke, they were absent. Somehow I understood it was too soon, that whatever had caused them hadn't occurred yet.

This wasn't my earliest memory, I realized. Impossibly, unbelievably, this was just *before* it.

I sensed a presence behind me, someone I couldn't see. A male voice spoke, rich and smooth as oil.

"What if I told you everything you thought you knew was a lie? What if I could show you? All you have to do is—"

"Wake up," Isaac said.

My eyes snapped open. I was groggy, the fleeting images in my head evaporating like so much steam. Had I been dreaming? Actually, genuinely dreaming? I'd never dreamed before, not anytime I could remember, and the fact that my first dream was slipping away so quickly filled me with panic. I struggled desperately to hold onto it, even a remnant of it, a single image, but it was already gone. It left me feeling like someone had died. But if I was capable of sleeping, capable of dreaming, it meant I was closer to normal than I'd thought. That was monumental.

As my grogginess wore off, I found myself seated in a luxuriant, antique chair. Isaac stood in front of me, his arms crossed.

"I told you you'd sleep," he said. He looked smug. I wanted to wipe the smirk off his face with my fists.

I tried to get up but quickly discovered I couldn't. My wrists were tied together behind the tall back of the chair. I struggled against the binding, but the more I pulled, the tighter it held. Whatever it was, I could tell right away it wasn't handcuffs. There was no bite from the hard edges, no cold metal against my skin. It didn't feel like rope either, or cable, or plastic wrist ties. Instead, it felt warm, buzzing with a slight vibration.

"Where am I?" I demanded.

"Welcome to Citadel," Isaac said, spreading his arms. "Welcome to my home."

So *this* was Citadel, their base of operations. Just the room we were in was big enough to live up to its namesake. Octagonal in shape and paneled with dark, finished wood, it spanned nearly three thousand square feet of floor space. Beneath the wrought-iron chandeliers that hung from the twenty-foot ceiling, glass display cases held crystal obelisks that throbbed with light, glittering multicolored geodes, and primitive carvings of creatures with human bodies and animal heads. Mahogany bookshelves were crammed to bursting with dusty old tomes bound in cloth and leather. The walls were adorned with framed oil paintings that looked centuries old; ancient shields and sigils of wood, clay, and metal; and multiple sets of masks, each wearing a more ghoulish expression than the last, fashioned from copper, bronze, and gold.

A marble sculpture stood in each of the eight corners of the room, statues of bizarre creatures atop stone pedestals. The largest was a rearing centaur, almost life-sized, his marble hand pulled back and clutching an iron spear as though he were about to hurl it at an unseen enemy. Beside it, a carpeted staircase led up to another floor, where I had no doubt there were more rooms just as big and cluttered as this one.

I'd never seen Underwood's home, only the fallout shelter where he conducted business, but I always imagined it looked very much like this, with every nook, corner, and shelf crammed with his own private collection of stolen goods. Isaac Keene was like Underwood in that way. He was a man who surrounded himself with strange, curious, and probably very valuable objects. It must have taken him years to put this collection together.

At the far end of the room, two tall, stained-glass windows arched, cathedral-like, to the ceiling. Between them, Isaac had set up some kind of workstation with six video monitors attached to the wall, their screens currently dark. Directly beneath them was a long, sturdy walnut table. Computer equipment, reams of loose paper, and numerous books had been cleared off it and stacked in piles on the floor to make room for the single item that now sat in the middle of the table. The box.

I whistled. "This is some hefty New York real estate. What'd you do, cast a spell on the co-op board?"

Isaac didn't so much as chuckle. "I've got a lot of questions for you, Trent. We'll get a chance to chat soon, very soon, but until then, I need you to sit tight." He turned and walked out through an open, polished cherry wood door across the room. Through it I could see a short hallway that led outside.

"Was that supposed to be a joke?" I called after him, struggling against my bonds. They held tight. I cursed under my breath. I thought about breaking the chair to get my hands free, but from the feel of it I knew the wood was too strong for that. I twisted around as far as I could and caught a glimpse of something bright glowing around my wrists. I sighed and slumped in the chair. Just my luck—Isaac had used magic to restrain me. I couldn't slip, unknot, or break my way out of it if I tried.

How had I let it come to this? Time was, I could have gotten the box off two people like Bethany and Thornton in thirty seconds flat. Instead, I'd held back and botched it. Why? Was I growing soft, or just growing soft for them? For *her*?

Isaac and Gabrielle entered from outside, supporting Thornton between them. They gently moved him toward an old-style, porcelain clawfoot tub that had been filled with water and set up in the middle of the room. Bethany and Philip came in behind them, staying close in case Thornton stumbled or fell. Gabrielle took the long coat off of Thornton's shoulders and let it fall to the floor. The remains of the Anubis Hand in the pocket hit the carpet with a muffled thud. Thornton could barely walk. He was so emaciated that he looked like he'd died weeks ago, not just last night. His eyelids drooped, half-closed. If any lights still pulsed on the amulet in his chest, I couldn't see them.

"It's called a Methusal spring," Gabrielle explained as they approached the tub. "It's the same spell the dryads in Central Park have used for centuries to extend their lifespan, ever since the pollution made them infertile. It has enormous regenerative properties. The dryads are very protective of it and don't normally share it with anyone. I had to call in a lot of favors for this."

Bethany paused, knitting her brow. "Gabrielle, maybe we shouldn't do this. It's only going to cause him more pain. He's been through enough."

"No, if anything can help him, the Methusal spring can." Gabrielle turned to Thornton and murmured in his ear, "It's going to work, baby. I know it is. There's so much more we're still going to do together. The annual naming of the manticore cubs, the mermaid migration down the Hudson River. Remember how much you liked that one last year? How the mermaids' song got stuck in your head for weeks?"

Thornton didn't answer. He was so far gone he couldn't anymore. Philip helped them lower Thornton delicately into the tub, still in his clothes. Bethany hung back, watching and chewing her thumbnail nervously. As soon as Thornton was fully submerged, the water lit up with a rich, golden glow that reflected off their faces.

Gabrielle knelt beside the tub and reached into the water to take Thornton's hand. Her voice cracked as she spoke. "If this is going to work, it's got to come from you, Thornton. You've got to want it. You've got to *fight*." She pulled his hand out of the water and kissed it. One of her braided dreads came loose and fell in front of her face, but she refused to let go of his hand to push it back. "Please, baby. I need you to stay with me."

There was a long silence. All I heard was the gentle sloshing of the water and my own breath. I looked from one face to the next. Any of them could be the one who'd betrayed us at the safe house. Gabrielle's full attention was on Thornton, her eyes full of hope and expectation. Isaac stared down at Thornton, the wrinkles around his eyes and forehead deepening with concern. Philip was unreadable behind his sunglasses. I didn't like the way he was still wearing them inside. It reminded me too much of Underwood.

I looked at Bethany next. Though she was facing me, she didn't meet my eye. She hadn't looked my way once yet. It bothered me. It bothered me a lot more than I was comfortable admitting to myself, but maybe it was a blessing in disguise. At least this way I didn't have to see the disappointment in her eyes again.

Then, suddenly, Gabrielle laughed, her face lighting up, and she wiped a tear from her eye. "He squeezed my hand. He heard me. He's still with us." She lowered his hand gently back into the glowing water. "I've got you, baby. I'm not going anywhere."

"I really don't think this is a good idea—" Bethany began.

Gabrielle cut her off. "Stop it, Bethany. Just stop it. It'll work. It has to."

Under the golden-hued water, Thornton lay like a corpse, his eyes closed and his hands clasped over his chest.

Twenty-four

With nothing more to be done for Thornton but wait and let the Methusal spring do its job, Isaac decided it was as good a time as any for a good old-fashioned interrogation. His questions ran the gamut of predictability: Who was I? Why had I lied to Bethany and Thornton? What was my mission? Who was Underwood, what was my connection to him, and what did he want with the box? Easy enough questions to answer—most of them, anyway—if I were at all interested in cooperating, but I wasn't about to tell him anything. Someone had sent the shadowborn to the safe house to kill us and steal the box, and the more I thought about it, the more Isaac became my prime suspect.

Bethany said mages like him were powerful enough to carry magic inside them without becoming infected, but what if she was wrong about that? I'd seen proof that Isaac carried magic inside him. What if it had infected him after all, made him decide he wanted the box for himself and the rest of us out of the way? The clues were as clear as day in my head. Isaac had sent us to the safe house. He knew where we would be, and with his knowledge of the safe house he could tell the shadowborn exactly where to go so the ward couldn't hide it from them. But why would Isaac send the revenant of Bennett to get me out of the way? What was the point of that?

"I asked you a question, Trent," Isaac said, interrupting my thoughts. He stood in front of me, crossing his arms over his chest. Philip and Bethany flanked him, waiting, their faces like stone. Bethany was finally looking at me, but there was a coldness in her blue eyes that felt like ice. I liked it better before, when she wasn't looking at me at all. "What were you planning to do with the Van Lente Box?" Isaac pressed. "Give it to Underwood? Sell it?"

I smirked up at him from where I sat tied to the chair. "You know, you didn't need magic to put me to sleep. Listening to you talk would have done the trick just fine."

"Just answer the question," Bethany said. "The sooner you do, the sooner we can figure out what to do with you."

Her voice was colder than I'd ever heard it. I'd blown any chance she would trust me again. She probably hated me. I deserved it, I supposed, but that didn't make it any better.

"You told me you wanted to destroy the box because it was the only way you'd be free," Bethany continued. "What did you mean? Free from what? Or was that just another lie?" I kept my eyes on Isaac and didn't answer. She continued, growing more frustrated, "So what was the plan, Trent? You knew the shadowborn were coming to the safe house, so you came back to . . . what? To look like a hero? To get us to trust you so we'd take you to the box? It's not like you were in any real danger from the shadowborn, right? You knew they couldn't kill you. Not permanently, anyway."

Damn, she really knew how to push my buttons. I wanted to tell her she was wrong about me, but I couldn't risk giving Isaac any information. Instead, I turned away from her. It was just as well. I couldn't stand the way she was looking at me.

"Bethany said you claim to have amnesia," Isaac pressed. "You'll forgive me if I don't believe it. Pretending not to have any memories is a long con to play, Trent. Sooner or later, you're going to slip up. It's inevitable. You might as well come clean now."

I looked up at him sharply, trying to bite back my anger, but the floodgates broke. "It's not a lie."

Standing next to Isaac, Philip said, "Sure it's not. You know who lies about who they are? Criminals. Thieves. Spies."

I glared at him, forcing myself to keep my mouth shut. Why couldn't the others see it? Why couldn't they piece it together the way I had? Maybe Isaac had cast some kind of spell on them.

Philip let out a frustrated groan. "This is bullshit. Give me five minutes alone with him and I'll get him talking."

"That's not how we do things," Isaac said. "You know that."

Philip shook his head. "Humans. I'll never understand you. Trust me, the best way to loosen his tongue is to tear part of it out. But if you're not going to do that, and he's not going to talk anyway, you might as well just get Gabrielle to do her Vulcan mindmeld thing and get it over with."

Isaac nodded, taking a deep breath. "I was hoping it wouldn't come to that, but I don't think he's left us much choice." He turned to Gabrielle, who was still kneeling on the carpet beside the clawfoot tub where Thornton lay submerged, still holding his hand in the water. "Gabrielle? I'm sorry, I wouldn't ask if it weren't important, but we need you."

She turned to Isaac, the golden hue of the water reflecting on her face. She looked angry. "Not now. Find some other way."

"I would if I could," he said. "None of us have your special talent. You're the only one who can get inside his mind and tell us what you see."

"Wait—what?" I stiffened in the chair. Were they serious? Could Gabrielle really do that? Of course she could, I realized. At this point it was foolish to be skeptical about anything these people were capable of. Still, withholding information from Isaac was the only leverage I had, and if she told him everything, I'd lose that.

Gabrielle let go of Thornton's hand and stood up with a sigh. "Fine, but let's keep it quick." She walked over to me, inhaled a deep, steadying breath, and held my face in her hands. One was still wet from the tub, the spell in the water tingling against my skin like the brush of a feather. I tried to pull away from her, but with my wrists bound behind the chair there was nowhere to go.

"Don't do this," I said.

But it was too late. She was already in my head. I could feel her there, leafing through the pages of my mind as effortlessly as she might a magazine on the beach. She closed her eyes and bent closer, close enough that I saw the wet trails her worried tears had left in the corners of her eyes and along the sides of her nose.

She pulled my memories to the surface, dredging them from the swamp of my mind. In my head, unbidden, I saw the abandoned Shell gas station on Empire Boulevard. She saw it, too. Then she peeled the image away like the outer layer of an onion, and beneath it was my room in the fallout shelter, sparse and dreary, the overhead light flickering dimly. She peeled that one away, too, and beneath it she found what she was looking for.

"It's Underwood," she said. "I see him."

The memory of Underwood's face hung like a ghost in my mind, remaining frozen there no matter how hard I fought to keep my mind blank. Gabrielle was too strong. Now that she was inside my head, she could look wherever she wanted and I couldn't stop her.

"Do you recognize him?" Isaac asked. "Is he someone you've seen before? Maybe under a different name?"

She shook her head, her eyes still closed. "No, I don't know him."

"But Trent does," Isaac pointed out. "Tell us what he knows."

She burrowed deeper into my mind, sorting through random images as if they were photographs: Underwood slapping my cheek and calling me a good dog. Underwood handing me a gun. Underwood sliding the address of the warehouse across the table to me. I was surprised at how vivid it all was, the colors, the sounds, even the smell of Underwood's plentiful cologne. With Gabrielle along for the ride, the memories felt as fresh as if I were living them for the first time.

She laid open my mind, picking over my most private memories like Thanksgiving leftovers. She effortlessly pried them free and told the others what she saw—a thief who couldn't remember his past, the low-level Brooklyn crime boss who took him in, and the mission to steal the box for an anonymous buyer in return for the information Underwood claimed to have found. I felt exposed, helpless, but most of all, hearing it spelled out so matter-of-factly, I felt foolish for having believed Underwood for as long as I did. He was a criminal, a master of lying to get what he wanted. I'd been an idiot to think he wouldn't lie to me, too.

"So Underwood gave him the address of the warehouse," Bethany said, talking about me as though I weren't there. "That explains how he got past the ward. I thought there was something off about his story. But how did Underwood know we were there?"

Gabrielle found another memory: Underwood disappearing behind the black door. "He heard it from a mobster named Bennett, who belonged to a syndicate that owns the warehouse," she said. "Underwood tortured him for the information. He killed him."

"So Trent was telling the truth about that, at least," Bethany said. "Bennett was the name of the dead man he saw at the safe house. He told me he knew Bennett, he just didn't say how."

"Now we know," Isaac said. "Bennett is connected to Underwood, too. They all are. So who is he, and why haven't we heard of him before?"

My breathing fell into sync with Gabrielle's, to the point where I couldn't tell which breaths were hers and which were mine. The longer she spent inside my head, the more our minds became entwined, knotting together like tree roots. Other memories began to bleed through into my own, memories I didn't recognize until I realized they weren't mine. They were hers. Most of them were of Thornton; her thoughts of him were still the rawest, closest to the surface. The fallout shelter faded from my mind, and I saw Gabrielle and Thornton kissing on a hilltop beneath a bright full moon and a sky full of stars. Their hands were clasped, their wrists bound by shiny white ribbons that reflected the moonlight. Figures moved around them, squat and low to the ground, dressed in ceremonial robes and intoning in high-pitched voices. Her memory filled in the blanks for me: They were goblins, and with that knowledge came a sudden understanding of what it was I was seeing.

Gabrielle and Thornton were engaged to be married. They'd done it in secret in Prospect Park, in a ritual the goblins called the Binding Oath, but they hadn't told the others yet. They'd planned to surprise them with the news once Thornton had finished securing the box, but now . . . Now she didn't know what would happen. Her concern for Thornton, her deep regret at not being at his side when he needed her, the overwhelming fear she felt at the prospect of her beloved dying in pain, the infinite sadness she'd pushed down just so she could function—it all put a crack in her heart, a crack that I felt, too. I knew with certainty now that she wasn't the traitor. She loved Thornton too much to ever put him in danger.

She winced suddenly, and the memory was yanked forcefully from my mind. I felt her defensiveness, her outrage that I had seen something so private. It shouldn't have happened. Distracted by her worries, she'd carelessly allowed her own memories to seep through.

Isaac spoke again. "Does Trent know who Underwood was planning to sell the box to?"

Gabrielle dug tentatively through my mind once more, this time making sure to keep her own memories shielded. "He doesn't know. Underwood never told him. The buyers are always kept anonymous."

Isaac grunted, frustrated. Suddenly I was very happy that Underwood hadn't told me anything. Probably, Isaac only wanted to know who his competition was so he could send the shadowborn after them, too. The longer he was in the dark, the harder it would be for him to keep up the charade. Sooner or later he would slip up and the others would learn the truth about him.

"He doesn't trust you, Isaac," Gabrielle said. "He thinks you're the one who summoned the shadowborn to kill them at the safe house. He thinks you want the box for yourself."

Damn. That was stupid of me. I should have realized Gabrielle could do more than see my memories while she was in my mind. She could hear my thoughts, too.

Isaac bent closer to me. "*You* don't trust *me*? That's a laugh, coming from a thief and a liar."

"So why did you do it?" I asked him. "Why send the shadowborn after the box when Bethany and Thornton were going to bring it here anyway? Was it because you wanted it all to yourself, or were you just impatient?"

His eyebrows lifted in indignation. "What? You're the one who summoned the shadowborn, not me. You were gone when they came to the house. That's a little suspicious, don't you think?"

"How long do you think you can keep this up?" I asked. "You've got them all trusting you, but sooner or later they'll figure out all roads lead back to you. What are you going to do then? Kill them all?"

The confusion on Isaac's face looked real. He was a good actor, I'd give him that. He straightened up and said, "He's lost his damn mind."

"No, he's just gotten very good at lying," Bethany said.

I ignored her and kept my focus on Isaac. "You almost got away with it, too. Luckily, I came back to stop you."

He shook his head. His eyes dipped down to the blood on my collar and shirt. "That blood is yours, isn't it? Bethany told us what happened, how you died and came back." He pulled something white and crumpled out of his pocket. It was an old, used bandage, stained dark on one side with dried blood. "We took this off your back while you were sleeping. There was nothing under it. No scratches, no scars. Your wounds were gone. No more games, Trent. I want the truth. What are you?"

I laughed in his face.

Isaac clenched his jaw. "This is getting us nowhere. Gabrielle, find out what he's hiding. He's obviously something more than human."

She dug deeper, a drill boring through my mind. Images sped by like a flip book as she moved back through days, weeks, months, a year—all the way back to my first memory: the brick wall. She tried to peel that memory back, too, to see what was under it.

She flinched suddenly, opening her eyes and letting out a small gasp. "I can't."

Isaac put a hand on her shoulder. "I know it's a lot to ask. I know you'd rather be with Thornton right now, but I wouldn't ask this of you if there weren't so much at stake. You have to try."

"It's not that," she said. "I can only see what Trent knows, and he doesn't know what he is. Beyond that, there's a barrier, a mental block I can't get past."

"Can you force your way past it?"

She blew out her breath. "I don't know."

"We need to know exactly what we're dealing with," he said. "Please try."

She sighed and closed her eyes again. Her mind pushed hard into mine, trying to force its way through the barrier to whatever lay on the other side. There was nothing I could do to stop her, and I wasn't sure I wanted to. Because if it worked and she got through, she could unearth the answers I'd been looking for.

Then the pain came. It was excruciating, like a razor-sharp knife filleting my brain. The harder she pushed the more a sharp pressure mounted in my head, as if someone had put my brain in a vise and was turning it tighter. Bright spots flashed behind my eyes.

"Push past it, Gabrielle," Isaac said. "Push past the barrier."

Blood trickled from my nostrils, and still she pushed. It felt like my head was going to explode.

Gabrielle screamed suddenly and broke contact with me, both physically and mentally. She stumbled suddenly, thrown back as if some invisible force had pushed her away from me. I slumped forward in the chair, as far as my bound wrists would let me. Breathing hard, I spat on the carpet between my feet. My saliva was tinged with blood. The pain in my head dampened slowly, the vise unwinding.

Gabrielle swayed, dizzy, and put her hands to her head. Bethany held her steady. "Are you okay?"

"What happened?" Isaac demanded.

Gabrielle shook her head and stammered, "I—I don't know. It felt like something attacked me. Pushed me away when I got too close. It was like touching a live wire."

Isaac turned to me, his face red with anger. "What did you do to her?"

I spat more blood onto the carpet. "What did *I* do to *her*? I'm the one who just had his brain squeezed like a sponge, and in case you hadn't noticed, you fucking overgrown leprechaun, I'm the one who's bleeding."

Isaac took a step toward me, his hands balling into fists. "If you hurt her . . ."

"Don't, Isaac, I'm okay," Gabrielle said. She shook her head like she was trying to clear out a thick layer of dust. "It wasn't his fault. Our minds were locked, I would know if he meant to do it. This was involuntary, some kind of defense mechanism. It was like feedback in my head. Psychic feedback." She stared into my eyes so intensely it was like she thought she could see into my soul if she just looked hard enough. "What *are* you?"

"If I had a nickel for every time I've asked myself that, I could buy this place," I told her. "You're the one who was digging around in my head. You tell me."

She stared at me for a long moment. "All I know is that there's something very powerful inside of you, Trent. Something I've never experienced before."

"All the more reason to keep trying," Isaac said.

"No," Gabrielle replied, shaking her head. "I've had enough, and so has he. It's time to let him go, Isaac. I know you're worried, I know how important it is that the box stays safe, but he's not a danger to us. I don't think he ever was. He didn't even know magic existed before yesterday."

"Are you sure we can trust him?" Isaac asked.

"He's a thief," Bethany interrupted angrily. "He tried to steal the box, remember? He pulled a gun on me, for God's sake! As far as I'm concerned, he can rot in that chair."

"Underwood was manipulating him, he knows that now," Gabrielle explained. "As strange as it sounds, he really was trying to protect you, Bethany. He likes you." Gabrielle smirked at me. "Also, he likes your tattoo."

Crap. What other memories had she seen in my head?

Bethany blanched. "He *what*?"

"Trent made some really stupid choices, I won't argue that, but he never would have hurt you. He's kind of sweet on you."

Oh God, could this get any worse?

"He's got a funny way of showing it," Bethany said.

"Can I just say something?" I interjected.

"No!" Bethany snapped.

Gabrielle turned to Isaac. "There's no need to keep him bound. Let him go."

Isaac took a deep breath. Then he did something I didn't expect. He freed me. With a wave of his hand, the magical bonds around my wrists vanished. I pulled my arms forward from behind the chair and rubbed my wrists and sore shoulders.

Bethany crossed her arms and turned away.

"You're going to have to trust me, Trent," Isaac said.

"You're going to have to trust me, too," I told him.

"I trust Gabrielle," he said. "She vouched for you, and that's good enough for me. But I'll be keeping a very close eye on you, Trent. Don't prove her wrong."

I turned to Gabrielle. "Thanks. I owe you one."

She shook her head. "You've had so many second chances, Trent. Most people don't even get one. Maybe it's time you started putting them to good use. You can start by stopping all the lies. And you, Isaac, instead of tying people up and using my abilities to satisfy your own curiosity, don't you think you should make sure the box is secured before the equinox gets here?" She walked back to the tub, knelt down beside it, and reached into the water to take Thornton's hand again. "Thornton went through hell to help you both get to this point. The least you can do is stop this pissing contest and make sure the sacrifice he made was worth it."

Isaac nodded, his jaw tight. With a quick, final glance at me, he walked to the desk at the far end of the room. Philip went with him, leaving me alone with Bethany. She still had her back to me. I couldn't blame her for being furious.

I stood up out of the chair. "Bethany, I'm sorry—"

She turned around and slapped me hard across the cheek. "If you *ever* point a gun at me again . . ."

I rubbed my cheek. It stung like a bastard. The others stared at us, the slap catching their attention, but they didn't interfere. I supposed they thought this was something we needed to hash out ourselves. I also supposed they were right.

"Okay, I had that coming," I said. "I'm trying to apologize, Bethany. I'm sorry. It was a stupid thing to do. I just—I didn't know how to tell you about Underwood. I didn't want you to . . ." I trailed off, feeling foolish. What was the point? She would never forgive me. Why should she?

"You didn't want me to what?" she demanded, her hands on her hips.

I struggled for the words. They didn't come easily. "If I told you the truth about who I worked for and the real reason I was at that warehouse . . ." I trailed off and started over. "You and Thornton are the only friends I've got, Bethany. I don't think I could have handled it if you turned your back on me."

"So you thought it would be better to pull a gun on me instead? How crazy are you?"

I sighed. "I wanted to get the box away from you before it was too late, before Underwood's enforcers showed up. That's who those two men were. It was clear you weren't going to just let me take it, so yeah, welcome to the way my brain works. It's kind of messed up in there. Just ask Gabrielle. She had a front-row seat."

"You really thought I'd turn my back on you? You didn't think I would help you?"

I shrugged. "It's not like anyone's ever given a damn about me."

She opened her mouth to say something, but then crouched down instead and took a tissue from her pants pocket. She used it to dab up the blood-tinged saliva I'd spat on the carpet. That was Bethany in a nutshell, I thought. Everything had to be just so. "You've got some on your face, too," she said, not looking up at me.

I touched under my nose and my fingers came back tipped in red. I wiped the blood off with my sleeve. "Thanks. I don't know what happened, only that it hurt like hell when Gabrielle tried to force her way into the parts of my life I can't remember."

"That's probably what made the defense mechanism kick in," she said. "Are you okay now?" The question came out robotically, a matter of courtesy, not concern. Maybe the chasm between us was too wide for a simple apology to bridge.

"I'm fine," I said. I crouched down next to her on the carpet, glanced over my shoulder at the others, and lowered my voice. "Bethany, whatever you think of me right now—and I wouldn't blame you if you hated me—I need you put it aside for a moment and listen very carefully. You can't trust Isaac. He's dangerous."

She kept dabbing the tissue over the stain on the rug and moving it in tight circles.

"Think about it," I continued. "He knew we were at Ingrid's house. He sent us there. You said yourself the enemy knows our every move. It could only have been an inside job, and Isaac is the only one who could have pulled it off."

She put the wadded-up tissue in her pocket and finally looked at me. "I know."

My eyebrows shot upward in surprise. "You know?"

"You're right that it could only have been an inside job, but you're wrong about Isaac. I know him a lot better than you do, Trent. He's a good man. He's done a lot for me. I spent my whole childhood being shuffled from one foster home to another, and after I turned eighteen they kicked me out onto the street. It was another ten years before Isaac found me. He cleaned me up and gave me a job. He's the closest thing I've ever had to a father. What you said before about no one ever giving a damn? That's how I felt my whole life, until I met him. He wouldn't betray us. I trust him with my life. I trust *all* of them with my life. I can't imagine any of them betraying us."

"But someone did," I said. "It's the only explanation."

She nodded. "Here's the problem, Trent. Someone tried to kill us at the safe house, someone who must have told the shadowborn we were there, but I know these people. It couldn't be any of them. There's only one wild card in the deck. Only one person it could be. You."

I blinked. "It wasn't, I swear."

"I know it wasn't," she said, standing up again. "But now you see the problem."

I did, and it was made all the more vexing by the fact that Bethany had an annoying habit of always being right. Frankly, she hadn't been wrong about anything yet. Which meant I probably owed Isaac an apology. I wasn't looking forward to that.

Still, if the traitor wasn't any of the others, and it wasn't me, who was left?

Twenty-five

At the table under the stained-glass windows, Isaac and Philip inspected the box. The windows flashed with a sudden bright light, followed by the distant boom of thunder. A heavy rain began to patter the glass, then wash down it in sheets as the storm clouds that had been gathering all day finally opened.

Isaac glanced up at me. He still didn't fully trust me. I couldn't blame him. It was going to take a long time to earn his trust. The question was, would I stick around long enough for that to happen? What was my plan, exactly? I didn't know. On the one hand, part of me wanted to stay. These people were freaks like me. I felt like I belonged with them, like I was a part of something in a way I never felt before. On the other hand, there were answers out there I needed to find, and I had unfinished business with Underwood.

Isaac ran his hand reverentially over the box lid, his fingertips tracing the words written along the metal crest. "*In de eenheid, sterkte,*" he read aloud. "Dutch for *in unity, strength.* It's the family crest of Willem Van Lente. The box is authentic, the same one Van Lente hid away four centuries ago. The question is, is it still inside? Because if it's not, we're all still in danger." He took a deep breath. "We're going to have to open it."

Bethany glanced nervously at the box. "Is it safe?"

"It should be. The equinox isn't until tomorrow." Isaac bent to inspect the lock. It was bulky and hinged, the kind of lock you'd see on a steamer trunk, but instead of a keyhole there were three rotating cylinders. A combination lock, only there weren't any numbers, just strange, blocky symbols.

Isaac tapped the lock with his finger, then narrowed his eyes and rubbed his tightly cropped beard in concentration. "It's hexlocked. The box can't be opened by force or by magic. Willem Van Lente didn't want anyone finding it, and he certainly didn't want anyone opening it. I should have known he wasn't going to make it easy."

Philip nodded, the box's reflection bouncing in his mirrored sunglasses. "So what's the combination? His birthday?"

"I doubt it's anything so mundane," Isaac said. "The symbols are a kind of puzzle. All we need to do is figure it out."

"Like in Gregor's tunnel," I said. "Could it be Ehrlendarr again?"

"It's not," Isaac said, "but it's definitely an older language. Hold on a moment." He took a hand mirror out of one of the table drawers and held it up to the combination lock. "Ah! I thought so! Look at this." All I saw in the mirror were the same symbols backward. Isaac, on the other hand, saw an epiphany. "It's so simple I should have known. They're Egyptian hieroglyphs, only reversed. Van Lente studied magic in Egypt with the Order of Horus before he relocated to New Amsterdam in the seventeenth century." He spun the cylinders, examining each of the hieroglyphs. Then he grinned. "Oh, you clever, clever magician. It's perfect."

"What is?" I asked.

"The combination," he said. "Back then, very few people would have known the password to the Order of Horus's inner sanctum, especially in the New World. That's how Van Lente ensured that even if the box were found, no one would be able to open it. Lucky for us, I've been to the inner sanctum myself. Now, let's see. It's been a while." He started turning the cylinders one at a time. "First is life, the ankh. Then growth, the papyrus stem. And finally Horus, the falcon."

The lock sprang open with a sharp *clank*. I moved closer. I wasn't going to miss this. So many people wanted what was inside it, were willing to kill or die for it, that I had to see with my own eyes what could possibly be worth all the trouble.

Isaac opened another drawer in the desk, took out a box of thin latex gloves, and pulled a pair over his hands. Then he gently opened the lid of the box. White wisps of steam drifted out and dissipated in the air around him, as if the box were full of dry ice. He squinted into it. Then he tipped the box over.

Something big, round, and as gray as gunmetal rolled out, landing on the table with a heavy *thud*. Tendrils of steam clung to its every fold, crease, and tip. My mouth dropped open in surprise.

It was a severed head. A gargoyle head, to be precise, only it looked a hell of a lot bigger than the head of any gargoyle I'd seen. Its eyes were closed but its mouth was open, frozen in a silent roar that revealed rows of sharp teeth. Its tusks had been broken off, though whether from injury or simply to make the enormous gargoyle's head fit within the confines of the box I couldn't guess. At the stump of its neck, bone and dried gray muscle tissue were still visible where a clean, precise cut had severed the head from its body.

I wasn't sure what I'd expected to see, but this wasn't it. Not the head of a giant, dead gargoyle. It didn't make sense. How could all the danger we'd faced, all the deaths, have been over *this*? Why would anyone want it?

Isaac lifted the head in his gloved hands and inspected it, as excited as an appraiser evaluating a rare, lost antique. "Ladies and gentlemen, you are in the presence of royalty. Meet Stryge, the first king of the gargoyles. It looks like he hasn't aged a day since Willem Van Lente cut off his head four hundred years ago."

Ingrid had mentioned Stryge was the king of the gargoyles before the Black Knight came along, I remembered, but that was all she'd said about him. "What happened?" I asked.

"For millennia, Stryge was the scourge of Europe," Isaac explained. "He viewed all human life as vermin, an infestation deserving nothing short of extermination. Finally, in the eleventh century, the magicians of Europe banded together and banished Stryge and his gargoyles across the ocean to North America. Stryge continued his reign of terror here, leading the gargoyles in attacks on the natives and, later, the Dutch settlers of New Amsterdam. By the time Willem Van Lente came to New Amsterdam in 1660, the gargoyles were regularly ambushing the trade routes between settlements. It was one massacre after another. No one came back alive. Some of the victims disappeared. Others were found in pieces, as if they'd been torn limb from limb.

"The authorities blamed the local Lenape Indians, but Van Lente suspected it wasn't the work of anything human. He decided to run his own covert investigation and learned from the Lenape elders that the attacks were perpetrated by creatures they called Mhuwe, man-eaters. Van Lente recognized them for what they were: gargoyles from the old country. He knew the only way to stop the slaughter was to cut off the head of the snake, as it were. Kill Stryge and leave the gargoyles powerless and in disarray without their leader. So he made a deal with the Lenape to fight Stryge together.

"The battle lasted weeks. The sacrifices Van Lente made were unbelievable. He cut off his own hand to create the Anubis Hand, the only weapon that could hurt Stryge, though even that wasn't enough. In the end, it took the combined might of all his magic and the entire Lenape nation to bring Stryge down."

I looked at the black, mummified fist of the Anubis Hand poking out of Thornton's coat pocket on the floor. Willem Van Lente's own hand. It was a crazy story. Completely unbelievable. But something itched in my mind, a kernel of a thought. Something about the Lenape Indians. I'd heard the name before.

"There are no records of Van Lente after the battle," Isaac went on. "He must have died from his wounds shortly after he hid the box. He gave his life to save New Amsterdam, but it was all in vain. Not long after, the Black Knight came out of nowhere, stepping in to fill the void as the gargoyles' new king and leading them in further acts of evil to this very day. Nothing changed. Willem Van Lente fought and died for nothing."

"Why did he bother hiding the head?" I asked. "I mean, we're talking about someone who cut off his own hand to make a magical weapon, right? If Van Lente was half the badass he sounds like, you'd think he would have stuck the head on a pike or something as a warning to the gargoyles not to mess with them anymore." Bethany and Isaac arched their eyebrows at me. "What? I'm not saying that's what *I* would do, but . . ."

Unlike the others, Philip smiled at me. "Nasty. I like the way you think."

I sighed. "Look, forget all that, you know what I mean. Why go through the trouble of a puzzle box and a hiding place? Why didn't he want anyone finding Stryge's head?"

Isaac gently replaced the head inside the box, closed the lid, and locked it again. "Lenape legend has it that if Stryge's head is reunited with his body during the equinox, he will awaken. Stryge has immense power, enough to destroy New York City and everyone in it. With his hatred of all humanity, I have no doubt that's exactly what he would do."

"Hold on, I thought you said Stryge was dead," I said.

"Not dead, exactly," Isaac replied. "Just dormant. Stryge is an Ancient. No one knows the full extent of their powers. Their magic is as alien to us as ours would be to the simplest single-celled organisms. The equinox, the precise moment when the Earth and the sun are perfectly aligned, is when the Ancients' powers are at their height. If Stryge's head and body are reunited at that moment, there's no telling what could happen. That's why we had to get this box to safety first."

"So Stryge's an Ancient like Gregor," I said.

"Only a hundred times worse," Bethany said. "Stryge was the most violent and hateful of the Ancients. If he were to wake up, he would be a destructive force the likes of which this city has never seen."

"But Ancient or not, how can he still be alive without his head? That doesn't make sense."

Philip pointed his thumb at me. "I agree with Mr. Head-on-a-Pike here. I've seen firsthand what taking off someone's head can do. You don't come back from that." I didn't want to know what he meant about seeing it firsthand.

"The shadowborn at the safe house weren't dead when we found them, were they? Not even after their heads were cut off," Isaac said. "The barrier between life and death isn't as easily definable as you think, and it only gets harder to define when magic is involved. Consider this. Gargoyles don't honor their dead or have burial rituals. They don't give their dead much thought at all, except to cannibalize them for food during the lean hunting seasons. If they're this keen on reclaiming Stryge's head, it can only be for one reason: The Lenape legend is true. But what's really got me concerned is that gargoyles don't do anything without orders from their king. That means the Black Knight himself must want it. The only question is why. The Black Knight has ruled over the gargoyles for four hundred years. Why would he want to bring Stryge back? The gargoyles won't serve *two* kings."

"What if you've got it all wrong?" I said. "What if the Black Knight wants the head to make sure no one brings Stryge back?"

Isaac nodded. "I thought about that. If that's the case, it's the first time the Black Knight and I have ever seen eye to eye. But I suspect there's more to it. Frankly, I'll be happy if the equinox comes and goes without us ever finding out."

He carried the box over to one of the cluttered bookshelves. Sitting on a shelf in front of a few oversized tomes was a small, ancient-looking leather globe of the Earth on a polished stone stand. He pulled the globe forward, tipping it on a hidden lever in its base, and the bookshelf swung open on concealed hinges. Behind it was a metal door. There was no knob or handle, only a keypad. Isaac pressed a few of the keys in sequence, and the metal door swung open to reveal a doorway in the wall. Light poured out it, and a strange, deep hum.

Isaac's vault. This was where he kept the dangerous artifacts he sent the others to secure. It was also what he was protecting, I realized. The reason he didn't want any of his operations traced back to him. Unlike what was displayed around the room, the vault contained the big-ticket items, the truly powerful artifacts the Infected would kill for. If they got their hands on this collection, they would have the magical equivalent of a nuclear arsenal.

I couldn't see much of the vault's interior from where I stood, just what was on a few of the shelves by the door: a sword in a scabbard that glowed bright emerald green; a small statuette of a multiarmed figure that seemed to be vibrating like it couldn't sit still; a fleshy, tentacled mass inside a Mason jar that thrashed its limbs angrily against the glass; and money. Stacks of it. I'd never seen so much money in one place before. I'd figured Isaac was loaded, he'd have to be to afford a place this big in New York City, but this was beyond the pale. If *Forbes* ran a list of the richest mages in the world, I was sure he'd be at the top.

Isaac emerged empty-handed from the vault, closed the metal door, and pulled the leather globe again. The bookshelf swung shut. "It's safe now. Good work, everyone."

A sudden, bursting splash of water came from behind us. I turned around. Thornton sat up in the tub with a guttural cry. Gabrielle, still holding his hand, nearly fell backward in surprise.

I rushed to the side of the tub with Isaac, Philip, and Bethany at my heels. What was left of Thornton's shirt was translucent from the water, and through it I could see his skin had healed itself. The discolored patches of necrotic tissue were gone. The stitches had dissolved, and his scars had vanished. His face looked healthier, too. Fuller and less corpse-like.

Gabrielle gripped his hand tightly in both of hers. "Thornton! Thornton, are you okay?"

"God!" he cried through gritted teeth. "It feels like I'm being skinned alive!"

"Your nerve endings are healing," she said. "Give it time. The pain will pass, I promise."

Thornton turned to her. He stared at her hands for a long moment, then murmured, "I—I can feel your hands." He put his other hand over hers and laughed. "I can *feel* them!"

She kissed his hands. Her chin quivered with emotion. "Oh, Thornton, I'm so sorry. I should have been with you. I should have come running."

"It's not her fault, it's mine," Isaac said, putting a hand on Thornton's shoulder. "But she put up one hell of a fight, believe me."

Thornton smiled and touched Gabrielle's face. "I bet you did."

"I'm so sorry, Thornton," she said again.

"I was worried I'd never . . ." He winced suddenly. ". . . see you again . . ." He grunted in pain. "Ungh . . . my whole body's . . . on fire!"

"That's just the Methusal spring doing its job," Gabrielle said. "Your body is healing. Hang in there, baby. It'll be over soon. You can do this."

Gathered around the tub, Isaac and Gabrielle wore the same hopeful expression. Philip looked as enigmatic as ever, his eyes hidden behind his mirrored shades, his face neutral. And then there was Bethany. No matter how hard she was trying to hide it, she didn't look happy. She'd had her doubts from the start that this would work. But she was wrong. She had to be. This time, just this once, maybe Bethany *wasn't* right about something.

She'd said there was no spell that could bring the dead completely back to life, but Gabrielle's plan was clearly working. Thornton looked like his old self again, the way he'd looked when I first met him. No, he looked better, actually—Thornton had already been dead the first time I saw his human form. Now he looked *alive*. This changed everything. It should have been impossible, but here he was, living proof that magic could conquer death after all.

Thornton finally noticed me squatting by the side of the tub. "You," he said weakly. "Did anyone check this son of a bitch for a gun? He's got a nasty habit of pointing one right at you."

"It's okay, baby," Gabrielle said, stroking Thornton's hair. "Everything's okay. He's with us now. We came to an understanding."

"I'm sorry about before, Thornton," I said. "I panicked and lost my judgment. I hope you can forgive me."

Thornton looked up at Bethany. She nodded and said, "It was classic Trent, acting without thinking first. But it's fine. Gabrielle read his mind. He's not a threat."

Thornton's eyes focused on me again. "Fine, but do it again and I'll bite your fucking face off. At least you stood up for us in front of those two creeps." He winced in pain. Through clenched teeth he added, "Just tell me you didn't give them the box. Tell me it's safe."

I nodded. "It's in Isaac's vault now, safe and sound."

"See? Everything's going to be okay," Gabrielle said.

Thornton cried out suddenly, an agonized sound. He must have been in intense pain. We looked at each other around the tub, not knowing what to do. Even Isaac seemed at a loss. Thornton writhed in the water and banged the side of the tub with his fist, making Gabrielle jump.

"What is it?" she asked, her voice high with panic. She gripped his free hand tightly. "Baby, what's happening?"

"The amulet," he groaned. "Ungh, something's wrong . . . Not now, I'm not ready . . ."

His whole body thrashed in the tub, the golden water sloshing over the sides. He was seizing. I tried to hold him steady, but he was shaking too hard. The others reached in around me, and together we stabilized him as best we could.

Tears streamed down Gabrielle's face. "Baby, talk to me, what's wrong?"

"It . . . stopped . . ." he said, his voice hoarse. His body thumped against the porcelain as another seizure rocked him. His contracting muscles felt as hard as rock under my hands. When the seizure passed, I let go of him, albeit hesitantly.

Gabrielle grabbed his head and turned his face to her. "Baby, look at me!"

He grimaced in pain. "I'm sorry, Gabrielle . . . I tried . . . I tried to stay . . ."

"Baby, don't talk like that!"

He touched her face with his hand. She held it to her cheek, her fingers wrapped around the leather bracelet she'd given him. "But at least," he said, "at least . . . I got to touch you again . . . and feel it. . . ."

He cried out suddenly. A shaft of blinding light burst out of the amulet. It shot from Thornton's chest up to the ceiling, where it turned to billowing white smoke, swirling like a maelstrom between the chandeliers. The light kept pouring from the amulet, the blazing column disappearing into the center of the smoky vortex. There was a loud, sharp crack, as if the world itself had snapped in two, and then, as suddenly as it started, the light stopped. The smoke curled in on itself and vanished, leaving only the sharp smell of ozone in the air.

Thornton fell back limply, his head lolling against the side of the tub. His eyes were open, staring at me, but there was nothing in them anymore.

"No, baby, come on," Gabrielle said. She took Thornton's head in her hands and tipped it toward her. "Come on, stay with me."

The room went quiet. We were too stunned, all of us, too shocked and grief-stricken to say anything. It looked wrong, how still Thornton was.

"Stay with me," Gabrielle said again.

A quiet mechanical clicking sound answered her. A moment later, the amulet dislodged itself, rising up out of Thornton's chest on its central spike. The four small red gems on its face, once so brightly pulsing with the amulet's energy, had turned smoky and dark.

Gabrielle shook her head defiantly. "No!" She put both hands on the amulet and pushed it back down, sinking the spike into the hole in Thornton's chest again. The amulet clicked and lifted itself out again. She pushed it back into his chest over and over like some horrible version of CPR compressions, but each time it refused to stay down. "Not like this," she insisted as she pushed it down one final time, tears streaming down her cheeks. "It doesn't end like this. Not until we're both old, not until we've done so much more."

Bethany put a hand on Gabrielle's arm, stopping her. In a hushed tone, she said, "The amulet only works once."

Gabrielle finally let go of it. She collapsed beside the tub, sobbing.

"I'm so sorry, Gabrielle," Bethany said. "The Methusal spring may have regenerated his skin and muscle, even his nerve endings, but Thornton was still dead. There was nothing you could do to change that. Nobody could."

Gabrielle clung to Thornton's hand. Even when Bethany tried to get her to let go of it, she wouldn't.

I looked down at him, my breath coming in short, startled bursts. I drew my hand gently down his face, closing his eyes.

The full weight of it hit me then. Until this moment, Thornton's death had seemed like a technicality—he was dead but still with us, still cracking jokes and fighting alongside us. The possibility that Gabrielle's spell could reverse his condition had seemed so feasible. But Bethany was right. From the start, she'd said there was nothing we could do to save Thornton. I hadn't listened, but I should have. Bethany was always right. It wasn't fair, but she was always goddamn right.

Now, long overdue, it struck me with the force of a sucker punch I should have seen coming.

Thornton was dead.

Twenty-six

I helped them move Thornton's body to the antique Queen Anne couch on the far side of the room. Philip went upstairs and brought down a white sheet. He covered Thornton with it. I felt like a hole had been torn inside me, a bitter, angry emptiness. Beneath that white sheet, Thornton's body was good as new from the Methusal spring. Fully healed, yet still dead. It was a cold and merciless irony, courtesy of a world that didn't give a damn.

Gabrielle sat on the edge of the couch, her head bowed in grief. The others gave her time alone with Thornton as they took the tub away and drained it someplace. I stood in the empty spot in the middle of the room where the tub had been. There were divots in the carpet from the tub's clawed feet, the only reminder of where Thornton had died. Soon they would fade away, as if they'd never been there at all, and that only made me angrier.

I watched Gabrielle and thought of the goblin Binding Oath she'd taken with Thornton. It'd been the happiest day of her life. I could only imagine what she was feeling now. Gabrielle peeled back the white sheet to reveal Thornton's face. With his eyes closed, he should have looked asleep, but instead he just looked . . . empty. She stroked his cheek.

The others came back. Bethany sat beside her, putting her arm around Gabrielle's shoulders. Isaac whispered words of comfort. I stood apart from them, still an outsider. The four of them had a connection that bound them tight, a shared history and a trust that had developed over time. Those were things I'd never had with anyone, things Underwood had taught me were weaknesses to be exploited, but now, seeing the way they cared for each other, I understood it was what I'd been missing all along. A sense of belonging, of family. I wanted it more than anything.

Isaac came over to me. His face was long, and even paler than before. He sighed and said, "We still need to find out everything we can about Underwood. I could use your help."

"Why bother?" I asked. "Stryge's head is safe now."

"Because I want to know why your boss wanted it," Isaac said. "How did he even know about it? It's not common knowledge."

I shrugged. "He has buyers, people who commission him to find valuable items. One of them must have been familiar with the story."

He nodded, but he didn't look convinced. "Come with me, there's something I'd like you to look at."

We returned to the long table beneath the stained-glass windows. Isaac pulled up a chair and opened a sleek, expensive-looking laptop on the table. He tapped a few keys. The six video monitors on the wall flickered to life.

Faces began appearing on the screens, a different one on each monitor, and a few seconds later they were replaced with new ones. Some were photographs, others were paintings and drawings. The faces were male and female, old and young, every color and ethnicity; some were human and others, such as the tentacle-faced monstrosity that appeared briefly on one of the screens, were definitely not.

"What is this?"

"I've been putting together a database of the Infected," Isaac said. "It's far from complete, but it's a good start. What I'd like you to do is watch the faces and keep an eye out for Underwood, or anyone you've seen him having dealings with."

"Underwood isn't infected," I said.

"How do you know that?" he asked. "If he knows about Stryge's head, odds are he knows about magic."

He had a point, though I found it hard to believe. If Underwood were infected it would mean he had magic—which meant he wouldn't need enforcers like Tomo and Big Joe. He wouldn't need me, either. But I dutifully watched the parade of faces for a while, studying each one closely before moving on to the next. One resembled a woman who'd been genetically crossbred with a bat. Another looked for all the world like the pickled remains of a human head in a glass globe. "I really don't think these are his kind of people," I said.

"Just keep looking," Isaac said. "Let me know if you see anyone you recognize, anyone at all."

Another image flashed onscreen. This one caught my eye. A figure in a red hooded robe with a golden skull mask over his face. "Wait, hold on."

Isaac tapped the keyboard and the image froze on the screen. "This one?"

"I've seen him before. I'm sure of it."

"Where?" Isaac asked.

"Outside the safe house. He was standing across the street, watching the house. And then he disappeared."

"Why didn't you say anything?" Bethany demanded. She came over from the couch to join us.

"There wasn't exactly a lot of time with the shadowborn trying to break down the door," I explained. "After that, with everything that happened, I guess it slipped my mind."

"He must have known we were in the house," Bethany said.

"How? The ward was still active."

Isaac tapped the keyboard, bringing up more information. The picture of the hooded figure appeared on five of the monitors, while the sixth filled with text. "He's called Melanthius," Isaac said, reading off the screen. "He's half high priest and half manservant to an entity called Reve Azrael, also known as the Mother of Wraiths, and the Mistress of the Dead."

"Sounds charming," I said. "What do you mean by *entity*? Or do I not want to know?"

"No one has ever seen her," he said. "No one knows what she looks like, or even what she is. All we know is that she's a powerful necromancer."

"So she can create revenants," I said. "Like the one of Bennett that came to the safe house."

"Precisely," Isaac said.

"But what would she want with Stryge's head?" Bethany asked.

He frowned. "That I don't know."

I stared at the picture on the monitor. Melanthius's golden skull stared back at me, expressionless.

I spent another half hour reviewing the rest of the faces in Isaac's database, but nothing else jumped out at me. No Underwood, and no one I'd seen him have dealings with. I wasn't exactly surprised. Underwood was a violent and dangerous criminal, but one of the Infected? No.

"Damn. It was worth a shot," Isaac said, leaning back in his chair. "So either Underwood's new to the game, or I'm wrong about him and he's not a player at all. Either way, we're no closer to an answer than we were before."

From the couch, Gabrielle said, "There might be another way." She covered Thornton's face with the sheet and came over to us, wiping away her tears.

Bethany touched Gabrielle's arm. "Are you sure you want to do this? You don't have to."

Gabrielle patted Bethany's hand and forced a thin smile. "It's okay. Thornton would want us to carry on. He understood the importance of what we're doing. Just . . . Philip, can you stay with him? I don't want him to be alone."

"He's dead, he's not going to care," the vampire said flatly. Isaac shot him an angry look. Philip crossed his arms. "Fine," he said, and went to sit beside Thornton's body. "Humans. I'll never understand you."

Gabrielle turned to Isaac. She was putting up a strong front, but I could tell she was still in shock and deeply hurting. "There's an old gas station in Brooklyn with a fallout shelter beneath it. That's where Underwood operates from," she said. Then, amazingly, she gave them the exact street address of the station on Empire Boulevard. She turned to me with a sheepish grin. "Sorry, I was in your head. I saw everything, even the street signs."

Jesus. It was a good thing I didn't have a bank account or I'd have to change my PIN number.

Isaac tapped furiously at the keyboard. A moment later, all six monitors lit up with images of the Shell station, each from a different angle, some far away, some as close as across the street. Rain fell across the images like strings of static. The sight of the station made my chest squeeze tight. I hadn't realized how much I hated that place until now.

"That's it," I said.

"These are live feeds from security and traffic cameras all over the area," Isaac explained. "I wish I could get closer, but this is the best I can—"

A bright flash on each of the video monitors interrupted him. The walls of the gas station blew apart in a huge, silent fireball—the cameras Isaac hacked into had no sound, only video. Towering gouts of flame shot into the sky. Weakened by the blast, the signpost tipped over, and I watched in shock as, from every conceivable angle, the broken HELL sign that had so aptly defined my life for the past year fell into the flaming wreckage.

Bethany and Gabrielle gasped in surprise. Philip came running from the couch. I stayed frozen in place, watching the gas station burn. "What happened?" I demanded. It came out as little more than a whisper. I turned to Isaac. "Did you do something?"

He looked back at me, his hands still on the keyboard of his laptop. "What do you mean, *do* something? It's a MacBook Pro, Trent, not NORAD missile command."

"Don't," I warned him. "You could have cast a spell, or—"

Philip appeared suddenly between us. "Back off," he snarled.

"It's all right, Philip, relax," Isaac said. He turned back to his laptop. Only then did I see how ashen his face was. He'd been as surprised by the explosion as I was.

"What happened?" I asked again.

Isaac shook his head. "I don't know. I'm seeing if there's a way to re-wind the feeds so we can find out. If the files are stored digitally on the same server, we might have a shot at it." His fingers danced across the keyboards. A moment later the images on the monitors reversed themselves. Flames and smoke retreated back into the building, the walls closing around them and sealing themselves whole again. The signpost lifted itself back up. Rain rose off the sidewalks into the sky, and cars sped backward along Empire Boulevard.

"Wait, there!" Bethany exclaimed. Isaac froze the images. She pointed at one of the monitors, where two shapes could be seen walking through the gas station parking lot. "Those are the men from the auto body shop," she said.

"Tomo and Big Joe," Gabrielle said before I had a chance to. It was eerie how much she knew about my life now.

Isaac began the playback again. Onscreen, Tomo and Big Joe walked with an aggressive gait, angry after their humiliation at the auto body shop. They weren't used to losing. The bravado and posturing also masked how worried they likely were about how Underwood would react once he learned the box had slipped through their fingers. Underwood didn't take kindly to failure. They entered the fallout shelter through the storm doors at the back of the station. Then all was quiet. No one else approached the gas station before it exploded.

"Whatever caused this, it must have happened inside the building," Isaac said.

We watched the feed unfold again. This time we could see that the blast didn't come from inside the abandoned gas station itself, but beneath it, from the fallout shelter.

There was no way anyone could have survived the explosion. I wondered if Underwood had been there, too. It was a possibility. After driving away from the auto body shop, he probably would have gone straight back to the fallout shelter to plan his next move.

Did that mean they were *all* dead?

"Wait, hold it," Gabrielle said suddenly. She'd been poring over the images on the monitors for clues, and now she pointed to one of the screens. The picture was angled from across Empire Boulevard, catercorner to the gas station and high above street level. A traffic camera. "Isaac, go back. Go back on this one."

The feed rewound as Isaac tapped the keyboard. The playback began again. This time I saw what had caught her eye. It was just barely visible behind the inferno, but it was there. It was unmistakable.

A flock of big, black birds taking off into the sky.

"Are those crows?" Bethany asked.

Isaac said, "The Black Knight."

I watched the birds fly into the sky until they were nothing but tiny digital dots. "What the hell was the Black Knight doing there?"

"Looking for you," Bethany said.

"Me? Why?"

"You're the only one who's ever taken him on and lived," she pointed out. "It's like Ingrid said, you got his attention. He must have traced your footsteps back to the gas station."

I looked at the raging fire on all six monitors. "So this was meant for *me*?"

Isaac shook his head, squinting at the screens. "Something's not right.

This kind of flagrant, wholesale destruction doesn't seem like the Black Knight's style at all—"

Philip interrupted, tensing suddenly. "Someone's here. Citadel's ward has been breached."

"What? That's impossible," Isaac said, standing out of his chair.

"Just like at the safe house," Bethany said. "It's happening again."

"What the hell is going on? Are wards just giving out all over the damn city?" Isaac demanded. "Philip, how many of them are there?"

Philip looked up at the ceiling, his lips pulling back from his sharp teeth. "I can hear them on the roof, but I can't see them. They're not giving off any body heat at all." He inhaled sharply through his nose, then cringed. "Ugh, they smell stale and dry, like dust."

A bright flash of lightning illuminated the stained-glass windows. Two silhouettes appeared in the light, one in each window, swinging down from the roof on long ropes. Just before they hit, the shapes vanished and the ropes thumped, empty, against the glass.

A second later, the two figures reappeared just inside the windows, somersaulting through the air above us. I caught a glimpse of lithe bodies clad head to toe in black leather. They landed together in the middle of the room in a graceful, wide-legged stance, turned their steel-masked faces toward us, and drew katanas from the scabbards on their backs.

Shadowborn.

Twenty-seven

Instinct had me reaching for my gun before I remembered I didn't have it anymore. Philip had taken it from me at the auto body shop, and he still had it. Not that it would do any good against the shadowborn anyway, but I felt naked without it.

Isaac acted quickly, not waiting for the shadowborn to attack first. Something bright and crackling burst from his outstretched hands and raced toward them. The shadowborn brought up their katanas, using the polished steel blades to deflect the blasts into the walls. They left seared, smoking holes in the wood.

Then the shadowborn vanished. Before we could react, they reappeared right in front of us. They pulled back their katanas, ready to strike. Philip moved like a bullet, his supernatural speed allowing him to get his arms around one for a moment before it dematerialized. He skidded to a stop halfway across the room, empty-handed. He turned, ready to go after the second shadowborn, but it chose that moment to vanish, too.

Gabrielle scanned the room nervously. "Where did they go?" Her voice wavered. She was terrified.

"How the hell did they find us?" Isaac demanded.

I turned to Bethany. "I thought we killed these assholes back at the safe house."

"There are a lot more than three shadowborn in the world," she replied. "Whoever summoned the others must have summoned more."

"Great," I said. "Maybe they got a bulk discount."

A shadowborn materialized behind Bethany. Before I could shout a warning, it grabbed her.

"Let her go!" I started toward the shadowborn on blind, furious instinct. It raised its katana blade to Bethany's throat. She flinched, sucking in her breath. The shadowborn shook the sword slightly, but didn't cut her. I stopped and put up my hands. "Okay, okay, I get it. Nobody moves."

Across the room, something banged on the closed door that led to the hallway outside, strong enough to rattle the door in its frame.

All I cared about was getting Bethany away from the shadowborn. I didn't take my eyes off its sword. The edge pressed against her neck, where a film of nervous sweat glistened with each panicked breath she took, but it made no move to slit her throat. For now, at least, the shadowborn was waiting for something.

Another bang shook the door, and another. The second shadowborn materialized in front of the door, and opened it.

A crowd of people spilled into the room like floodwater bursting through a dam. Amid the confusion I smelled the stench of rancid meat. Then I noticed their torn, dirt-smeared clothes and rot-mottled skin. They were dead, all of them. Dead but moving, crowding into the room like an angry mob. A sharp red light glowed inside their pupils. A light I'd seen before.

They were revenants, and there were dozens of them. They smashed the display cases, pulled paintings and artifacts off the walls, knocked over a few of the statues, and sifted through the wreckage. They were looking for something. The box, I figured. Everyone was after that damn thing.

Two revenants came forward and grabbed Isaac. They held his arms behind his back and slipped a heavy chain over his neck. A large iron medallion dangled from it, old and round and carved with weird sigils. Another pair of revenants grabbed Bethany, and the shadowborn who'd been holding her blinked out of sight. Philip and Gabrielle were restrained as well. Everyone had been brought under control but me. For some reason they'd left me alone. Why?

I didn't have to wait long for an answer. I felt a tap on my shoulder and turned around.

Bennett stood behind me, a toothy grin on his pale, dead face. "Surprise."

A pair of revenants came forward and took me by the arms. They were in bad shape, these two, half-faced corpses that looked like they'd died in a meat grinder. But they were unbelievably strong. I couldn't move in their grip at all. Up close, the odor of rotting flesh wet from the rain was so strong it made my eyes water.

The red glow in Bennett's pupils flashed. "And so the captor becomes the captive. We've come a long way since you had me tied up in the back of your car, haven't we, errand boy?"

"You can stop calling me that," I said. "I know you're not really Bennett. You're just pulling his strings, making his dead body dance for you. It's sick."

The thing with Bennett's face stopped smiling.

"So why the charade?" I asked. "Why come to me at the safe house in Bennett's body?"

When the revenant answered, it was still Bennett's vocal cords at work, still his voice, but the speech patterns were all wrong. Whoever was controlling his corpse had stopped pretending to be Bennett and was now speaking freely. "I chose this body precisely because it was known to you. It was a face you would respond to."

A chill fell over me. "How did you know that?"

"I know much about you."

"How?"

"It helped that Bennett's body was freshly dead," the revenant continued, ignoring my question. "His brain hasn't deteriorated yet. It made impersonating him that much easier, drawing upon the memories and information locked in his head. This body was the perfect shill. But every good con needs a mark. So tell me, what does that make you?"

"I don't understand, what does any of this have to do with *me*?"

With a grin, Bennett's corpse walked away, joining the throng of revenants.

I struggled to free myself from my two half-faced guards, but their grip was like iron, and just as cold.

The crowd of revenants parted like the Red Sea, leaving an aisle down the center of the room. There, standing at the far end, was the red-robed figure I'd seen outside the safe house. His hood shaded the golden skull mask over his face. He was flanked by the two shadowborn, their swords back in their sheaths. They walked with him as he crossed toward us. I studied the mask over his face, but I couldn't see any of the person behind it. There were no eyes in the empty black sockets of the skull mask, no mouth visible behind its leering grin.

Isaac lifted his head, struggling against the weight of the heavy chain around his neck. "Melanthius."

"You know of me?" Melanthius said. His voice seeped out from behind the mask like poison gas. "Good. Then you know I am not to be trifled with. A point of interest: The amulet around your neck is called the Hangman's Damper. Can you guess why?"

Isaac scowled. "I have a feeling you're going to tell me. You seem the type who enjoys the sound of his own voice."

The revenants guarding Isaac dug their sharp finger bones into his shoulders and arms. He winced in pain and gritted his teeth.

"Watch your tongue, mage, or I will see it cut from your mouth." Behind Melanthius, the shadowborn's featureless steel masks turned toward Isaac. "The Hangman's Damper was a favorite tool of the magician hunters of the Spanish Inquisition. It earned its name for two reasons. First, it keeps the wearer's magic safely in check. So long as it is around your neck, mage, you can neither cast nor summon."

Isaac glared at him, his face reddening and twitching with exertion as he tried to cast a spell, presumably one that would flatten Melanthius to a smear on the carpet. Then he let out his breath and slumped forward, panting. "Get this thing off me and let's see how tough you really are."

"I prefer it this way," Melanthius replied. "The second reason for the name is that the Hangman's Damper had a side effect the Inquisitors found most useful. The spell tightens around the wearer's neck with each lie he tells. One lie and you feel as if all the air has left the room. Two lies and you feel you're being strangled. Three lies and you're dead. I would caution you not to put that to the test. But I know you're no fool. You know what we have come for as certainly as we know that you have it. It's somewhere in the building. Remember what I've told you about the amulet, and answer our questions truthfully."

"*Our* questions?" Isaac said. "I take it you're not alone?"

Bennett stepped out of the crowd to stand with Melanthius.

"Ah." Isaac's eyes narrowed. "Reve Azrael, I presume."

Shit. The entity Isaac had mentioned earlier, the necromancer Melanthius served, was controlling Bennett's body. And she *knew* me somehow.

"Enough talking, mage. Where is Stryge's head?" Reve Azrael demanded through Bennett's mouth.

"Why don't you show yourself, instead of hiding behind the dead like a coward?" Isaac taunted. "Or do you not have a body of your own? Is that it? Are you a floater, just some random consciousness without a form to call home? It must be so lonely, not being able to touch anyone except with the cold, numb hand of a corpse."

"Stryge's head," she repeated.

"Never heard of it," Isaac said. He choked suddenly and gasped for air. Red-faced, he slumped forward in the grip of his revenant guards. I could hear his desperate breathing as he fought for air.

Reve Azrael smiled down at him as he choked. "You know how the Hangman's Damper works, mage. Even you would not be so foolish as to risk the consequences of another lie, would you? Now, tell me where it is."

Between his coughs and gags, Isaac managed to squeeze out the words, "I'd sooner die."

"To what end? If you did, I would simply take your body for myself and find the answer within your tiny, pitiful brain," Reve Azrael said. "I will not be denied, not even by death. Not when a weapon of this magnitude is so close at hand. Not when it assures me limitless power, and limitless control."

"What weapon, what are you talking about?" Bethany demanded.

"Why, the most powerful weapon there is, of course. An Ancient," Reve Azrael said. The discolored lips on Bennett's dead face twisted into a smug smile. "With Stryge's power, I can unmake this wretched city. I can bring it all down."

Isaac sucked air into his lungs. "You're insane . . . Stryge won't do your bidding . . . He's an Ancient, practically a force of nature."

Reve Azrael grabbed his hair and pulled his head back until she was staring into his face. "I did not come here for advice. I came for the head. Where is it? Tell me and your pain will end."

Isaac locked eyes with her, the defiance in his gaze burning like fire. "I don't have it."

He choked again, wheezing and gasping as his face turned red as a brick.

"It must be getting very hard to breathe," Reve Azrael said. "Two lies is usually all anyone can muster before they die. Save yourself, mage, and tell me what I need to know."

Isaac gasped like a beached fish.

"Stop it!" Gabrielle cried. "You're killing him!"

"You mean I should show him mercy?" Reve Azrael asked. "I already have. I could have killed him, killed *all* of you, the moment we arrived, but I did not. I have no more mercy in me than that. But you can end this, woman. Any of you can. Just tell me where he has hidden Stryge's head." Her request was met with stony silence. She bent her ruined corpse face toward Isaac. "You've earned their loyalty. How endearing. I wonder, how will your loyal companions feel watching you die, knowing how unnecessary it is? Be smart, mage, and speak, because each moment that passes only makes me more determined. I can hear the heartbeat of this city in my head like a constant drum, the din of breath and metal, the cracking of its skin underfoot. It never stops, never gives me a moment's peace, but soon it will. Soon there will be silence."

"Seriously?" I interrupted. "You want to destroy New York City because it's too loud? Why can't you just move to Westchester like everyone else?"

Reve Azrael glared at me. "Because then I would not see its streets fill with blood, nor its buildings become tombs."

I shouldn't have bothered. You can't reason with crazy.

She turned back to Isaac. "Feel free to die, mage. I do not need you alive. I am very good at finding things. After all, I found this place."

Isaac looked up at her. "How?" he gasped. "The ward . . . should have . . . stopped you . . ."

Reve Azrael smirked. "We had help."

"What do you mean?" Bethany demanded. "Who helped you?"

Melanthius stepped forward. "When soldiers scour the battlefields for their dead, they do not waste valuable time searching blindly through the tall grass. Instead, they let themselves be guided by the sound of flies."

Beside me, Philip scoffed. "That Halloween mask must be cutting off your air supply. You're not talking sense."

"He means something led them right to us," Bethany said. "Here, and at the safe house."

I thought back to the safe house. The protective ward Morbius had cast around it had stood unbroken for more than thirty years, until last night. Now Citadel's ward had been breached just as easily. Both locations, I realized, had one thing in common when their wards had been compromised. My stomach dropped. I should have realized from the start. Maybe I would have if it weren't so awful.

"Something didn't lead them here, Bethany. Some*one* did," I said. "When the shadowborn attacked the safe house, I thought we'd been betrayed by someone on the inside. Ingrid thought so, too. But you were right, it wasn't Isaac or any of the others. It's just like you said, there's only one person it could have been. Me."

The color drained from Bethany's face. "What are you saying?"

I turned to Reve Azrael. "I'm right, aren't I? You said you know me. I'm guessing that means somehow you know how to find me, too. You found the safe house because I was there, the same way you found this place. You used me like a homing beacon. So what is it, do I just light up like a flare to you?"

"Come to me," Reve Azrael said, and the revenants dragged me forward. They shoved me onto my knees in front of her, letting go of me in the process. I looked up at her. She gazed back at me, the telltale red glow of her magic filling Bennett's dead eyes. She smiled a terrible smile. "Tell me, little fly, how does it feel to know all your buzzing has brought nothing but pain and suffering to those around you?"

The revenants had made a big mistake letting me go. I sprang to my feet and wrapped my hands around her neck. She didn't try to stop me as my hands squeezed the cold, dry flesh. Instead, she laughed in my face. Coming from the mouth of Bennett's corpse, it was a chilling sound.

"Who are you?" I demanded. "How do you know me?"

With a single swipe of her arm, she knocked my hands from her throat. Her strength was incredible. "Perhaps we can strike a deal, little fly. The answers to your questions in return for what I want."

"Been there, done that, it didn't work out," I said. "I'm done playing the patsy."

Her triumphant grin melted away. "So be it."

From where he knelt on the carpet, Isaac croaked out, "Philip, now!"

In a flash, the vampire was gone. The revenants that had been holding him tumbled backward, tossed as effortlessly as paper dolls. A dark blur sped toward Isaac, and then Isaac was gone, too, leaving something spinning in midair where he'd stood. For a moment, a silence hung over the room. Then the object hit the floor with a heavy *clank*.

It was the Hangman's Damper.

After that, all hell broke loose.

Twenty-eight

A moment after the Hangman's Damper hit the floor, a blazing fire erupted in the far corner of the room. Its flames whirled like a funnel cloud, and through the conflagration I caught a glimpse of Isaac in the corner where Philip had deposited him, fire bursting wildly from the mage's hands. The spinning cone of fire barreled forward and engulfed the nearest revenant, transforming it instantly to smoldering ash. This had to be the flaming dervish spell he'd mentioned earlier, I thought. Then the fire, like a living thing, moved on to engulf the next revenant.

I ducked as my two half-faced guards came up behind me and tried to grab me again. I bolted for cover behind a nearby marble statue of a woman wearing a toga and some kind of battle helmet. From behind the statue, I looked at Bethany and Gabrielle still held fast by their revenant guards, and wondered how the hell I was going to get them free without my gun.

On the other side of the room, Melanthius and Reve Azrael shrank away from the raging flames, retreating to the wall. The shadowborn went with them, their blades drawn, covering their retreat.

I didn't see Philip anywhere, but I hoped he was still close by. With Isaac busy on the other side of the room, Gabrielle and Bethany still being held prisoner, and me stuck behind a statue without a weapon, our odds of making it out of this mess without the vampire's help were slim to none.

A group of revenants rushed Isaac, too many for the flaming dervish to take out at once. A pale, emaciated corpse slipped past the fire and came up behind him. Philip appeared out of nowhere, dropping down from above like a spider, and tackled the revenant to the floor. He sank his sharp teeth into the revenant's throat and tore out a chunk so large that its head flopped off its neck at a peculiar angle. The revenant stopped moving. The red lights inside its eyes snuffed out. Then Philip was gone again, nothing but a dark blur moving through the chaos.

A split second later, he was standing in front of me. He wiped something dark and oily from his mouth with the back of his hand, and spat on the floor. "For the record, revenants taste like shit. Here, catch." He pulled my gun out of the back of his pants and tossed it to me. He was gone again before I even snatched it out of the air.

With my Bersa semiautomatic in hand, I jumped out from behind the statue and ran toward Bethany and Gabrielle, lining up a shot to start blasting their revenant guards. I hardly made it half a dozen steps before I was clotheslined by a thick, meaty arm. I fell on my back. Above, one of my old pals, the half-faced revenants, reached to grab me. I rolled away and came up on one knee, squeezing the trigger and putting a bullet in Half-Face's shoulder. The revenant didn't stop, but it did slow down. I spun around and saw that from this angle I had a clear line of sight to Melanthius and Reve Azrael, sandwiched between the shadowborn and the wall. There would only be time for a single shot before Half-Face was on me again. I had to make it count. Reve Azrael was the one calling the shots from inside Bennett's body. I drew a bead on Bennett's head and squeezed the trigger.

Bennett's skull was already fragile from decay. It burst like a melon from the bullet's impact. His body crumpled to the floor.

Throughout the room, the revenants jolted and spasmed like they'd been hit with ten thousand volts, then went still as statues. They were blank, empty, like radios that had lost their reception. My shot must have broken Reve Azrael's connection to them. Putting a bullet in Bennett's brain while her consciousness had occupied it must have shattered her hold, stunning her, weakening her control over the other revenants. That was the key. Destroy a revenant's brain, or sever its head from its body like Philip had done, and Reve Azrael couldn't control it anymore.

The shadowborn drew back to create a tight, protective circle around Melanthius. He didn't move, didn't attack or cast any spells. I wondered if he had any magic of his own.

The broken connection only lasted a few moments, but it was long enough for Gabrielle and Bethany to squirm free of their guards. As Reve Azrael's consciousness slowly took control of the revenants again, the two women didn't waste any time. Bethany ran toward me, while Gabrielle picked up a small, tubular object that had fallen out of one of the smashed display cases. She clasped her hands together around the artifact and chanted a few words in that same weird magical language Bethany had used. A bright glow seeped out from between her fingers, then grew longer, until finally she was holding what looked like a sword in her hands, only its blade was made of fire instead of metal. One swing sliced the head clean off the first of her revenant guards, and another finished off the second.

Bethany stopped suddenly, her gaze moving past my shoulder. "Behind you!"

I turned to see Half-Face coming at me again. "Come to me, little fly," it said. Reve Azrael had found a new host body.

I swung my gun around, aiming for the head, but Reve Azrael swatted the weapon from my hand so hard my fingers stung. The gun landed on the carpet a few feet away. I backed away, and bumped into another revenant. It tried to grab me in a bear hug, but I ducked out of its reach and ran. Unfortunately, the only direction I could run in was *away* from my gun.

I sprinted across the room, narrowly avoiding the cold, grasping hands of revenants. Each dead thing whispered to me as I passed, Reve Azrael's consciousness following me through the room, jumping from one corpse to the next. "I know you. I know the power you possess," one said. "I would not be so foolish as to try to kill you," another said. "Yet you amuse me so," said a third. I ran past each of them, twisting and jumping to evade their clutches. I searched the crowd, but I couldn't see Bethany anywhere. I'd lost her in the chaos. I caught a glimpse of Isaac. His flaming dervish spell had only reduced six revenants to ash so far, and was starting to peter out. More walking corpses crowded toward him.

Distracted, I didn't see a revenant come up on me until it was too late. It grabbed me by the shoulder and turned me toward it. "Perhaps I will keep you as a pet," Reve Azrael said through its crumbling mouth. "Have you kneel before me in the blood of your companions."

Something flashed in the corner of my eye. The revenant's hand released my shoulder and fell to the floor, severed cleanly from its arm. Gabrielle stood beside me, the burning sword in her hands. She swung it again and lopped off the revenant's head.

"Where's Bethany?" I asked.

"Just keep moving," she told me. "Get to higher ground. The stairs."

Then she was gone, running back into the fray. I charged for the staircase, but I only made it to the base of the steps before another revenant blocked my path. This one was a dead woman in a pantsuit, wisps of thin white hair floating above its bloated and discolored face. One eye was nothing but a dark, empty hole. The other fixed me with an unyielding gaze, the red glow of Reve Azrael's magic burning in its pupil. Its bony, clawlike hands stretched toward me.

I jumped back, out of its reach, and accidentally knocked into the sculpture of the centaur that stood by the staircase banister. The iron spear rattled loosely in its marble hand. Loose enough to give me an idea.

I grabbed the top half of the spear and pulled it toward me. It slid easily free from the statue. It was awkward and heavy but well balanced, a good enough weapon for now. The revenant lunged at me again. I swung the spear. The tip caught the side of its head, tearing a chunk of flesh from its cheek.

"You should be thanking me," Reve Azrael said through the dead woman's cracked lips. "It is not everyone who knows what the future holds for them. The full measure of their destiny. Yours is to be in chains and crawl at my heels."

"Lady, I'm done being anyone's pet." I stabbed the sharp tip of the spear through the revenant's forehead and into its brain. It fell to the floor. The red light in its eye went out. I pulled the spear out of its head, stepped over the body, and ran up the stairs.

Bethany was already on the stairs, standing near the landing halfway between the first and second floors. Philip was there, too, pulling a revenant's head away from its shoulder and sinking his teeth into its neck. He bit out a big chunk of rotting flesh, pulled the revenant's head free of its body, and tossed both down the stairs. He spat again, his features twisting in disgust. "Ugh, I'm going to need a breath mint after this." His mirrored sunglasses were spattered with dark blood. Even now, he still wore the damn things.

I hurried over to Bethany. "Are you okay?"

She was holding the guns she'd confiscated from Tomo and Big Joe, one in each hand. "I've had better days," she said.

Isaac came bounding up the stairs next. Below, the room looked like a slaughterhouse, the floor littered with chunks of skull, bone, and severed body parts. But there were still far too many revenants still on their feet for us to get comfortable. Over by the bookcase, Gabrielle hacked away at them with her burning sword.

"You cut that one much too close, Isaac," Philip said. "I thought they were going to kill you with that damn amulet."

Isaac nodded, catching his breath. "Sorry about that. I had to get her talking, find out what she was planning and how she got through the wards. Now we know."

"Bullshit," I said. "You wanted to know what I was going to do. You were testing me."

"Maybe some of that, too," he said. "You could have told her where the box is and spared yourself a world of trouble, but you didn't. I'm sorry I misjudged you."

"Yeah, well, I'm sorry I thought you were crazy and trying to kill everyone," I said.

Below, four revenants lurched toward the staircase, their glowing eyes fixed on us. Bethany lifted her guns and fired them both repeatedly. The revenants' foreheads blew apart, and they fell to the floor.

"Not bad," I said. "Where'd you learn to shoot like that?"

"The Saint Aurelius Home for Orphaned Girls." She raised the guns again and blew the heads off two more approaching revenants.

I looked across the room at the polished wooden door that led outside. It was the only exit I knew of, but it was too far away to do us any good. Even if we managed to destroy all the remaining revenants, we wouldn't even get close before the shadowborn stopped us. I scanned the room, searching for another way out. When my gaze fell on the couch near the door, my blood went cold.

Thornton's body sat up slowly. The white sheet slid off him as he stood up. His clothes were still wet from the Methusal spring, dripping onto the carpet and leaving a trail behind him as he crossed the room toward Gabrielle. She didn't see him. Her back was to him as she chopped and swung her blazing sword at the other revenants, sending heads, arms, and hands flying. They were no match for her, but they kept coming like cannon fodder, keeping her distracted.

"Gabrielle, behind you!" I shouted.

She spun around, raising the burning sword in her hands, expecting to see just another revenant. She froze the moment she saw it was Thornton.

"Hello, baby," he said. "Did you miss me?" Pinpoints of red light burned in his eyes.

Twenty-nine

Bethany started down the stairs but didn't make it far. Both shadowborn vanished from Melanthius's side and reappeared at the bottom of the steps. They lunged. Bethany stopped short and fell backward, their blades passing over her. She pulled herself upright and scrambled back up the steps.

The shadowborn charged up the steps toward us, their katanas cutting the air so sharply the blades practically sang. Bethany leveled the handguns at them, double-fisted, and started squeezing off shots. The shadowborn disappeared, reappeared closer. She shot at them again, forcing them to vanish once more. As long as she kept them on the defensive they couldn't launch an outright attack, but it was only a temporary fix. Eventually she would run out of bullets. As it was, the shadowborn were already adapting. They split up, one appearing above us on the landing between the first and second floors, the other appearing right in front of me.

I still had the iron spear in my hand, and brought it up to block the shadowborn's katana. I lunged before it could swing again. The shadowborn vanished a split second before the spear pierced its chest.

Chaos raged around me. Bethany's gunshots echoed in my ears. Isaac blasted fire from his hands. The shadowborn popped in and out of the material plane all up and down the stairs. And through it all, I watched Reve Azrael in Thornton's body creep closer to Gabrielle down below. Gabrielle had finished off all the revenants but one, a skinny corpse with a mohawk and a leather vest. It backed away as Reve Azrael approached.

"You can put the sword down now, baby," Reve Azrael said. Her approximation of Thornton's speech pattern was eerily perfect.

"Don't call me that," Gabrielle said, shaking her head defiantly. "You're not Thornton."

Reve Azrael smiled. The red glow danced in her eyes. "No. Even you would not be so foolish as to fall for that. But the memories housed in this body, his thoughts of you are so sweet. So exposed. Did he ever tell you the nickname he had for the mole on your lower back?"

Gabrielle's face hardened. She drew back her burning sword. "You leave him be!"

"Or what? You'll strike me down? Do it, and you'll destroy your lover's body. All that remains of him. Are you prepared to do that?"

Gabrielle gritted her teeth, the muscles of her arms tensing.

"Your beloved, cleaved in two by your own hand," Reve Azrael said. "Could you perpetrate such violence on him? Could you live with the memory of it for the rest of your life?"

The burning sword seemed to tremble in her hands, and her face registered a mix of emotions: confusion, outrage, revulsion, grief, and a paralyzing uncertainty.

Swing the damn sword, I thought, but I could tell she wasn't going to. Reve Azrael had gotten to her. She couldn't bring herself to destroy the body of the man she loved, the man she'd planned to marry. If we didn't do something to help, she was going to get herself killed.

I hurried down the steps, but Philip sped past me. But as fast as he was, the shadowborn were faster. One materialized in Philip's path and swung its katana in a wide, forceful arc. The blade caught Philip in the chest, knocking him backward onto the steps. His shirt had been sliced open to reveal an angry red gash across his chest.

It could have been a lot worse. Frankly, I was surprised it wasn't. A blow like that from the shadowborn's katana probably would have cut me in half, but Philip, who looked skinny enough to wriggle through a roll of paper towels, only seemed to have suffered a flesh wound. Just how hard was a vampire's skin?

Bethany opened fire at the shadowborn again, covering Isaac as he bolted down the steps. He grabbed Philip under the arms and dragged him back up the stairs to the landing.

"If you're going to strike me down, do it now," Reve Azrael taunted Gabrielle. "Cut Thornton's head from his shoulders."

Gabrielle's eyes glistened with tears. She slowly lowered the blazing sword. "I can't."

Shit. I started down the steps again, but this time both shadowborn appeared before me, blocking my way. Damn. The higher ground of the stairs had been perfect for fighting the revenants earlier, but now we'd inadvertently trapped ourselves. I backed away. Bethany came storming down the steps, pulling the triggers on both guns, but they were empty. She tossed them away and reached for her vest. The shadowborn stalked up the steps toward us.

I'd lost track of the mohawked revenant below, but now I saw it again. It was holding something in its hand. A gun. *My* gun. It must have picked it up from the floor. Now it was pointing it at Gabrielle's back.

"Behind you!" I shouted.

Gabrielle spun around, lifting the burning sword again, but it was too late. The gun went off. She jerked back, a red splotch blossoming in the spot between her shoulder and chest. She spun from the shot, and the burning sword took off the mohawked revenant's head. Gabrielle crumpled to the floor. The burning sword extinguished itself. She lay so still that I was worried she was dead. Then I saw her take a shallow breath and knew she was only unconscious. I felt a surprising amount of relief. Apparently, I was starting to care about these people. It was a new feeling.

Reve Azrael loomed over Gabrielle, a cruel smile twisting Thornton's features. She picked up the gun, and aimed it squarely at Gabrielle's head.

"No!" I shouted.

Reve Azrael pulled the trigger. The gun clicked, empty. I let out my breath. I'd never been so relieved to run out of bullets.

She tossed the gun aside. "No matter. She will be dead soon enough, just like the rest of this accursed city." She looked at Thornton's hands, clenching and unclenching his fingers. "Oh, but I like this body. Dead, yes, but whole. Strong. Thank you for making it so much better than the rotting carcasses I'm used to. I think I'll keep it a while. It has so many useful memories to draw from. And one in particular that I am most thankful for." She walked to the bookcase that hid Isaac's vault, and pulled the small leather globe. The bookcase swung open. Isaac's face remained defiant as he watched her punch in the combination on the keypad of the metal door behind the bookcase. Then the metal door swung open, too, and bright light spilled through the doorway from the vault, accompanied by the strange, deep hum I'd heard before.

"Ah, such marvels," Reve Azrael said. She walked inside.

With the shadowborn between us and her, there was nothing we could do to stop her from helping herself to the contents of the vault. All we could do was retreat up the steps to the landing. The shadowborn stayed where they were at the bottom of the steps, keeping us penned in. Either they were awaiting further instructions, or they were just toying with us, knowing they'd won.

Isaac was crouching over Philip, keeping pressure on the vampire's wound. "We can't just let her take it," I said, but Isaac didn't answer me. Philip groaned in pain. "We can't just let her win!" I insisted.

"Did you really think it would end any other way?" Melanthius asked, stepping forward. The rictus smile of his golden skull mask looked like a smirk.

Reve Azrael emerged from the vault, carrying the box. My heart sank. This was it, then. We'd lost. Reve Azrael had Stryge's head.

"Picture it, mage," she said as she joined Melanthius in the center of the room. "An entire city of the dead. It's almost enough to make me want to spare your life, just so you can see it before you die. Almost."

Isaac's eyes were cold and hard. "There are ten million people in this city, Reve Azrael. Someone will stop you. If not us then others, but someone *will* stop you."

Reve Azrael laughed. "Who? The Guardians? They do not care. They will sit on their hands and watch, as they always do. Or perhaps you think the wretched denizens of this city will rise up to stop me, these selfish, blind, and craven fools who swarm the sidewalks like mindless vermin, who cower in their homes in fear of each other? None of them will move against me. No one will risk their own lives. Even you never did, mage. Oh yes, I am aware of your clandestine activities, the thefts of artifacts from all over this city. I have been aware of you and your operation for some time now. Did you really think no one would notice? How foolish you are, how shortsighted. No wonder I defeated you so easily. Next, I expect you will beg for your life."

Isaac remained quiet.

"No? Very well, mage." Reve Azrael turned to the shadowborn. "Kill them. Then bring our buzzing little fly to me."

The shadowborn climbed up the stairs toward us. I backed up a few steps, holding the spear in front of me. The shadowborn vanished. I spun one-eighty, desperate to see where they'd gone, clutching the spear so hard my knuckles looked like snow. Philip was still lying on the landing, half conscious, but Isaac was on his feet again, scanning the room intently.

The shadowborn appeared again, one on the landing right behind Isaac, and the other on the steps just above Bethany and me, cutting us off. Damn. Divide and conquer. There was a reason it was a classic strategy. It tended to work.

The first shadowborn was about to stab Isaac through the back when the mage spun, dropped, and rolled, sending a blast of fire from his palms. The shadowborn dematerialized before the flames hit it.

The second was already coming down the steps toward me and Bethany. I feinted at it with the spear, feeling about as intimidating as an extra in a Tarzan movie, but the shadowborn vanished. I guess if you're able to phase out of the material plane whenever you want, you don't have to be big on courage.

"Trent, give me the spear," Bethany said. I tossed it to her. She caught it, took a small charm out of her vest, and threw it to me. "Take this. When they come back, do your thing."

I looked at what she'd given me. It was the displacer charm. The bean-shaped burlap pod was still pierced through the middle by the rusty old nail she'd driven into it. "Do my thing? What does that mean?"

She didn't have time to answer before the pair of shadowborn reappeared again a few steps below, storming up toward us. I pointed the charm at them and pressed the nail in its center. A dark red blast erupted from the charm's tip, and the whole room tinted carmine like I was looking through stained glass. Both shadowborn recoiled, stumbling dizzily back down the stairs. They lost their grip on their katanas and put their hands to their heads. Good. I hoped it hurt.

Bethany didn't waste a moment. Holding the spear out in front of her like the world's shortest Amazon, she leapt off the stairs directly at the shadowborn. The spear pierced the chest of the nearest one and came out its back with a dry *chuk*, as if it had gone through a bag full of hay. The shadowborn lurched back, yanking the spear out of Bethany's hands, still skewered through the middle like a cocktail olive.

"They can't phase!" Bethany shouted.

From behind me, Isaac sent out a crackling beam of energy that made the hair on my neck stand on end. It struck the second shadowborn and blew it back across the room, where it crashed into one of the few display cases still standing, and landed in a shower of glass, metal, and small glowing crystal obelisks.

But it would take a lot more than that to put the shadowborn out of commission. I ran down the stairs, grabbed the spear handle sticking out of the first shadowborn with both hands, and pushed it backward. Stuck through with the spear, the shadowborn kicked and dragged its feet as I pushed it farther and farther, but momentum was on my side. With nothing in its leather jumpsuit but very old bones, it wasn't strong enough to stop me. I kept running, kept pushing, and drove the tip of the spear into the second shadowborn, which had just gotten back on its feet. I kept moving, pushing with everything I had until they hit the wall. The spear went through them both and embedded itself in the wood, pinning them there like butterflies.

I stepped back, moving out of their reach as they clutched at me. Without the ability to phase, the shadowborn were stuck fast and not going anywhere. They looked absurd, pathetic even, but I had no sympathy for them. As far as I was concerned, if I ever saw another one of these undead ninja assholes, it would be too soon.

I turned around, expecting to see Reve Azrael and Melanthius, but they were gone. The polished wooden door that led out of Citadel was open. They'd run off, escaping into the same city they wanted so badly to destroy.

Thirty

I ran outside into the rain. The storm clouds had turned the late afternoon as dark as night. It took me a moment to get my bearings. I hadn't been awake when they brought me to Citadel, so I didn't know where I was. There was no street outside, no sidewalk or lamps either, just grass, and a thick forest in the distance. The familiar skyline of Fifth Avenue loomed above the trees, illuminated windows glittered against the clouds. I was in Central Park, I realized, closer to the East Side than the West.

There was no sign of Reve Azrael or Melanthius. Not even footprints; the grass had already been pounded flat by the small army of revenants they'd brought with them. I scanned the forest edge in the dark, but I knew they could be anywhere by now. Central Park was more than eight hundred acres of forests, grottos, and hidden paths. I couldn't even tell which direction they'd gone.

I turned to go back inside, and got my first view of Citadel. An imposing three-story building of gray stone and stained-glass windows, it took my breath away. At each corner, a stone tower topped with crenellated battlements rose two additional stories above the domed roof. Suddenly the name Citadel made sense. It looked more like a fortress than a home. A paved path, just wide enough for a Parks Department vehicle, snaked past and forked in two. One path led back into the woods. The other ended in a patch of dirt beside Citadel, where the Escalade was parked.

Funny, I'd been through the park numerous times and never noticed this building before. But then, I wasn't supposed to. No one was. That was the point of wards.

I went back inside. Isaac had burned the shadowborn while I was out, leaving only a spear sticking out of the wall and a mound of ashes beneath it.

"Reve Azrael is gone," I reported.

"Of course she is, she got what she wanted," Isaac said, his tone bristling with anger. He cast another spell to burn the bodies of the revenants scattered on the floor—either as a precaution or because he was so furious, I couldn't tell—and in a flash the carpet was so thick with ash the room looked like the inside of a cremation furnace.

"Isaac, I need your help," Bethany said. She was crouched over Gabrielle's unconscious body on the other side of the room. She'd torn open the shoulder of Gabrielle's shirt and was applying pressure to the bullet wound to stop the bleeding.

Isaac hurried to her, telling me to go look after Philip.

The vampire was still on the middle landing. He'd regained consciousness but was weak. I helped him down the steps. He leaned his weight on me, his body as hard and heavy as stone. I finally got him onto the antique Queen Anne couch where we'd laid Thornton's body earlier. Even as he settled onto the couch, breathing hard and sweating, he never took off his mirrored shades. I took that as a sign that he was probably okay.

Philip winced as he adjusted himself to get comfortable. "Hurts like hell," he said. "Take it from me, never be on the wrong end of a shadowborn's sword."

"Too late," I told him.

"Oh yeah, that's right. You're the man who doesn't stay dead. Must be nice not having to worry about it."

"Not as nice as you'd think," I said. "Anyway, what's it to you? I thought vampires were supposed to be dead already."

"You've been watching too many movies, man. I'm as alive as you are. Vampires just live longer, that's all. And we're a hell of a lot harder to kill." He poked gloomily at the long tear across the fabric of his shirt. "Damn. This was the last of my black turtlenecks."

"If it's any consolation, my shirts get ruined all the time, too," I said. "You learn not to get attached."

Philip pointed at a small marble box sitting on an end table. "Do me a favor and hand me that box?" I got it for him. When he opened it, I saw it was filled with dirt, as rich and dark as coffee grounds. He took some in his fingers and smeared the dirt on his wound. He winced again, like someone putting antiseptic on a fresh cut, but the dirt seemed to lessen his pain.

"Is that . . . *magic* dirt?" I asked. This was what my life had become. Asking if dirt was magical.

"It's just dirt," he said, but didn't explain further. He rubbed some more on his chest. "I'll be fine now. You don't need to stand over me like a mother hen."

"Suit yourself," I said.

Philip seemed to be recovering fine. Gabrielle had me a lot more worried. I went over to where Isaac and Bethany were crouched over her. They hadn't moved her off the floor yet. They didn't dare move her at all until she was stabilized. Isaac was holding a wooden bowl filled with some kind of fibrous green goop, while Bethany scooped out handfuls and patted them over the bullet wound. I knelt down beside Gabrielle. Her face was coated in sweat from shock, but she was still breathing and I could see the faint throb of her pulse in her neck. "Is she going to be all right?"

"She hasn't lost too much blood," Bethany answered. "The Sanare moss will stop the bleeding and help the wound heal faster."

"The bullet went right through her," Isaac said. "The exit wound is pretty bad, but at least the bullet missed the brachial artery in her shoulder."

She was lucky. It would have been a lot worse if the bullet had stayed inside her. I knew that from personal experience.

I watched Bethany apply more of the Sanare moss to Gabrielle's shoulder. "Why did you give me the charm instead of using it yourself?" I asked her.

"It wouldn't have worked otherwise," she said. "There was something wrong with my containment spell, remember? Reverse engineering is never as good as using an original spell."

"But still, you gave it to me," I said. "You thought it would work if I used it?"

She looked up at me. "It did, didn't it? That's what happened last time, so I took a chance it would happen again." She shrugged. "Somehow, magic just seems to work better for you."

"That was a hell of a chance to take," I said. "If it hadn't worked . . ."

"But as she said, it did," Isaac said. "How often does that happen to you?"

"How often does what happen?"

He looked at me curiously. "Is magic *always* more powerful when you're in contact with it?"

I shrugged. "Damned if I know."

"It happened with the Anubis Hand, too, didn't it? When you used it, it didn't just stun the gargoyles, it killed them. Burned them up, that's what Bethany said. And then there's the shock Gabrielle experienced when she went too deeply into your mind. She said it was like feedback. Her own psychic energy coming back at her, but stronger . . ." He trailed off, tapping his short red beard in thought.

Great, I thought, more reasons to think of myself as a freak. But I'd seen magic in its rawest form, and it was terrifying. If it was connected to me somehow, I had to know. "Okay then, so what does all this mean?"

"I'm not sure," Isaac said with a sigh. "Magic is an element of the natural world, no different from wood or fire, even if it has been tainted by the Shift. Casting a spell is just channeling and transforming that elemental energy, but even so, the energy should remain constant. If the charm didn't work for Bethany, it shouldn't have worked for you either."

"What about you?" I asked. "You're a mage. Aren't your spells supposed to be stronger or something?"

He shook his head. "It's not the same thing. Mages have access to a different level of magic, and through study and a greater understanding of the element we're manipulating, it can be carried inside us with less chance of infecting us—"

"Wait, less *chance*?" I interrupted. "I thought mages were immune."

"Nothing is foolproof," he said. "There have been mages who've become infected. Some were weak-willed, or had an affinity for darkness already. Others . . . well, fending off the infection can be a struggle even for the most powerful among us." I didn't like the sound of that. Did it mean Isaac could become infected, too? At any time? "But, Trent," he continued, "even a mage can't make a faulty charm work, let alone operate with the kind of increased intensity that one did. That was all you. Somehow, you're like a shot of caffeine to magic. A supercharger."

"How?" I asked. "I don't even know when I'm doing it."

"The real question isn't how, Trent, it's *why*," Isaac said. "Why does magic become stronger around you? Why can't you die? And why is Reve Azrael able find you whenever she wants?"

Isaac had studied magic enough to become a mage, and yet even he didn't know what to make of me. That wasn't exactly comforting.

"Guys, she's coming around," Bethany said.

I looked down at Gabrielle. Her eyes fluttered open.

Isaac smiled at her. "Welcome back. You gave us quite a scare."

With her good arm, Gabrielle pushed a few loose dreadlocks out of her face. When she spoke, her voice was hoarse, gravelly. "I'm sorry. I saw his face and I—I just couldn't do it."

"It's all right," Bethany said. "Don't move. Just try to relax."

Gabrielle groaned as the pain of the gunshot wound finally sank in. "At least tell me you stopped them."

Bethany scooped more of the Sanare moss onto Gabrielle's bullet wound. "I wish I could, but they got away. They took Stryge's head with them."

"They took Thornton, too," I said.

Tears welled in Gabrielle's eyes, and she turned away. "So that monster is still walking around in Thornton's body, doing God knows what with it?" She choked back a sob, but then she couldn't hold it in anymore and her body shook as she wept.

"I need you to keep still," Bethany said.

"Keep still?" Gabrielle demanded, her sadness shifting to anger. "How the fuck am I supposed to keep still? She has his body, Bethany. She's wearing him like a fucking dress. We have to go after her."

"Opening that bullet wound again isn't going to get Thornton back," I said. "Let them fix you up."

"While she takes him farther and farther away?" Gabrielle raged. "How can you say that? You know what he was to me. You fucking *saw* it!"

"It doesn't change anything," I said. "You're not in any shape to go running after her."

"What is she talking about?" Bethany asked me. "What did you see?"

"Something happened when she was inside my mind," I explained. "Somehow, I got inside hers too for a second, and I saw . . . something." I stopped myself there. It didn't feel right that it should come from me.

"He saw that Thornton and I were engaged," Gabrielle said, closing her eyes. I couldn't imagine how hard it was for her to say the words out loud. How much it hurt. But she braced herself, opened her eyes again, and said, "It happened a few days ago. He wanted to tell you all right away, but then the new job came up. Securing the box. Thornton only took the job so we'd have money for the wedding." She closed her eyes again, and a tear rolled down her cheek. "It was my idea to wait until after the job was over to tell you, so we could celebrate properly. I thought we had time."

"Oh, Gabrielle," Bethany said, stroking her hair. "I'm so sorry."

"I'm sorry, I didn't know," Isaac said.

"You want Stryge's head back. I want *Thornton* back," Gabrielle said. "We have to go after them."

Isaac didn't answer.

"I won't let her use Thornton like this," she insisted. "I won't let her desecrate his body. He deserves better than that. Isaac, we have to go after them!"

Isaac looked down at the floor. I could see in his eyes that he was wrestling with something inside. A promise he'd made long ago.

"She said to tell you she was wrong," I said.

Isaac looked up at me. "What?"

"Ingrid," I said. "She was still hurting from Morbius's death when she told you to keep your head down and not get involved, but she regretted it. Right before she died, she asked me to tell you to keep fighting the good fight. To not let Morbius's dream die with her. She said she was wrong. She wanted you to know that."

Isaac nodded and closed his eyes, as though a great weight had been taken off his shoulders. When he opened them again, he said, "I spent so much time worrying about drawing attention to myself that I asked others to risk their lives for me, and all the while I stayed hidden away here in Citadel. Thornton paid the price for that. No more. It ends today. Reve Azrael brought the fight to us. Now we're going to bring it to her. Together." He started pacing the floor, thinking out loud. "She's crazy if she thinks she can just wake Stryge up and make him do her bidding. He'll kill her the moment he opens his eyes."

"So why don't we let him?" Philip asked, coming over from the couch. He'd taken off his black turtleneck and draped it over his shoulder like a towel. Remarkably, the wound had already closed and scabbed over, leaving only a thin white scar across his hairless, dirt-smeared chest. Apparently dirt helped vampires heal faster. Good to know. I filed it away with the hundred other ridiculous and impossible things I'd learned over the past twenty-four hours.

"And then what?" Isaac asked. "Once Stryge is awake, there's no way to stop him."

"Willem Van Lente did it four hundred years ago, right?" I pointed out. "We could do it again."

"How? No one knows how Van Lente brought Stryge down, and he didn't leave any clues behind."

"Reve Azrael's plan doesn't make any sense," Bethany said. "There's no way to control an Ancient."

"Maybe she found a way," I said. "Maybe there's a spell no one knew about."

"It's possible," Isaac said. He sighed and brushed his hands through his cropped red hair. "Reve Azrael craves control. It's why she surrounds herself with revenants. All that nonsense about the city being too loud, that's just a symptom of her madness. It's *life* she hates. Life is messy and loud, and she can't control it the way she controls the dead. She wants to snuff it out."

From the start, Bethany had insisted that if the box fell into the wrong hands it could be used as a weapon. I couldn't think of any worse hands for it to be in than Reve Azrael's. She was planning the full-scale destruction of New York City. I couldn't even fathom it. I had as strong a love-hate relationship with New York City as anyone else who lived here, but no matter how many times I cursed this city while sardined into an overcrowded subway train or stuck in endless Midtown traffic, actually trying to destroy it never crossed my mind. You'd have to be completely insane. The people who'd tried to destroy this city before—and even with my limited memories I knew about that; you couldn't live in New York without knowing—only proved the point. Now Reve Azrael was proving it again. She was even more unhinged than I thought.

"She makes revenants from the dead," Bethany said. "The more people she kills, the larger her forces grow. If she wakes Stryge up and really can control him somehow, the death toll would be astronomical. She'll have an army of the dead, with each new revenant another weapon in her arsenal. The slaughter would spread exponentially, until eventually there wouldn't be anyone left alive in New York City but her and Melanthius. Reve Azrael and her servants in five boroughs of rubble."

"My guess is, once she gets a taste for destruction on that scale she won't stop with just New York City," Isaac said.

"All the more reason to go after her," Gabrielle insisted.

"She could be anywhere. No one has seen her true form. No one knows anything about her, including where her lair is. We'll never find her in time," Isaac said. "But that doesn't mean we can't stop her. We just have to beat her to the punch."

"I'm not following," Bethany said.

Isaac began pacing again, thinking out loud. "If she's going to make Stryge whole again, she has to join the head to the body at the moment of the equinox. The *exact* moment. And that's tomorrow at . . . Philip?"

"Eleven twenty a.m.," Philip answered.

"Tomorrow morning, eleven twenty. She won't miss that window. If we're going to stop her, our best chance is to get to Stryge's body before she does."

"Fine, so where's the body?" Gabrielle asked.

"That's the million-dollar question," Isaac said. "It's got to be somewhere in the city. Come on, Keene, think. After the battle, Willem Van Lente tried to destroy Stryge's head, but he couldn't, it kept putting itself back together again. So he hid it instead, and while he was doing that the Lenape Indians hid Stryge's body. They knew what would happen if the two were brought together again, so to be safe neither party told the other where they were hidden. They didn't tell *anyone*. To this day, there are no historical documents, no scrolls, not even any oral histories that give away the locations. Reve Azrael must have some clue where the body is, or she wouldn't go through all this trouble to steal the head this close to the equinox." He stopped pacing and took a deep breath. "For four hundred years, magicians, researchers, and scholars have tried to find Stryge's body and failed. We have until eleven o'clock tomorrow morning."

"And how exactly are we going to pull that off?" Bethany asked.

Isaac tented his fingers under his chin. "Over time I've amassed the most extensive library of arcane and secret knowledge in the city. If there are clues anywhere, it's there. We'll search every book, front to back. We'll start with the major works, *The Libri Arcanum*, *The Book of Eibon*, then work our way down from there. It's got to be there somewhere."

Gabrielle struggled to her feet, gritting her teeth through the pain and putting one hand on the bandage Bethany had affixed to her shoulder. A second, larger bandage covered the exit wound near her shoulder blade. "Then let's get started. I don't want to waste any more time."

"Hold on," Isaac said. "For God's sake, Gabrielle, you just got shot. You need to rest until you're strong enough—"

"Try to stop me and you'll see how strong I am," she said. "Don't argue with me on this, Isaac. I can't just sit on the sidelines while she's got Thornton's body. When she shows up to put Stryge back together, I want to be there. I'll pull that bitch out of his body with my bare hands if I have to."

"If you go after Reve Azrael half-cocked, you're going to get yourself killed," Isaac said. "We've already lost enough people today."

She narrowed her eyes at him. "Don't you dare lecture me on what we've lost. I know better than anyone."

While they continued arguing, I walked over to the monitors on the wall. They were still broadcasting the feed from the traffic cameras. Fire trucks had gathered outside the burning Shell gas station now, cordoning off the area and turning their hoses on the flames. I'd put the fallout shelter out of my mind during the fight, but I hadn't forgotten. Now that things had quieted down, it demanded my attention again.

"I'll catch up with you guys later," I said. "There's something I need to do."

Isaac turned to me, his eyebrow raised in surprise. "We could really use your help, Trent."

"You know what you're looking for in those books, but to me it's all gibberish," I said. I nodded toward the monitors. "I have to go back to Brooklyn. I have to see it for myself. I have to know."

"Know what? If Underwood's dead?" Bethany asked. "No one could have survived that."

"What if he's not dead?" Isaac asked. "What then?"

I didn't have an answer for that. I didn't want to think about what I would do to Underwood if I ever saw him again.

Bethany touched my arm, the unusual warmth of her hand coming through my sleeve. "Trent, you don't have to do this. You can walk away from that life."

"No, I can't," I said. "Not until I'm sure."

She frowned. She didn't like it, but she didn't argue, either. Even Bethany knew when she couldn't win.

Isaac pulled a small cell phone out of a drawer in a table by the door. He handed it to me. "It's got my cell number in the contacts. If you run into trouble, call. I'll call you if we find anything. Otherwise, let's regroup here in a few hours."

"Sounds good," I said.

He shook my hand. "We may have gotten off on the wrong foot, Trent, but you're one of us. You proved that today."

"I'm full of surprises," I said.

"So I'm learning," he said. "Stay safe out there, and don't stay away too long."

I said my goodbyes. Gabrielle said, "Don't take too long. We can't do this alone."

Philip said, "Go already. What do you want, a hug?"

Bethany crossed her arms and wouldn't look at me. "This is stupid," she said.

I left. Walking out the door was harder than I thought it would be. Part of me already knew I belonged with them and wanted to stay. Outside, the afternoon was wearing on toward evening and the storm clouds hadn't budged. The sky was as dark as coal. The rain had grown chillier, and as it battered me I hugged myself, shivering as I walked away from Citadel. I had almost reached the paved path when I heard Bethany's voice.

"Trent, wait!"

I turned around. She left Citadel's porch and walked across the grass toward me. She looked even smaller soaked to the skin like that, her long black hair plastered to the sides of her face.

"Look," she said, "you're stubborn and annoying, and you've been nothing but trouble since I laid eyes on you, but that doesn't mean I want to see you go and get yourself killed." She paused a moment, then said, "Okay, killed *again*. Someone needs to keep an eye on you. I'm coming with you."

I shook my head. "I'll be all right. I know how to take care of myself.

I've been doing it for a long time. Besides, I thought *I* was the one who kept saving *your* life."

"What, are you keeping score now? Put the headstrong macho crap aside for a second and just accept that I'm not letting you do this on your own."

"It's too dangerous," I said. "The Black Knight is still out there looking for me. I can handle him if he comes for me, I've done it before, but you . . ." I shook my head. "I don't want anything to happen to you."

"You have to stop thinking of me as someone you need to protect. I can take care of myself, too."

"People keep dying because of me, Bethany," I said. "Ten people I barely know died just so I could keep living. Ingrid is dead because of me, because Reve Azrael followed me to the safe house. She followed me here, too, and nearly killed Gabrielle. Now she's got the box, and she's got Thornton's body, and it's all because of me. I'm tired of getting people hurt. I'm tired of all the death." She just looked at me, her bright blue eyes shifting slightly as she looked into mine. "You'll be safer here with the others," I said.

"It's not me I'm worried about," she said. "Who's going to protect *you*? You'll be out there on your own."

I recognized the words, and smiled. It was the same thing I'd said to her when she'd tried to get rid of me after the warehouse. It already seemed like a lifetime ago. But I shook my head. "You can't come with me, Bethany. The others need you."

"And you don't?"

I hung my head. That wasn't what I'd meant. "This is something I have to do alone. It's a part of my life I have to close the door on, once and for all. I'm no good to anyone until I do."

She looked at me like she wanted to say something but didn't have the words. I knew the feeling. There were things I wanted to say to her, too, starting with thanking her for showing me there were good, decent people out there, not just men like Underwood. People worth going to the mat for. But just then my tongue felt too thick to move.

Finally, she said, "Have I mentioned how annoying you are?"

"I picked up on it," I said.

She stood up on her tiptoes, and kissed my cheek.

"Try to come back in one piece," she said.

I wanted to say something witty, something charming and memorable, but all I could manage was, "Okay."

Then she went back inside, and I walked away, into the storm.

Thirty-one

I took the 2 train to Brooklyn. By the time I got to Empire Boulevard, the fire had been completely extinguished. All that was left of the Shell gas station was wet, charred wood and exposed metal beams poking out of the wreckage like the ribs of some enormous dead beast. I stood across the street and watched the firefighters pull what was left of the furniture out of the station and pile it all in the parking lot. There wasn't much. I was angry at myself for it, but I couldn't help feeling a pang of regret. This was the only home I'd ever known, and now it was gone. Gone, too, was the list of names I'd kept inside my mattress, and the old TV that had kept me company through countless sleepless nights. Even my copy of *The Ragana's Revenge* was ash now. All of it, nothing but ash.

Two ambulances were parked nearby, their lights flashing, their back doors closed and guarded by police officers.

The sight of cops made me nervous. Old habit. I backed up deeper into the big crowd of locals who'd gathered on the sidewalk to gawk at the show. But the cops weren't the ones I had to worry about. The Black Knight had come looking for me. He'd done this, and there was a good chance he was still nearby. There was also a good chance this was a trap, that he was waiting for me to come back and walk right into his clutches. Losing myself in the mass of umbrellas and rain parkas on the sidewalk might keep me hidden from the cops, but it wouldn't hide me from him. It was dangerous to be here, stupid even. But I had to see it with my own eyes. I had to know for sure that Underwood and his crew were gone.

I turned to the person next to me, a thin, West Indian man wearing a plastic poncho, and I put on my best innocent act. "What's with the ambulances? I thought that old gas station was closed a long time ago."

He crossed himself and answered in a thick Jamaican accent, "They found four bodies inside, God rest their souls."

Four bodies. So it was true, then. Tomo, Big Joe, and Underwood were dead. The dark-haired woman, too. The one who used to stare at me all the time, silent and watchful, like a cat focusing on its prey. It occurred to me then that I'd never even learned her name.

"They found an old fallout shelter from the sixties under the station, with a bed and some furniture," the man continued. "There must have been some homeless people in there."

"And you can bet they're the ones who started the fire," an old woman in a rain hat interjected, *tsk*ing loudly. "Probably doing drugs. I heard the police say they kept a faulty generator down there. One spark and the whole thing blew up."

Bullshit, I thought. I'd gassed up that generator myself dozens of times. Underwood always kept it in meticulous condition. He was too smart, too careful, to let an accident take him out. No, if the firefighters had traced the explosion to the generator, the Black Knight must have done something to it. Isaac was right, sneaking around and sabotaging machinery didn't seem like the Black Knight's style, but I'd seen the crows on the video feed myself. I knew what it meant.

"I hear they found other things down there too, bad things," a second man said. He was tall with dark, craggy skin and a curly beard.

"What're you talking about, Winston?" the first man scoffed, rolling his eyes. It was clear Winston was the local gossip, the busybody nobody quite liked. Every neighborhood had one. "What *bad things*?"

"Drugs," the woman said with unshakable certainty.

"Guns," Winston corrected her. "Enough for an army. Makes you think about what was going on down there. Who they were. Why they needed so many guns. Too many suspicious people in this neighborhood, you ask me."

That was my cue to leave. I slipped away, leaving Winston and the others sharing their theories about everything from street gangs to terrorist sleeper cells, but I didn't get far before the back of my neck started tingling. Someone was watching me. I scanned the crowd and picked him out immediately.

There are a lot of dead things in New York City, things you usually don't see. Dead rats in the sewers. Dead roaches under floorboards. Dead squirrels in the park bushes. The dead are everywhere, and in New York you probably aren't more than a few feet from a dead thing at any given moment. I just never expected that rule to hold true on a crowded sidewalk. Still, when you're dealing with an entity with the power to raise and control the dead, you have to stay flexible.

The revenant stood half a block away. It wore a maroon, zippered hoodie, its gaunt, male face mostly hidden in the shadows of the hood. But even if I hadn't been able to make out the dark patch of rot on its cheek, the red glow from its pupils, muted as it was behind tinted horn-rimmed glasses, told me everything I needed to know.

Reve Azrael was keeping tabs on me. How long had the revenant been following me? All the way from Central Park?

I waited until a group of onlookers passed between us, then made a break for it. I hurried toward the subway station, flipping open the cell phone Isaac had given me. His number was the only one in the contacts. He picked up after one ring.

"Reve Azrael is tailing me again," I told him. "I just saw one of her revenants in a crowd here in Brooklyn."

"Damn. Can you lose it?" he asked.

I glanced back at the crowd. I didn't see the revenant anywhere, but that didn't mean it wasn't still following me.

"You don't get it," I said. "It doesn't matter if I shake this one. It doesn't matter where I am or how many wards I'm behind, it won't stop her."

"Come back, Trent, we can protect you—"

"I can't, Isaac. I'm the fly on the battlefield, remember? The only way your plan is going to work is if you've got the element of surprise. If I'm with you, she'll know what you're doing. She'll see you coming. You won't stand a chance."

"Trent," Isaac started.

I reached the subway steps. "Look, it's me she's got a bead on, not you.

I can draw her away and buy you some time. Use it. Get to Stryge's body before she does."

"No, Trent, I don't want you doing this alone—"

I snapped the phone shut, ending the call, and hurried down the steps to the subway platform. A plan was already forming in my head. If Reve Azrael insisted on shadowing me, I would lead her as far away as I could. I'd lead her out of the city entirely, and give Isaac and the others enough time to figure out where Stryge's body was. But if I was going to do that I would need a car. The Explorer was already ancient history, probably sitting in some impound lot or Staten Island junkyard. What I needed was another car.

Luckily, I knew just where to find one.

I took the subway north, back into Manhattan, then transferred at Times Square to the R train to Queens. It was already standing-room only when I got on, but the closer we got to Queens the more it filled up with twentysomething hipsters returning to their trendy neighborhoods. They were boisterous and remarkably carefree, all unkempt hair, neck beards, and moth-eaten flannel over ironic 1980's T-shirts. I watched them and wondered if they had any idea what kind of danger they were in, how close they were to death. I wondered if it mattered to them.

To get away from the crowd, I moved all the way to the end of the subway car. I could see into the next car through the rear window, and caught a glimpse of the revenant in the maroon hoodie again. It must have followed me from Empire Boulevard, keeping out of sight even when I changed trains. Good. As long as Reve Azrael's attention was on me, it wasn't on the others.

At my stop, I got off the train amid a teeming throng of passengers. As the rest of them swarmed up the steps, I slowed down on the platform to give the revenant a chance to catch up. If I was going to lead Reve Azrael on a wild-goose chase, I had to make sure her revenant didn't get left behind. But I didn't see it anywhere, not on the platform, and not through the train windows as it pulled out of the station. That made me nervous. I didn't like not knowing where it went. I climbed the steps quickly and exited the station.

I turned off the main streets and soon found myself on a desolate stretch of old, vacant apartment buildings. In the middle of the block, the buildings gave way to a small, abandoned playground. Maddock's body had been taken away, I saw, and the front gate taped off with yellow police tape. I lingered a moment, watching the dragon spring rider wobble gently back and forth on the wind, gazing back at me with its big, painted eyes that were nothing like Gregor's. The world had grown so much larger since I'd last been here.

Bennett's black Porsche was still parked where he'd left it around the corner. A sopping wet parking ticket lay beneath one of the windshield wipers, and a neon-yellow sticker on the passenger's side window proclaimed that the vehicle had violated parking regulations and the street couldn't be cleaned properly. I was lucky it hadn't been towed away yet. I walked to the Dumpster near the car, got down on my hands and knees, and looked under it. Bennett's key chain was still there. I fished it out and hit the unlock button. The Porsche's doors unlatched with a satisfying *ka-thunk*. I peeled the orange parking ticket off the windshield, tossed it aside, and got in. The car started without an argument.

There was no GPS system in the car, so I drove around looking for signs for the 695, which would take me north to Westchester. As the rain began to taper off, I found myself alone on a barren stretch of road far from the residential neighborhoods. It was a part of Queens I wasn't familiar with. There wasn't much to see but trees, overgrown fields, and the occasional streetlamp lit up against the dark.

Was this what it felt like to be free, I wondered? Truly and completely free? Part of me wanted to just keep driving and leave everything behind. What would it feel like to aim this stolen Porsche for the horizon and never look back? I was surprised to find the thought didn't appeal to me.

I touched my cheek. I could still feel her kiss there.

I shook my head. What the hell was wrong with me? When had I become so goddamn sentimental?

A roar came from behind, startling me. In the side mirror, I saw a flame-red Ferrari speeding toward me. If the damn fool didn't slow down, he would crash right into me. I moved to the side to let this moron pass. The sports car accelerated to come up alongside me, but instead of passing it stayed beside me. I glanced over to see who was behind the wheel. The revenant in the maroon hoodie returned my glance, a twisted grin on its face. A mess of exposed wires sat on its lap like noodles, spilling out from the bottom of the dash where the car had been hotwired.

A corpse driving a Ferrari. Even with amnesia, I was pretty sure now I'd seen everything.

I sped up, but so did the revenant. It steered its car into mine. The sound of metal scraping against metal made me grit my teeth. I pulled my seat belt on, floored the accelerator, and yanked the steering wheel to the side, slamming into the Ferrari and nudging it to the opposite side of the road. It came back a moment later to sideswipe me again. This time I made a hard turn, driving right into it, and before I knew it we were both spinning out of control.

I thought I heard the sound of a car hitting a tree, but since I was still moving, I assumed it was the revenant. A second later, my car hit something I couldn't see. I crashed through it with the sound of rending metal. The impact jolted me, the seat belt biting into my chest as it strained to keep me in place. I heard the sound of breaking glass as both my headlights went out. I hit the brake, and the car finally screeched to a stop. I leaned forward, resting my forehead against the wheel and tried to catch my breath. In the side mirror, I saw that I had crashed through a tall, wrought-iron fence. I'd taken down an entire panel. It lay on the ground behind me, its spiked tips pointing my way like accusing fingers.

I undid the seat belt, opened the car door, and stepped out onto the wet, spongy grass. I was still dizzy from the accident and had to lean against the car to pull myself together. The Porsche was totaled, its hood crumpled like scrap paper, the engine block battered and steaming. It wouldn't take me anywhere now. As the dizziness passed, I looked up from the car to get my bearings. A crowded field of graves, headstones, monuments, and crypts stretched over gently sloping hills all the way to the horizon.

Shit. There were dozens, maybe hundreds of cemeteries in Queens, and it was just my luck to end up in one with a goddamn necromancer on my tail.

I turned and ran for hole in the fence and the road beyond it, but the revenant in the maroon hoodie was already crawling through it toward me. It was legless now from the crash, trailing thick black ooze as it pulled itself along the ground with grim determination. The red glow from its pupils speared the dark.

Slow and low to the ground, it didn't pose much of a threat. Its friends, on the other hand, were a different matter. Behind the crawling revenant, three more pairs of red, glowing eyes appeared in the dark and moved closer.

I had a flash of my gun lying empty on the floor back at Citadel. Damn. Like a fool, I'd gone into this completely unprepared.

I backed away from the approaching revenants, retreated up a shallow hill, and bumped into something. I turned around. A winged skull grinned back at me, and my heart jumped in my chest before I realized it was only an etching on an old granite headstone. I turned back to the revenants. They crept closer. In another few seconds I'd be within their reach.

I took off through the maze of headstones, running deeper into the cemetery. This was Reve Azrael's turf, not mine, but I didn't see any other choice. I was weaponless, and though the revenants were tireless and supernaturally strong, I did have one advantage over them. I was faster. I ran as fast I could toward the fence that surrounded the cemetery. There had to be a gate in it somewhere, or a hole that hadn't been fixed yet. Some way out.

Hands burst up out of the ground, snagging my feet and ankles. I fell, eating a mouthful of dirt. I rolled onto my back and kicked at the hands, but it was no use, revenants were coming out of the ground everywhere around me, vomited forth from the earth. Ragged and vile, they clawed their way up from beneath headstones, or pushed their way through the rusted gates of family crypts. By the time I got back on my feet, I was surrounded.

They grabbed me and pushed me forward up a small hill. We stopped in front of a stone monument shaped like a sarcophagus. Standing on top of it was the emaciated corpse of an old woman. She wore a torn and dirty white gown, and her long, thin white hair blew around her head like a halo in the breeze. She fixed me with her red-glowing eyes and said, "Hello, little fly."

"Reve Azrael," I said. "We have to stop meeting like this. People will talk."

"I told you, there is no place you are safe from me."

"Is that so? So tell me, how do you keep finding me?"

The corpse smirked, not the prettiest sight in the world. "You may as well ask how I am able to speak with the dead, or raise them from their graves and fill their empty husks with my will. It is in my nature to do so."

The revenants crowded closer. I could smell their sickly sweet rot all around me. I ignored them. They were a sideshow. Reve Azrael was trying to intimidate me and I wasn't going to let that happen. "I see you've got yourself a new body. Did you get tired of Thornton's already? Because I know someone who'd like it back."

"Your flippancy does a bad job of hiding your true feelings," she said. "You are not used to being afraid, are you? But you are wise to fear me. Had I no need of you, little fly, I would have my revenants tear you limb from limb, just to see how your body would resurrect from that."

Revenants brushed their rotting, skeletal hands across my arms, my chest. I suppressed a shudder of disgust. I wouldn't give her the satisfaction. "What do you want with me? I told you before, I'm not big on being your pet."

"We could not be more different, you and I," she said. "I am death, and you are deathless. Can you not see how you confound me? I cannot kill a man who refuses to die, nor can I make into a revenant a man who won't stay dead. And yet, for all the challenges you pose, I have need of you."

"What are you talking about?"

"The dead speak of you. Did you know that?" she asked. "Beyond the veil of darkness that separates our world from theirs, they gather in plains of mist and seas of ash, and they see you, each time you die, like a fly trapped in amber, floating there in the darkness. You fascinate them. They even have a name for you. They call you the Visitor, because you come but never stay."

A chill crept its way up my back. The dead spoke about me? They *saw* me?

"But do you know what *I* call you?" Reve Azrael continued. "An omen. A sign that the end of all things has finally come. A glorious end, to which you are the key."

"I'm not a sign of anything," I said. "And if you think I'm going to help you, you're even crazier than I thought."

"Ah, but when the time comes, you will not have a choice."

The revenants began to drag me away. I dug my boots into the ground, but it didn't do any good. There were too many of them, and they were too strong.

"Where are you taking me?" I demanded.

"Sometimes you find your destiny," Reve Azrael said with a wry smile, "and sometimes your destiny finds you."

Her host body jerked suddenly, as if something had hit it from behind. The blade of a long black sword burst through its chest. Reve Azrael looked down at it in anger. "No, this one is mine. He is *mine!*"

The sword sliced upward through her host body. The corpse broke apart, shattering in a mist of blood, and falling to the ground in chunks. The Black Knight stepped forward out of the darkness, his curved and barbed black sword coated with blood and tissue.

My heart crowded into my throat. I tried to yank my arms free from the revenants' grasp, but their immense strength held me fast. There'd been no interruption in Reve Azrael's control this time. She must have transferred her consciousness to another host body before the Black Knight destroyed the first.

The Black Knight jumped off the sarcophagus onto the ground. The revenants swarmed him immediately, but he didn't seem deterred in the slightest. He chopped the closest one in half, then grabbed another around the neck with his gauntlet. It laughed at him, and Reve Azrael spoke through its ruined mouth, "Wretched thing, there is no life in these bodies for you to suck out!" The Black Knight swung his sword and cut the laughing corpse's head from its body with a single blow.

A moment later, something big fell out of the sky and landed amid the revenants with a heavy *thud*. It was followed by another, and another. Gargoyles, half a dozen of them, dropping out of the sky like paratroopers from a plane. They laid into the revenants with their sharp claws, one after another, shredding them to pieces. It would have been a massacre if the victims weren't already dead.

Two more gargoyles landed directly in front of me. I recognized one of them from the warehouse—Yellow Eye, with its withered, battle-scarred eye. The second had an elongated, almost horselike face, and together the two of them made short work of the revenants holding me. The moment I was free I started running, but Yellow Eye and Long Face hadn't freed me out of the kindness of their hearts. They flew after me, scooped me up in their claws, and carried me into the sky. I struggled to get free, but they were strong, even stronger than the revenants. Within seconds we were up so high that it became safer *not* to struggle. Below, more revenants streamed out of their graves and crypts like a tidal wave, a sea of glowing red eyes that lit the darkness crimson. The last thing I saw before the cemetery dropped out of view was the revenants surrounding the Black Knight, and the Black Knight cutting them down on every side.

Yellow Eye and Long Face carried me across the East River, then the northern tip of Manhattan, and the Hudson River. Finally, as we passed over the white steel hulk of the George Washington Bridge with its stream of headlights far below, I saw where we were headed—the enormous, stony cliffs of the Palisades.

The other gargoyles from the cemetery soared past us, followed by a flock of crows. They all flew into a gaping black cave mouth in the cliff-side. I was carried inside after them.

Thirty-two

There was a cage waiting for me just inside the cave mouth, a construct of thick wooden poles lashed together with strips of dried, treated animal hide. Yellow Eye and Long Face threw me into it before my feet even hit the ground. I landed on my side instead of my legs, and pain flared through my ribs. Yellow Eye fixed me with his withered half-gaze and latched the cage door shut, securing it with a heavy chain and lock. I got to my feet. The Black Knight had gone through a lot of trouble to find me, blown up the gas station and taken on a cemetery full of Reve Azrael's revenants, all to bring me back here. Why? What did I matter to him?

Around me, an enormous cavern stretched deep into the Palisades cliff, dimly lit by veins of glowing green lichen that grew upon the stone. Thick, knobby stalagmites rose from the floor like obelisks. Stalactites hung from the ceiling like gigantic teeth. In a handful of places the two met to form natural columns. Shapes crawled along the walls and clung to the stalactites overhead. Gargoyles, hundreds of them, all focused on me. The air stank of their breath as they hissed and chittered excitedly.

I'd been pulled from Reve Azrael's clutches only to be brought right to the heart of Gargoyle Central. Out of the frying pan and into the nuclear fucking explosion.

Yellow Eye and Long Face lifted my cage effortlessly between them, and carried it deeper into the cavern. I was jostled against the bars for a few moments, unable to tell exactly where we were going. Then I was put down again.

In front of the Black Knight.

He sat upon a tall throne fashioned from hundreds of skulls, both human and gargoyle, bonded together with some kind of crude cement. Standing beside him was a wizened, stoop-backed old gargoyle, its ancient, leathery hide stretched tight over its bony frame. The gargoyle leaned its weight on the gnarled wooden walking stick it clutched in one claw. A single long, twisted fang drooped from its mouth. Its deep-set black eyes watched me inscrutably, sphinx like. I couldn't tell if it regarded me as a prisoner or as dinner.

The Black Knight rose from his throne and approached the cage. The old gargoyle's walking stick tapped the floor as it hobbled forward. The Black Knight reached one gauntlet through the bars, grabbed my wrist, and pulled my arm toward him.

"What are you—?" I started to say, but I was cut off by the sudden, freezing darkness that filled me up inside. He was sucking the life force out of my body. He'd tried to kill me this way once before. It seemed he was determined to try again.

I gritted my teeth and tried to pull my arm back, but his grip was too strong and I was already too weak. I was freezing from the inside out, faltering, and then, just like before, the bluish-white light burst out of my arm. It was too bright for the gargoyles. They shielded their eyes with their wings and hissed angrily. It crackled like lightning across the Black Knight's armor. He released me, stepping back from the cage quickly, and the light dissipated. The gargoyles folded their wings back and chittered among themselves, confused and alarmed. The only gargoyle that didn't seem fazed was the old one. It leaned on its walking stick and narrowed its black eyes thoughtfully.

I doubled over against the bars, catching my breath as the freezing darkness ebbed from my body. I glared at the Black Knight. "Don't blame me, you knew what would happen."

The Black Knight's only reply was to motion for the gargoyles to lift the cage once more and follow him. I was carried through tunnels that led deeper into the cavern. There was less of the glowing lichen in these depths, and I couldn't see much through the cage's bars except the wings of the gargoyles carrying me and the long, forked stag horns of the Black Knight's helmet. We passed chambers hewn into the stone walls, and passages that branched off in other directions. We crossed what appeared to be a natural stone bridge, and though I couldn't see what it spanned or how far down the drop was, I could smell what was down there. It was like the stench of a Dumpster behind a butcher shop, the stink of rotting meat.

Finally, the Black Knight entered a chamber off the side of the tunnel. The gargoyles carried me in after him and set the cage down against one wall. The room was hot and dry, in stark contrast to the cool dampness of the rest of the cavern. A pungent, sulfurous smell clung to the walls. Across from me, on the far side of the chamber, was a long table cluttered with what looked like laboratory equipment, if the lab happened to be from the Dark Ages. There were ceramic vessels connected by looping glass tubes, a brass balance scale, a collection of mortars and pestles of various sizes, and numerous earthen pots and crucibles nestled in a sand-filled box. Suspended from hooks above the table were glass globes filled with liquids and powders of all different colors. Beside the table sat a stone furnace, a fire roaring in its belly and a small, controlled flame gouting from a hole in its top.

The Black Knight waved the gargoyles away. They filed out, shutting a thick steel door behind them and leaving us alone in the chamber.

"Why did you bring me here?" I asked.

The Black Knight didn't answer. He removed one of the glass globes from its hook, and poured out a fine yellow powder into one of the crucibles. Then he moved the crucible onto the furnace, above the spurting flame. While his back was to me, I quickly inspected the cage door, looking for a weakness in the latch or hinges. I rattled it, put my shoulder into it, but it was no good, the thing was too solid. It was the same with the joints where the bars were lashed to the frame. I wasn't going anywhere.

Even with all the noise I made trying to bash through the cage door, the Black Knight didn't turn around. Instead, he watched intently as the powder in the crucible began to smoke.

"So you *are* an alchemist," I said. "The one from the history books, the one who vanished, just like Ingrid thought. Only you didn't disappear for long, did you? You came back to Fort Verhulst to kill everyone you knew. Why? Was it because they knew something about you? It must have been something big, something dangerous. That's what Ingrid thought. She thought they'd discovered your weakness, a way to kill you. Of course you couldn't allow that, could you?"

The Black Knight kept his back to me, showing no sign that he heard me or cared what I had to say.

"The name Ingrid doesn't mean anything to you, does it?" I said. "Let me refresh your memory. Older woman with a penchant for white gloves and fire magic. Forty years ago, you murdered the man she loved, and if she were here she'd kill you for it herself."

The Black Knight took the crucible off the flame and carried it to the cage. I wished I could see more through the visor of his helmet than just an empty darkness, if only to know if I'd gotten through to him on some level, but he was as unreadable as a blank wall. He put the steaming crucible on the floor in front of the cage, then grabbed my arm again and pulled it toward him.

"Really, this again? You're like a dumb kid who keeps touching a hot stove."

This time, the Black Knight pried open my hand. I didn't notice the long, thin dagger until he was already bringing it toward my palm. I sucked in my breath as he drew the blade painfully across my palm, leaving a red line of blood along the skin.

He picked up the crucible and squeezed my fist over it until the blood dripped onto the hot, yellow powder. As soon as the blood touched it, the powder began to sizzle and smoke. Then he let me go and brought the crucible back to the furnace.

I cradled my bleeding hand to my chest. "What did you do that for?"

The Black Knight put the crucible over the flame again and watched it steam.

"Damn it, what do you want from me?"

It was pointless. The Black Knight only continued to ignore me, focusing his attention on his work. My palm was throbbing where he'd cut it, but the bleeding slowed as the blood began to clot. Frustrated, I sank down against the cage bars and watched the Black Knight work. What was he doing? What did he want with my *blood*?

He lifted a glass globe filled with an ice-blue liquid off its hook and poured a few drops into the steaming crucible. It flared like flashpaper, then sputtered and died. The Black Knight balled his gauntlets into angry fists. With a sweep of his arm he knocked the crucible off the furnace and onto floor. The experiment must have failed. The Black Knight spun quickly, his tattered black cape billowing out behind him. He stormed out the steel door, slamming it closed again behind him. I heard a heavy clank as the door's lock slid into place.

It was tempting to think the experiment's failure was a good thing, but I knew that was shortsighted. Given my situation, the only thing more dangerous than the Black Knight was an angry Black Knight, with *me* as the cause of his frustration. What would he do when he came back? Drain the rest of my blood? Dissect me like a frog?

I stood up and tried to get the cage door open again. I kicked it, slammed my shoulder into it, but the damn thing still didn't budge. Finally, I hit the door at the wrong angle and a jagged bolt of pain shot through my arm. Wincing, I wiggled my fingers and bent my elbow until I was satisfied I hadn't broken anything. Then I sighed and slumped to the floor again. I had to face facts, there was no way out. I was at the Black Knight's mercy, and something told me the cut on my palm wasn't the worst of what he had in store.

I hoped the others had found what they were looking for. I pictured Bethany bent over a book, scouring it for clues. The image put a pang of regret in my chest. It was likely the Black Knight would keep me here as his prisoner-slash-guinea pig for . . . well, forever, I supposed, considering neither one of us was exactly mortal. I'd never see Bethany again. At least I'd managed to keep Reve Azrael and the Black Knight distracted so the others would be safe, even if only for a while. It wasn't much, and it didn't make up for everything I'd done, but maybe it was some small bit of redemption. Or maybe there was no redemption for someone like me. There was a string of bodies in my wake, and maybe this was what I deserved, my punishment, to be dissected and studied by the Black Knight until there wasn't enough of me left to come back from the dead. And then the world could breathe a sigh of relief, finally wash its hands of me, and say good riddance.

I don't know how long I sat there staring at the guttering furnace fire through the bars of the cage and feeling sorry for myself. Hours, maybe. The blood on my palm had dried when I heard the chamber door unlock. I stood, my heart in my throat as I watched it swing open, but it wasn't the Black Knight. It was the wizened old gargoyle I'd seen standing beside him in the throne room. The gargoyle limped into the room, its walking stick tapping the floor quietly. The long, saliva-wet snaggletooth that hung from its mouth glistened in the firelight.

I stepped back from the cage door, but it wasn't like there was any place I could run if Snaggletooth decided to turn me into a meal. "What do you want?"

Surprisingly, the gargoyle answered in English. "Be fearless. I bring you liberation." I frowned. Not only did the words not make sense, they sounded wrong coming from a mouth that wasn't meant to speak them. It was like listening to a dog trying to talk. The gargoyle shook its head and tried again. "Please forgive. Your language is difficult and I have not spoken it in many years. Do not be afraid. I have come to free you." Snaggletooth unlocked the cage and held the door open for me.

I stepped out of the cage hesitantly. I didn't know if I could trust a gargoyle, but I wasn't going to let an open door go to waste. "Why would you help me?"

"For the good of my kind," Snaggletooth replied, leading me toward the chamber door. "We are an ancient race, old before yours was even born. Yet there are so few of us left who remember the old days, before the usurper came." Snaggletooth opened the door carefully, and peered into the tunnel outside. The gargoyle stepped out and motioned for me to follow.

I still didn't know if trusting Snaggletooth was a safe thing to do, but I didn't see much choice. It was either that or wait for the Black Knight to return for a new game of Operation. I followed the old gargoyle into the tunnel, making sure to tread lightly. The tunnel was empty, but I doubted it would stay that way for long. The whole cavern was crawling with gargoyles, and the Black Knight could already be on his way back. As we walked, I whispered, "Who's the usurper? Are you talking about the Black Knight?"

Ahead of me, in the dim light of the glowing lichen, Snaggletooth nodded. "Bad enough he is not of our kind, but his cruelty is unbridled, his tyranny unmatched. He rules through fear and intimidation. Those who fail him are publicly executed as a warning to the rest of us, to keep us meek and obedient."

I cringed, remembering the gargoyle skulls cemented into the Black Knight's throne. Failure and disobedience got you the best seat in the house, only in the worst way. It reminded me of some of the crime bosses I knew. Anger them, don't follow their orders, and you got two in the back of the head. The Black Knight would have felt right at home in the Brooklyn underworld.

"Many are too young to remember the time before the usurper," Snaggletooth continued. "Many remain loyal to him. But not all. There are others like me who would be free of him. Our numbers grow by the day. The time will soon come when we will rise up, but still we are not enough. We need . . . I do not know the word. We do not have our own word for it. We have need of you. That is why I have done this."

The words were garbled but the meaning was clear enough. In return for freeing me, Snaggletooth was asking for my help.

"What is it you want me to do?"

Another chamber opened off the corridor. Snaggletooth paused by the doorway and peeked inside. The gargoyle turned back to me, put a long, clawed finger to its jaws, and waved for me to follow. Snaggletooth crept silently past the doorway. I did the same, risking a quick glance through the opening. Inside, a throng of gargoyles surrounded something wounded and bleeding on the floor. I heard the sounds of gnashing teeth and the bleating of an animal, and caught a glimpse of blood-tinged fur. Dinnertime. I hurried past.

"The usurper must not be allowed to wake Stryge from his slumber," Snaggletooth said as we continued through the cave tunnels.

"Wait a minute. I thought you said you liked it better under Stryge's rule, before the Black Knight came along."

"You misunderstand. Stryge was as cruel a tyrant as the usurper. We do not wish his return. But that is not the usurper's intention anyway. He would never allow Stryge to reclaim the throne. All the usurper craves is power. It is all he has *ever* craved. He plans to steal Stryge's power for himself, just as he planned to steal yours."

Damn, was there anyone who *didn't* want a piece of Stryge? Still, what Snaggletooth said gave me pause. "He wants to steal *my* power?"

The tunnel bent around a corner. Snaggletooth motioned for me to wait before we turned. A cluster of gargoyles flew down an intersecting tunnel. Then it was safe to move again.

Snaggletooth continued, "He tasted your power when you bested him last night. After that, he grew obsessed. He yearns to take that power for himself, and he surely would have had I not freed you."

That explained why the Black Knight had tried to drain the life out of me a second time. Alchemists were scientists, after all, and like a scientist he'd tested me to see if the same results would occur again. After that, he'd tried to figure out why, testing my blood to find the answer. The test had failed, but what if it hadn't? What would he have done then? Distilled it out of me like salt from water? Cut it out like a tumor?

"I didn't think it was possible to steal someone's power," I said.

"Oh yes, power can be stolen, provided you have the right spell and equipment—" Snaggletooth stopped suddenly and waved me back, eyes wide with sudden terror. We had come to another chamber doorway off the tunnel. I was too far back to see inside, but whatever was in there had set Snaggletooth's nerves on edge. The old gargoyle motioned for silence, then darted past the doorway. Snaggletooth stopped me with a raised claw, then a moment later gave me the all clear. I ran past the chamber, risking a quick glance inside. My chest squeezed tight.

It was the Black Knight. He was surrounded by old wooden chests, their lids flung open, and their contents rummaged through. His back was to me as he bent over one of the chests and searched through the objects inside it. I saw him pull out a long steel blade like a bone saw, and then I was past the doorway and hurrying after Snaggletooth. The old gargoyle was running remarkably quickly, the walking stick now tucked under one arm.

The tunnel forked in three different directions. I followed Snaggletooth down one, and when we turned the corner, we stopped to catch our breath.

"You're faster than you look," I said. "Do you even need that walking stick?"

Snaggletooth's face twisted hideously in what I could only assume was the gargoyle equivalent of a grin. "It is better if the usurper believes I am weak. No one would suspect rebellion from one so feeble." The gargoyle looked up at me then, its black eyes hard and serious. "We wish only to be free. Not to be ruled, but to rule ourselves in peace, without fear, and without constant strife with the outside world. Surely that is the right of every living thing."

I couldn't argue with that. I had to admit, Snaggletooth had surprised me. I'd thought the gargoyles were senseless killing machines, mindless servants of the Black Knight that reveled in carnage. Everyone had said as much. Yet there was so much more to them.

Snaggletooth continued, "Long ago, the oracles spoke a prophecy, one that claimed we would be granted our freedom by an immortal storm. For a time, many of us believed this was a reference to the usurper himself, but now we know better. The usurper did not bring us freedom, and the prophecy remains unfulfilled. These old eyes of mine have seen centuries born and die, but there is a limit to even my patience. The time has come to stop waiting for freedom to be granted to us, and claim it for ourselves."

The immortal storm again. It seemed to be on everyone's lips today. Gregor had called it a danger to all existence. Snaggletooth thought it would bring the gargoyles their long overdue freedom. Two completely different interpretations of the same prophecy. Just another reason not to believe in prophecies, as far as I was concerned.

"I think it's best not to put too much stock in these things," I said.

The gargoyle nodded. "I agree. I have lost faith that the immortal storm will ever come."

That wasn't exactly what I'd meant, but it was close enough.

We came out of the tunnel at the foot of the natural stone bridge. Now I could see where the overpowering stench of rotting meat came from. Far below was a wide crevasse filled with bones and what looked at first like mud, though the smell told me otherwise. It was liquefying flesh, rotting off the bones with the help of the maggots and beetles that crawled through the muck. This was the gargoyles' garbage bin, I realized, the place where they threw the bones of their prey when they were finished eating.

Snaggletooth dashed across the bridge, once again tucking the walking stick under one arm. When I joined the old gargoyle on the other side of the bridge, I said, "Look, I'd help you if I could, but I don't know what I can do."

"You have already shown you are immune to the usurper's magic, and you have caused him pain in a way no one else has. You are our best chance. Our only chance."

"Best chance to do what?" I pressed.

"To kill him," Snaggletooth said.

I paused, surprised. A gargoyle asking me to kill its king didn't make sense. It also didn't seem doable. "No one's been able to kill the Black Knight in four centuries," I pointed out.

"They simply did not know how."

"And you do?"

"I do, though the opportunity has never come to me. His heart is his lone vulnerable point. Destroy his heart and you destroy him." Using the walking stick again, Snaggletooth led me down another tunnel.

"His heart?" I scoffed. "That's his big secret? That's the information he killed those Dutch settlers in Fort Verhulst over? It hardly seems worth it. *Everyone's* heart is their vulnerable point."

"You know nothing of what you speak. I was with the usurper at the human settlement called Fort Verhulst. Like the others, I killed at his command." Snaggletooth's voice softened then, and the old gargoyle nodded, its eyes filled with regret. "Yes, back then I obeyed without question, foolishly. Would that I had known better. Still, those humans did not die for any reason but one: They knew the usurper's name."

"His name? What's that got to do with anything?"

"Names have power," Snaggletooth said. "To know someone's name is to have an advantage over him. It can be the most dangerous information of all."

"Then tell me his name," I said.

Snaggletooth sighed. "Would that I could remember, but the point is moot now. Too much time has passed. No one remembers his name. Not even the usurper himself."

It figured. Nothing was ever that easy. And yet I had the strangest feeling that the answer was dangling just out of reach, a missing puzzle piece I could almost see.

I hurried after Snaggletooth. "Even if I managed to get a shot at his heart, how would I pierce his armor? Everyone says it's impenetrable."

"It is not armor," the old gargoyle corrected me. "It is a shell, a carapace containing only his essence. All that remains of the usurper's original form within is his heart, and the feathered fragments of his soul."

"Feathered . . . ? Oh, the crows," I said. "But that still doesn't tell me how I can get to his heart."

"The usurper carries with him the only spell that can pierce his carapace."

"A spell? How am I supposed to get it from him?"

"That is up to you."

We came out of the tunnel at the cave mouth. Snaggletooth went first to check if the coast was clear, then waved me forward. "We must get you to safety. The time will come soon for you to face the usurper again, and when you do, remember what I have told you."

"Come with me," I said. "If the Black Knight finds out you helped me, you'll wind up part of his throne."

"No, he will never suspect me," Snaggletooth replied. "I am his vizier, his trust in me is absolute. As is his trust in others he ought to be more cautious of."

Another gargoyle emerged from the shadows. I stiffened, but when Snaggletooth didn't react I realized it was one of his allies. To my surprise, it was Yellow Eye. I remembered Yellow Eye spotting me on the street in Manhattan but backing off instead of attacking. Now I understood why. Yellow Eye had been part of Snaggletooth's underground resistance all along.

The two gargoyles chittered at each other for a moment, and then Snaggletooth turned back to me. "You will be taken to safety, but you must go now. The usurper will notice your absence soon and come looking for you. His rage will make him even more dangerous."

"Let's hope he doesn't blow up any more gas stations," I said.

"Once again you know nothing of which you speak," Snaggletooth said. The old gargoyle spoke quickly, knowing there wasn't much time. "The fire was not his doing. I followed the usurper this day as he searched for you, though the cover of the storm clouds could not fully shield me from the painful rays of the Dayburning Hellstar above. Yet follow him I did. Your trail led him to the building you speak of, this gas station, but it was destroyed *before* he reached it. The death of those inside is one crime the usurper is not responsible for."

"What?" If the Black Knight hadn't destroyed Underwood's base, who had?

A loud gargoyle screech emanated from deep within the cavern. Snaggletooth and Yellow Eye looked back in alarm.

"We have run out of time," Snaggletooth said. "Your absence has been discovered. Even now, the usurper will be sending guards to find you. You must go!"

Yellow Eye took to the air above me, flapping its wings hard enough to cause a strong downdraft that almost knocked me over. It grabbed me under the arms with its prehensile hind claws and lifted me off the ground. Below, Snaggletooth turned and started walking back into the tunnel.

"Wait," I said. "You never told me your name."

The gargoyle turned to face me. "It is Jibril-khan, fourteenth hatchling of Khan-maku. Go now, and may the Guardians show you favor this night." Then Snaggletooth—Jibril-khan—disappeared into the darkness of the tunnel.

Gripping me tightly, Yellow Eye flew us out of the cave mouth. The gargoyle's claws dug through the fabric of my trench coat and shirt and into my shoulders. It hurt like hell, but at least it kept me from falling into the Hudson River as we flew toward the distant shore of Manhattan. I breathed a sigh of relief as the cavern—and the Black Knight—fell farther behind.

I looked up at Yellow Eye. "I remember you from the warehouse. We fought there, didn't we? I'm sorry if I hurt you."

Yellow Eye looked down at me with its one good eye and grunted dismissively, as if to tell me I was flattering myself.

Just then, another gargoyle came hurtling out of the cave mouth behind us. Yellow Eye saw it the same time I did and immediately took evasive maneuvers, diving and banking while I held on for dear life, but we couldn't shake our pursuer. The second gargoyle flew high, then dove in front of us, causing Yellow Eye to pull up in order to avoid a collision.

The other gargoyle screeched, loud and angry, and I saw that it was Long Face, the same gargoyle that had helped Yellow Eye carry me from the cemetery. Now that Yellow Eye's betrayal had been revealed, Long Face was enraged. The two gargoyles shrieked, bit, and clawed at each other like bitter enemies. Yellow Eye twisted in midair to slash at Long Face, jostling me dangerously in its rear claws. I held on as tightly as I could.

Long Face let out a high-pitched screech of pain and fell back. Yellow Eye flapped harder, propelling us toward the far shore. We didn't get far before Long Face came at us again, though this time the gargoyle flew directly at me. I got my legs up and kicked, striking Long Face in the snout and knocking it back a few feet in midair. The kick jostled me in Yellow Eye's grip again. I glanced nervously down at the dark water far below.

Long Face came back at us. Yellow Eye banked to one side, trying to get around Long Face, but it was no use. Long Face attacked Yellow Eye again, and the next thing I knew we were spinning out of control. Blood rained on me from above, but from which gargoyle I couldn't tell. Given the ferocity of their attacks, probably both of them. They snarled and shrieked and clawed at each other, and all the while we fell, twisting and spinning, toward the frothing black waves below. I held on tight and scissored my legs in a futile attempt to try to stabilize us, but I had no leverage. We were out of control.

I looked up in time to see Long Face tear out Yellow Eye's throat with its teeth. More blood rained all around me. Yellow Eye's body went limp in midair. Its claws relaxed their grip on my shoulders, and suddenly I was in free fall. Long Face snarled, folded its wings against its body, and dove to catch me.

The gargoyle's claw reached for my arm, its fingers starting to close around my wrist, and then all three of us slammed into the Hudson River.

Thirty-three

The force of hitting the water was as painful as landing on a hardwood floor. The freezing cold waves of the Hudson closed over me instantly. Swallowed me whole. Underwater, it was too dark to see. I was too stunned and disoriented to know up from down. I thrashed and twisted in the cold, black void until my lungs burned for air. I was panicking, I realized, and if I didn't stop I would drown. I went as still as I could and let myself rise like a buoy to the surface. It seemed to take forever, my lungs like overinflated balloons threatening to burst. When I finally broke the surface, I sucked in so much air that the astrophysicists at Columbia University probably thought a new black hole had formed off the coast of Manhattan.

I hadn't dropped far in that final free fall, maybe forty feet, but still, I was lucky I hadn't broken my neck on impact. Yellow Eye's dead body floated a few feet away. Damn. The gargoyle had been trying to help me, and had gotten killed for its trouble.

I treaded water, keeping an eye out for Long Face, but there was no sign of the gargoyle. They were tough creatures, though. I knew that if I survived, Long Face probably had, too. I didn't like not knowing where the gargoyle was, but I had other priorities at the moment, like getting the hell out of the freezing cold water.

I swam toward Manhattan, fighting against the strong current that kept trying to pull me downriver. I was sore all over, a man-shaped contusion, but I didn't let myself slow or stop. I kept reaching for the city lights twinkling in the distance like a beacon, until finally I felt the bottom of the river under my feet. Then I stood and stumbled like a madman through the surf. Cold, wet, exhausted, and in pain, I collapsed onto the slick, unyielding rocks that formed a narrow ribbon along the shoreline.

I didn't pass out. I never do, it's one of drawbacks of my condition. I lay there a long time, though, and was conscious for all of it. I was also painfully aware of something poking me in the thigh, something that felt different from the hard stones underneath me. I reached into my pocket—a simple, commonplace action that suddenly took Herculean effort—and pulled out the object that was poking me. It was the cell phone Isaac had given me. I almost laughed, but all I could manage was a throaty cough. I flipped the phone open. Water poured out of it. The display screen stayed dark. The phone was dead. That's what it got for hanging around the likes of me. That's what everyone got, in the end.

The cell phone dropped out of my hand, and my hand dropped to my side. I didn't have the strength to move anymore. I knew this feeling, and I knew what would come next. I'd wondered on occasion what would happen if I died and there was no one around whose life force the thing inside me could steal. Would I just lay there, inert, until some unlucky soul wandered by? What if no one did? How long could I stay dead before it was irreversible? I had a feeling I was about to find out.

I waited to die, but I was wrong. Death didn't come for me. Rejected again. Maybe it was done trying at this point.

Once my strength had recovered enough that I was able to get up and leave the shore, I stumbled inland. I made my way through trees and up a slight incline. I heard the distant sounds of traffic on the Henry Hudson Parkway, but the first road I arrived at was something else. Narrow and deserted, it was little more than a paved path. An access road, probably designed for emergency or sanitation vehicles. A single lamppost beside the road struggled to fend off the dark all on its own. I sympathized.

I stepped onto the road. Aside from being cold and wet, my bones ached and my legs shook, barely able to support my weight. The idea of walking very far was a joke, though I wasn't sure what the punchline was. Still, I forced myself to put one foot in front of the other and hoped I would wind up somewhere.

Something dropped from above, crashing through the treetops and landing on the road in front of me. It was Long Face. The gargoyle was bruised and battered, but still alive. We had that in common, at least.

Too weak to run, I just stood there, wobbling, and said, "Oh. It's you."

I braced myself for the gargoyle's inevitable attack, hoping that if Long Face killed me he would at least stick around long enough to contribute to my resurrection. Provided it worked with gargoyles. I didn't know if it would. The thing inside me had only ever stolen the life forces of human beings before. It's funny, the things you wonder when you're about to die.

I thought I heard the revving of an engine in the distance, growing louder and nearer. Long Face chittered angrily. The gargoyle crouched like a jungle cat ready to spring.

A big black Escalade came roaring out of the darkness, barreling down the road right for us. Startled, I threw myself out of the vehicle's way on a surge of adrenaline. A moment later, it slammed into the gargoyle like a battering ram. The Escalade's front grille crushed inward and a single headlight shattered. The vehicle skidded to a halt while Long Face was sent somersaulting through the air. The gargoyle collided with the metal lamppost with a painful-sounding clang. Long Face tumbled to the ground, but the gargoyle was a resilient bastard. Almost immediately it rolled back up onto its feet.

The driver's-side door opened, and Philip stepped out, the streetlamp's light reflecting in his mirrored shades. He marched grimly up to Long Face, undeterred by the gargoyle's threatening hisses, and punched it in the face. Or rather, *through* its face. Philip's fist, covered in blood and gargoyle brain matter, came out the back of Long Face's head as if the gargoyle's skull was made of papier-mâché. Long Face stopped hissing, twitched a bit, then fell still.

I got up on wobbly legs. "You should be more careful. You almost hit me when you were aiming for the gargoyle."

"Aiming for the gargoyle? Sure, let's go with that." Philip pulled his hand free from Long Face's skull and shook the gore off of it. "Get in the car."

I wasn't about to argue with someone who could punch a gargoyle to death, so I went around the other side and got into the passenger's seat. I shrugged out of my sopping wet trench coat and tossed it in the back. It didn't help much. The rest of my clothes were wet, too, and I was still cold.

"What are you doing here?" I asked Philip as he got behind the wheel. "How did you know where to find me?"

He started driving, following the access road. The light of his one working headlight briefly lit up Long Face's body on the side of the road, then left it behind. "The cell phone Isaac gave you has a GPS chip inside it. I followed it until the signal died, and after that . . ." He paused and glanced at me. "Let's just say you have a peculiar smell for a human. Spicier, like gumbo. Definitely not the same as everyone else's. All I had to do was follow my nose."

I lifted my arm and sniffed my armpit. I smelled like the Hudson River, but I had a feeling that wasn't what Philip meant. First Ingrid had said my aura was wrong, and now Philip said my scent was wrong, too. Just more unanswered questions for me to obsess over instead of sleeping.

"You shouldn't have come for me," I said. "I told Isaac Reve Azrael was following me. I can't go back."

"It was his idea. Me, I think if someone wants to run off and get themselves killed that's their prerogative, but Isaac doesn't leave people behind. Ever."

"He should have this time. He knows it's safer for me to stay away."

"Let me tell you something about Isaac Keene," Philip said. "I was in the Towers the day they came down. The South Tower, the first one that fell. I was trapped for hours with the sun coming through a hole in the rubble above me and burning me alive. It was Isaac who pulled me out. He'd been there all day, rescuing people from the wreckage, never stopping, never resting. He didn't care that I was a vampire, or that the only reason I was there was because I was feeding on a janitor when the shit went down. All he saw was someone who needed help. Isaac saved my life."

"Yeah? Is that why you stuck around?"

"According to the laws of my kind, I owe him one hundred years of servitude in return, and I give it gladly. Isaac may have his flaws, but he doesn't give up on anyone."

I arched an eyebrow. "Flaws? I thought he was Mr. Perfect."

"Oh, he has his flaws," Philip said. "For instance, he won't let me feed the way I want to, and that is a definite flaw. I haven't had fresh human blood in over a decade. It's unnatural. Do you know what happens to a rutting bull when he's not allowed to mate?" He glanced at me. "You have no idea how close I came to tearing your throat out when we met. The smell of your blood . . ." He trailed off. I was glad not to hear the rest of that sentence. "You have Isaac to thank for keeping your throat intact. He gave you a second chance because that's who he is. It's what he does. He did it for me, and he did it for Gabrielle and Bethany, too. They have their own stories about how Isaac found them at their lowest points and gave them a purpose. He cares. In fact, he cares too much, and that's his biggest flaw. It makes him weak. It will get him killed one day. Luckily, he's got me around to make sure that doesn't happen."

Isaac had surrounded himself with special people from the start, I realized, each with his or her own talent. He'd been putting this team together for a long time now. He'd been preparing all along to take up the fight, even if he didn't know it.

Philip found an exit off the access road that brought us onto the Henry Hudson Parkway, where we merged with traffic heading downtown. I was starting to feel much better, almost fully recovered. Even my bones hurt less. The sun wasn't up yet, but it was getting close as the black sky brightened toward gray. The headlights of oncoming traffic speared through the dark and reflected off Philip's mirrored shades.

"Can you see in the dark with those glasses on?" I asked.

"I'm a vampire," he said. "I can see in the dark with a blindfold on."

"Do you ever take them off?"

He turned to me with a slight grin. I could see the tips of his fangs. "Trust me," he said, "you wouldn't want me to."

Something in the tone of his voice told me to drop the subject.

He continued, picking up the thread of our conversation, "Isaac didn't just send me to get you because you were in danger. He needs you, Trent. Just like he needs the rest of us. It's all-hands-on-deck time. The question is, are you going to be a man and step up, or are you going to keep running?"

I sighed and looked out the window. "All I ever wanted was to find out who I am and where I came from. I snuck into a warehouse to steal a box because I thought it would get me the answers I needed, but instead it turned my world upside down. Made me question everything I thought was true. As if that wasn't enough, now you're asking me to help stop an unkillable million-year-old creature from waking up and destroying everything?"

"Welcome to New York," Philip said. "You didn't say no, so I take it you're in?"

Outside the window, I saw the passing lights of the city. How much longer would those lights burn if Stryge got loose? How many thousands, millions of people would die? I already had too many deaths on my shoulders. "Fine," I said. "I'm in."

He dug his cell phone out of his pocket and tossed it to me. It was identical to the one Isaac had given me. "Isaac's number is in the contacts. Call him and put it on speakerphone. We need to know what our next move is."

Once again, Isaac's number was the only one programmed into the contacts. I put it on speaker and hit the send button. A moment later Isaac's voice filled the inside of the Escalade.

"Philip, tell me you found him." He sounded harried, like he'd had a long night. That made two of us.

"It's me, Isaac, I'm here," I said.

"Trent! Thank God you're all right." He actually sounded relieved. That surprised me. I still wasn't used to people giving a damn.

I filled him in as quickly as I could on everything that had happened since we last spoke: Reve Azrael's ambush in the cemetery; the Black Knight's plan to steal Stryge's power, and mine; and the brewing gargoyle rebellion. He wanted to know if I was okay, and I told him I was fine, but that the Black Knight was pissed. "Right now, I bet every gargoyle in the Tri-State area is out looking for me," I said. "Once the sun comes up it'll buy us some time, but right now I'm more worried about Reve Azrael. She's a lot harder to shake. She could be tailing me as we speak, or she could already be with Stryge's body. Either way, I don't like it. Tell me you found something useful in the books."

"Nothing," he said. "Unfortunately, the conspiracy to keep the location of Stryge's body a secret was executed perfectly. We have a couple more shelves of books to look through, but I'm not feeling hopeful."

"Reve Azrael isn't the only one who knows where Stryge's body is," I said. "It stands to reason the Black Knight knows, too, or he wouldn't be planning to steal Stryge's power."

"Are you suggesting we ask the Black Knight?"

"Actually, I was thinking maybe we should just hang back and let them kill each other."

Isaac laughed, but it sounded weary, exhausted. "Believe me, I'm tempted, but it's way too dangerous. Still, I think you're on to something. The gargoyle that helped you . . ."

"Jibril-khan," I said.

"Funny, it never occurred to me that gargoyles would have names. I always thought of them as animals," Isaac said.

"You and everyone else. But they're not. They're a lot more complicated than anyone gave them credit for."

"Gargoyles have a centuries-long lifespan," he said. "Jibril-khan told you he was alive back when Stryge was king, right? Which means he was probably at the battle where Willem Van Lente defeated Stryge."

"Along with who knows how many other gargoyles still alive today," I said. "That's how the Black Knight knows where Stryge's body is. Oh shit, it just occurred to me. I bet that's how Reve Azrael knows, too. She probably killed an older gargoyle and plundered its memories for the location."

"Did Jibril-khan say anything about where the battle was or what happened to Stryge's body? Think back. Anything could be a clue. Anything at all."

"I didn't exactly have time to ask," I said. "Wait, there was something. Jibril-khan mentioned oracles, and a prophecy about an immortal storm. Gregor said the same thing. That can't be a coincidence, can it?"

"I don't know what an immortal storm is," Isaac said, "but the oracles . . ." He paused. I could practically hear him stroking his beard in thought.

"They must know something. So where do we find them?"

"Whoa, hold on," Philip interrupted. "I'm not going anywhere *near* the damn oracles!"

"Philip's right, I can't let you do this," Isaac said. "If it's going to be anyone, it should be me."

"Forget it." I glanced at the clock on the dashboard. "It's just after six a.m. We have five hours until the equinox. Five hours before Stryge wakes up and everyone dies. You need to stay where you are and keep looking through those books. Leave the oracles to us."

"Oh, hell no," Philip said, shaking his head adamantly. "You want to see the oracles, you're on your own."

"Fine," I said. "Just point the way."

"Trent, listen to me," Isaac said. "The oracles aren't human, not even remotely."

"So what are they?"

"They're . . ." He paused, trying to find the right word. "They're unknowable. They're beyond our understanding. They have their own ways of doing things, their own rules about who they'll see and who they won't—"

"Maybe you haven't noticed, but I don't give a damn about rules," I said. "Like it or not I'm going, and one way or another I'll get an answer out of them."

"Trent, you'll be in way over your head—" I heard a muffled voice interrupt him on the other end of the line. Isaac sighed and said, "Fine, here, maybe you can talk some sense into him." He passed the phone to someone, and then Bethany's voice came on the line.

"I thought I heard someone being stubborn and exasperating. I should have known it was you. So, are you still in one piece?"

I smiled at the sound of her voice. I couldn't help it. It was an involuntary reaction. Philip caught me smiling, shook his head, and groaned.

"I hate to disappoint you, but I'm not that easy to get rid of," I said.

"The day's still young," she replied.

Philip rolled his eyes and muttered, "Get a damn room."

"Philip, can you hear me?" Bethany asked.

"Unfortunately."

"Meet me on Second Avenue, between Second and Third Street. You know the spot."

Philip blanched. For a vampire who was already quite pale, it was a remarkable feat. "You can't be serious, Bethany."

"What's on Second Avenue?" I asked.

"I can't allow this," I heard Isaac say.

Bethany said, "Look, Isaac, the oracles may be the only chance we've got left, and Trent shouldn't go alone. Someone needs to go with him, but it can't be Philip, and you and Gabrielle need to keep looking through those books. That leaves me as the obvious choice."

I looked at Philip. "What does she mean, it can't be you?"

"Bethany, you can't ask me to do this," Philip said, ignoring me. He almost sounded frightened.

"I don't like this," Isaac said.

"I think we're all going to like being dead a lot less," she replied.

Isaac sighed. "You have a point. Okay, do it, but be careful, both of you."

"This is crazy," Philip said.

Bethany said, "Philip, if you get there first, keep Trent in the car. Trent, no running off on your own again. I'm coming with you. I mean it. No arguments this time."

"No arguments," I said, and ended the call.

Philip shook his head. "Taking you to see the oracles. I must be out of my damn mind."

He turned off the Henry Hudson Parkway onto Ninety-Sixth Street, heading east into the city. As we drove down the canyon of concrete and glass, a ball of fire burned before us on the horizon, dimmed to a shimmering egg yolk by the Escalade's heavily tinted windows.

The sun, rising on what, if we failed, would be the last day of New York City.

Thirty-four

Philip pulled the Escalade up to the curb on Second Avenue between Second and Third, just as Bethany had instructed. She was there already, leaning against one of the supporting poles of an awning, the faded words PROVENZANO LANZA FUNERAL HOME emblazoned above her head. With her bulky cargo vest and the morning sun on her face, she looked like a five-foot-tall jungle explorer waiting to enter the bush. All she was missing was a machete and a pith helmet. I opened the passenger door and stepped out onto the sidewalk. Bethany looked up at me with a half-smile. I'd thought of her eyes as sky-blue before, but now, seeing the way they sparkled in the sun, I realized just how apt that description was.

"For someone who spent most of the night in a gargoyle cage, you don't look any worse for wear," she said. "Pity. You could stand to be taken down a peg."

"I've spent the night in worse places," I said. I turned back to the Escalade, where Philip watched us from behind the wheel. "You coming?"

He shook his head. "I told you, you're on your own. Vampires aren't welcome here."

"You're going to let that stop you?"

He looked up through the tinted windshield at the morning sky. "Even if I wanted to come with you, I couldn't. Not *everything* you've heard about vampires is a lie. We have . . . issues with the sun."

"Like the gargoyles," I said.

"We are *nothing* like those mindless vermin," he snarled, turning to me angrily.

"They're not all like that," I reminded him. "Besides, you were outside yesterday during the day. I saw you."

He sighed and seemed to relax. "That was different. Storm clouds covered the sun yesterday. I won't be so lucky today. But it doesn't matter. Vampires can't enter. I'll wait for you here." I nodded and started to close the passenger door, but he stopped me. "Be careful, Trent. If I were you, I wouldn't trust a word the oracles say."

"I don't believe in prophecies. I don't think the world works that way," I told him. "But if they know anything that can help us, I'll get it out of them."

I closed the door and turned back to Bethany. She stooped to pick up a metal birdcage I hadn't noticed down by her feet. Inside, two small starlings sat on the perch. They let out a few chirps as she lifted the cage, then sat quietly again.

"What's with the birds?" I asked.

"Payment," she said. "The oracles don't work for free."

"You were able to get two birds on short notice at six in the morning on a Sunday?"

She shrugged. "I know a guy. Come on."

I followed Bethany down the sidewalk. Just past the white brick funeral home was a tall, wrought-iron gate that covered the mouth of an alley. Running along the top of the gate were the words NEW YORK MARBLE CEMETERY, INCORPORATED 1831. Through the bars I saw a long brick alleyway lined with fire escapes and windows with air-conditioning units, and at the far end, a glimpse of the cemetery in the form of a green sliver of grass. Bethany handed the birdcage to me and glanced over her shoulder to make sure no one was watching. While I studied the starlings and wondered who exactly could supply birds to the needy at odd hours, she pulled a key from her jeans pocket and used it to open the padlock on the gate. She opened the gate quickly, and we went through. As soon as we were in, she closed the gate again and reached through the bars to squeeze the padlock shut. It was clear she didn't want anyone following us inside.

We walked down the alley, the sound of my boots echoing back at us from the brick walls. "How do you have the keys to this place?" I asked. "Your bird man give you those, too?"

"I borrowed them," she said, "from the Library of Keys."

I stopped walking. "There's a library of *keys*?"

She didn't break her stride, just shook her head and grinned. "I keep forgetting you're new to all this. Tell you what, if we get out of this alive, I'll take you on a tour of the *real* New York. There's a lot more to this city than the Statue of Liberty and Famous Ray's."

"So I'm learning," I said, catching up to her. "A tour sounds good. I'm going to hold you to that."

We walked on, neither of us saying anything, though I imagined we were thinking the same thing. Time was running out, and even if the oracles told us where Stryge's body was, the odds were still stacked against us. By this time tomorrow, it was likely there wouldn't be a New York City left to tour.

Another locked gate stood at the end of the alley. Bethany pulled out the key and opened this one, too. Once we'd passed through, she made sure to lock it again behind us, just like before. She took the birdcage back from me. I looked around, expecting to see a cemetery, but it looked more like someone's backyard. A meadow of neatly cut grass, a few shrubs and trees, and some plastic outdoor tables and chairs, all fenced in by stone walls. There wasn't a single headstone or monument anywhere. Either the bodies were buried in unmarked graves or they'd been interred in the walls, behind the engraved marble tablets affixed to the stone.

We continued walking, making our way to the far end of the lawn. "I always wondered what was back here," I said. "I must have passed this place a hundred times, but the gate was never open."

"You weren't meant to know what's back here," Bethany said. "No one is. It's too dangerous."

"Because of the oracles?" I asked. "Are they really that bad?"

"If you believe the stories, yes," she said. "They say hundreds of years ago the elder of a vampire clan got some bad news from the oracles. It upset him so much he sent assassins to kill them. The assassins never returned. The entire clan disappeared. Just wiped out, like that." She snapped her fingers. "Ever since, no vampire has been allowed inside. More to the point, no vampire has dared enter."

I'd seen the way Philip reacted, and he was certainly no shrinking violet. It was the only time I'd ever seen the vampire scared of anything. Maybe the stories were true after all. But even if the oracles were badass enough to frighten vampires, I still didn't know what to make of them. I'd seen too much suffering and injustice to believe in destiny or prophecies. And yet, the oracles kept coming up, and so did their prophecy about an immortal storm. Even if they were charlatans, it had to mean something.

At the far wall of the cemetery stood a low, corbel-roofed stone structure covered in moss and vines. It looked like the tower battlements of a castle, if that castle had sunk deep into the ground a long, long time ago. A heavy iron door was set into the side facing us.

Bethany turned to me. "When we get down there, let me do the talking, okay? This is a very tricky situation, and the last thing you want to do is tick off the oracles."

"What makes you think I'll tick them off?"

She arched an eyebrow at me. "Who *don't* you tick off? You act without thinking. You use your fists more than your words. Right now we need to be a little more respectful. So just leave this to me, okay?"

I shrugged. "Fine."

She pulled opened the iron door. Inside, a spiral staircase descended into the darkness.

"Oh, before I forget, I have something for you." Bethany pulled an amulet out of her cargo vest and handed it to me. At the end of a silk cord hung what looked like a slab of quartz, so thin and fragile I was worried it would shatter if I stared at it too hard. A vein of light pulsed inside it.

"A charm?" I asked.

"I've been giving some thought to your . . . condition," she said. She started down the steps, using her mirrored charm as a flashlight, and I followed her. "Remember the shock Gabrielle experienced when she tried to read your mind? And what happened when the Black Knight tried to kill you? I think they were both the same thing, a kind of magical feedback. In some ways, magic is like electricity. It can flow from one source to another. The power inside you isn't magic, or at least it isn't like any magic we know, but it obviously works the same way, taking the life force from one source and giving it to another. So why can't it be channeled the same way we channel magic?"

"You're losing me," I said. Our footsteps echoed off the close walls as we descended. I wondered how deep we were going. The staircase seemed to spiral endlessly downward.

"Okay, let's put it a simpler way," she said. "What if you could come back from the dead without anyone else having to die in your place? What if we could create a circuit that captures your own life force as it leaves your body and lets the power inside you simply take it back? A feedback loop, essentially. You wouldn't *need* to take anyone else's life force."

I lifted the amulet to look at it again. It was so delicate I couldn't believe it could be capable of something so monumental. "This can do that?"

"You told me you were tired of all the death. I figured maybe we could do something about it, starting with your own." We reached the bottom of the steps at the mouth of a dark, musty corridor. She turned to me and said, "It's made from the shell of a giant volcanic ammonite. Their shells are known for their conductive abilities, especially with magic. There's also a stasis spell inside the charm to trap your life force before it escapes, but I had to tune the charm specifically to you to keep the circuit whole."

"How did you do that?"

"It's got your DNA in it," she said. Then she turned quickly on her heel and started walking down the corridor.

"Wait, what? How did you get my DNA?" But even as I asked, the answer came to me. Back at Citadel I'd watched Bethany clean my blood off the carpet with a tissue, then pocket it. I hurried after her again, half shocked and half revolted. "The blood on the tissue?"

She sighed. "I know, it's disgusting, I don't even want to talk about it. Look, just be careful with the amulet. No one has ever engineered one of these before. It's utterly unique, and giant volcanic ammonites are extremely rare. There are only two of them left in the world, and I don't have any more shell on hand, so don't lose it and don't break it."

"Are you sure it'll work?"

"There's no way to test it short of killing you, and right now I need you focused and upright. So even when you're wearing the amulet, try not to die, okay?"

I slipped the silk cord around my neck and tucked the amulet inside my shirt, letting it rest against my chest. It felt unexpectedly warm. I thought of the little boy in the crack house, and the homeless man in the CHILD OF FIRE T-shirt. If the amulet worked, Bethany had given me a way to put an end to all the needless death. No one would be in danger from the thing inside me anymore.

"Thank you," I said. The words sounded embarrassingly feeble, unworthy of the gift she'd given me, but I didn't know what else to say. Maybe she was right about me being better with my fists than my words.

"Let's just hope you never need it," she said.

I watched her walk in front of me, silhouetted by the glowing charm in her hand. There was no way I could ever repay her, not for something this big. I owed her so much, this stranger who'd befriended me from the start, who'd fought beside me and forgiven me for betraying her. I had the overwhelming desire to pick her up in my arms and—

"You're awfully quiet back there," she said.

I took a deep breath and collected myself. "So, um, what are you going to call it? All magic charms have names, don't they?"

"Most do," she said. "Usually it's a combination of the primary engineer's last name and the function of the spell, like the Avasthi phalanx or the Mamatas silencer."

I thought about it a moment. "I suppose the Savory lifesaver is out of the question?"

"Yeah, I think we can do better," she said. "But I don't care what they call it. I only care that it works."

"You knew I'd come back," I said. "Even though I told Isaac I wouldn't."

"Of course I knew. You're like a bad headache, Trent. There's just no getting rid of you."

"If I didn't know better, I'd think you actually missed me."

She barked out a sharp laugh. "Actually, I was enjoying the relative quiet in your absence. You weren't gone long enough to miss."

"But if I had been, you *would* have missed me."

"Keep it up and I'll put that amulet to the test after all," she said.

We walked through an arched doorway into an enormous, underground Gothic chapel. We passed through rows of tombs arranged along the floor, stone sarcophagi with carvings of knights, kings, and queens lying in repose on the lids. In the light of Bethany's charm, I saw more sarcophagi inside the numerous nooks carved into the walls. We went through a door on the far side of the chapel and descended more stairs. Once more I had the feeling we were descending into the depths of a great tower that had been swallowed by the earth. At the bottom of the steps, the corridor branched off in three different directions. Without a moment's hesitation

Bethany started down the passageway on the right, and I realized then what I should have from the start: Bethany knew exactly where she was going. In a dark underground labyrinth like this, with no map and no guide, that could only mean one thing.

"You've been here before," I said.

"Once, a few years back," she answered. "I had questions about my parents, who they were, why they abandoned me. I thought the oracles could tell me, or at least help me find them."

"Did they?"

"They wouldn't see me. They didn't even open the door." She stopped, shining her light on a pair of huge metal doors that towered before us. "Let's hope this time they do."

The doors stood nearly twenty feet tall, coming together at the top in a pointed arch. The knockers, two heavy bronze rings, hung low enough on the doors for someone of average height to reach. Bethany, not being of average height, had to stand on her tiptoes to swing one. The knocker fell against the door with a loud, deep noise that reverberated in my chest and echoed through the corridor. We waited. And waited. The doors didn't open. Bethany knocked again, and again nothing happened.

She couldn't hide the disappointment in her face. "They still won't see me," she said. She sounded ashamed, as if she were being punished for some imagined infraction. "Isaac was right, he should have come, not me. This is my fault."

"The hell it is," I said. I grabbed the knocker and slammed it hard against the metal. "Open the damn door!"

The doors opened this time, swinging inward on ancient, creaking hinges. We looked at each other, surprised. Even more surprising was that no one was waiting on the other side of the threshold. Apparently, the doors had opened on their own.

"Okay, that's not creepy or off-putting at all," Bethany said.

We walked cautiously inside. The doors swung closed behind us, once again seemingly on their own. The light from Bethany's charm snapped off suddenly, plunging us into pitch-blackness.

"Turn it back on," I whispered.

"I didn't turn it off," she answered. She cursed and shook the charm like it was a flashlight with dying batteries, but it stayed dark.

A moment later, the room lit up as the flames of dozens of candles sprang to life around us. We were standing in a circle of tall candelabras arranged in the center of a large chamber. And yet, despite the plentiful candles, everything outside the circle remained as black as night, as if the light itself refused to go there.

Dozens of birdcages were interspersed with the candelabras, hanging on hooks at the end of long chains that stretched down from the darkness above us. A few of the cages had birds in them, pigeons, warblers, and sapsuckers that hopped or fluttered their wings. The rest of them were empty. The chamber floor was carpeted with shed feathers, so many they could have come from whole flocks. They must have kept a lot of them as pets over the years.

A voice boomed out of the darkness, thunderous and echoing. "Speak." It seemed to come from high above us, as though the oracles were up by the ceiling, or perhaps giants stuffed into the chamber somehow. I couldn't see a thing, though. Looking up into the dark was like looking into a starless night sky.

A pigeon cooed nervously. Bethany cleared her throat. "My name is Bethany Savory—"

"We know who you are," the voice interrupted.

"You are not of interest to us," a second voice said, somewhere to the right of the first.

"Nor is the question of your heritage," said a third, off to the left.

"I'm not here about me," she said. I had to hand it to her. She was remarkably calm. It wasn't everyone who could keep their composure after being told the biggest question of their life didn't matter. "We've come in search of information."

"You have questions," the first voice said.

"Questions you believe we can answer," the second voice said.

"Yet we answer no questions without payment," said the third.

"I brought an offering," Bethany said.

"Bring it forward."

At the far edge of the circle of candles, a chain descended suddenly from the darkness above. On its end was a thick metal hook. Bethany walked to it, hung the birdcage on the hook, and stepped back again.

The darkness on the other side of the candles seemed to swell, billowing forward to envelope the birdcage. In the dark I heard the starlings struggle, flapping their wings in panic. Their shrill birdcalls were cut off a moment later with a sickening crunch.

I looked down and noticed the tiny bones scattered among the feathers on the floor. The birds weren't pets. They were snacks.

The darkness receded, leaving an empty birdcage behind. Another, smaller circle of candelabras appeared suddenly, deeper inside the chamber, illuminating an old wooden table with an hourglass on top of it. As I watched, the sands in the hourglass began to fall.

"Ask your questions and we will answer," a voice said. "When the sand runs out, we will answer no more."

Bethany took another deep breath, steeling herself. "We seek the location of Stryge's body."

"You will find him to the north, in the same place where he fell in battle."

"Stryge still sits upon his throne, entombed deep beneath the stones of Saint-Michel-de-Cuxa."

"And the stones of Saint-Guilhem-le-Désert."

"And Bonnefont-en-Comminges."

"And Trie-en-Bigorre."

"And Froville."

Bethany shook her head. "Wait, I don't understand. I don't know those names. Please, we don't have time for riddles. Can't you just tell us where his body is?"

"We have answered your question already. We will not answer it a second time. Yet the sand still runs. Time remains for other questions, and other answers."

Bethany swallowed hard and nodded. She thought for a moment, then said, "If we're too late and Stryge wakes up, how can we kill him?"

"What you ask is impossible. Stryge is an Ancient."

"A primal entity forged in magic and eternity."

"You may as well ask how to kill the sky, or the wind."

"But there *has* to be a way to stop him," Bethany insisted. "Willem Van Lente managed to cut off Stryge's head. How?"

"The answer to that question is shielded even from us."

"Shielded by Willem Van Lente's own will."

"Perhaps you should ask him yourself."

"We can't," Bethany said. "He's been dead for centuries."

"No. Willem Van Lente yet lives."

"He's alive?" Bethany demanded, incredulous. The oracles didn't reply, presumably because they'd answered that question already.

I blurted out, "Where is he?" Bethany tried to stop me, but it was too late.

"At last, it speaks," the first voice said.

"The mighty warrior has returned," the second said.

"Returned in the guise of a man," said the third.

"A man that is not a man."

I stared up into the darkness. "What are you talking about? What does that mean?"

"It has forgotten."

"It has forgotten what it is."

"It remembers nothing of its past."

"I'm not an *it*," I said, growing angry. "And frankly, I'm tired of people treating me like one."

"It does not even know what it is."

"It is a threat, that is what it is."

"No," I said, "you're wrong."

"It is a danger to all who live."

"You're wrong!" I shouted up at them. "I have an amulet now. I'm not a danger to anyone anymore."

The oracles remained silent for a long moment. I thought maybe I'd gotten my point across. Then, out of the darkness came a booming voice. "It thinks it has a choice. It does not."

"What does that mean?" I demanded. "What am I?"

"An abomination."

"A menace."

"It is a combination of elements that were never meant to be combined."

"As long as it walks upon this world, as long as it dwells among us, it puts us all in peril."

"No, you're lying!" I yelled. "God damn it, if you know what I am, tell me!"

"We have answered your question."

"Like hell you have!"

"Then seek out the Mistress of the Dead," the first voice said.

"The Mother of Wraiths," the second said.

"She knows," the third said. "She knows all who have passed through the dark that separates the cities of the living from the cities of the dead."

"You mean Reve Azrael?" I said. "How does she know what I am? What's the connection between us?"

"We have answered your question."

"Tell me!" They remained silent, which only made my blood boil more. "Tell me, God damn it! You think I'm dangerous now? Keep pissing me off and you'll see just how dangerous I can be!"

Bethany grabbed me by the arm. "Don't," she said. "You've got to keep it together. This isn't why we're here."

I was beginning to understand why the vampire clan elder had wanted to kill the oracles. I wanted to wring their necks myself, but Bethany was right. This was getting us nowhere, and we didn't have the time to waste. "They're wrong about me," I told her, but doubts were already starting to sneak into my mind. How could I be so sure? Everything about me was wrong, my aura, my scent, my memories. I was so wrong even death wouldn't take me. What if the oracles were right? What if I really was something awful?

Bethany let go of my arm and looked up into the darkness. "I'm sorry about my friend. He didn't mean it. Please, we need your help."

"It is too late," the first voice said. "The sands have run out."

I looked over at the table. The sands of the hourglass had emptied into the lower half.

"No, wait, please," she begged them. "If Willem Van Lente is still alive, you've got to tell us where to find him. He's the only one who can stop Stryge."

"Your time is up."

"Your questions have been answered."

The candles extinguished, plunging us into darkness. Behind us, the doors swung open on their own.

"Please, you're our last chance!" Bethany cried into the dark. "You have to help us!"

No one answered.

Thirty-five

"Did the oracles help?" Philip asked as Bethany and I returned to the Escalade.

I crawled into the backseat. "It was a colossal waste of time."

"I figured," Philip said.

"They weren't exactly forthcoming, but I wouldn't call it a waste of time," Bethany said from the front passenger seat. She was more optimistic than I was, but I didn't see any reason for it. The oracles hadn't given us anything but gibberish and bad attitude. "They said Stryge's body was in a tomb somewhere to the north." She gave him the five names the oracle had supplied, but he'd never heard of them.

She pulled out her cell and got Isaac on speakerphone. She ran the names by him, too. "Do they mean anything to you?" she asked. "Were they in any of the books?"

"No, but hold on a moment, let me get to my computer," Isaac said. The sound of tapping keys came over the speaker. "I put the names into a search engine, but it's weird, none of them have anything to do with New York City. Saint-Michel-de-Cuxa is a Benedictine abbey in the Pyrenees. Saint-Guilhem-le-Désert is a medieval abbey outside Montpellier. Trie-en-Bigorre is a Carmelite convent near Toulouse. They're all religious sites in France."

"That doesn't make sense," Bethany said. "Stryge's body has to be here. The Lenape Indians hid it somewhere after the battle."

"Maybe they shipped the body to France instead," I said. "It's a lot harder to join the head and body when they're on two separate continents."

"Impossible," she said.

I leaned back in my seat and crossed my arms. "Fine. Here's something that's more possible: the oracles don't know what the hell they're talking about."

She ignored me, turning back to the phone sitting open in her hand. "Are you sure there's no connection between those names, nothing that applies to New York?"

We heard Isaac's fingers on the keyboard again. "This might be something. It's from a Web site of New York City walking tours. Listen to this. 'Throughout the grounds, visitors will find the authentic hallways, chapels, and gardens that once stood in such famous French cathedrals and abbeys as Saint-Michel-de-Cuxa, Saint-Guilhem-le-Désert, and Bonnefont-en-Comminges. Each structure was disassembled brick by brick before being shipped to New York and reassembled in the 1930s as a public museum.'"

"Where is this?" Bethany asked.

"Fort Tryon Park, up in Washington Heights," Isaac said. "It's the Cloisters. That's where Stryge's body is. They built the Cloisters right on top of his tomb."

Bethany nodded. "Of course, Washington Heights. That must be where the battle took place. 'To the north.' The oracles were right."

"Lucky guess," I said. Even to my own ears I sounded as petulant as I felt. Even if it meant the end of New York City, part of me didn't want the oracles to be right, because if they were right about this, it meant they were also right about me.

"How many millions of people visit the Cloisters every year, completely unaware of what's sleeping right under their feet?" Isaac said. "Good work, guys. Get back to Citadel, we've got work to do. And Trent?"

"Yeah?"

"I've got something you need to see," Isaac said.

I leaned forward in the backseat. "What?"

"Get here now, guys," he said, ignoring my question. "We don't have a lot of time. The equinox is coming."

Bethany ended the call. Philip started the engine and pulled the Escalade into traffic.

I watched the New York Marble Cemetery grow farther away in the rear window, and heard the oracles' voices in my head again. I couldn't help harping on the things they said about me.

A threat.

A danger.

An abomination.

They weren't all that different from the things I'd wondered about myself in the dark of my room during all those sleepless nights when my thoughts got tangled in knots and turned on themselves like rabid dogs. But even if the oracles *were* right and I was some kind of menace, it still didn't answer the big questions hanging over me.

Why couldn't I die?

How did I know how to fight as if I'd been doing it all my life?

Why couldn't I remember anything from before?

I put it from my mind. If I hadn't been able to answer those questions in the past year, I wasn't going to do it now. Besides, something else the oracles said had stuck with me too, something more pressing.

Willem Van Lente yet lives.

That Van Lente was still alive after all this time was impossible. It was insane. But by now I was willing to believe a lot of crazy things I wouldn't have thought twice about before. In fact, the more I thought about it, the more sense it suddenly made, and pieces of the puzzle began to slip into place.

When we got back to Citadel, Isaac took me up to the second floor. At the end of a hallway lined with marble busts and draped with heavy, red cloth panels was a simple wooden door. He took me inside to a small, cluttered study. Crowded bookshelves lined one wall and a leather couch covered with loose papers stood against another. An Oriental rug covered most of the hardwood floor. The morning light filtered through a stained-glass window on the far side of the study and fell on the cluttered desk, illuminating two objects resting on the blotter. The first was a big, empty, glass Erlenmeyer flask stopped with a thick cork. The other was my Bersa semiautomatic.

"My gun!" I said, as excited as if I were seeing an old friend for the first time in years. I picked it up off the desk. Even with an empty clip, it was remarkable how much better I felt with it back in my hand.

"You left it here last night," he said. "But the moment I touched it, I knew something was wrong with it."

I looked at it, inspecting the grip and the barrel. "It looks fine to me."

"It is, now," he said. He pulled over a standing magnifying glass on a brass stand, and positioned it in front of the Erlenmeyer flask. "This is what I wanted to show you. Look inside the flask."

"It's empty," I said.

"Use the magnifying glass."

I tucked the gun in the back of my pants and bent closer, putting my eye to the magnifying glass. The flask wasn't empty after all. Inside it, a tiny shape flittered around on thin, batlike wings. I blinked, surprised, certain I was imagining it, but when I looked again, the winged shape was still there. Somehow, it was aware I was watching it because suddenly it stopped flying, clung to the wall of the flask, and turned its head toward me. I sucked in my breath. It resembled a tiny naked man, albeit horned, tailed, and winged like a child's idea of what the Devil looked like. Its skin was the color of mud or clay, and it seemed to be coated in clear, slick goo. Instead of hands and feet it had barbed suction cups at the ends of its limbs. The creature flicked its forked tongue at me disdainfully.

I turned to Isaac, amazed. "What is it?"

"A homunculus," he explained. "It's a very advanced, very special kind of spell. It acts as the eyes and ears of its creator. It's a way to spy on someone without being detected. I found it attached to the grip of your gun. It's so small it's no wonder you never knew it was there." He bent down to look at the Erlenmeyer flask. "I believe this is how Reve Azrael found you at the safe house, and how she found Citadel."

I took a quick step back from the desk. "Then she can see us right now?"

"Don't worry, the psychic link has been severed," Isaac said. "Without it, Reve Azrael is flying blind. She won't know where you are or what you're doing, not anymore."

I looked at the flask again. With only my naked eye, I couldn't even see the homunculus inside. How could something so small have caused so much trouble?

"How did it get on my gun?" I asked. How many times had I held the Bersa without knowing the homunculus was right there on the grip, stuck there like glue just centimeters from my hand? Even right *under* my hand, so small I wouldn't have felt it?

"One of her revenants must have put it there," Isaac answered. "Bennett, I'm guessing. That's the only revenant who could have gotten close enough."

Isaac's theory sounded good on the surface, but it didn't hold up under scrutiny. Reve Azrael had already found me at the safe house before she could have gotten close enough in Bennett's guise to slip the homunculus onto my gun. No, I was convinced there was something we weren't seeing. Something we'd overlooked.

I studied the homunculus through the magnifying glass again. Inside the flask, it flitted back and forth like a restless mosquito. "You said it was a spell, but it looks alive."

"It's not," a voice said from the study door. I looked up. Gabrielle walked into the room. She had one arm in a sling, but otherwise she looked pretty good for someone who'd been shot just last night. Whatever was in the Sanare moss they'd put on her wounds had worked wonders. "The homunculus is made of paper, clay, and magic, nothing more. Think of it as a machine. And like a machine, it can be reprogrammed."

"How?" I asked.

She picked up the flask with her good arm. "Reve Azrael can't use the homunculus anymore, but with just a few tweaks to the existing spell, *we* can." She walked back to the door. "Give me five minutes and I'll have it ready, Isaac."

"Be quick," he said. "The others are gearing up downstairs. We're leaving in ten."

When Gabrielle was gone, I said, "Why do I get the feeling you've got something up your sleeve?"

"It's always good to have a Plan B." He led me back out into the hallway, then closed and locked the door to the study. "Trent, after everything you've already done for us, I hesitate to ask you this. It's a lot to ask of someone I've only just met, but we need all the help we can get."

"You're asking if I'm coming with you," I said.

"Are you?"

I nodded. "But she'll know I'm with you. She'll know you're coming."

"Not anymore. Not without her homunculus."

"I wouldn't be so sure of that," I said. "I don't think we're seeing the whole picture. Reve Azrael could just as easily have used the homunculus to track Bethany or Thornton, right? But she chose me. She knows things about me that a homunculus can't explain. The oracles said she knows who I am. I want to know how."

"She's not going to sit still for an interrogation if that's what you're thinking," Isaac said.

"I know, but I aim to get the truth out of her, one way or another."

He shook his head. "Let it go, Trent. Reve Azrael is dangerous. Not just to us, but to this whole city. If we have the chance to put her down once and for all, we can't risk waiting around. We have to take it. You would be smart to do the same."

Not without getting some answers first, I thought, but I nodded as if I agreed with him.

"Good," he said. We started down the hall toward the staircase. Halfway there, I noticed an open door to a room off the hallway. Bethany was inside, standing at a metal table in the center of the room, her back to me. The room was small, its walls covered floor to ceiling with little drawers, as if it were one big apothecary chest. I told Isaac I'd join him downstairs in a minute, then leaned against the doorway and crossed my arms. I watched her pull open a drawer and take out a small, tubular charm with a glass bead on one end. She placed it on the table next to a selection of charms she'd lined up there.

"This is a familiar sight," I said. "Tomo, Big Joe, and I used to do this all the time before a job. Only we were loading up on guns and ammunition, not charms."

She glanced at me over her shoulder. "The principle's the same, I suppose." She opened the pockets in her vest and started unloading charms from it onto the table. "Gabrielle told me about the homunculus."

"Isaac showed it to me," I said. "Ugly little thing."

She smirked. "They say homunculi take on the physical features of the people they're spying on."

"Really? Come to think of it, the little guy *did* have a sort of rugged charm to him."

She rolled her eyes. "The important thing is that you know the truth now. You know what happened wasn't your fault."

"Wasn't it? Reve Azrael would never have gotten the box if she hadn't followed me here."

"That's not what I'm talking about," she said. "You blame yourself for Ingrid's death. You have from the start, even if you won't admit it. I can see it in your eyes every time someone says her name. Maybe now you can stop beating yourself up over it."

"If I'd known about the homunculus . . ."

"You couldn't have," she said. "It's not your fault Reve Azrael used the homunculus to find us. It's not your fault you weren't there when the shadowborn came. You need to start believing that, or the guilt will eat away at you. Believe me, I know. Guilt was a constant companion throughout my childhood. When I wasn't busy hating my parents for abandoning me, I was busy blaming myself for driving them away. The guilt ate away at me a little more every day, until I couldn't feel anything else. Don't let it do the same to you. Find a way to move past it."

"That's easier said than done."

"Maybe," she said, "but it's worth it." She turned away from me again and took off her vest. Beneath it was a dark blue, formfitting turtleneck top. The material was snug, clinging to the planes and curves of her body like a second skin, and it turned sheer where it stretched across her shoulders. I could just make out the phoenix tattoo covering her back, bisected by the black band of her bra.

I caught myself staring and looked away. "The others are waiting downstairs. I should probably—"

"You okay? You sound weird." She turned around to face me again. Her eyes were as bright and blue as the clearest water.

"I'm fine," I managed to say.

She handed me a small cardboard box about the size of a wallet. "Here, this is for you." I opened the box. Inside were seven nine-millimeter bullets. I grinned about a mile wide. "I found it in one of the drawers and thought of you. They probably won't do you much good, but I figured you might like them anyway. If I didn't know better, I'd say your gun was your talisman."

I loaded them into the clip of my gun. "First the amulet, now this," I said. "What would I do without you, Bethany?"

"Probably die a lot more," she said.

I looked into her eyes again. She looked back at me. Something passed between us then, a moment where it felt like I could do or say anything because anything was possible. I opened my mouth to speak, not even sure what was going to come out, but the oracles' words started banging around in my head again. *Danger. Threat. Abomination. A man that is not a man.* I closed my mouth again. Who was I kidding? Bethany wouldn't waste her time on someone like me. I felt like a fool, and the moment was gone.

"We should get downstairs," she said. She put on her vest, its pockets bulging with charms. We went downstairs in silence.

Downstairs, the main room was still a shambles from Reve Azrael's attack, the floor covered in shattered crystal obelisks, books knocked from their shelves, and broken statuettes, all covered in a coarse layer of ash. The others had already gathered amid the mess. Gabrielle was holding a morningstar she'd taken from Isaac's vault, weighing the balance of the spiky-headed mace in her good hand. Philip had a long-handled broadsword, its elaborate hilt carved in the shape of a roaring dragon's head. The vampire was covered head to toe in a flowing black hooded cloak to protect him from the sun. Even his hands were shielded inside black gloves. If I didn't already know him, I would have found him terrifying.

Isaac came up and tossed me a staff. "Catch!"

It was the Anubis Hand, new and improved. The blackened, mummified fist had been mounted to the tip of a metal staff this time. I tapped the staff against the floor. It was solid, strong. There was no way this one was getting chopped in half.

Isaac checked his watch and addressed the group. "Two hours until the equinox. Two hours to stop Stryge from waking up and destroying New York City. I'm not going to lie to you, this isn't going to be easy, and it isn't going to be safe. We're severely outnumbered by Reve Azrael's revenants and the Black Knight's gargoyles. I can't guarantee we're all going to come home from this, or that any of us will. I wanted to take a moment to tell you that you've all done your jobs remarkably well. I couldn't be prouder to work with each one of you. But what we're about to do is more dangerous than any job I've sent you on. This isn't like securing an artifact. This is Stryge we're talking about. He has all the powers of an Ancient, and he revels in death and destruction. If something goes wrong and Stryge is awakened, there's no amount of money I can pay you that'll be worth the danger you'd face."

"This isn't about money, not anymore," Gabrielle said.

Isaac nodded. "A very wise man once told me there comes a time when you have to rise up and make a stand, even if no one else will. I didn't listen. I sent you all out into danger instead. You risked your lives for me, while I hung back. No more. But this is the most dangerous thing I have ever asked you to do, so if you have any reservations, if you've changed your mind about coming, leave now. The door's right over there. No one would blame you." He looked at each of us. No one spoke. No one left.

"Fun speech," Philip said. "So, are you gonna drive, or am I?"

Philip drove us north on the West Side Highway toward Fort Tryon Park. Seated in the back of the Escalade, I watched the city roll by and gripped the staff tightly. I didn't know what would be waiting for us on the other end of the ride, but I had some nasty ideas. Were we strong enough to handle it? Prepared enough? I wondered if this was the same trepidation Willem Van Lente had felt as he'd approached the battlefield to face Stryge four hundred years ago.

It was Willem Van Lente's own fist that had become the Anubis Hand. He'd used magic—dangerous magic—to transform his own flesh into a weapon. The more I thought about that and everything it implied, the more the puzzle pieces slid into place.

The oracles were right when they said Willem Van Lente was still alive. And if I was right, he would be at Stryge's tomb today, too.

Up front, in the passenger seat, Isaac shared his plan. "Reve Azrael will most likely have already gone underground to the tomb by the time we get there, but it's a sure thing Melanthius will be lurking somewhere close, acting as lookout. We can use that to our advantage. Wherever Melanthius is, Reve Azrael won't be far. He's our signpost. Find him, and we'll find Stryge's tomb."

Fort Tryon Park sat at the north end of Manhattan like a small island of green amid a vast sea of concrete, nature's last gasp at the top of an over-developed urban landscape. The Cloisters loomed over the treeline in the distance as we approached, an enormous brick and stone Gothic fortress. When we reached the park, we pulled into the public parking lot.

The lot was surprisingly crowded. It took us a few minutes to find a parking spot, weaving through the cars and big white trailers before we finally found a space to pull into. A family walked by, two parents and three kids, the father pushing the smallest one in a stroller. Isaac shook his head. "Damn it. I didn't think there would be this many people here today. We have to be careful."

We got out of the Escalade and started toward the park entrance. Philip pulled the hood of his cloak lower over his head to keep himself protected from the sun. The people standing by their cars watched us as we passed. Their eyes went to Gabrielle's morningstar, my staff, Philip's cloak and sword, but instead of doing something sane like backing away and calling the cops, they just nodded and gave us the thumbs-up. I scowled at them, confused, but kept walking.

"The Cloisters are on the other side of the park from where we are now," Isaac said. "That gives us a lot of ground to cover. Keep your eyes open and your weapons handy. Melanthius is out there somewhere, and I'm guessing the Black Knight is, too."

"Piece of cake," I said. "How hard can it be to spot a man in a wizard's cloak or a knight in armor? They'll stick out like a sore thumb."

Then I looked up and froze.

A dense throng of people waited at the park entrance. There were men in tights and doublets, cloaks, chainmail, and full suits of armor, and women in Renaissance gowns and cone-shaped princess hats. Above them, a banner stretched from one side of the park entrance to the other. It read, WELCOME TO THE MEDIEVAL FESTIVAL AT FORT TRYON PARK.

"Oh," I said.

Thirty-six

We entered the park, trying not to draw attention to ourselves, but after a couple of minutes it was obvious no one was giving us a second look. There were others in the crowd drawing much more attention than we were, women in colorful, cleavage-baring satin corsets and men dressed as knights riding upon flag-draped horses. There were Renaissance noblemen chatting on cell phones, and armor-plated squires gnawing on oversized barbecued turkey legs. Children ran by with foam rubber swords, giggling with delight, followed by a handful of adults walking with poleaxes and sheathed sabers that looked a lot more real. I caught a glimpse of a man in a peaked, storybook-style wizard's hat, a curved wooden pipe in his mouth and a whittled walking stick in his hand. He reminded me of the twins in the photo of the Five-Pointed Star. It made me wonder if there were others at the festival who were like us, walking unnoticed amid the thousands who had no idea magic was real. What would the festivalgoers think if they knew? If they understood how dangerous magic was?

When I read *The Ragana's Revenge*, I'd scoffed at the idea that magic could be real. I wished now that I'd had the chance to finish the book before losing it in the fire. Seeing as how my life had started to mirror the novel in ways I never would have imagined, it suddenly felt very important to know whether or not it had a happy ending.

We followed the paved path deeper into the park, surrounded on either side by booths of jewelers, gamers, purveyors of period clothing, and one booth labeled, oddly, YE OLDE LONG DISTANCE SERVICE, where a woman wearing a velvet gown and a wreath of flowers in her hair took customers' applications on a decidedly anachronistic laptop. So much for escapism, I thought. The path was so packed with festivalgoers that we could only move at a crawl. As I weaved my way through, I almost collided with a group of college-aged men and women in forest-green tunics and dresses. They laughed at some private joke and touched their comically big, prosthetic pointed elf ears to check that they were on straight.

Next to me, Bethany adjusted her hair self-consciously.

A flash of red caught my eye in a small field just past the booths, where the crowd was less thick. A figure in a hooded red cloak was moving swiftly across the grass, his face hidden from me. He wasn't browsing the booths or studiously checking the festival-grounds map like the others around him. He walked with speed and purpose, definitely heading somewhere specific.

Melanthius. I took off at a sprint after him.

"Trent, wait!" Isaac shouted after me, but I wasn't about to let Reve Azrael's manservant get away.

I zigzagged through the crowd and ducked past a blacksmith presentation at the edge of the path. I tried to keep my eyes on Melanthius as I ran, but every time I thought I was close, I lost him in the crowd, only to catch a glimpse of his red cloak again even farther away. I ran up the grassy hill toward him. Suddenly a unicorn appeared in my way, snorting and stamping one hoof. I paused, startled, then realized it wasn't a unicorn at all, just a white horse with a long fake horn attached to a part of the bridle that covered its forehead. The long-haired, long-gowned woman riding atop it smiled down at the children who had gathered around her, blocking my path. I went around them and kept running. Ahead, Melanthius had paused near the edge of the forest, his back to me. I ran up, grabbed him by the shoulders of his cloak, and spun him around to face me.

A startled man with fat, ruddy cheeks and a patchy beard gaped back at me from inside the hood.

I let him go. "Sorry, I thought you were someone else."

"The fuck is wrong with you, dude?" He walked off cursing as the others came running up behind me.

"It wasn't Melanthius," I said.

"I can see that," Isaac replied angrily. "Don't go running off like that again. We need to stick together."

I scanned the crowd, only half listening. I saw red cloaks everywhere—on a teenage boy walking by, on a young woman buying something at a jewelry booth, on an older woman standing near the path and singing madrigals. "We're never going to find him in this crowd," I said.

A loud scream startled us. We took off running, following the commotion to the side of the park grounds, where a low stone wall overlooked the Hudson River. A crowd had gathered by the wall, pointing at the Palisades cliffs across the water. A thick, dark gray column billowed out of a cave in the cliffside and drifted across the river toward the park.

"Is that smoke?" Isaac asked.

"No," I said. "It's gargoyles."

There were hundreds of them, all pouring out of the cave en masse and stretching like a ribbon across the sky. They followed the path of the river northward, flying inside a thick cloudlike cover of steam. It took me a moment to realize what the steam was. Their flesh was burning in the sunlight. They must have been in immense pain, but they had their orders direct from their king, and from what Jibril-khan had told me, if they didn't obey they would end up dead. This was the Black Knight's endgame, his final push to acquire Stryge's power for himself, and he wasn't the kind to let a tiny detail like his subjects' painful aversion to sunlight stop him.

"We have to get everyone out of the park, right now," Isaac said. "Philip, Gabrielle, you're with me. Bethany and Trent, you follow the gargoyles, find out where they're going. If I'm right, we won't need Melanthius after all. The gargoyles will lead us right to Stryge's tomb."

The three of them took off, shouting at everyone they saw to evacuate the park. Bethany and I ran north with the gargoyles. In the distance, the single tower of the Cloisters peeked over the trees like the battlements of a mighty castle. The gargoyles were making a beeline right for it.

We ran past the tournament field, a long meadow of grass and dirt enclosed by a semicircle of portable bleachers on one end and a small picket fence on the other. I caught a glimpse of the jousting tournament inside, a man in an armored breastplate and plumed cap atop a chestnut stallion. He was holding a lance in front of him and galloping toward his opponent. The bleachers were filled with hundreds of cheering festivalgoers, oblivious to the gargoyle army flying past. I hoped like hell the gargoyles stayed over the river and didn't come inland. The people here were sitting ducks, locked in by the bleachers and the fence with only a handful of narrow exits. If the gargoyles chose to attack, it would be a massacre.

But they ignored the tournament field and kept flying. Finally, they turned inland, sailing over the forest that surrounded the Cloisters. Bethany and I followed them, running into the woods and up a hill. At the top of the hill, Bethany stifled a cry of surprise, and we both skidded to a halt.

Below, the woods were filled with revenants, more than I'd ever seen in one place. There had to be a hundred of them, all shambling toward the Cloisters. They wore leather sheaths on their backs, and as one they stopped and turned their ragged forms toward us, until we were looking out upon a field of glowing red eyes. I reached for my gun, but as a great shadow fell over them, I realized it wasn't us that had caught their attention.

Overhead, a pack of gargoyles had broken away from the others. They swooped down through the treetops and attacked the revenants with their claws, teeth, and tusks. Undeterred, the revenants fought back, pulling machetes from the sheaths on their backs and hacking at the gargoyles.

Bethany grabbed my arm and started pulling me away. "Come on! Back this way!"

I looked up. The sky was filled with gargoyles flying toward the Cloisters. The ones at the head of group had already reached the tower and were circling it like a funnel cloud. "But the tomb, we must be close," I said.

"We'll never make it," she insisted. "You saw all those people back there in the bleachers. It's only a matter of time before the fight spills over to where they are. You think either side cares how many humans get caught in the crossfire? We have to get them out of there before it's too late."

I took one last look at the battlefield below, already running with gargoyle blood and littered with chunks of mangled revenants, then ran with Bethany back to the tournament field. We squeezed through the narrow gaps between bleachers to get inside. There were three hundred people in those seats, at the very least. There was no way the two of us could get them all out of there as fast as we needed to.

Bethany looked overwhelmed. "What are we going to do?"

On the other side of the field was a dais where a man dressed as a medieval king was announcing the tournament standings into a microphone.

"There," I said, pointing. "That mic is the only way we're going to reach everyone."

"But what are you going to—?" she started to ask, but I was already running out onto the field. I darted between the horses as they galloped toward each other, the chestnut stallion rearing in surprise and throwing its rider. The other horse, a black mare, whinnied and slid to a quick stop. I kept running. Security guards appeared from the sidelines, chasing after me. I broke for the dais, raced up the stairs beside it, and hip-checked the announcer away from the microphone.

I grabbed the mic with my free hand and raised the Anubis Hand with the other to make sure I had the crowd's attention. "Everyone! You need to get out of here! Clear the stands!"

A murmur rippled through the crowd, peppered with a few nervous chuckles and some drunken applause, but no one moved.

"Damn it, listen to me! You have to get out of here *now*! You're all in danger!"

Below, the security guards surrounded the dais but didn't climb the steps. They barked into walkie-talkies, and a moment later a cluster of police officers came out onto the tournament field, walking toward me. On instinct, my chest tightened at the sight of them, but I pushed the feeling away. This time, the cops were just what I needed. Provided they would listen to me.

"Officers, you have to evacuate the park, everyone is in danger!" I shouted into the microphone.

The cops kept coming toward me. One look at their stern, stony faces told me they didn't care what I had to say. Their hands hovered at their belts between their guns and their handcuffs, waiting until the last minute to decide which one they'd need to subdue the raving nut with the big metal stick.

I stepped back from the mic and looked around, trying to find a way out. The security guards were still at the bottom of the steps, blocking any exit that way. On my other side, the costumed announcer had found his courage and grabbed the mic again.

"No need to worry, folks. We'll get the show back up and running in a moment," he said. The crowd cheered. The announcer looked at me, then said into the mic, "Just another reason they shouldn't serve alcohol at these things anymore. Am I right?" The cheers turned to boos.

The cops looked up at me from the field below. One of them spoke around the wad of chewing gum he was working over, "Drop the metal pipe, sir, and come on down."

I backed away, clutching the staff tight. I had to make them listen, but I didn't know how. "Please, get them out of here!"

The cop sighed. "I don't like having to repeat myself, sir." The group of officers started toward the dais stairs.

A commotion arose at the far end of the field. A handful of gargoyles and revenants smashed suddenly through the low picket fence and onto the tournament field, locked in a desperate struggle. It was too late. The fight had spilled over already.

The officers, not understanding what they were seeing, ran toward the fight to break it up. "No, get back!" I yelled, but it was too late. As soon as the officers got close, the revenants attacked them with their machetes, hacking them to pieces.

Like a spark hitting a tinderbox, it set off a scream of terror through the crowd. People stampeded for the exits. The costumed announcer jumped off the dais and ran across the field, where the horses were panicking, kicking and running in circles. The jousters didn't stick around to try to calm their horses before scrambling away. But only one end of the field was safe from the battle, the side with the bleachers, and the exits between them were too narrow. People pushed and shoved, and before long shouts of pain and anger joined the screams of terror. It was pandemonium.

I jumped off the dais, gripping the Anubis Hand tight in case any gargoyles came at me. I scanned the surrounding chaos for Bethany, but I didn't see her anywhere.

A vast shadow fell over the tournament field, as if something immense had passed over the sun. I looked up. The whole sky swarmed with gargoyles, so many that the heavens themselves were blotted out, relegated to bright flashes of blue between the winged bodies overhead.

"Bethany!" I shouted, looking for her again. Then, finally, I spotted her near the other end of the field. She was helping an older woman with a cane out of the stands and away from the fight. I started running toward her. Bethany got the woman to the nearest exit, then saw me. She started toward me across the field, shouting something I couldn't hear over the din.

A flash of black caught my eye. A dozen crows descended from the sky and swooped down to the field. A moment later they were gone. In their place was the Black Knight, sitting astride his armored black horse.

Right behind Bethany.

I shouted, "Look out!"

She looked over her shoulder, saw the Black Knight, and started running. The Black Knight urged his horse into a gallop, chasing after her.

"No!" I shouted, running toward them. "It's me you want! Leave her alone!"

The Black Knight drew his sword.

Damn it, they were too far away. I heard the distressed whinny of another horse and saw the chestnut stallion standing nearby, digging a hoof in the dirt and flicking his tail nervously. I grabbed the saddle strap, hooked a foot into the stirrup, and swung myself up into the saddle. The jouster who'd ridden him had left his shield behind, hooked to the saddle on the horse's back. Perfect. I picked it up in my free hand. It was made of a thin metal, possibly tin. Fine for a jousting exhibition, but not so great against the Black Knight's sword. Still, it was better than nothing, and I didn't have time to complain. The Black Knight was already bearing down on Bethany.

I leveled the Anubis Hand in front of me, a makeshift metal lance with a mummified human fist for a point, and squeezed my knees together to signal the horse to move. The stallion broke into a gallop, his panic subsided as his training took over.

"Over here!" I shouted. "I'm right here, you overgrown tin can!"

But I was still too far away. The Black Knight swung his sword, the barbed blade striking Bethany in the back. She cried out in pain, her legs giving out beneath her, and fell facedown to the ground.

My heart crammed into my throat. I couldn't breathe, couldn't release the anguished cry building like a head of steam inside me.

Bethany lay still in the dirt. Very, very still.

My lips pulled back in an angry snarl. I spurred the horse to run faster. The Black Knight turned the impassive, expressionless face of his helmet toward me just as I bashed the Anubis Hand into his chest. I'd hoped to knock him off his horse, but the Black Knight only rocked in his saddle a moment. Then I was past him, the chestnut stallion's momentum taking me several yards away before I managed to slow the horse and turn him around.

The Black Knight charged at me, the pounding hooves of his night-black horse throwing up divots of dirt and grass. He held his sword high, ready to strike. I spurred my horse to a gallop, the stallion's taut muscles flexing beneath me as I closed the gap between us. The Black Knight swung his sword. I raised the metal staff to block it. The blade clanged against it, nearly knocking it out of my hand. Then we were past each other as our horses continued galloping.

I turned my horse around. The Black Knight did the same, and we rode at each other once more. This time the Black Knight knocked the staff out of my hand completely, and as we passed each other, he brought his sword around to strike again. It crashed against my shield with more force than I'd expected, throwing me off my horse. The shield went flying. I landed hard on my back in the grass. Apparently, I didn't have much of a future in jousting.

Or maybe not much of a future at all. The Black Knight slowed his horse and dismounted. The chestnut stallion deserted me, galloping off to the other end of the field. I couldn't blame him; just then I wanted to be on the other end of the field, too. The Black Knight held his sword in both gauntlets and walked toward me, his heavy boots flattening the grass beneath them.

I stood up, holding my head. It felt like the fall had knocked something loose in there. "Wait," I said.

The Black Knight swung the sword at me. I jumped back, narrowly avoiding getting cut in half at the stomach.

I put my hands up as if to ward him off. "Whoa! I thought you wanted me alive. What happened to stealing my power for yourself?"

He swung again, and I jumped back to avoid the blade. Clearly he wasn't interested anymore. Maybe he'd decided I wasn't as enticing a source of power as Stryge. It was hard to feel bad playing the bridesmaid in that particular contest, but unfortunately it meant the Black Knight had no use for me anymore, no reason not to hack me to pieces.

"Stop," I said. "I know who you are. I figured it out. It doesn't have to be like this."

The sword cut through the air at my midsection as I jumped back again. The Black Knight came forward, his metal boots stomping the dirt.

"Please, listen to me," I said. "No one put it together before because the clues weren't all there. They didn't know you were still alive, or that you'd forgotten your own name. Four hundred years ago, an alchemist vanished from Fort Verhulst. It was you, but you didn't vanish, you snuck out to go fight Stryge, to stop him from killing your fellow Dutch settlers. You made the Anubis Hand so you could save your home and the people you cared about. You're Willem Van Lente." I pointed at the staff lying in the grass. "The fist on the end of that staff is *yours.*"

The Black Knight swung again, and I jumped back again. I wished I knew how much more room I had behind me, but I didn't dare take my eyes off him to turn around. I hoped I wasn't about to pin myself against the bleachers.

"In order to fight an Ancient like Stryge, you had to carry so much magic inside you. Every spell you could think of," I said. "But after the Shift, that was a dangerous thing to do. All that magic changed you. It turned you into this."

He swung again. I couldn't tell if he was listening, but I refused to believe it didn't matter to him. I refused to believe I couldn't get through to him.

"In time, the infection twisted your mind. It made you forget who you are, forget everything about yourself. Except, maybe not *everything.* Somehow you remembered there were still people out there who could connect the Black Knight to Willem Van Lente, so you went back to Fort Verhulst, and you killed them. The infection made you kill the very same people you fought to protect."

The sword cut through the air again, so close I could feel the breeze it made against my shirt.

"Willem, damn it, listen to me!" I yelled. "The infection made you forget the battle with Stryge. It made you forget so completely, buried the knowledge of how you did it so deeply, that even the oracles couldn't see it. You forgot the man you used to be, the *good* man. You forgot your own name."

The Black Knight drew back his sword to swing again, but hesitated. Was I finally getting through to him?

"I told you it doesn't have to be like this. We can help you, Willem. If there's a way back, we can help you find it, but first we need your help. Reve Azrael is about to wake Stryge up and undo everything you did. Please, you've got to help us. You're the only one who can."

The Black Knight tilted his helmet as though he were listening.

"I know how hard this is," I said. "Believe me, I know better than anyone, because we're in the same boat, you and me. Because if you want to put things right, if you want to save the city you love again . . . all you have to do is remember who you were."

The Black Knight regarded me in stoic silence.

"There's got to be something left inside you, Willem," I said. "Some part of you that still gives a damn."

By way of an answer, he drove his sword into my stomach.

I gasped and fell to my knees. The sword's hilt and half the blade stuck out of my body like a third appendage. Blood poured out of me. The Black Knight pulled the sword out again, the barbs on the back of the blade shredding my insides even more. If the sword hurt going in, it was a hundred times more painful coming out. The Black Knight backed up a step but didn't leave, preferring to watch me die. I looked up at him, desperately searching the cold, emotionless black helmet for some sign of the man he used to be, but there was nothing left of him in it. The infection had destroyed everything of the man he'd been, and replaced it with madness and cruelty.

The oracles were wrong. Willem Van Lente had died a long time ago.

I fell backward, landing right next to one of the bleachers. Bethany's charm rattled against my chest under my shirt. As blackness crawled from the corners of my vision to spread over everything, I caught a glimpse of four small faces staring in horror at me from under the bleachers. They were children, three boys and a girl, their faces streaked with dirt and tears. They must have been hiding there since the moment all hell broke loose. They were so close I could reach out and touch them—too close, and too frightened to run.

Oh God, no, not again. In my mind I saw the little boy in the crack house, dead in his mother's arms, and then the darkness came to swallow me whole.

Thirty-seven

I gasped air into my lungs and opened my eyes. I didn't know where I was. I'd been dead again, that much I could tell, but what had happened? Above me, the sky was dark, rippling and swelling as though I were looking at an ocean wave from the bottom of the sea. A moment later, my vision cleared. What I'd thought was the sky was actually a mass of gargoyles circling overhead.

I looked down and saw a hole in the front of my shirt. The whole lower half of my shirt was soaked with blood, but as usual, I had come back whole and uninjured. I sat up quickly, the memories rushing back. The Black Knight was already gone, I saw, a dozen crows flying up into the gargoyle-filled sky.

I turned and looked under the bleachers, dreading the sight of a mummified husk of a child, but the four kids were still there, all of them still alive. Relieved, I let out a sigh. Amazingly, miraculously—impossibly—Bethany's charm had worked. The children shrieked at the sight of me, this big, blood-soaked man who'd come back from the dead before their eyes. It was enough to finally get them to leave their hiding place and run for safety.

I pulled myself up to my feet, still sore and disoriented. The tournament field was empty. The crowd had dispersed. The fighting gargoyles and revenants were gone, leaving their fallen behind. Bethany lay face-down in the grass farther down the field. I started toward her and heard what I thought was a cough. She moved, just slightly, and coughed again. I broke into a run, and knelt down beside her. I could see the wound on her back, only it wasn't what I'd expected. The Black Knight's sword had cut through her cargo vest and shirt, but beneath it, her skin was unbroken. There was no injury, no blood, just the fiery feathers of her phoenix tattoo peeking out at me.

"You're alive! Oh my God, you're alive!" I couldn't stop myself from laughing with relief.

I turned her over gently and cradled her against my knees. She blinked at me, groggy. "Trent? What happened?" She glanced around the tournament field. "Where's the Black Knight?"

"He killed me and left," I said.

"How rude of him," she said fuzzily. Then she shook her head clear and said, "Wait, what?"

"The amulet worked, Bethany. No one died when I came back," I said. "By all counts, you should have been dead, too, but the blow only knocked you unconscious. I think your tattoo saved you."

"Don't be absurd," she said. "The sigil of the phoenix only protects me from magic, not from swords."

She had a point. So why hadn't the Black Knight's sword cut her in two? It had sliced through the chassis of my Explorer like it was cream cheese. A single swipe had knocked a police car right off the road. The sword could probably cut *anything*, so why had it spared her? I didn't know. And frankly, at the moment I didn't care why it hadn't killed her, I was just relieved that it hadn't.

I looked down into her eyes, marveling again at how bright and clear they were. "For a while there, I thought I'd lost you," I said. "I didn't like it."

"It wasn't a whole lot of fun for me, either," she said. If she meant to say anything after that, she didn't have the chance. I was already kissing her. It'd been building up in me, riding the crest of the immense relief I'd felt that she was still alive, and I simply couldn't contain it anymore. I kissed her, and she put one hand on my cheek and the other on my neck, smaller and warmer than any hands I'd ever known. She pulled me closer, kissing me with a ferocity I hadn't expected from her. Time seemed to slow, then stop altogether. But then she broke away, and pushed me gently back. "Wait. I—I can't do this."

I wasn't expecting that. I leaned back on my haunches, confused. "I'm sorry, I thought . . ."

"Don't," she said. "This is hard enough already, please just let me say this, okay? Remember what you told me when you left, how you weren't any good to anyone until you knew for sure that Underwood was out of your life? Well, I've got something like that, too, something that makes me no good to anyone either until I can put it behind me."

I nodded. I had a feeling I knew what it was. "Your parents," I said.

She nodded back at me. "I have to know who they were, what happened to them. I can't get involved with you, Trent. I can't get involved with *anyone* until I can put it to rest. It's too big, it takes up too much of me. There's just no room for anyone else right now. I'm sorry. Does that make sense?"

I sighed. It did make sense. If anyone could understand what it was like having big questions hanging over you, it was me. "Just do me a favor and let me know when some space opens up in your life again. Because this thing we were doing just now? I kind of want to do that some more."

She laughed, her cheeks reddening, and brushed her hair back from her face. "I'll take it under consideration. Provided Stryge doesn't kill us all first."

She had a good point. We were running out of time, and we still hadn't figured out how the hell we were supposed to stop an unkillable Ancient before he took us all out. Only one man had done it before, and he was so infected he couldn't even remember—

And then, suddenly, the answer came to me. It was like a lightbulb switching on in my head. I snapped my fingers and said, "The Black Knight's sword!"

She knit her brow. "What about it?"

"It's no ordinary sword," I said. "It's magic. It's as much a magical artifact as the Anubis Hand is. I figured out that the Black Knight is Willem Van Lente, or what's left of him anyway, and that sword must be what he used to cut off Stryge's head."

"The Black Knight is Willem Van Lente?"

"Was," I clarified. "I don't think there's anything left of him in there anymore."

I heard someone call out to us and looked up. Isaac, Philip, and Gabrielle were walking toward us across the field. I stood up, held out my hands to Bethany, and helped her to her feet. Her hands burned warm in mine.

For a moment, our bodies were pressed together. Her breath hitched, and she pulled away quickly.

"Are you two okay?" Isaac asked.

"We're fine," she said tersely. We filled them in on everything that had happened.

"Everyone's evacuating the park," Isaac said. "We've only got half an hour before the equinox, and we still haven't located the entrance to Stryge's tomb. Show me the woods where you saw the revenants. They had to be heading *somewhere* before the gargoyles attacked them."

I picked up the Anubis Hand and started to lead them out of the tournament field. A piercing shriek from far above stopped us in our tracks, followed by more, a cacophony of screeches and cries. In the sky above us, the gargoyles had broken into two warring factions, grappling in midair. The rebellion had begun.

"What the hell is happening up there?" Isaac asked.

"Civil war," I said. "It's been a long time coming. Come on, we'd be smart to stay out of the way."

We returned to the woods and climbed the hill from which Bethany and I had seen the battle between gargoyles and revenants unfold. Below, the forest floor was carpeted with hacked-up gargoyles and shredded revenants. The air smelled foul and coppery from blood. Nothing moved. In the distance, the Cloisters rose like an ancient stronghold. The swarm of gargoyles above it roiled and undulated with clashing factions, their wings steaming in the sunlight. The gargoyle civil war was spreading across the sky.

We descended the hill, making our way carefully through the dead bodies and across the field toward the Cloisters. I stepped over bones and body parts, broken tusks and crushed skulls. Pools of blood sucked at the soles of my boots like mud. This was only the start, I knew. The whole city was on the verge of becoming a killing field. The end of everything was breathing down our necks, and we only had half an hour to stop it.

A flash of movement between the trees caught my eye. A figure in a hooded, bloodred cloak walked quickly in the direction of the Cloisters. He turned to look back at us over his shoulder. A golden skull mask peeked out from within his hood.

"Melanthius!" I took off running.

Melanthius ran, too, weaving confidently through the trees. Apparently he knew the terrain well. He moved fast, but it wasn't hard to keep my eye on him. His vibrant red cloak stuck out against the brown, yellow, and green of the autumn forest. I jumped over tree roots and skirted around boulders, pushing myself faster. Ahead, Melanthius ran toward a rock outcrop in the distance. I hurdled over a log, only taking my eyes off him for a second, but that was all he needed. When I looked up again, Melanthius was gone.

I drew to a halt, breathing hard as the others caught up to me.

"What did I tell you about running off like that?" Isaac said.

"Sorry," I said, scanning the woods for Melanthius's telltale red cloak, but there was no sign of it. Where could he have gone? That cloak was impossible to hide. My eyes went to the rock outcrop again, a formation of boulders poking out of the earth. It was the last place I'd seen Melanthius before I lost him. "Wait here."

I approached the outcrop cautiously, pulling my gun with my free hand. The carpet of dead leaves crinkled loudly under my boots. If Melanthius was waiting for me on the other side of the rocks, he knew I was coming. I circled around to the other side, holding the gun out, ready to fire, but he wasn't there. Instead, I saw an old, rusted iron gate standing framed within the rocks. It was unlocked and slightly ajar. Wide stone steps led down into the dark. I waved the others over.

"Do these stairs go where I think they go?" I asked.

Isaac looked over his shoulder at the Cloisters towering above us. "Stryge's tomb must be right below us," he said. He pulled the gate open wider, its hinges surprisingly quiet considering how old they looked, and we entered, descending the steps inside. The sunlight coming through the open doorway lit the way, but the deeper we went the murkier it got. By the time we reached the bottom, nearly a hundred feet down, there was more shadow than light.

We found ourselves in a wide tunnel of rough-hewn stone that extended off into the inky black distance. The walls were pitted with dark recesses, vaulted nooks that at one time must have held statuary or treasure, but now stood empty.

A shadowy figure stood in the dark before us. I lifted my gun. "Melanthius."

"Not this time," came a familiar voice. The figure stepped closer, out of the shadows, and Gabrielle gasped.

It was Thornton, his eyes glowing red with Reve Azrael's magic.

Gabrielle ran at him, hefting the morningstar with her good arm. "Get out of him, you bitch!"

A hulking revenant stepped out of the dark between them. It grabbed Gabrielle's neck with one beefy hand and yanked the morningstar out of her grasp with the other. More revenants appeared, crawling out of the darkened nooks like roaches. They surrounded us, took our weapons, and tied our hands behind our backs with thick cords of rope. I felt two revenants behind me tightening the knot around my wrists. Others pulled back Philip's hood and slipped a thin chain over his neck. He cried out and fell to his knees, clutching at the chain until they tied his hands behind his back as well.

"It is silver, vampire, to keep you in your place," Reve Azrael said. "You will find I do not make the same mistakes twice."

Isaac struggled to break away from the revenants that had tied his hands. His palms began to sizzle and glow.

"Stay your hand, mage, or my revenant will snap Gabrielle's neck like a matchstick," Reve Azrael said. Isaac stopped struggling. The glow faded from his palms. Reve Azrael turned to Gabrielle, who was gasping for air in the revenant's strangling grip. "That *is* your name, isn't it? Gabrielle? It's the name your lover Thornton has for you in his mind, though there are others as well. Private names; names that exist only between you. He has so many memories of you, Gabrielle, each with such strong emotions attached that I feel almost as if they are my own." With Thornton's hand she stroked the side of Gabrielle's face.

Gabrielle flinched away. "If you're going to kill me, you better do it quick," she said. "Because if I get free, this time I won't hesitate. I won't hold back."

"No," Reve Azrael said. "I imagine you wouldn't."

The revenant let go of Gabrielle's neck. She doubled over, coughing, but before she could recover and make a move against Reve Azrael, the revenant pulled her injured arm out of its sling. She cried out in pain as the revenant yanked both her arms back and tied them together.

"You sent Melanthius to lead us right to you," Isaac said. "Why? What do you want with us?"

"I have use for this one." Reve Azrael stepped up to me, studying my face. She was so close all I could smell for a moment was the rot of Thornton's dead body.

"What do you plan to do with the rest us?" Isaac demanded.

"Watch you die," Reve Azrael answered. A revenant clubbed Isaac in the back of the head with the metal Anubis Hand. The mage fell to the floor, unconscious.

"Stop!" I shouted. "I'll stay, I'll do whatever you want, just let the others go."

"But I already have you, my little fly. Why would I strike a bargain now? I've waited so long for this moment. I even prepared for your arrival. As you see, I wanted you to feel at home."

The revenants behind me spun me around to face them. They were both severely burned, their faces reddened and charred. Yet even grossly disfigured by the fire that had killed them, I recognized them. How could I not?

"How you doin', T-Bag?" Big Joe's corpse said. The red glow of Reve Azrael's magic danced in the burned wreckage of his eyes. Next to him, the corpse of Tomo started laughing.

Thirty-eight

Watching Tomo and Big Joe's half-burnt corpses laughing at me, I thought I was going crazy. How could they be here? Why? Then, finally, I put it together. I turned back to Reve Azreal. "You're the one who blew up the gas station," I said. "Why? You were keeping tabs on me, you must have known I wasn't there, so why kill Underwood and his crew? Was it just for the thrill of it?"

She didn't answer. "Bring them," she said, and she turned and walked deeper into the tunnel. The revenants pushed us forward. One grabbed the collar of Isaac's duster and dragged the mage's unconscious body behind it like a duffel bag.

"Life, death, it's all just some sick game to you, isn't it?" I called after her. She continued to ignore me.

The tunnel ran for several hundred feet before it terminated in a huge archway. Reve Azrael passed through, and her revenants pushed the rest of us through after her. On the other side was an enormous chamber.

The first thing I saw was the massive throne carved out of rock that stood at the far wall. Seated upon the throne was the headless body of an enormous gargoyle, as gray as stone, and chained to the throne by thick metal links that crossed over his chest and looped around his shoulders.

This, I realized, was Stryge. If he'd been standing upright instead of sitting, and if he'd had a head, he would have hit thirty feet tall, easy. But it wasn't just his size that was intimidating. Stryge was so powerful it had taken all the warriors of the Lenape Indian nation and every spell in Willem Van Lente's arsenal just to chain him to this throne and chop off his head. And even that hadn't killed him, only put him into some kind of supernatural hibernation.

Somehow, it was brighter in the chamber than it had been in the tunnel outside. Looking up, I saw why. Sunlight streamed through a hole far above us in the ceiling, coming in at an angle and hitting the wall to our left like a spotlight. Rings of concentric circles had been carved in the wall, each of them decorated with strange symbols. All but the circle in the center, which had been left blank. Lenape Indian glyphs, I guessed, left by the warriors who'd hidden Stryge's body here. As the sun moved across the sky, its light traveled along the wall, inching closer to the empty circle at the center of the rings.

A metal cage had been set up across from the throne. The revenants herded Philip, Gabrielle, and Bethany inside, then threw Isaac's unconscious body in after them. They closed the door. The *thunk* of the lock sliding into place echoed through the chamber.

For some reason, they left me on the outside. Reve Azrael had said she had special plans for me, but I wasn't exactly eager to find out what they were. I started working the ropes that bound my wrists. They'd been tied by the clumsy, numb hands of revenants and the knot felt sloppy. If I could just loosen it . . .

Inside the cage, Philip knelt down beside Isaac's unconscious form, keeping watch over him as he had sworn to do, but with his hands tied and the silver around his neck, the vampire wasn't capable of anything else. Gabrielle leaned against the bars, a sheen of sweat coating her face and a spot of blood dotting the shoulder of her shirt where the bullet wound had reopened. If she felt any pain from it, she didn't show it. Instead, she watched Reve Azrael in Thornton's body with a red-hot intensity. And then there was Bethany. She was working her wrists like I was, trying to squeeze them out of the knotted rope, but she wasn't getting very far. She was still wearing her cargo vest. The revenants had confiscated our weapons and tossed them in a pile off to one side of the cage, but they must not have known her vest was full of charms.

Not that she could reach any of them with her hands tied behind her back.

Melanthius entered from the tunnel outside, walking purposefully toward Reve Azrael, who stood at the foot of the throne. In his hands was the box.

I spat on the floor. That fucking box. I wished I'd destroyed the damn thing after all.

I worked the ropes again and felt a loop slip free.

Melanthius knelt before Reve Azrael and held the box out to her, his golden skull mask betraying no emotion. Reve Azrael opened the lid, reached into the box, and pulled out Stryge's severed head.

"At last," she said, holding the head aloft. "Now you will bear witness to my triumph. By day's end, this city will be unmade. Nothing will make a sound, nothing will *move* without my will commanding it."

Another loop of rope loosened and slipped, and then my hands were free. I tossed the rope on the ground and ran for Reve Azrael. I had to get Stryge's head from her before she could join it to his body. Big Joe got in my way. His cold, meaty, dead fist knocked me down. He sprang at me, but I rolled away and he landed in the dirt.

"Stop this," Reve Azrael ordered, but I was already on my feet and running again. The other revenants formed a protective circle around her. That would have been bad news if I'd wanted to get at Reve Azrael, but she wasn't where I was headed anymore. By gathering around her, the revenants had left the stash of weapons unguarded.

The chrome plating of my Bersa semiautomatic glittered at the top of the heap, its magazine full again thanks to Bethany. I made a mental note to buy her something nice, and reached for the gun.

Big Joe tackled me from behind before I could pick it up. I got a faceful of dirt as I went down. The heavy revenant pinned me to the floor. I managed to squirm onto my back, and face him. His glowing red eyes stared into mine. "This is foolish, my little fly," Reve Azrael said through him. "You cannot escape. Not from me."

"I'm not your little fly," I said. My fingers scrabbled along the dirt floor until I found a good-sized stone. I brought it up and smashed it against the side of Big Joe's head. It tore a chunk of skin off his skull. He tumbled off me.

I moved quickly, scrambling on all fours for my gun. I grabbed it and spun around just as Big Joe came at me again. I pulled the trigger. The top of Big Joe's head blew off in a spray of blood dust, bone, and brain matter, and he keeled over. This time, he stayed down.

"Trent, behind you!" Bethany shouted from inside the cage.

Before I could turn around, a dead, foul-smelling arm snaked around my neck in a sleeper hold. I glanced over my shoulder and saw Tomo's half-burnt face glaring back at me. "Enough," Reve Azrael said through Tomo's mouth. "Why do you keep trying to thwart me? Give up. You cannot win."

The sleeper hold tightened, cutting off my oxygen. I started to feel light-headed. I had to act fast. In another few seconds I would black out. I brought up the Bersa, positioned it under Tomo's chin, and blasted a nine-millimeter slug straight up through his skull. Tomo's hold relaxed, and he fell off me. I wiped his thick, sludgy blood off my face and looked down at the bodies.

God, I'd just killed Tomo and Big Joe. My hands were shaking.

"Do not lie to yourself," Reve Azrael said, back in Thornton's body. "It gave you pleasure to destroy those two. No doubt it is something you wanted to do for a very long time. There is so much anger in you. We have that in common, you and I. There is much anger in both of us. The only difference is that you keep yours bottled up, while this wretched city will soon feel the brunt of mine."

Just the sound of her talking infuriated me. I pointed the gun at her and cocked it. "We have *nothing* in common." She was using Thornton as her host body, and though I didn't want to, if I got past the revenants surrounding her I was going to have to put a bullet in Thornton's head.

But not before I got some answers out of her.

Her revenants came at me in a rush. I only managed to squeeze off a couple of shots, neither of which did any good, before they were upon me. Cold, bony fists struck my face, stomach, and sides. Overwhelmed, I doubled over to protect myself from the pummeling. The gun was pulled out of my hand, and finally the beating stopped. I was pulled upright again, my arms pinned behind my back. I was winded, weak, and in pain. There was nothing I could do to stop her.

"Now," Reve Azrael said, "let us proceed."

The beam of sunlight coming through the hole in the ceiling moved to the middle of the rings on the wall, where it illuminated the blank circle at the center. As soon as the light touched it, the stone circle spun around on hidden gears. The blank side disappeared into the wall, and on the reverse side was the carving of a grotesque face, like something out of a nightmare, its tusked maw open in a roar, its eyes hollow black pits. A loud grinding noise came from above, echoing through the chamber. A huge stone slab began slowly lowering along the wall above the archway, held by thick ropes attached to an ancient pulley system. It was a system designed to seal Stryge inside at the moment of the equinox, I realized, a backup plan in case anyone was foolish enough to awaken him. The Lenape Indians had been clever. Maybe a little too clever. I didn't see us getting out before the stone slab blocked the exit.

"The time has come," Reve Azrael said. She climbed up onto one of the throne's armrests and lifted Stryge's head toward the stump of his neck.

"Don't!" I shouted. The revenants pulled my arms back harder to shut me up. It did the trick. I winced in pain.

Reve Azrael placed Stryge's head over his neck. A bright, sizzling light appeared between the two ends. The head and neck began to knit together, tendrils of flesh, muscle, and bone reaching toward each other, joining and pulling tight. Reve Azrael let go of the head and jumped down to the floor.

"Awaken, Stryge!" she said, looking up at her handiwork. "Awaken and become my weapon!"

The light that had filled the seam between Stryge's head and neck vanished, as did the seam itself, and the Ancient became whole again. His chest swelled suddenly, filling with air. Stryge's first breath in centuries, and the sound of it was like the howling of the wind.

"What have you done?" I said.

"Given birth," she replied, "to my glorious city of the dead."

Surprisingly, the revenants let go of me then. Reve Azrael turned away, and she, Melanthius, and the revenants walked to the archway. Above them, the stone slab continued to lower slowly.

"Wait, where are you going?" I demanded, hurrying after them. A fat revenant like a walking boulder pushed me back. The message was clear: This was as far as I went. I watched them file out into the tunnel.

"The rest is for you to do, my little fly, not me," Reve Azrael said.

"What am I supposed to do?"

"Why, kill Stryge, of course."

I blinked at her, dumbfounded. "What? How? He already had his head cut off four hundred years ago and he's not dead yet. There isn't a weapon on Earth that can kill him!"

"Isn't there?" she said. "You'd better figure it out quickly, unless you want to see your companions die. Stryge despises all humans with a bitter passion. What do you think he will do when he wakes up and the first thing he sees is a cage full of them?"

"Why did you bother waking him if you just . . . ?" I trailed off as I pieced it together. In that moment, her plan spread out like a roadmap in my mind, and it all became horribly clear. "Oh, God," I said. "You woke Stryge in order to kill him. You're going to turn him into a revenant."

She smirked at me. "And then all Stryge's power as an Ancient will be mine to command. My most powerful revenant yet. Undead. Unstoppable. A perfect storm of destruction."

A chill ran down my spine. Gregor had warned us an immortal storm was coming, a force so powerful it threatened everything. Even if I didn't believe in prophecies, I had to admit this one was starting to sound pretty damn accurate. Stryge as a revenant under Reve Azrael's control would very much *be* an immortal storm.

"You're insane," I said. "I won't help you."

"Then your companions will die, and this city will be destroyed regardless."

"He'll kill you, too," I pointed out. "You won't be safe from him."

"You think I fear death?" Reve Azrael said. "Death bends to *my* will, I do not bend to *its*."

The stone slab dropped down over the archway then, striking the floor with a heavy thud. It cut me off from Reve Azrael and sealed me inside.

I looked back at Stryge. He sat on his throne, his eyes still closed, his chest swelling and falling with breath. How much time was left before he was fully awake? Not a lot, I guessed. And was I imagining it, or did the broken stubs of his tusks suddenly look longer than they had before, as if they were growing back?

I grabbed my gun off the floor and pocketed it. I pulled Gabrielle's morningstar off the pile of weapons, then ran to the cage. "Stand back from the door!" I shouted. I swung the weapon's spiked head into the lock.

The door didn't budge. Damn. If Isaac were awake he probably could have blown the door off its hinges with a wave of his hand, but the mage was still unconscious on the floor, bleeding from the back of his head. I hit it again, with no effect.

Bethany came up to the door. "You're just going to bend the lock out of shape like that, and then you'll never get it open. There's a charm in my vest, third pocket down, right over my stomach. It can get the door open, but you're going to have to reach in there and get it. I can't."

She pushed herself up against the bars. I dropped the morningstar and tried to put my hand in her pocket, but the angle was off. She pushed herself closer, as close as the bars would allow, and I did the same, until we were so close I could smell a faint floral scent coming off of her hair. I managed to slide my hand into the pocket over her stomach. I could feel the unusual warmth of her skin radiating through the material.

"We just keep finding ourselves like this, don't we?" I said.

Bethany looked past me at Stryge. "Trent, hurry!"

My fingers grazed something inside the pocket, a long, thin, metallic object. I pulled it out. It was the same charm I'd seen her take out of the drawer at Citadel, the small metal tube topped with a beveled glass bead.

"Touch the glass to the lock," she said, stepping back. "Gently," she added.

I did. There was a sudden shower of sparks, and the door swung open. I ran into the cage and untied Bethany's hands. Once she was free, she rushed to untie Gabrielle. I freed Philip and took the silver chain from around his neck, tossing it aside. He breathed a sigh of relief, rubbing the red marks it had left on his neck. Then he picked up Isaac, and ran like a blur for the stone slab blocking the exit. By the time the rest of us caught up to him, he had already laid Isaac gently on the ground and was trying to push the stone aside, but even his immense strength wasn't enough to move it.

"Help me," Philip said. "We've got to move this thing—"

A low rumble of a growl echoed through the chamber.

I froze, then turned around very slowly. We all did.

Stryge's eyes were open. They burned like fires in their sockets—cold, white fires, the same as Gregor's eyes. Maybe those were traits all Ancients shared, I thought, invincibility and freaky eyes. Then Stryge stood up out of the throne, effortlessly snapping the chains that bound him. His tusks had regrown to their full length. His vast wings unfolded from his back.

The last of the broken chains slid off his shoulders and crashed loudly to the floor at his feet. Then Stryge noticed us, and let loose an angry, deafening roar that shook the chamber's walls.

"Guys," I said, "I think we should run."

Thirty-nine

Stryge charged, his enormous, clawed feet pounding the floor so hard it felt like the whole chamber would collapse. Philip slung Isaac's unconscious body over his shoulder, and sped to the other side of the room. The rest of us scattered out of Stryge's way. The Ancient slammed into the stone slab that covered the archway. The stone cracked, a long fissure that ran lengthwise from top to bottom, but Stryge himself was unharmed. He turned toward us, bellowing his rage.

We ran for the weapons. Bethany snatched up the Anubis Hand, Gabrielle grabbed her morningstar, and I picked up Philip's broadsword. I shouted his name and tossed it across the chamber to him.

Philip moved quickly. He jumped for it, grabbing the sword in midair, flipped, and landed on Stryge's back. The Ancient batted him with his wings, trying to knock him off, but Philip held on. He stabbed the sword into Stryge's back, but the blade snapped, the tip shattering against the Ancient's invulnerable hide and leaving Philip holding a hilt with half a blade.

Stryge pulled him off his back with one claw and tossed him away like a toy. The vampire struck the wall where the circles had been carved, and then tumbled to the floor, landing in the column of sunlight that streamed through the hole in the ceiling. He screamed as the sunlight touched his bare face, reflecting like spotlights in his mirrored shades. His skin reddened into boils and began to steam.

"Philip!" I shouted, but I couldn't reach him. He was all the way on the other side of the chamber, and a pissed off, thirty-foot-tall Ancient stood between us.

Philip thrashed in pain. He covered his face with his gloves and managed to drag himself out of the light. He pulled his hood up to protect himself, tried to stand, and fell back down. After that, he didn't move. I hoped he was still alive, but there was no way to tell how badly injured he was.

Bethany ran at Stryge, preparing to strike him with the Anubis Hand. He kicked her away. The staff flew from her hands as she tumbled through the air and landed hard, headfirst, against the wall near me. When she slumped over, I saw blood in her hair.

I picked up the Anubis Hand and gritted my teeth angrily. "All right, you ugly son of a bitch." I ran at him, clutching the Anubis Hand so tightly my knuckles went hot. But before I had a chance to swing it, he knocked me aside with a single sweep of his enormous hand. The sheer force of the blow sent me sliding across the floor until my back hit the wall next to Philip. I winced in pain. Next to me, the vampire was curled on the floor, unconscious but still breathing. That was the good news. The bad news was that Gabrielle and I were the only ones left conscious to fight an enormous, unkillable Ancient, but she only had one good arm and I wasn't feeling all that solid after Stryge's backhand. Frankly, the odds sucked.

Gabrielle pointed her morningstar at Stryge. In my dazed state, I thought it a strange way to hold what was essentially a club. But she'd taken it from Isaac's vault, and Isaac didn't keep ordinary weapons in there, only magical artifacts. The spiked ball at the end of the morningstar began to glow, and a bright sunburst of light exploded from it, like a flashbulb going off directly in Stryge's face. Stryge bellowed in rage, throwing one arm over his eyes and flailing angrily with the other. Apparently he didn't like bright light any more than other gargoyles did. Disoriented and in pain, he stumbled and fell, crashing into the enormous stone slab a second time.

This time, the slab broke apart, crumbling into rubble under his weight and revealing the tunnel outside. Unfortunately, I was still too stunned to get up and run. But that didn't mean Gabrielle couldn't.

"The door's open! Go!" I shouted to her. She didn't listen. She blasted Stryge with more light from the morningstar. The Ancient roared in pain. As her confidence built, she moved closer to him, intensifying the light. Stryge shrieked in agony. One wing unfurled and, before Gabrielle saw it coming, it swatted her away. She flew backward through the air and slammed into the metal bars of the cage. She yelped in pain and dropped the morningstar.

Stryge stood up again. He didn't look seriously injured, just a whole lot angrier than before.

Damn. We'd gone up against an Ancient and had our asses handed to us. What more could we do? There was no way to stop him. I wished I had Van Lente's sword so I could at least cut off Stryge's head again. It wouldn't kill him, but I'd settle for dormant at this point.

Stryge towered above us as we lay injured and pathetic on the floor of his tomb. I thought for sure he would stomp us into hamburger, but the Ancient hardly took notice of us. Instead, he looked up at the ceiling. He took a deep breath, the sound like the rush of a waterfall, and his whole body swelled. The shadows seemed to gather around him, pulled from the corners of the chamber, flowing into him. Then he exhaled with a mighty roar, and a beam of dark red light exploded out of him, shooting up to the ceiling.

And through it.

The light, or whatever it was, broke effortlessly through the rocks and earth, raining stones and clods of dirt down into the chamber. I covered my head. Boulders crashed to the center of the room, smashing the throne to rubble and sending up a cloud of dust. I couldn't see Bethany on the other side of the chamber anymore. I had no idea if she was alive or dead after the rockfall.

The chamber kept shaking. It felt like an earthquake, like the whole world was tearing itself apart. The red beam coming out of Stryge's form continued shooting past the enormous hole it had blasted in the ceiling, rising higher and higher into the sky itself. The warring factions of gargoyles, so far up from where I lay that they looked like tiny black bats, scattered out of its path. Finally, the beam seemed to explode in midair. The blue sky turned dark with clouds that billowed out of nowhere. Red and black clouds, like nothing I'd ever seen before, roiling like an angry sea.

The strange beam disappeared, but the quaking didn't stop. Stryge spread his wings and began to flap, lifting off the ground toward the hole he'd blasted in the ceiling.

No, I thought. I wasn't going to let it be that easy for him.

I forced myself to stand, and ran toward him, scooping the Anubis Hand off the floor. It was hard to keep upright with the whole chamber shaking. I jumped and clung to the lower half of Stryge's leg as he flew up toward the hole. Stryge roared at me, angry that my weight was throwing him off balance. He tried to kick me off. I held on for dear life with both arms wrapped around his enormous calf, trying not to fall, and trying not to let go of the Anubis Hand, either. Unfortunately, holding on this tight, I didn't have the leverage to use the staff against him.

We rose to the top of the chamber. I looked down but couldn't see the others through the dust in the air. I could see the open archway, though, and hoped they'd get the hell out of there as soon as they could. I thought I heard voices below, calling out to each other—was that Bethany?—and then Stryge flew through the hole and was loose in the city. I didn't know how I was going to stop him, but I knew it had to be done, and soon.

He landed on the park grounds at the foot of the Cloisters. I let go of his leg and ran for the treeline. The ground was shaking up here, too, not just in the chamber below. Stryge was causing it somehow, I was sure of it. The Ancient's enormous foot came crashing down behind me as I ran, trying to squash me like a bug, but I darted into the forest. I went in deep, dashing around trees, then stopped when I didn't hear Stryge follow. Only then did I notice all the leaves around me had turned red. The tree trunks and the ground, too. Everything was tinted the color of blood from the light filtering through the red and black clouds above. The air suddenly felt thick, soupy, difficult to move through, as though it were turning solid. It was as if the laws of physics were being altered. Somehow Stryge was doing that, too.

I looked up to see why he'd stopped chasing me. He'd become distracted, looking around with a strange, stunned expression on his face. I guessed a lot had changed since the last time he'd seen this plot of land. His surprise turned to anger when he saw the Cloisters. Stryge hated humans, and they'd built the Cloisters right over his tomb. It must have been like a slap in the face to him, a reminder of how much humankind had thrived in his absence. He roared in rage, and the Cloisters burst apart as if a bomb had gone off. But it was like no explosion I'd ever seen. The stones, bricks, and rubble didn't fly in all directions from the force of the explosion, nor did they fall to the ground—they just hung in the thick, red air, slowly spinning.

Stryge hadn't just destroyed the Cloisters, he'd taken the place apart. Unmade it. God, was *this* what Reve Azrael had meant when she said Stryge would unmake the city?

I couldn't let it happen. I didn't know what I could do to stop him, but I had the Anubis Hand and that was a good start. I started running toward him, but the quaking ground made it hard to keep my balance. The air was like rubber cement, any move I made felt like swimming against a strong current.

Stryge bellowed angrily again. He turned to a nearby copse of trees. They uprooted and floated into the air. With them came three shrieking figures, two men and a woman. They wore familiar green tunics and a green dress that I recognized immediately. If I'd been closer I probably would have seen their prosthetic elf ears, too. Damn it, I thought everyone had evacuated the park. What were they still doing here?

The trees broke apart as Stryge unmade them, and then, suddenly, horribly, the shrieking stopped as Stryge unmade the people, too. Their pieces hung in midair, torsos, heads, arms, legs, all floating and spinning like the remains of the trees and the stones from the Cloisters. I felt sick. Some of the Dutch traders Stryge ambushed in New Amsterdam had been found in pieces, I remembered. I had a pretty good idea now what had happened to them.

This had to end before anyone else got killed. Stryge was still facing away from me, as good an opportunity as any to take him by surprise. I ran out of the woods, ready to swing the Anubis Hand, but Stryge spun around and fixed me with his coldly burning eyes. Suddenly I was floating up off the ground. I felt an invisible force stretching me like taffy, pulling at my limbs. I felt a terrible pressure inside, as if my whole body were about to burst.

Stryge was unmaking me.

I gritted my teeth against the pain. In a moment it would be over, and then I would be nothing but a collection of body parts spinning in the air like some macabre children's mobile. Would I come back from that, I wondered as the pressure in my head built, or would it really be the end this time? I was surprised at how much a part of me welcomed the idea of a lasting death, how much it embraced an end to this unending life.

The pain built, and just when I thought I couldn't take it anymore, I heard the flapping of wings. A lot of wings. Out of nowhere, I was surrounded by big, black crows. They pecked and clawed at Stryge. He roared and tried to swat them away. The sensation of being unmade instantly subsided. I fell to the ground, then rolled to the edge of the trees. I stayed down, hoping Stryge wouldn't see me.

The crows flew toward me in a swarm, and then, suddenly, I was looking up at the Black Knight sitting upon his armored horse. I scrambled backward, away from him. I didn't know why he'd saved me, but I didn't trust him. He'd already killed me once. Maybe he'd come back for an encore performance.

But the Black Knight only looked down at me with his usual stoic silence.

"Um . . . thanks?" I said. It didn't sound convincing.

He lifted one black gauntlet and pointed at me.

"Yeah, I know, I'm alive even though you killed me. You're not the first to be confused by that."

He didn't answer. Then I realized it wasn't me he was pointing at. It was the Anubis Hand lying on the ground beside me.

"You want the staff?"

His black helmet tipped forward. That was a yes.

I looked at the Anubis Hand. It *was* his, after all. But there was no way he could have remembered it, or what it could do against Stryge, unless—

Unless something had changed.

I turned back to the Black Knight. "You remember! You finally remember!"

His helmet tipped again. He held out his gauntlet. I stood up and passed the Anubis Hand to him.

"Give him hell, Willem," I said.

He nudged his horse forward. Holding the Anubis Hand in one gauntlet and the heavy chain reins in the other, he charged Stryge. The tremendous Ancient roared at him, clenching his claws into mighty fists. For a moment it was as though I'd stepped back in time to the seventeenth century, back before New York City even existed, to when the battle between Willem Van Lente and Stryge had played out for the first time.

Van Lente swung the Anubis Hand and struck Stryge just above the knee. There was a bright flare at the point of impact, and Stryge howled in agony. The earth seemed to tremble harder with his anger. He swiped at Van Lente with a massive claw, but he was sluggish from the pain. Van Lente galloped past him, out of reach.

Van Lente turned and rode by a second time, swinging the Anubis Hand again. It hit Stryge in the other leg. Again there was a bright flash, and Stryge stumbled. Van Lente struck him in the chest, and Stryge roared in pain and fell onto his back. He stayed down, his breathing ragged. Was it over? Would Van Lente take his head again and leave the Ancient dormant once more?

Van Lente dismounted, and his black-armored horse vanished like an illusion. He approached Stryge, carrying the Anubis Hand in one gauntlet, and with his other he drew his sword. Stryge's arm lashed out suddenly, knocking the staff out of Van Lente's grasp. The Ancient stood, bellowing in rage, and picked up the staff. He effortlessly snapped it in two, as if the metal were no stronger than rotten driftwood. Then he crushed the pieces to dust, including the mummified fist, destroying the Anubis Hand utterly.

Shit, I thought, but Van Lente wasn't finished yet. He slashed Stryge's forearm with his sword, and the Ancient's impenetrable skin sliced open under the sharp edge of the blade. Stryge bellowed in pain, and my heart leaped in my chest. I'd been right about Van Lente's sword—it was the only weapon that could penetrate Stryge's hide.

But then, with an angry swipe of his other arm, Stryge knocked Van Lente to the ground. The Ancient loomed over his dazed, prostrate form.

Damn. History should have told me Van Lente couldn't do this alone. Four hundred years ago, the Lenape Indians had had his back. Today, I was all he had. I started running, but it felt like I was moving through molasses. Stryge lifted his giant foot over Van Lente, then brought it crashing down to the ground. A second before it struck, Van Lente disappeared and a dozen crows flew away into the sky.

The crows stopped in midflight, stuck in the air like flies on a glue strip, and Stryge unmade them. The crows came apart into little black pieces—beaks, wings, legs, feathers, all spinning in place in the red-tinted air. Stryge released them, and the pieces fell to the ground like discarded trash.

I ran to where they'd fallen. When I got there, the birds were gone and Van Lente was lying on the ground, whole once more, but broken. Both his legs and one of his arms were twisted at odd angles, and he couldn't move them. His helmet remained bent to one side, as though his neck were broken. He didn't speak or make a sound, but looking at him I could tell he was in agony.

I knelt beside him. "Willem."

He pointed with his good arm at his sword lying on the ground near me. It had fallen free of its scabbard.

"You want your sword?" I asked. He shook his helmet ever so slightly. "You want me to use it?" He tried to nod, then struck the gauntleted fist of his good hand against his chest, over his heart.

I knew what he was asking me to do, and I shook my head. "No, I won't. Even if I wanted to, I couldn't. Your armor—your *shell* is too strong."

He pointed at the sword again, more emphatically this time, and I understood. Jibril-khan had said Van Lente carried with him the only spell that could kill him. I realized now the gargoyle had meant the sword. Strong enough to cut off an Ancient's head, it was also strong enough to penetrate Van Lente's shell, to pierce his heart, his one vulnerable spot.

I looked down at his mangled form. "But you can fix yourself, can't you? You have magic."

Van Lente shook his head again, then tapped his chest plate once more. The infection had turned him into this. It had remade him as a monster and kept him alive for centuries. It would likely continue to keep him alive, even now, broken and in agony. He wanted me to put him out of his misery. He'd been a hero once. He'd sacrificed everything, even his own humanity, to save the city he loved. Didn't he deserve some peace at last? How could I deny him that?

With a heavy heart, I picked up the sword. "I'm sorry, Willem," I said. He shook his head as if to tell me I shouldn't be. I took a deep breath, lifted the sword high, and then drove it into his heart.

Van Lente's form erupted in a fountain of fire, smoke, and crackling, strobing lights. I backed away from the blaze, a hand in front of my face to shield me from the heat. Within the flames I saw his silhouette, the stag horns of his helmet burning like lightning-struck trees, his tattered cape going up like flash paper, his black form now glowing orange from the intense heat. And then all I could see was the burning fountain of fire.

The flames died down almost immediately, fading to a blackened circle of glowing embers and charred grass on the ground. In the middle of the circle, a bearded, middle-aged man lay naked and still, his eyes closed, his face peaceful beneath close-cropped white hair. Willem Van Lente in his true form. I knelt down beside him and reached out to touch his face, but he faded like an apparition before I could, leaving nothing behind but a patch of burnt earth.

And his sword.

I picked up it up, and stood. I turned around to face Stryge.

He was walking away from me, toward the south end of the park, as though Van Lente and I had been nothing but minor distractions. With each step he took, rocks, plants, and trees lifted off the ground and broke apart in the air. Great columns of water exploded out of the Hudson River alongside the park and hung shimmering in the air. Stryge was unmaking everything.

"Hey, asshole," I called.

He kept walking.

"Stryge!" I shouted.

That got his attention. He turned around, snarling with rage. My courage dropped into my belly. Shit. Now that I had his attention, what the hell was I going to do?

A peculiar feeling came over me then, a sense that I wasn't alone. I felt others behind me—Morbius, Ingrid, Thornton, even Willem Van Lente— all those who had made a stand against evil before me. They stood with me now as if to say, for better or worse, I was a part of something bigger. Bigger than me, bigger than Isaac's team, bigger even than Stryge. It was what Ingrid had called the good fight, what she'd begged with her dying breath not to let end with her. It was the mantle she'd asked Isaac to take up, and by extension all of us to take up. And then, like an answer to my question, I knew what I had to do.

No matter what, no matter how this turned out or what happened to me, I had to keep fighting the good fight.

I ran at Stryge, the sword held out high in front of me. I rose off the ground as Stryge's magic caught me up again, but my momentum kept me moving forward, too. He tried to unmake me—I felt my joints stretching, weakening—but before he could, I plunged the sword into his stomach. Stryge howled in pain. As formidable as Van Lente's magic sword was, I knew it couldn't kill the Ancient, but it hurt him a lot and that felt pretty damn satisfying in its own right. Stryge stopped, releasing me from his spell. I would have fallen nearly twenty feet to the ground if I hadn't held onto the sword hilt like a mountain climber dangling from a piton.

Stryge swatted at me, his claws tearing open one side of my trench coat, but I managed to hang on. From the ripped pocket of my coat, my gun fell out and tumbled to the ground. Damn. I knew bullets couldn't hurt Stryge, but I didn't like losing my gun. Underwood had done too good a job drumming that damn Golden Rule into my head.

"Trent!" a voice called from below.

I looked down and saw Bethany standing near the tree line. Then Isaac, Gabrielle, and Philip came through the branches behind her. They were bruised and bloodied, but they were alive. I felt a surge of relief. Then Stryge swatted at me again, tearing off the rest of my coat as I struggled to keep my grip on the hilt.

"Little help here?" I shouted.

Isaac raised his hands, Gabrielle raised her morningstar, and Bethany pulled the mirrored charm from her vest. From each of them burst a bright light. Stryge reeled back with another loud howl, and covered his eyes with his arms. He unfolded his wings and started flapping. We began to rise off the ground.

"Trent, get down from there!" Bethany cried.

"No," I shouted back. "We can't let him get away! He'll unmake the whole damn city!"

With great beats of his enormous wings, Stryge tried to lift himself higher, but couldn't. The light and pain were distracting him, and my added weight kept him off balance. But these were only temporary diversions. It wouldn't be much longer before he found a way to take flight for real.

"Come down!" Bethany shouted again. "There's nothing you can do up there!"

She was wrong. There was something I could do. The one thing I was good at. The one thing I'd always been able to do.

I called to Bethany, "The gun! Use the gun!"

She looked down at my gun on the ground, then back up at me. "Bullets won't kill him!"

"Not him!" I yelled back. "Me! It's the only way to stop him!"

"What?" She'd heard me, she just couldn't believe what I was saying.

Carefully letting go of the hilt with one hand, I reached into my shirt and pulled the amulet she'd made for me from around my neck. I hated to take it off, especially now that I knew it worked, but just this once I needed it not to.

Stryge swatted at me again, trying to knock me off of him. I held onto the hilt, swinging my body out of the way of his claws, but as I did the amulet slipped from my fingers and dropped. It tumbled down to the grass below. I hoped it survived the fall, but there was no time to worry about it now.

"Now, Bethany, before it's too late!" I called to her. "Then run as far from here as you can! All of you!"

Bethany slowly picked up my gun. Damn it, I needed her to move faster. Every second she wasted, Stryge brought me farther out of range. She aimed the gun me. I couldn't make out her features anymore, we were too high up, but I heard her voice.

"I'm sorry!" she cried, and she pulled the trigger.

She was a good shot, even at long range, though I already knew she would be. The bullet hit me square in the chest. The pain ripped through me like a scalpel, but it was mercifully brief. I died almost instantly, but not before I saw Isaac, Gabrielle, Philip, and Bethany start running, the smoking Bersa semiautomatic still in her hand.

Forty

For a moment, there was only blackness, an empty void. Was this the dark that separated the worlds of the living and the dead, some part of me wondered? Were the dead watching me even now? Then, suddenly, there was light again. Way too much light. Even before I sucked the first gulp of air into my lungs, I knew something was wrong. I opened my eyes, and what came out of them was a coldly burning white fire, the same fire that had burned in Stryge's eyes. The fire of the Ancients. I exhaled, and more of it erupted from my mouth and nose.

I felt like I'd swallowed a nuclear reactor. It flowed like lava through my veins, burned inside me like the heart of the sun. I felt . . . altered. Changed.

It is a combination of elements that were never meant to be combined.

I got to my feet, but I couldn't stand for long. I dropped to my hands and knees, vomiting up more gouts of cold white fire. It just kept coming. There was more of it in me than my body could hold.

It is a danger to all who live.

Had the oracles foreseen this? Had they been trying to warn me?

As long as it walks upon this world, as long as it dwells among us, it puts us all in peril.

The fire burned and burned and felt like it would never stop.

Bethany's voice came from a distance. "Trent? Are you okay? What's happening?"

She'd come back to check up on me. I squeezed my burning eyes shut and turned away from her. "Stay back! I don't know what's happening to me!" I heard her footsteps running toward me, and shouted, "Damn it, stay away!" Something powerful coursed through me, something frightening and building in pressure. "The plan worked, but something's wrong, it's different this time." Then I couldn't contain it anymore. I leaned back and screamed, the white fire jetting from my eyes, nose, and mouth. Before I knew what was happening, I was floating into the air, as though I were being lifted. I stopped myself somehow, hovering a dozen feet above the ground.

Above, the red and black clouds Stryge had summoned were gone, replaced with a far more normal-looking gray cloud cover. The warring factions of gargoyles were gone, too, probably frightened off by Stryge. In the near distance was the wreckage of the Cloisters, its broken stones littering the hillside. The bits of trees and rocks and body parts had fallen to the ground as well, the laws of physics restored with Stryge's death.

As for Stryge himself, the once mighty creature lay on his back below me where he'd fallen to the ground. A thirty-foot-tall mummy, shriveled to bone and dried tissue. Once again, I'd done the impossible. I'd killed an Ancient.

Out of habit, I added his name to my mental list.

11. Stryge.

Eleven names. Eleven lives I'd stolen. God. My heart felt heavy at the number, and even heavier when I thought about how many more had died over the last couple of days. More than I could count, and most of them had died because of me. It felt like there was so much blood on my hands they would never be clean. The oracles were right. I was a threat.

Bethany stared up at me in awe, which angered me. Didn't she know what a monster I was? What an abomination?

But of course she did. She'd seen it firsthand. The thing inside me had almost killed her. *I* had almost killed her.

My anger boiled inside me. Everything around me changed, as if a filter had been put over my eyes. Suddenly I didn't see Bethany, or the park grounds, or the wreckage. I saw *through* them, *into* them. I saw the millions of silken threads that bound their atoms together, and the more I looked at them, the more I understood how easy it would be to sever those threads, to break those atoms apart. As an experiment, I chose one of the threads in the ground directly below me. I plucked it with my mind. It was a gentle pluck, not even a break, and the ground crumbled. A sinkhole formed as the dirt poured into the darkness below. It was so easy. I could make it bigger, I thought, and plucked again. The sinkhole grew into a crevasse that cut through the ground like a wound. I laughed at how easy it was. I could pluck all the strings if I wanted, even break them and bring everything crashing down, and it would hardly take any effort at all. Perhaps I ought to. Maybe that was what I was meant to do. I could unmake everything and start over from scratch. Or maybe skip starting over altogether. Maybe I would just float in the void I'd created, endless, deathless, until I was as old as Stryge.

Bethany stepped back as the expanding crevasse crept toward her. "Trent, what are you doing?"

"Fulfilling my destiny," I told her. "You heard what the oracles said, you were there. I'm a threat to all life." I looked at the Bethany-shaped silhouette where she stood, filled with a thousand silken strings connecting all the little sunbursts of atoms inside her. It looked like she was made of comets and stars. It would be so easy to stop them cold, to just sever the threads inside her. The urge to do it shocked me, but maybe it shouldn't have. "They said I was an abomination. They were right. I always was. And now this abomination has the power to unmake everything."

"Trent, listen to me," she said. "Somehow you absorbed Stryge's magic when you got his life force. I don't know how it happened, but the magic of the Ancients is different from ours. It's not meant for us, our bodies can't contain it. If you don't get rid of it somehow, it'll kill you."

"But it can't. Nothing can kill me, not even this." I looked up at the sky, and saw through it, saw the gears of the universe moving like clockwork. It was filled with spheres, gorgeous, singing, rotating spheres decorated with mystical symbols and designs that made my heart soar. The spheres circled each other like dancers. It was so beautiful. So pure and unsullied by all the horrors of our world. "I have the powers of a god, Bethany. I can unmake it all. I can put an end to the suffering and cruelty, to the killing and the pain, and all I would have to do is pull a loose thread."

"Don't. You'd only be proving the oracles right. But they're not right, Trent, this isn't who you are. You're not a killer."

"I have a list of names that says otherwise," I said. "But even so, it wouldn't be murder to unmake this world. It would be *mercy*. Watch."

It took no effort at all to reknit the threads below me with a thought, joining them together in a new pattern. The ground shook, and long, sharp fragments of stone burst up out of the crevasse, forming a crooked fence of giant stone spears. Bethany gasped and took a step back from it. She was afraid of me. She was right to be.

Philip came at me from out of nowhere, moving so fast I almost didn't see him. I'd been wondering where he was. Had he reached me, he could have done some serious damage, but I didn't let him get that far. There were threads all around him. I bent two of them, and Philip came to a sudden stop in midair, as if he'd hurled himself into an invisible wall. I plucked a thread, and down he went, tumbling to the ground. The threads inside a vampire were different, I noticed, darker in hue, and the atoms they bound burned colder, brighter. It was beautiful, in its own way.

Isaac came at me next, running over a nearby hill. The mage's entire body crackled with an energy only I could see—magic, shimmering inside him like a star, pure, uninfected. He threw a spell my way, a bright burst of searing light, but I worked a few threads and the spell dissipated. Gabrielle attacked then, wielding the morningstar with her good arm. I sent her sprawling into the dirt next to Philip.

"Stop it!" Bethany yelled. "Stop it, all of you!"

There was so much anger in her voice that it pulled my attention back to her. Isaac's, too. He lowered his crackling hands, and Philip and Gabrielle stood up, brushing dirt off their clothes.

"You're not going to unmake the world, Trent, because you're *not* a killer," Bethany insisted. "That's not who you are. I know it's not."

"You don't know me," I said.

"But I do." She walked closer, skirting around the jagged spears of rock until she was right under me. She wasn't afraid anymore. "Do you want to know why I kept you around after the power inside you almost killed me? Or why I didn't kick you out after you drew your gun on me? It's because despite everything, I saw something good in you. I saw who you could be if you only gave yourself a chance."

I looked down at her, concentrating until the atoms-filled silhouette was gone and I could see her face again. "But the oracles . . ."

"To hell with them. Believe me, I've been called every name in the book. I know what it's like. When you're a kid and you're different, the other kids make sure you know it, every single day. It's hard not to let it get to you when someone calls you an abomination. It's hard not to internalize it, but it's normal. It's human."

"What if I'm not human?" I asked.

"What if you *are*? Would it make your life easier? Would it make you a different person? You still have free will, Trent. What matters isn't *what* you are, it's *who* you are, right now, in this moment. What matters are the choices we make. That's what defines us. Nothing else."

I felt myself calming, and sensed the new power inside me growing calmer, too. A moment later, the white fire in my eyes, nose, and mouth sputtered and died out.

"Now," Bethany said, putting her hands on her hips, "are you going to stop this and come down from there, or am I going to have to pull you down myself?"

The threads around me started to vanish, but a split second before my vision returned to normal, the world seemed to break open, and I saw what lay behind its mask. I saw seven titanic figures, seven pairs of eyes watching, always watching, and an empty space where an eighth figure should have been. Then it was gone, and everything took on solid shapes again. Unable to stay afloat, and unsure how I'd managed it in the first place, I fell out of the air and onto the ground at Bethany's feet.

She knelt beside me and helped me up. I stumbled on weak legs, and she steadied me. "I've got you."

"Thanks," I said. "I don't think I could have stopped if you hadn't . . ." I trailed off, words failing me again.

Bethany gave me a wry smile. "See what happens? I leave you alone for five minutes and you almost destroy the world."

I smiled back, but it was halfhearted. Inside, I felt unstable and unsure of myself. Was my self-loathing so strong that I'd nearly taken the world apart because of it?

"Is it gone now?" she asked.

I shook my head. The power was still with me, I could feel it burning inside me like a low flame, but I couldn't reach it, couldn't make it do what it did before. It was as if the power had gone dormant. "It's still in me, but it's under control."

"Be careful," she said. "I'm serious. There's a reason no mortal has ever tried to carry Ancient magic. It's volatile. Dangerous."

I nodded to let her know I understood. She went to make sure Isaac, Gabrielle, and Philip were all right. I was going to have some apologizing to do to the team. Again. At this point, it was practically a pastime.

My boot kicked something that tinkled along the ground. I looked down and saw the thin, delicate ammonite shell lying shattered on the ground where it had fallen. I knelt and sifted through the tiny pieces, but there were too many of them for the amulet to be salvaged. Damn. I hadn't had a choice, taking it off had been the only way to stop Stryge, but Bethany's little charm had changed everything, even if only for a moment. Losing it stung. We hadn't even had the chance to come up with a name for it. I sighed, and was about to stand up again when the sound of something cutting rapidly through the air caught my attention. Before I could react, an arrow embedded itself in the dirt right in front of me.

I jumped to my feet. Melanthius stood on a mound of broken Cloisters stones, an archer's bow in his hands. He pulled another arrow from the quiver strapped to his back, notched it into the bowstring, and sent it flying at Bethany. She jumped aside, but the arrow tore the sleeve of her shirt and drew a line of blood across her shoulder. She gasped, but it was only a flesh wound. She ran for cover behind one of the big, jagged stones sticking up from the crevasse.

Either Melanthius was a bad shot or he was trying to get our attention. I figured it was the latter. Well, now he had it.

He reached for another arrow, but before he could pull it out, a dark blur rushed out of nowhere and slammed into him. Philip ripped the bow from Melanthius's hands and punched him across the golden skull mask. Melanthius stumbled backward and almost fell, but Philip grabbed him by the front of his cloak and pulled him back up. While Melanthius was still dazed, Philip took a piece of rope out of his pocket, the same rope his own hands had been tied with earlier, and used it to tie Melanthius's hands behind his back. It struck me as a fitting irony.

The rest of us gathered by Stryge's body as Philip approached with his captive. Melanthius's golden skull mask regarded me stoically, emotionlessly.

"This isn't over," he hissed.

"Wanna bet?" I asked.

"As a matter of fact," Melanthius said, "I do."

On the ground between us, Stryge sat up suddenly. I jumped back.

Stryge's eyes opened, and where they had once blazed with white fire, they now glowed red with Reve Azrael's necromancy. The thirty-foot-tall revenant rose to its feet, towering over us.

"My God," Isaac breathed.

"Stay back, all of you!" I shouted. They backed away. Melanthius chuckled inside his mask.

Reve Azrael looked down at me through Stryge's eyes. She spoke through the Ancient's wide, tusked mouth. "I owe you a debt of gratitude, little fly. My plan would never have worked without the one weapon that could kill an Ancient. You."

"You knew what I would do to stop him," I said, fuming. "You used me."

"You *exist* for me to use." She turned her enormous host body to the others and said, "Release Melanthius."

"Why don't you come and get him?" Philip snarled back.

Bethany, still holding my gun, lifted it and squeezed off two shots. The bullets bounced off Stryge's withered skin.

Reve Azrael laughed. "Tiny, foolish thing. You think because this body is dead its hide is any more vulnerable? It is still the body of an Ancient. It contains vast, inexhaustible power. There is no limit to what I can do." She started toward Bethany. Bethany backed up, but Reve Azrael stopped suddenly. She looked down at her host body. "Wait. Something is wrong. This body is nothing but an empty shell. What has become of Stryge's power? Where is it?"

I looked up at her. "Take a guess."

She turned her glowing red eyes to me. There was so much anger in them, so much rage, that they glowed all the brighter for it.

"You thought you had the perfect plan, but there's one thing you forgot to take into account," I said. "Ancients aren't like the rest of us. Their magic is different from ours." She stared at me, still not comprehending. "Ancients were the first living creatures in the world, right? They're millions of years old. Magic alone couldn't have kept them alive all this time. It's the strength of their life force; it's part of what they are. Their life force *is* their magic. And now it's in me."

"Of course," she sneered. "That is what you do, isn't it? Absorb their life forces for yourself? Steal what rightfully belongs to others? You are a thief, little fly, in more ways than one."

"Maybe," I said. "But what does that make you? Just another talking corpse."

Reve Azrael bellowed in rage, furious that she'd been denied Stryge's power. Her anger distracted her, and Isaac took advantage of it. He pushed out his hand. Crackling arcs of electricity flared from his palms and hit Reve Azrael in the back. She roared louder and turned to face the mage. He hit her with the spell again. This time it knocked her backward. Arms spinning wildly, she fell onto one of the huge, sharp stone fragments. The weight of her body coupled with the unyielding strength of the stone drove it into her back and out through her chest.

She struggled and squirmed to pull herself off the sharp stone, but she couldn't. She was stuck. Good. I wanted her to suffer the way she'd made others suffer. I wanted her to hurt. But this was only a host body, not the real thing. I had no idea if she could even feel pain through a revenant.

She stared at me angrily. "You have Stryge's power, so why do you not use it? Why hesitate? You could unmake me in a heartbeat, break me apart into dust!"

As tempting as that sounded, it wasn't an option. I couldn't control the power inside me. But she didn't have to know that.

"Because you have something I want," I replied. "No more games. No more evading the question. Tell me the truth. What do you know about me?" She didn't answer. I tried again. "Who am I?"

"Trent, just end this," Isaac said, coming forward.

"Wait," I barked at him. He stopped where he was, but he didn't retreat. "We found your homunculus, Reve Azrael. I know that's how you kept tabs on me, but it doesn't explain everything. The only time you could have hidden it on me was when you came to the house in Bennett's body, but that doesn't make sense. You wouldn't have come to the house unless you already knew I was there. How did you know?"

She stayed silent.

"Trent," Isaac warned again, but I lifted my hand to stop him.

"Tell me the truth," I demanded. "How do you know me? Who am I?"

"Allow me to take Stryge's power back from you, and I will give you all the answers you seek," she said.

"Stryge's body is ruined," I said. "His power is useless to you now."

"I can still read his memories," she said. "These wounds and broken bones mean nothing. Once Stryge's power is returned to his body, they won't matter."

"Trent!" Isaac shouted. His palms began to glow. "End this, or I will!"

"It still burns inside you," Reve Azrael said. "But it is not made for mortal bodies. In time, the power will consume you from within. It will destroy you. Give it to me, save yourself, and I will tell you everything."

I watched her lips curl into a smile, and felt cold inside. She was using me again, manipulating me to get what she wanted, and she would keep on doing it as long as she had something she could hold over me. I'd been down that road before, and I didn't like it the first time. Isaac was right, it was time to put an end to this.

Willem Van Lente's sword lay on the ground nearby. I walked over to it and picked it up.

"Listen to what I am offering you," Reve Azrael insisted.

I carried the sword back over to her.

"Fool, this is the body of an Ancient," she sneered. "A sword forged by man will do nothing."

"It's no ordinary sword," I said. "Search Stryge's memories. I'm sure you'll recognize it."

Her eyes went wide as it came to her. "No," she shrieked. "I have worked too hard and waited too long to be cheated like this! It's not fair!"

"Lady, if you've got a problem with the way life treats you, get in line." I lifted the sword up over my head, its blade pointing down between her eyes.

"Wait! Do this and I will never tell you what you want to know! You will live out the rest of your days knowing how close you came to the truth before you threw it all away."

"I'll live," I said, and drove the sword deep into Stryge's forehead, into his brain, severing Reve Azrael's link to his body. The red glow faded from Stryge's eyes as her consciousness fled. I pulled the sword free, the barbs on the back of the blade caked with thick grue.

God, I thought, we did it. I couldn't believe it. Somehow, against all odds, we'd actually saved New York City. I laughed with relief, and nearly dropped to my knees in exhaustion.

A sudden, pained cry startled me. I turned around to see Melanthius standing behind Philip, holding a small silver dagger to the vampire's neck. Loops of severed rope dangled from Melanthius's wrists. He inched backward toward the ruins of the Cloisters, keeping a firm grip on his hostage. Bethany lifted the gun again, drawing a bead on Melanthius's gold skull mask over Philip's shoulder, but she didn't fire.

"Shoot him," I said.

She shook her head. "I can't. It could hit Philip."

"He'll be fine, he's a vampire."

"Silver saps a vampire's powers. The bullet could kill him." But she didn't lower the gun. She kept it trained on Melanthius, waiting for him to slip up and give her a clean shot.

"Let him go," Isaac warned.

"Stay where you are, mage," Melanthius said. "Make a move, any of you, and the vampire dies."

"Drop the knife," I said. "It's over. Reve Azrael is gone."

Melanthius laughed. "My mistress is never far." He pulled Philip up onto the rubble.

We followed, keeping a cautious distance. "You're outnumbered, Melanthius," Isaac said. "There are only two ways out of this. You stop, or we stop you."

"No, there is another way." Melanthius plunged the silver dagger into Philip's chest, then shoved the wounded vampire toward us. Isaac caught Philip before he fell.

Melanthius ran into the ruins of the Cloisters. I sprinted after him, Gabrielle right behind me. We chased him into a crumbling, dark corridor of stone. Each step I took brought a cloud of dust raining down on my head, making me wonder if the whole structure was going to come down on top of us at any moment. In the distance, Melanthius produced something small from a pocket inside his cloak. I was too far away to see what it was before he threw it down on the ground in front of him. It broke open, and a hole appeared above it, an opening in the air itself that swirled like a vortex and flickered a bright blue. I'd seen that flickering light before, I realized, the first time I saw Melanthius outside the safe house. The same light had been coming from the alley he disappeared into.

Melanthius leapt into the flickering hole. At the same time, Gabrielle threw something at him, though I didn't see what it was. A weapon of some kind, I supposed, but she must have missed because Melanthius didn't cry out or slow down for a second. Then the vortex swallowed him, and the hole in the air closed. He was gone.

I stopped, putting my hands on my knees and catching my breath. Gabrielle did the same. The front of her shirt was red with blood from the reopened wound in her shoulder.

"What the hell was that . . . that hole?" I asked.

"He had a charm that opened a portal," Gabrielle said. She winced and touched her bleeding shoulder. "Damn it. I should have guessed he would have an escape plan."

We walked back to where Isaac and Bethany were tending to Philip. Bethany was cradling his head against her knees while Isaac rubbed dirt on the knife wound. The vampire's face was twisted with pain and glistened with sweat.

Gabrielle told them about the portal. "But a portal to where?" I asked.

Isaac shrugged and shook his head. "Who knows? Another dimension. Some other part of the city. Timbuktu. It could be anywhere." He turned to Gabrielle. "Did you get him?"

Gabrielle nodded. "I think so."

"Get him with what?" I asked.

Isaac looked at the ruins where Melanthius had disappeared. "Plan B."

Forty-one

We made our way back through Fort Tryon Park toward the parking lot. The northern half of the park was in ruins, the Cloisters destroyed, the grass littered with body parts from revenants, gargoyles, and the three festivalgoers. I wondered how they were going to explain it to the press, or the authorities for that matter, but I was so exhausted I didn't really care.

Philip wasn't in good shape, not even after Isaac rubbed dirt into his wounds. Between the burns he'd suffered from the hit of direct sunlight and Melanthius stabbing him with the silver dagger, the vampire was weak and barely conscious. That he could walk at all was a miracle, even with Isaac propping him up as we talked.

"You're saying Willem Van Lente remembered who he was?" Isaac asked.

I nodded. "I think so, right at the end."

"If that's true, it means the infection can be broken," he said. "It can be reversed. At least the hold it has over people's minds can be. I wonder if, given time, the physical changes could be reversed, too. Trent, you have no idea what a breakthrough this is."

"Let's not start celebrating yet," I said. "Van Lente was a powerful mage. It may not work with everyone."

"But it's *hope*," he said, and I couldn't argue with that.

Because it meant something else, too. It meant that forgotten memories, even those wiped away by something as strong as the infection, could come back. If Willem Van Lente could remember who he was after forgetting for four centuries, it meant there was a chance I could remember, too. It meant nothing was truly lost.

I walked farther ahead and came up beside Bethany. She looked over at me and asked, "Are you okay? It's been a hell of a morning."

I nodded. "I'm fine. I know I freaked out a little back there . . ."

She arched an eyebrow and gave me a skeptical look. She'd already given me that look so often she could have trademarked it.

"Okay, I freaked out *a lot,* but it's over now. Just don't ask me to explain it. I can't. I don't fully understand it myself." That was a lie. I understood just fine. Part of me had wanted to die, and since I couldn't, I was going to take down everyone and everything else instead. The new power inside me was dormant for now, but it was still there, waiting. I had no idea if and when it would surface again. It had brought out something dark in me, something frightening. What if it had changed me in ways I couldn't control? Magic infected people when it got inside them. Was I infected now?

Bethany didn't pry any further, but I felt the need to change the subject anyway before I drove myself crazy. "I'm sorry I broke the charm you made for me. It was a good charm. It worked."

"Of course it worked," she said. "I'm good at what I do. So are you, provided it involves punching, shooting, or breaking things." She looked at the bullet hole in my shirt. "Did it hurt?"

"Nah," I said.

"You're a terrible liar," she said. "I've never killed a friend before. Don't ask me to do that again, okay?"

"I'm not dead yet," I told her. "Besides, if it's any consolation, it was a good, clean shot. You killed me like a pro. The Saint Aurelius Home for Orphaned Girls would be proud."

"Don't joke," she said. "Not about this."

"Sorry, but I've died eleven times already. Joking is the only way I can deal with it without losing my mind."

She squinted at me as though she wasn't quite sure what was about to come out of her own mouth. "I'm sorry if I hurt you when I shot you. Is that a weird thing to say?"

"I've heard weirder," I said. "But I suppose I'm getting used to all the weird stuff now. Anyway, the way I see it, I almost killed you yesterday, and today you got to shoot me, so we're even."

To my surprise, she put her arm through mine as we walked. I liked the way it felt. It let me put the questions about the darkness inside me aside for a while. I wondered if this was what people meant when they used words like *happy*. I'd never really felt happy before.

A sudden downdraft lifted the dead leaves off the ground. A shadow fell over us. I pushed Bethany back with one arm, and looked up. A pack of gargoyles hovered against the gray cloud cover, two dozen of them at least, the wind from their wings blowing my hair back.

"Bethany, Trent, get behind me!" Isaac cried. He crouched down, laying Philip gently on the ground. Beside him, Gabrielle pointed the morningstar up at the gargoyles, but I waved at her to put it down.

"Don't," I said. "I don't think you're going to need it."

She looked puzzled, but she lowered the weapon.

The gargoyles landed in the open field before us, folding their wings behind their backs. I could feel Isaac and the others tensing, preparing to fight, but the gargoyles didn't attack. Instead, they remained still in an almost military formation. One gargoyle moved through the ranks toward us, a walking stick tapping the ground at its side.

"Jibril-khan," I said, smiling. "I take it your side won."

"There are no sides, not anymore," the wizened old gargoyle replied. "We are unified now, under our new king."

The smile faded from my face. "What new king? I thought you said you wanted to be free."

"That is for our new king to decide," Jibril-khan said. The gargoyle bowed before me, bending down on one knee and lowering its head. The other gargoyles did the same.

"Wait . . . what?" I said.

Jibril-khan looked up at me. "It is our tradition. He who slays our king takes his place upon the throne. What you decree, we must do."

"So that's how the Black Knight became your king," I said. "He defeated Stryge when he was still Willem Van Lente. You know, if you'd just told me that from the start, it could have saved a lot of time."

Jibril-khan bowed again. "If I have displeased you, my king—"

"Oh for God's sake, I'm not your king!" I protested.

"I don't think you have a choice in the matter," Bethany said, stifling a laugh. "King of the gargoyles. As if your ego isn't big enough already."

"No, forget it," I insisted, shaking my head. Then a thought occurred to me. "Wait, wait, okay then, yes. If I'm your king, here's my first decree. My only decree. No more kings. You're free."

Jibril-khan looked up at me. "You would grant us our freedom?"

"You don't need me. You don't need *any* king," I said. "You've been ruled over, controlled, and coerced for long enough. I know what it's like to feel like you have no choice. It's time you made your own destinies and lived your own lives. It's time you were free."

"Trent, are you sure this is a good idea?" Isaac asked. "What if a king was the only thing keeping them in line?"

"Under Stryge's rule, and again under the Black Knight, they didn't have a choice about who they could be, or what they could do. Now they do," I said. "They deserve that, just like everyone else."

Jibril-khan and the other gargoyles rose to their feet. "You have our gratitude. We will never forget what you have done for us."

"So what's next?" I asked.

"We will leave this place," Jibril-khan said. "Go somewhere else, somewhere less populated where we can live our lives in peace. Somewhere with good hunting." The gargoyle saw the expression on my face and added, "Not humans."

"I think a change of scenery sounds like a good idea," I said.

Jibril-khan hobbled closer and held out one hand. In the gargoyle's palm was a whistle carved from animal bone. "Use this should you ever have need of us, and no matter where we are, we will come. We are forever in your debt." I pocketed the whistle. Jibril-khan knelt again, and the other gargoyles joined in. They crossed their arms over their chests in what I figured was a gargoyle salute. "All hail the Immortal Storm, giver of freedom."

"But there *was* no storm," I pointed out. "The prophecy didn't come true."

"Didn't it?" Jibril-khan asked. "For centuries we assumed the Immortal Storm we waited for was an event. It was not. It was a person. *You* are the Immortal Storm, and as the prophecy foretold, you have given us our freedom."

My face fell. "What? No, there must be some mistake . . ."

"There is no mistake. May the Guardians show you favor, Immortal Storm. Always."

My chest felt tight. I had trouble breathing. Me? I was the Immortal Storm? How was that possible? But before I could ask Jibril-khan anything else, the gargoyle spread its wings and launched itself into the air, followed by the others.

"Goodbye," I called after them, waving. "Try not to eat anybody."

Bethany elbowed me in the ribs. "Don't be rude," she said. Then, snickering, she added, "Your Majesty."

I watched as they flew back over the Hudson River toward New Jersey. The rest of the gargoyles streamed out of the Palisades cliffs to join them, abandoning the cavern they'd called home for so long and flying westward to a new life.

A moment later, they were tiny specks in the sky.

A moment after that, they were gone.

Forty-two

"What will you do now?" Isaac asked. We were in his study on the second floor of Citadel. He sat at his desk, sunlight streaming through the stained-glass window behind him and casting him in a multicolored glow. On the desk between us, the empty Erlenmeyer flask caught the light from the window and refracted it in pretty fragments that scattered in every direction.

"I told the gargoyles to go make their own destiny," I said. "I suppose it's time I did the same. It's just . . ." I paused, "I'm still carrying Stryge's magic inside me. Does that mean I'm infected?"

"I don't know," he said. "I wish I could tell you, but the Ancients' magic is too different from ours. It's never been studied or tested. I don't know what it means, or what's going to happen."

"Great," I muttered. "So for all anyone knows, I could be a walking time bomb."

He tented his fingers under his chin. "What would you say if I were to offer you a job and a place to live?"

"I'd say I've heard that one before."

"We worked well together as team," Isaac said. "And now that we've stepped out of the shadows, we've been noticed. Not just by Reve Azrael, but by other Infecteds all over the city. If we're going to make this work, if we're going to keep up the fight, we need all the help we can get. Specifically, we need someone to take Thornton's place."

I frowned. "I don't think anyone can really replace Thornton."

He nodded. "Truer words. But what do you think, Trent? A new Five-Pointed Star. We could use your help."

It was a tempting offer. I liked these people, and he was right, we worked well together. At least, we worked well together when I wasn't using the stolen power of an Ancient to knock them around like rag dolls. I sighed. "Isaac, I don't know who I am, or what I am. After today, I don't know what I'm becoming. Jibril-khan said I was the Immortal Storm, but I don't know what that means. All I know is that it could be bad."

Isaac stood up and came around the desk. "I'll tell you the same thing I told Philip the day we met. No matter who you are, or what you are, everyone deserves a second chance. What we choose to do with it is up to us, no one else. Nothing is set in stone. Not even prophecies."

"Tell that to the oracles," I said. I rubbed my face. "God, I don't know. Maybe it's better not to know what I am."

"It's always better to know the truth," Isaac said. "And if you'll let me, I'd like to help you find it."

He held out his hand. I looked at it for a long moment. It was the same deal I'd made with Underwood, a job, a place to stay, and an offer to help me find the answers. Did I want to go down that road again? But it wasn't really a fair comparison. Isaac wasn't Underwood. He was a lot more trustworthy, and I got the sense he really did want to help me. I took his hand and shook it.

"Okay," I said. "Let's see how this goes."

"Glad to have you aboard," he said.

The study door opened, and Bethany poked her head inside. "Oh, excuse me, Your Majesty," she said. I was never going to live this down. "I thought you two might want to know that Gabrielle is starting to get a signal from the homunculus."

Bethany went back out into the hall, and Isaac went with her. I turned to follow them, but a small, circular object on a table by the door caught my eye. I recognized it right away. It was Thornton's leather bracelet, the one Gabrielle had given him as a token of her love. They must have taken it off his body after he died. I missed him, I realized, missed his quick humor and bravery, and my heart broke a little to see his bracelet sitting there on the table, alone and empty. I remembered how sentimental he'd been about it, how he'd never let anyone else touch it.

What had Thornton said when I asked if he was afraid to die? That nothing was ever what it seemed. Death wasn't the end, just another plane of existence. I remembered hoping he was right. I still did.

I reached out to touch the bracelet. It moved, sliding away from me. I yanked my hand back. What the hell? I looked around the empty office. There were no open windows, no breeze that could explain it moving like that. It was almost as though the bracelet had moved on its own.

Goose bumps lifted the hair on my arms. I whispered, "Thornton?"

Isaac called my name from downstairs. I took one last look around, decided I was being foolish, and went downstairs to the main room.

Philip lay on the couch, covered in fresh dirt and bandages. "What are you looking at?" he groused at me.

"Boris Karloff as Imhotep?" I answered. If Philip got the reference, he only growled in reply. Same old crabby vampire. He was going to be fine.

Gabrielle was at the desk, huddled over the laptop. She hit a button and the wall of monitors flickered to life. "I used a transfer charm to patch the homunculus's psychic link into the computer so we could all see it," she explained. "It's coming through now."

"If I'm right, Melanthius will have gone right back to Reve Azrael's lair," Isaac said. "Whatever we see now will be our best chance of finding her. Maybe our only chance."

The screens of all six video monitors flickered and jumped. An image appeared, accompanied by ambient noise through their speakers, but everything was shaking, making it hard to decipher what I was looking at. The image spun, shook again, and then stabilized. Gabrielle explained the homunculus had jumped off Melanthius's cloak and was clinging to a wall, granting us a much better view.

On the monitors was what appeared to be a small room with bare walls. There was a table in the center of it. On it lay a human male corpse.

Gabrielle stiffened. "It's Thornton." Her voice hitched. Before leaving the park, we'd helped her search the grounds for Thornton's body. We found the other bodies Reve Azrael had discarded once she didn't need them anymore, but not Thornton's. That one she'd kept for herself.

"Where are they?" Isaac asked, studying the monitors.

"I can't tell yet," Gabrielle said.

Melanthius came into view then, walking over to the table where

Thornton's body lay. His back was to us. He took off his gloves and laid them on the table. He pushed back his hood. He gripped the skull mask with both hands and pulled it off his face. He reached into a pocket of his cloak, pulled out a pair of dark sunglasses, and put them on. Then he turned around.

My breath caught in my throat. I went instantly cold, as if someone had dropped me into an ice bath.

The face I saw duplicated on all six monitors was unmistakable.

"It's him," I said, barely a whisper. "It's Underwood."

The house of cards Underwood had built so carefully fell down then. I remembered him sliding the Bersa semiautomatic across the table to me, and how often he'd repeated his Golden Rule: *Never lose your gun.* No revenant had hidden the homunculus on my gun. It had been there from the start, put there by Underwood himself so he could keep tabs on me. *That* was how he'd found me so quickly after I was teleported out of the safe house, and again after we picked up the box from Gregor. He'd gone so far as to blow up his own base at the gas station just to throw us off the trail. He'd killed Big Joe and Tomo in the same explosion because their faces had been seen at the auto body shop. Two birds with one stone. It was ruthless, monstrous, and nothing less than I expected from him.

My hands clenched into fists. On the monitors, Underwood came forward so suddenly that I took an involuntary step back. His face filled the screens. I knew he was looking at the homunculus, but it felt like he was staring directly at me.

"It's you, isn't it?" Underwood said. "Poor Trent. You really have no idea how far this con goes. Or how long it's been going." He took off his sunglasses, revealing the eyes I had never seen the whole year I worked for him. His pupils glowed with pinpoints of red light.

Oh, God. My mouth went dry. The freezing cold temperature of the fallout shelter. The gallons of cologne. Underwood was a revenant. He always had been.

"What you did today can't go unpunished, Trent," Underwood said. "We'll be seeing each other again soon. Very soon. Surely you don't think I need this two-bit homunculus to find you? It was nothing but a fail-safe. I know where you are. I *always* know where you are. It's like I've been telling you all along. You're my go-to guy."

A shape came onto the screen, drifting into frame from the right-hand side. At first it was a dark blur, indistinct. Then I realized what I was seeing was hair—long, ragged black hair that fell in wisps across a thin face, and eyes so dark they looked like bottomless black pits.

Reve Azrael. She stared at me through the homunculus.

Stared at me the way she always used to back in the fallout shelter.

She waved her hand, casting a spell. There was a brief flash as the homunculus was destroyed, and then the screen went blank.